ASHES
OF
BRITANNIA

ASHES
OF
BRITANNIA

HALEY ELIZABETH GARWOOD

2000
THE WRITERS BLOCK
BRUCETON MILLS, WEST VIRGINIA

ASHES OF BRITANNIA

The Writers Block/published by arrangement with the author

First Printing, June 2000

All rights reserved.

Copyright © 2000 by Haley Elizabeth Garwood

Cover concept by Mel Graham

Sword researched/art work by Tell Hicks

Cover art by Richard Hill of Pioneer Press of W. Va., Inc.

ISBN: 0-9659721-7-8
LCCN: 00-132192

THE WRITERS BLOCK

The Writers Block books are published by The Writers Block,
Laurel Run, Route One, Box 254, Bruceton Mills, WV 26525-9748
Designed by Pioneer Press of W. Va., Inc., Terra Alta, WV

Publisher's Cataloging-in-Publication
(Provided by Quality Books, Inc.)

Garwood, Haley Elizabeth
    Ashes of Britannia / Haley Elizabeth Garwood. — 1st ed.
    p. cm.— (Warrior queen series; 3rd)
    LCCN: 00-132192
    ISBN: 0-9659721-7-8

    1. Great Britain—History—Roman Period, 55
B.C.-449 A.D.—Fiction. 2. Boadicea, Queen, d. 62
—Fiction. 3. Paulinus, Gaius Seutonius—Fiction
4. Romans—Great Britain—Fiction. I. Title.
II. Series: Garwood, Haley Elizabeth. Warrior queen series

PS3557.A8417A8 2000   813.6
                      QBI00-361

Printed in the United States of America
10 9 8 7 6 5 4 3 2 1

DEDICATED TO

my husband,

Charles Edward Wales

December 20, 1928-May 16, 1999

ACKNOWLEDGMENTS

This book would not have been possible without the help of many people involved in the production of a novel.

First, I would like to thank Marilyn and Tom Ross who work tirelessly for small publishers through their non-profit organization, Small Publishers of North America (SPAN). Their advice, expertise, support, and humor has helped bring this novel to fruition.

I'd also like to thank the people who work at Pioneer Press— Lynda Hopkins for rapidly proofing the manuscript as it came off the computer and for catching some real author made boo-boos. I want to thank Rich Hopkins for his infinite tolerance, his leadership in design of the book, and his cheerful demeanor. I am lucky that Richard Hill works at Pioneer Press. He's an artist in many ways.

The Morgantown, WV writers group deserves a huge thank you for the support they've shown throughout the writing and production of my three Warrior Queen Series novels. There is a tremendous amount of talent in that group of serious writers.

Thanks to Catherine Cometti, historical novelist and short story writer, who read the manuscript and made suggestions that were invaluable.

Gerald Swick, author of *Lincoln and His In-Laws*, not only supported me as a friend, but also edited the manuscript. He made excellent suggestions regarding the structure of the novel.

Janet B. Peltz, editor, is not only valuable as a grammarian, but also as an historian. Her knowledge of Britain is extensive, and I am lucky to have her help. Any errors in the manuscript belong to the author, not the editors.

Bob Duncan, historian, was instrumental in explaining the proper nomenclature for the Roman Legions. Thanks for the detailed emails!

Carol Miller deserves a huge thank you for sending me packing.

A thank you goes to Teresa Hearl, Frank Hearl, Renee Hearl, Heidi Hearl, Otto Hearl, Patricia Patteson, and Candace Jordan for helping me to save face!

Kathryn Falk, Lady of Barrow, CEO of *Romantic Times Magazine*, was a tremendous help in getting my career off the ground and rolling. Without her support, there would have been no Warrior Queen Series. She is a terrific person.

As usual, Mel Graham was there as a good friend.

And, of course, my family gets a big thank you for believing in the Warrior Queen project.

ABOUT
ASHES OF BRITANNIA

Boadicea is a symbol of freedom in Britain. Although we don't know about her from her own records, the Romans kept extensive information on all their battles and interactions with other peoples. Fortunately, we know of this great Iceni queen through the writings of her enemy.

This novel is fiction although the main characters are not. It is difficult to develop a character from notes made by the Romans, who although they admired her, were the enemy. Over time, historians attributed Boadicea's greatness to her man-like qualities. I prefer to think that she was brilliant, not because she had male qualities, but because she was intelligent, a leader, fearless, and capable. These are qualities that both great men and great women possess. It is not a gender identifier.

I've tried to follow history as accurately as possible and to develop characters who were true to their actions. Why did her husband try to live in peace with the Romans? After his death why did Boadicea feel compelled to attack them? I had to research for days to answer all the why questions. Only then did I feel that I could continue to develop my characters honestly. I tried to think like a first century Iceni or Roman. I tried to immerse myself in their different religions, views on life, politics, locales, society, and even the weather to try to develop accurate characterizations of a people from long ago.

I hope you enjoy my effort, for my first wish is to entertain the reader with a good story that adds another piece of history to our growing repertoire.

ABOUT THE AUTHOR

Haley Elizabeth Garwood was born in Indiana a long time ago. She has had a variety of careers that included being a stewardess, a special education teacher, and a high school principal. She gave up these high flying careers to concentrate on writing historical novels.

Dr. Garwood's goal is to write the forgotten warrior women back into history in an entertaining manner. She diligently researched each novel in the Warrior Queen Series to give an accurate accounting of the characters and the times in which they lived.

Dr. Garwood recently left her mountain home in West Virginia for a farm in southern Kentucky where she raises dairy cattle. Barn cats, who refuse to be herded, comprise the rest of the menagerie on her animal farm. Each novel depicts one of her barn cats in a cameo appearance.

DRUID ZODIAC
Thirteen Months—28 Days each

DRUID SIGN	MONTH	SYMBOL

Birch   December 24–January 20   Eagle or stag
Those born under this sign are reliable, trustworthy, and determined.

Rowan   January 21–February 17   Green dragon
Humanitarian, kind, and progressive describes the Rowan tree person.

Ash   February 18–March 17   Trident
An ash tree person is compassionate, intuitive, and adaptable.

Alder   March 18–April 14   Pentacle
Alder tree people are courageous, loyal, and natural leaders.

Willow   April 15–May 12   Serpent
The willow tree person is tenacious, protective, and resourceful.

Hawthorn   May 13–June 9   Chalice
Those born under this sign are charismatic, innovative, and creative.

Oak   June 10–July 7   Goldenwheel
The oak person is philosophical, generous, and charming.

Holly   July 8–August 4   Flaming spear
Strong-willed, affectionate, and trustworthy describes the Holly person.

Hazel   August 5–September 1   Rainbow fish
Hazel people are perceptive, clever, and great organizers.

Vine   September 2–September 29   Swan
Those born under this sign are gentle, harmonious, and creative.

Ivy   September 30–October 27   Butterfly
Ivy people are loyal, generous providers, and thrifty.

Reed   October 28–November 24   Stone
Persistence, imagination, and visionary are qualities of Reed people.

Elder   November 25–December 22   Raven
Those born under this sign are patient, self-disciplined, and tenacious.

The Nameless Day—December 23

THE TRIBAL TERRITORIES
IN A.D. 60

CHAPTER

I

BOADICEA STOOD IN FRONT of the altar and lifted high a glass flagon filled with blood-colored wine. She'd participated in so many Druid rituals here, so many celebrations of life. Now her chalice held only death; wine kissed with hemlock. Fragments of rainbow colors danced up and down the cool glass sides and taunted her with memories.

There would be no more memories for her. Nor for her daughters. Would there be memories of them?

Her Irish servants talked of a new religion in which their priests remembered a man named Jesus. Six decades ago he had died at the hands of the Romans. Six decades from now would anyone know of Boadicea and how she had fought the Romans? Or six centuries? Or never? Would her beloved island become lost beneath a mantle of Roman ways? Boadicea shivered at the thought of Romans bathing in the sacred waters. She hated the thought of them sailing up the Thames and riding through sacred forests that had belonged to her people from the beginning of time.

Boadicea put the pitcher on the altar, ran her finger from the lip of the opening down the narrowed neck and followed the ribbed design to the bottom. She let her finger rest on the stone slab that formed the top of the altar. With her left hand, she grasped the handle, but did not lift the container of death. The handle felt cool. She wondered if the poison would be hot. She loosened her grasp and let her fingers ripple down the row of glass beads from the handle to the bottom of the flagon.

She turned, the white robes of the Druid priesthood flowing about her like a heavy fog, and looked at both daughters who knelt before her. She smiled at Sydelle, auburn-haired and so different in temperament from her younger sister and from Boadicea herself.

Boadicea's glance slid from Sydelle to her youngest child. Neila's dark ringlets curled so tightly that they were difficult to comb. Her hair matched her headstrong personality. The child was most difficult to control, but Boadicea liked Neila's strength.

As if she could read her mother's thoughts, Neila looked up and stared into her eyes. Boadicea was dismayed to see the girl's eyes glisten with tears. Her strongest child's resolve seemed to have weakened. A tear worked its way slowly down Neila's cheek and dripped onto her tunic. Boadicea watched the spot of life soak into the material like blood soaking into the earth during a battle.

Boadicea was more unsettled by the tentative smile that Neila gave her than by the tears. "May my gods forgive me," Boadicea said to herself using a sing-song whisper as a prayer to mask her pain.

Sydelle, a gentle and loving daughter, reached for Neila's hand. The two girls intertwined fingers to fence off their fears. It was a gesture that Boadicea recognized. Whenever her children had had to face misfortune, Sydelle had always reached for Neila. Boadicea used to think Sydelle needed to be comforted by her stronger sister, but over the years, Boadicea had discovered Sydelle's capacity for comforting others. It was interesting to see that although Sydelle was paler than usual, her eyes were tearless. She even had a tilt to her chin that reminded Boadicea of the defiance Sydelle had shown to the Roman soldiers who had . . .

Boadicea shook her head to rid herself of bad memories. She would not let thoughts of the Romans taint her last moments in this world.

Boadicea turned abruptly from the sight of her two daughters, on the threshold between childhood and womanhood, about to be forever youthful. She clamped her lips together in determination and quickly poured the poisoned wine into two cups and a bowl. The burnished silver cups were identical. Two delicately curved handles in the shape of an oak branch complete with leaves and acorns enhanced a fragile pedestal base. An ethereal pattern of curved vines decorated the chalice bowls. Boadicea's mother had told her the chalices had been a wedding gift from a king in a far away land. Boadicea set the death chalices aside and viewed the contents of the bowl. She poured more poisoned wine in a rose-red bowl that was her favorite. A careless hare hid beneath a carved broad leaf. Life was so simple for the ignorant. Once she had been ignorant, but her stupidity had complicated, not simplified her life. Maybe the gods dealt more harshly with humans who failed.

Boadicea stared into the deep red wine and saw her past. Perhaps she could find a reason for the events that led her to this point. Perhaps there would be triumph in her death. She braced herself against the altar to gather strength. On a sunny and happy day many years ago she had stood before this altar and begun the progression to this end. As a child, she always had a weapon in hand or a horse under rein.

Boadicea hung over the arm of her father's throne and listened to his deep, low voice as he told her who each tribal leader was and where they were from.

"Tremain's country is Catuvellauni. Do you remember where that is?"

"It is south across the River Stour. It runs west of Trinovantes and both countries go all the way to the Thames." Boadicea liked this game of geography. She had learned to draw maps in the dirt that pleased her father. "I know that Coritani is our western neighbor."

"You learn quickly and do not forget." Her father, Garik, pointed out other tribal leaders as they entered the great hall. "It is important that you remember these tribes. If ever we have war with the Romans, then we will need these tribes to help protect the Iceni people."

Boadicea clenched her fists. She didn't know who the Romans were, but if the Romans crossed the Narrow Sea and sailed up the Thames to invade her country, she would kill them with her bow and arrows.

Her father absent-mindedly stroked Boadicea's hair as he argued with men and women who had come from far away to talk about the Romans. "The Romans are marching closer and closer to the channel that separates our island from the rest of the world," Garik said. He looked at Boadicea. "My daughter has seen five summers. We must prepare to fight for our lands so our children will not become slaves. The Romans invaded three generations ago under a man they called Julius Caesar. We sent them back across the Narrow Sea then. We have to do so again."

"We can let them have the south part of our island," Alinna tugged at the pendant that showed her status as a tribal chieftain. "It is far from here. Maybe the Romans will be content." She rubbed her ancient fingers on her temples as if to dismiss the thought of an invasion.

"That's preposterous!" Dearg bellowed. "That's our land. Who are you to give Durotriges land to an enemy to save your own?"

Mabina jumped up and leaned across the table, her dark braids swinging. "You said you didn't want to fight, Dearg!" she yelled. "If you don't have the heart for a little war, then give up your lands to the Romans!"

Garik pounded once on the table with his fist. The room was deadly still. "Sit down."

Mabina sat and scowled at Dearg. Boadicea stared at the two tribal leaders. She had never known Dearg and Mabina to fight. They were friends. The Romans must be important for the different tribes to argue so much.

"Our spies have told us that the Romans do not take a small amount of land and quit," Garik said. "They keep marching and conquer all the land. The Romans would not be content with the unsettled land in the south; they'll want ours. They are halfway here. We have perhaps a dozen years to plan for an invasion by these Romans."

Boadicea slipped out from under her father's hand and left the great hall. Talk of the Romans tired her. Her mother had said that there was talk of Romans year after year, but no one could see the threat except Garik.

The sun was bright and the day warm. Boadicea picked up her bow and arrows that were next to the visitors' weapons and went outside. She would practice shooting Romans.

Boadicea pulled hard on the bowstring, holding her left arm straight as her father had taught her. She closed her left eye, sighted down the arrow, and stopped breathing. She waited for a bird to hop closer. A bead of perspiration ran down her forehead and slid into her eye. She blinked impatiently, still not breathing, and watched as the black and white bird moved away from her. It was annoying. She let the pig-gut string go, listening for the thud that should have come after the twang. The thud did come, but it didn't have the softness of iron against flesh. She saw tail feathers scatter as the squawking bird flew to safety, the arrow vibrating in the dirt.

"You were too impatient, Little One."

Boadicea turned toward her father and bowed her head. She could not speak to the giant man. There was a soft snapping of pebbles as he moved toward her, then she felt the warmth of his hand on her head. She leaned against him, felt the roughness of his tunic, and smelled the melilot ointment that her mother rubbed on his swollen joints.

"Do not feel bad, Boadicea. You have the strength of boys and girls twice your age and the keen eyesight of a falcon."

Her heart filled with hope. Without raising her head, she looked at his brightly colored tunic and focused on a bright red stripe that ran diagonally across her field of vision, making her forget the other colors.

"You need not bow your head in shame, daughter. You are of the Iceni people. Look at me."

He raised her face toward the sky with his rough hand under her chin. She blinked as the sun glinted off the gold shoulder brooch that held his tunic together. It was as if a piece of the sun had perched on her father's shoulder to favor him. Even on cloudy days the brooch shone like the sun. Her mother had said that the brooch was a reminder that the sun would always return no matter what.

"Of course," her mother had said, "we must pray to the goddess of the sun so that she knows we haven't forsaken her for the moon."

Boadicea loved the sun, so she prayed earnestly every morning to the sun goddess before running outside. She imagined that the sun goddess had hair to match her father's, for his hair was the color of the hearth flames in winter.

Boadicea glanced from the brooch to her father's eyes, serious and gray like thunder clouds. His smile, showing beautiful white teeth, belied the storm-like eyes. His skin was smooth, except for a small cut on his chin from a shaving. Boadicea liked his skin; it was almost as dark in color as the copper kettles in the kitchen.

"Your aim will improve as your patience improves. Come inside. I have a surprise for you. Instead of your Greek lessons, you have something else to study."

Her father took her hand. She liked the strength of it. He was tall—twice as tall as she was and taller than any of the other men in their clan. Boadicea looked up at her father, who was blocking the sun. At the summer solstice gathering of all the clans in her father's kingdom, none of the men had been as tall as he.

Boadicea walked beside her father, taking giant steps to match his stride. She was surprised to see that they had not entered the small door that led to the kitchen, but the front door that led to the great room.

Inside it was cool. Thick, clay walls kept the summer heat at bay and prevented the winter winds from seeking shelter. Boadicea's eyes took only a moment to adjust to the darkened room. The walls were painted white, but the windows were small and not much light could enter. The oiled goatskin that was used in winter to keep out the wind had been taken down.

Boadicea looked across the rectangular room toward the altar and was startled to see her mother dressed in her traditional robes of the priesthood. Boadicea stared at her mother's flowing, white robe that she had seen but a few times. Around her neck hung the heavy golden torc of her mother's family. Boadicea liked the tubular links that held a large burnished brooch adorned with stones of turquoise and red. Curved lines wound round the gems, flowing like the rivers near by.

Whenever her mother wore the robes and the torc, it meant there would be an important ceremony. Boadicea glanced around, but no one else was here. Usually when her mother donned the robes, there were many people present who banged animal bones against metal gongs and chanted sacred prayers.

"You and your mother have a ceremony to perform. I leave you to the secrets. When you have finished, we will go to the sacred oak trees to give thanks."

Boadicea turned and looked at her father framed in the timber doorway. "I don't understand, Father."

"You will. Now go to your mother, who at this moment is Priestess Durina. She stands at our sacred altar, waiting to give you the beginnings of wisdom." Her father left.

Boadicea stared at the altar. Huge stones had been placed so as to make a table. On this table lay the traditional oak branch, a blue and white marbled bowl with holy water, and an amber flagon that held dark red wine. A shaft of sunshine filtered through the window and embraced her favorite clay bowl. She liked the rose-red hue and the relief of a hare hiding under a broad-leafed plant, its ears up to listen for the approach of an enemy.

The earthen floor felt hard and cool beneath Boadicea's feet as she walked toward the altar. It was quiet, so quiet she could hear herself breathing. Her mother's face didn't have its customary smile. In fact, a slight frown creased her normally smooth forehead. Boadicea thought back over her own deeds of the past few days, but she could think of nothing she'd done wrong except not show patience in hunting.

She stopped in front of her mother and stared at the tangle of black hair that stood out from her mother's head as if she were racing across the fields in a chariot. Her mother held a silver bowl of yellow-green paste. From the time she could walk, Boadicea had been allowed to gather the best acorns from their family's sacred oak tree. She had never wondered until now what her mother did with the acorns, for she never made soup as did the peasants.

"Boadicea, I stand before you not as your mother, but as the priestess of your clan. Five summers ago your birth, at the exact moment of summer solstice, was the first cipher given to me. The second was that you were born under the sign of the oak tree like your father. The next omen was within you. Remember when the mad bull charged you? You were only in your second summer, yet you stood there, waved your arms and shouted at that bull until it fell dead at your feet, your father's spear embedded in its heart."

Boadicea shifted from one foot to another. She didn't know whether or not she should speak, so she whispered, "I remember laughing at the spear. It quivered like a reed blowing in the wind." Boadicea blushed from having spoken out of turn.

Durina's mouth twitched as she pushed a smile away. "There was the sign of greatness in all you did. I saw signs that told of your compassion. For these reasons, you have been chosen to begin studies that will make you a priestess, providing you pass the tests."

From the look on her mother's face, Boadicea knew that what had just been said was important. She watched as her mother placed her hands on a wreath of oak leaves.

Durina held the wreath above Boadicea's head. "By the god of thunder, Taranis, the goddess of the moon, Kynthia, and the goddess of the sun, Kira, I pray that you will accept this child into training. An omen is needed to show your approval."

The spicy odor of her mother's ever-present perfume tickled Boadicea's nose, as it always did.

Boadicea's attention was diverted by a scraping, fluttering sound to her right. Not daring to move her head, she let her eyes dart sideways. Through the window a light and dark shadow moved, scraped again, and dropped to the floor. A bird stared at Boadicea, unblinking, weaving to and fro a moment before hopping toward her. Boadicea's eyes widened when she noticed some tail feathers missing.

Durina lowered the oak leaf wreath onto the auburn-haired child. "The gods guide and protect her."

The bird squawked at Boadicea, fluttered upwards, and found its way out the window. Boadicea stood still as her mother held the blue and white bowl above her head.

"By this sacred water, I protect the life of this child in order to serve the gods while she is on this earth." Durina let the water flow slowly out of the bowl onto Boadicea's head until her thick hair was plastered against her scalp.

Glass scraped against stone as Durina returned the empty bowl to the altar. Boadicea's priestess-mother put her fingers in the oak paste, scooped out a portion, and made a stripe of oak paste down each of Boadicea's arms. It felt cold as did the stripe of oak paste that was placed across her forehead, down her nose, and chin. All the while Durina chanted in a sing-song voice. Boadicea listened carefully. She had never heard the words before.

"Protect my daughter, mighty acorn, and help her become as old, as strong, as beautiful, and as wise as the great oak tree that is sacred to us." Durina moved gracefully as she washed the acorn residue off her fingers in the rose-red bowl. To be trained like her mother was an honor.

"The testing will be done each year on the day of your birth." Durina stared into Boadicea's green eyes, her own dark eyes a contrast. "You will be taught the stories of the gods and goddesses and their ways. You will be taught the magic that we hold sacred. You will be taught the philosophies of our religion. You will be taught the ways of the ancients from far off lands. All this will have to be memorized, for we do not believe in writing the sacred word. The sacred word is to be known to those who are worthy and to no others. Do you understand?"

Boadicea wasn't certain she understood everything, but she worried that if she didn't say she did, something awful might happen because the gods would be angry. She especially didn't want Taranis, the thunder god, to be angry. She nodded, furiously bobbing her head up and down so that the gods would be sure to see.

"You must answer with a voice, so as to be heard, Boadicea."

"I understand, and I am ready."

"You must know that if you miss one question, you will be refused the priesthood."

Boadicea's eyes widened, and she stared at her mother. To be refused the priesthood would be tragic. She chewed her lower lip, then realizing she was engaged in the very habit her father was trying to break her of, she stopped. She stood straighter. "I will not fail." Boadicea's voice echoed off the whitewashed walls of the great hall.

Durina held out her hand. "Come. Your father waits for us by the path that leads through the woods to our sacred oak tree."

Boadicea took her mother's hand, the usual softness covered by the acorn paste. Boadicea tried to match her mother's strides with her own now that she was going to be a priestess, but since her mother was almost as tall as her father, she could not. Every third step Boadicea had to do a little hop to catch up.

They walked from the coolness of the great hall into the sunshine, across the grassy yard and past the wooden pole fence that stood upright and kept the goats and sheep separated. Usually Boadicea would stop and climb the gate to watch the animals, but today she wasn't interested. They passed the animal pens and crossed the pasture where their horses were kept. Boadicea counted them, a habit she had learned from her father, and was always relieved to see that they were all there including this year's foals. She looked back over her shoulder at the horses who stood quietly under the trees swishing their tails back and forth to ward off persistent flies. The stallion, under another tree away from the mares and foals, watched for signs of an intruder. He nickered softly in welcome as

Durina and Boadicea came within his territory, but when they did not come toward him, he lowered his head and nibbled on the grass. There would be no friendly scratching of his ears today.

Garik waited at the edge of the woods. He leaned against his staff, in his usual position, his hands folded across the burled top and watched them. Boadicea waved at him, dropped her mother's hand, and ran the rest of the distance with auburn hair flowing out behind her like hundreds of ribbons.

"Father! I am to be a priestess like mother. If I pass all the tests to be given on the date of my birth, then I will be allowed to wear the beautiful robes." Boadicea turned toward her mother who had come up behind her. "Will I wear the torc of your family?"

Durina's hand touched the turquoise stones set in the gold torc that was wrapped about her neck. "This sacred relic has been handed down for generations. The time will come when you have earned the responsibility for its care. To wear this heavy ornament will be a reminder that you will have a heavy duty in the priesthood."

"Come, Boadicea. It is time to visit our oak." Her father took Durina's hand.

Boadicea's laughter sliced through the quietness of the immense forest. She bounced up and down on her toes, her bare feet raised the dust in imitation of the clouds in the sky.

"Thank you, Father. I know I can find it." She turned, her short tunic swirling in a myriad of hues like flower petals in a storm.

She bounced down the familiar path, stopping finally to search for the hidden path that veered off to the left. She found the gnarled pine tree with the broken branch that pointed toward the bushes. As soon as she saw her parents, she pulled aside the branches of the bush.

Their presence frightened a fox, and a streak of red flashed before the trio. Boadicea clapped her hands together and jumped up and down. "Let me catch him, Father. He will make a great pet and keep the mice away."

"Do you not think that his family would miss him?" her father asked.

Boadicea's mother leaned down and looked into her eyes. "Perhaps he is really a mother and has kits hidden close by. Would it be proper to deny the kits a mother?"

Boadicea watched the streak of red disappear into the woods on the other side of the clearing. She shook her head. "I would not want to do that."

"Perhaps our great oak is protecting the fox," Durina said. "Come, let's go to our tree. I see that it still stands in the middle of the clearing unscathed by lightning."

Boadicea stared at the great oak tree. Her mother had told her that it was older than her mother's mother and had powers of healing and protection. The branches spread out and covered the sky, and Boadicea wondered whether or not it could eat the sun. She didn't want to disturb the tree and make it angry, for she was afraid it would snatch her off the earth and throw her to the sky. She walked softly through the grass, waist high for her, and held the hand of each parent, content to be in the middle instead of running ahead.

"Garik, the oak is even more beautiful than the last time we were here," Durina said.

"Your great-great-grandmother must have chosen a fine acorn to plant, for it is a magnificent tree," Garik said. "I have always believed that the priesthood is strong in your line. I find that even with Boadicea's youthful age, she has an uncanny ability to heal the sick. Remember when she saved the orphan kittens? And our piglets?"

"I do remember. We both had given them up for dead."

"But Boadicea put them in her bed and got up throughout the night to feed them. She will be a priestess."

"All the better to protect her." Durina frowned. "We live in the beginnings of difficult times for the Iceni. I have seen it in the veins of the oak leaves. Today I will show you what I see."

Boadicea looked at her mother's pretty face, the scattering of fawn-colored freckles across her nose and cheeks making their appearance in the light of the sun. She wished she had freckles like her mother, but whenever she took the mirror outside to see, she had none.

The shadow of the great oak fell across the three of them. It was more than twenty times taller than she, its branches reaching out towards the edge of the clearing that had been kept open for generations by her mother's people and now by her father.

Boadicea liked its shape, for the branches were evenly matched on each side, making the tree look like the giant plumed tail of a hawk.

Her mother removed a tiny flagon from a deerskin pouch and poured the contents at the base of the tree.

"I have brought you Boadicea for your guidance and protection. May she do honor by you. This sacred water is our gift." The clear liquid sparkled and danced its way out of the blue bottle. It soaked into the ground leaving only a small, damp spot.

Durina turned to her. "The prayer for your protection is as follows: 'Your branches are strong to give me strength, your leaves hold the secrets of the future to give me wisdom, and your trunk stands tall to give me honor.' You must repeat that prayer each time you're in the presence of our sacred tree."

Boadicea listened intently, her mother's voice obliterating all other sounds and all other things except the oak tree. She thought about the words carefully and repeated them slowly with perfection. She was pleased to see her parents nod their approval. She concentrated on the moment, for she never wanted to forget it.

"It's time to wash the acorn paste from your face and arms in our sacred stream," Durina said.

"It will be cold," her father said.

Boadicea nodded. She had never been happier.

Grass whipped around Boadicea's knees as she skipped across the meadow behind Rhys. At twelve she was nearly as tall as he.

"I will not teach you how to use a slingshot, Boadicea. I don't like little children following me around." Rhys folded his arms across his chest, the straight stick with its three leather thongs in question almost hidden from sight.

Boadicea's mouth dropped open. How dare he! "I am not a child, Rhys. I am twelve summers on this earth and only two summers younger than you. I am old enough to be a priestess."

"You are not a priestess, yet. You may fail the next test for all you know." Rhys turned and walked away from the angry girl.

Boadicea lunged and knocked Rhys to the ground. The two of them rolled and Boadicea got in a few good blows with her flailing arms.

"Stop that. Get off me." Rhys rolled over onto his back trapping the furious girl beneath him, but not before she hit him twice in the face. Even though he was taller and outweighed her he could not hold her down, and she squirmed out from under him in one smooth motion.

Boadicea's rage blinded her, and she continued to strike her friend. Rhys pushed her, but she did not feel it. He leaped to his feet, but she fell forward and knocked him down again. She sat on him while assaulting him in the face and chest with both fists.

"Stop it, Boadicea. Stop that or I'll have to really hurt you." Rhys let fly a fist that connected with her eye.

The squishing sound followed by a throbbing pain only fueled Boadicea's anger. "I won't until you promise to teach me how to use the slingshot." With that, she delivered another blow. Blood squirted from his nose and splattered her now dirty tunic with a ragged pattern of red. She ignored the hand that gripped her shoulder and hit Rhys again. He swung back and connected, fist against jaw, and she heard a crack. It hurt, but she willed her tears back.

She drew back her fist, ready to pound Rhys into the ground when she heard him chuckle, then laugh out loud. She held her blow and looked down at him uncertain of this abrupt change of mood. She frowned. "Are you laughing at me?"

"I can't help it, Boadicea. You look terrible! Your hair is flying in all directions and your eye is swelling shut. You look like an old crone rather than a priestess."

Boadicea tried to frown, but her face felt stiff. "You don't look very good yourself. I think I broke your nose, and I know I put bumps and bruises all over your ugly face."

Rhys continued to laugh. "Your jaw will be purple, too. You'll be able to frighten even the Furies." He reached up and took Boadicea's fist in his hand. "You're caving in my chest. Get off me, will you?"

"Not until I get what I want." Boadicea glared at him with her one good eye.

Rhys still held her fist tightly in his own. "You have always given me trouble, you stubborn . . . stubborn . . ."

"I don't care what you call me. I do care that you teach me to use the sling." Boadicea leaned closer to Rhys, her hair falling forward and blocking the sun from his face. "You are the best with the sling. Why should you not want to teach me?"

Rhys turned his head away from her and loosened the grip on her fist.

"Come on, Rhys, why don't you want to teach me?"

"Because."

"That's no answer. Do you think I'm too stupid to learn?"

"Get off me, Boadicea. You're as heavy as the boars in the woods."

"I won't until you tell me why you won't teach me the slingshot."

"All right! I won't teach you because you'll do better than me. Now will you get off?"

Her mouth fell open in astonishment, and she rocked back on her heels.

Rhys seized the opportunity and rolled over, dumping Boadicea to the ground.

She stared at him, his head in his arms and his back to the sky, then she got up and walked away.

Boadicea didn't know how she got to the stream next to her sacred oak tree, but she was there. A pool had formed behind a row of rocks she and Rhys had piled up to make a place to swim. She leaned over and looked into it. Her face looked like chopped meat before cooking. She dipped her hand in the water, brought it up to her eye, and winced when the cold water touched the swelling. She looked at her hands, caked with blood and dirt, then unpinned the filigree brooch at her shoulder and let the soiled tunic drop to her feet.

The water was cold and her breath caught in her throat as the dark liquid closed over her head. She touched bottom and came up quickly, swimming slowly.

She ducked under and held her breath until the cold water made her eye and jaw feel better. She popped to the surface and held out her hands. The right hand was swollen, but the dirt and blood were gone. She swam to the bank, reached for the hidden soap root, and rubbed it into her hair until she had a lather. She laid her head back and let the water carry the soapy bubbles away.

Although she felt better physically, she still hurt. It was wrong to let her temper cause another person pain, for her parents had taught her better. She was shocked to discover that she had enjoyed hitting Rhys. He had always been her very best friend—until now. He would probably never cross shadows with hers again.

A twig snapped and Boadicea looked toward the path she had come down an hour before. She was not afraid, for no one had ever tried to harm any of her father's people. The Iceni were known as powerful friends, but formidable foes.

She knew it was Rhys before she saw him because of his gait. He barely limped from the accident he had had two years ago. Boadicea believed her mother's medicines and the birch bark cast she put on Rhys' broken leg kept him from being a cripple.

He had come to her, and Boadicea could feel her face turn red from shame. She tried to sound the same as she always did when she called to him. "Rhys! Come join me."

Rhys appeared at the edge of the creek, his nose swollen to twice its normal size. Bruises covered his face, and his once colorful tunic was muddy brown.

Boadicea wanted to laugh at the sight, but remembering that she was the cause of his discomfort, felt the laughter fade to be replaced by sympathy. "Come in and swim. It'll make you feel better."

"I didn't come to swim. I came to apologize, and to tell you that I will teach you to use the slingshot."

"What?"

"I said that . . ."

"I heard you, but I don't believe the words that were flung from your mouth." Boadicea cocked her head and looked at Rhys with her good eye. "Why did you change your mind? Is there some trick to this?"

Rhys shook his head. He stared at his feet.

"Did I make you so angry that you don't ever want to see me again?" Boadicea held her breath and waited for his answer. If he hated her, she would die.

"No."

"Why do you stare at your feet? You've done nothing to be ashamed of." Boadicea wanted to touch him, but he seemed so distant. "We are friends, aren't we? You can tell me anything. I promise I won't hit you."

"I am ashamed of my jealousy. I wanted to be better in just one thing. Even if it's just the slingshot."

Boadicea frowned. She didn't understand, but she couldn't lose Rhys. He meant the world to her. She loved him above all her other friends.

"Then I shall never ask you again, Rhys," she whispered.

"That's not right. You will be the chief of the Iceni. It's not for me to deny you knowledge especially when you will rule me one day. I have been selfish." Rhys looked at her, then bent down and threw a pebble into the water.

Boadicea watched rings form, then dissipate. "I am the one who was selfish. I always want what others have. I always want to be the best no matter who it hurts. I am not fit to be a chief or a priestess. I have failed to learn the lessons of my parents."

"I have come to ask your forgiveness, Boadicea."

"I don't want forgiveness from you, Rhys. I want you to be my friend, and friends don't have to forgive. That's what my father told me. Please come swim with me and let's forget our fight." Boadicea swam over and tugged at the bottom of Rhys' tunic. "Cold water makes the flame of hurt die away."

"I am not worthy to share your sacred pool."

"You're being stubborn again. You helped me to build this pool, and it is as much yours as mine. Please do not make me beg. I have already had to beg for something from you once today."

"The water makes the wounds of war feel better?" Rhys asked.

Boadicea nodded. "I'll even give you the soap root to use."

"You will not hit me?"

Boadicea almost failed to notice the twinkle in Rhys' eyes. She stood and put her hands on her hips. "I will only strike you if you don't come into this water at once."

"All right. I can't take a second fight today. There isn't a place on my body for another bruise." Rhys unpinned his tunic and let it fall to the ground. He jumped into the pool with his legs folded close to his chest and as near to Boadicea as possible and splashed her with a great wave. He came up sputtering from the cold.

Boadicea held out the soap root. "Here, wash your hair. It's a mess, for now you've made it muddy and no longer is it the color of wheat. It's the color of cow dung."

"So was yours." Rhys took the root and rubbed it in his hair. "Your face, your tunic, and your arms were the color of cow dung."

"Not now. Here, let me wash your back. Look at this mess. There's dirt ground into your skin." Boadicea took the root and scraped it across Rhys' back.

"It's only ground in because you weigh as much as that mother pig you have penned up. Ouch! Don't rub so hard." Rhys squirmed away and dove under the water, leaving a residue of brown bubbles on the surface.

When he was out of reach, he popped to the top of the water. He snatched his tunic off the bank and slapped it down on the water, causing a spray to fly into Boadicea's face.

"Don't start a water fight, Rhys."

"A water fight? I am cleaning my dirty tunic, thanks to you." He slapped the water again, sending rainbow droplets into the air that rained down on Boadicea.

"That's not how you do it." Boadicea slipped under the water, gliding toward Rhys. Before he could get away, she grabbed his legs and pulled him under, and backed out of reach.

She laughed when he came sputtering to the surface. "That's how a tunic is washed."

"Thank you very much for the lesson in laundering. I shall repay you by teaching you the slingshot."

"No, Rhys. It would not be fair."

"Are you afraid you wouldn't become as good as I am?"

"Of course not. I could become better than you any time I choose. I could learn on my own, too, but you're the best, and I want to learn from the best."

"Then you'd better be up at dawn tomorrow for your first lesson," Rhys said. "I won't be easy on you like I am with my little brother and sister. I will make you beg for a rest."

"Be quiet. It isn't polite to brag," Boadicea said. "Come here and I'll wash your hair for you."

"And snatch me bald? No, thank you. Throw me the root, and I'll take care of myself." Rhys held up his hands and caught the root with ease.

Boadicea shivered, the coldness of the water finally permeating to her bones. She climbed out of the water and stood in the sun, wringing the water from her hair. She looked up to see Rhys watching her.

"You're getting the beginnings of womanhood," he said.

Boadicea looked down. It was the first time she had noticed.

"It won't be much longer before we can be married." Rhys smiled at her.

She smiled back. "I know. We shall have many children, I assure you. The veins in the oak leaves promise that I shall have many to follow me."

Rhys watched as Boadicea let the stone pop from the sling at the perfect moment to hit the knot on the pine tree dead center. "Good."

She stuck out her lower lip and blew upwards to move a coppery strand of hair out of her eyes. "You've taught me well, Rhys."

"I showed you a few things, but you have a natural instinct for the sling."

Boadicea laughed. "You sound unhappy."

"May the gods forgive me, but I would like to see you fail—just once. Only once, Boadicea."

"Really? Why?"

"Because I'm stupid, that's why." Rhys kicked a stone, and winced as it stung his bare toe.

"I've always wanted to be able to ride a horse as well as you do."

"You ride all right."

"I don't ride as if I am one with the animal. Father says that you think like the horse you're on and ride him from inside his own head. Father says that I should learn to ride like that, but to be honest, I . . . I am a little afraid of riding. I feel as if I'm about to fall off. Father says I am just an appendage to a horse and not a part of the horse as you are."

"Your father said that about me?" Rhys looked at Boadicea from the corner of his eye.

"He thinks you're the best rider in our tribe. He said even after you fell, you weren't afraid. I wish I could be as easy around horses as you are," Boadicea said.

Rhys stared at her. "I never would have guessed you didn't like horses. You're always around them."

Boadicea wrinkled her nose. "That's because Father makes me. Actually, I'm not afraid of them, but I've never found a horse that I could feel close to."

"The problem is that you haven't found a horse that fits you."

Boadicea placed another stone in the pouch of the sling, whirled it around, and listened for the tale-tell thud. A piece of bark flew off the tree as the stone hit it left of center. "A horse that fits? It sounds like making shoes."

"I want to show you how to find a good horse."

"You do?"

Rhys nodded. "I might as well. If you decide you want a horse, you'll just go to the pasture and get one without considering anything you should."

"I'm not that bad."

"What do you look for when you get a horse?"

"I . . . I make sure it's not lame. I look to see that its ribs aren't showing." Boadicea pursed her lips. "What else is there?"

"There are a lot of things," Rhys said.

Boadicea's eyebrows arched upwards. "Such as?"

"Such as checking his tendons, joints, the condition of his coat." Rhys shook his head. "I don't suppose you ever consider a horse's temperament."

"What's that?" Boadicea asked.

"I guess I have a lot to teach you."

"You make me sound stupid. You don't have to teach me anything. I can learn on my own if I want to know something." Boadicea whirled her arm around again and let go with another pebble. It made a resounding thud against the tree, the flying chips underscoring her rising anger.

"I do not make you sound stupid. You're acting so . . . so . . ." Rhys kicked a clump of dirt, sending miniature clods flying. He turned and grabbed Boadicea by both shoulders and shook her. "Why do you always turn a favor from me into a contest?"

Boadicea jerked away from Rhys. "It's not a contest. You don't owe me any favors, and I certainly don't want to owe you any."

Rhys frowned and stepped back. "I seem to bring out the worst in you. I don't mean to do that. Listen to me for a minute, and I'll try to explain."

Boadicea lowered the slingshot to her side. "I'm sorry."

"We both know that you're going to be chief of this tribe. It only makes sense, as I've told you before, that you should know more than the rest of us together." Rhys smiled. "Besides, when we are married, I want a wife who can keep up with me."

"Keep up with you? I would think that it would be the other way around." Boadicea grinned.

"Come on, Trouble. Let's go out to the south pasture where all the horses are. I'll show you what makes a good horse. If you have the right horse, you just might become a better rider and a better hunter."

Boadicea tied the slingshot to her belt and trotted along with Rhys, her long legs matching him stride for stride, which was not easy, for even though Rhys had a limp, he refused to let it slow him down. She looked sideways at him and admired his profile with his straight nose, long lashes, and strong chin.

They walked through the village and down the main road that had been beaten so hard by wagons and people that little dust was raised as they passed. Round mud and timber huts lined both sides of the road. Boadicea liked the white-washed huts with their neatly thatched roofs and square windows. Laundry hung outside most of the huts, and women brought their looms or their pottery wheels outdoors to work in the sun.

Knee-babies clutched their mothers mesmerized by spinning wheels. Puppies chased their tails, enemies impossible to catch no matter how fast they were pursued.

Chidren ran after Rhys begging him to play. Boadicea smiled at their grimy faces and grass-stained tunics.

"They like you, Rhys. You'll be a good father."

"I like children. They're simple and honest."

Boadicea considered what he had said, turning it over again and again in her mind, wondering exactly what he meant. There was nothing wrong with children, but since she had neither brother nor sister, she wasn't at all certain about them.

Once she had asked her mother why there were no brothers or sisters for her. Her mother turned to Boadicea, her eyes misty, and said that the babies born before Boadicea had died at birth or had been born early and after Boadicea, there were none. Then her mother had smiled and said, "It proves that you are special."

Boadicea wrinkled her nose as they passed the lower end of the village, where her father had decreed that all the people live whose work created unpleasant odors. Hides were tanned with urine. The pungent smell caused her nose to sting as she and Rhys crossed over the bridge that spanned the tiny creek. The dyer's cottage was next to the tanner's hut and the creek was colored deep brown from the run off of both their homes. Long strips of brightly colored material stretched across pole frames set up in front of the dyer's cottage and offset the unpleasantness of the smell.

Boadicea waved at Gwendolyn whose rainbow-colored arms contrasted with her brown hair. Gwendolyn was able to nod in acknowledgment since her arms were full of wet cloth and dye ran down her tunic, a deep brown from layers of bright colors that ran together to form non-colors. When Gwendolyn turned to hang the cloth on the poles, the back of her tunic was bright with slashes of color.

The tanner was nowhere in sight, but steam rose from the huge kettles in his front yard, and the stench made Boadicea press her nostrils together with her fingers. Her eyes watered and she wanted to run, but it would be impolite.

The pasture was close to the village, for horses were used often for riding, plowing, and pulling chariots. Rhys and Boadicea leaned against the fence that had been built of woven tree branches held together by upright posts. Bushes had been planted on the field side of the fence to discourage horses from jumping.

Boadicea watched the horses and their foals as if she were seeing them for the first time. She looked hard to find differences.

Rhys pointed. "See that one over there. . . ."

Boadicea put her fingers to his lips. "Wait! Don't tell me. Let me watch first, and I'll tell you what I see." She glanced up at his eyes that were lake-water blue and turned back toward the horses, barely aware that her heart was beating faster.

"I like that filly. See, the bay," Boadicea said.

"Why?"

"I don't know. She's pretty."

"That she is, but her chest is too narrow. She's too small boned. She wouldn't be good in battle." Rhys clapped his hands and shouted. The filly skittered sideways, then ran to the far side of the pasture.

"She would be hard to train?"

"Not necessarily, but she'd be hard to keep calm in battle." Rhys shaded his eyes and scanned the field. "See the colt that runs along the far fence line? He seems to have more energy than the others his age. What do you think of him?"

"He's large even for his age," Boadicea said.

"That one was sired by the strongest stallion in the village. That year old has a love of competition. See, he taunts the others into racing with him." Rhys pointed at the young colt. "Now watch. There! He pretends he cannot run any faster than they do. When he has them fooled, he pulls away and leaves them behind. That would be a good horse to train if he can be calmed. Do you want to come back tomorrow with a rope?"

"How do we train him?"

"We start by feeding him by hand, then petting him, smoothing his coat. Eventually we'll lay across his back. Next is a harness. Each step we take is done slowly and gently. A harsh broken horse does not love its master. It'll take long hours of hard work. Are you willing?" Rhys asked.

Boadicea folded her arms on the top rail of the fence and tucked her chin down. She watched the colt as sun glinted off his sorrel coat, highlighting the reddish-gold flecks of hair. He chose that moment, as if he knew he was the center of her attention, to stare at her. He trotted toward her, tantalizingly close, and with a toss of his head, turned his rump toward her and cantered away. Boadicea laughed at his audacity emphasized by the switching of his tail.

"Let's work with that one, Rhys. Now I know what you mean by choosing a horse that fits." She laughed again, leaning against Rhys.

"I have this peculiar feeling that you and that horse have similar personalities. You're both difficult to put in harness."

Boadicea looked to see if Rhys were joking. He was not. She looked back toward the yearling that raced across the pasture, kicking up little clumps of grass. "It's because we have a need to be free, totally free. Do you think it's wrong to harness a creature who loves freedom so much?"

"I can't answer that. Perhaps you would be better able tell me." Rhys smiled at her. "However, with the loss of freedom comes comfort. He will be well-tended."

Boadicea chewed on her lower lip. "There is nothing that can replace freedom."

"There is one thing," Rhys said. "I've heard in songs that love can do anything, even make you want to give up freedom."

"Oh, Rhys! A person who truly loves another would never ask him to give up freedom."

Boadicea stared across the pasture to the hills beyond. "I'd rather be dead than to be enslaved."

"And if the Romans come as your father predicts?"

"I will fight them as long as I have life."

Rough laughter from behind them caused Rhys and Boadicea to turn. She frowned when she saw Gryffyth.

"Why do you always sneak up on me?" Boadicea glared at the boy who was near her age. He'd bullied her for as long as she could remember.

"The great chief's daughter admits that I sneak up on her?" Gryffyth laughed again.

"Go away, Gryffyth," Rhys said. "We're busy."

"That's the trouble with both of you. You're too good to talk to us lowly ones." He spat at their feet. "Someday you won't be so high and mighty. Someday you'll beg me to be your friend."

"I'd rather be dead than be a friend to the likes of you. You don't know the meaning of honor or loyalty," Rhys said.

Gryffyth raised his fist and shook it in Rhys' face. "I will fight you any time you say."

"I won't waste my time with you." Rhys turned his back to Gryffyth and leaned on the fence.

Gryffyth bent down and picked up a rock and brought his hand up above Rhys' head.

Boadicea screeched and kicked Gryffyth between his legs. He groaned, bent double, and, clutching his crotch, fell to the ground.

"Let's go, Rhys. I have no use for cowards." Boadicea pulled her surprised friend from the fence. When she glanced over her shoulder as they walked away, she could see Gryffyth still cringing on the ground.

"Did you kick him?" Rhys asked.

"Yes. I'm glad I did. I wish he'd go away and never return. He was going to crush your head with a rock!" Boadicea looked at Rhys. "I would hate for anything to happen to you. In spite of all your faults, I couldn't live without you."

"He handles well after just two months, doesn't he?" Boadicea patted the horse.

"Yes, but never trust a horse. Never." Rhys said.

"I named him Thayne so that he'd want to follow me."

Laughter erupted from Rhys. "Don't count on it."

"He likes me."

"That's because you feed him apples every day. I wonder that your cook hasn't noticed the fruit cellar is almost empty."

"It isn't. I just give him the withered ones that wouldn't be used." Boadicea cantered the colt up a hill and waited for Rhys to catch up. "Your mare does very well. She's lovely."

"I raised her. From the minute she was born, I knew she'd be a good horse."

"Why did you name her Ella?"

"She's like a sprite, so I gave her an elfin name," Rhys said.

"Look! There's a dust cloud across the valley? Does a storm come?"

"I've never seen a storm like that." Rhys shaded his eyes with his hand. "I see riders. Dozens of them. Maybe close to a hundred."

"The Brigantes! Father said that they refused to sign a new peace treaty." Boadicea shivered. "They're fierce warriors and always seem to want to fight someone."

"I think it's our turn. Head for the woods before they see us. We have to warn your father." Rhys slapped Ella on the rump and she shot forward.

Thayne took his head quickly, and it was all Boadicea could do to hang on. She squeezed her legs against Thayne's belly and lay low across his mane. In less than half an hour they were in their village. Rhys reached the edge of the settlement first and shouted a warning. Someone rang the bell, and workers raced from the fields that circled the huts. Weapons, always handy, were brought forth by those who had stayed at home to work.

"Father! Father! The Brigantes are close behind us!" Boadicea slid off her horse as her parents ran from their hut. "I need my sword!"

"No!" her father yelled. "You are not ready to use your sword against the likes of them."

"But Father, you allow others my age to fight."

"They are ready. You are good, but are not a warrior yet."

Boadicea, shocked at her father's denial, felt hot tears sting her eyelids. "Father, I want to fight. I need to fight. Mother, tell him!"

Durina shook her head. "Your father knows the way of war."

"But Mother!"

"I don't have time to argue. I must prepare for a battle." Garik strapped on his sword and waved at Rhys who had already saddled the chief's horse.

"I am ready to fight." Boadicea watched her father ride to the head of the army and down the main road through the village.

"You are good with medicines. That will be our war—to fight to save our people." Durina tugged Boadicea's sleeve. "Come. Let's get our potions ready. You start the water to boiling."

"How can you be so calm when Father could be killed?" Boadicea's chin quivered.

"I am an Iceni Queen." Durina gave her daughter a kiss, then entered the kitchen.

Boadicea ran to the well and drew two buckets of water. She banked the coals, blew on them, and added more peat and wood. It would take a long time to boil that much water. She stared at the pots. Would they never steam? Boadicea sprang to her feet and raced to the front door. She heard nothing.

"Wait a minute. Father said I wasn't ready to use my sword. He said nothing about the slingshot."

Boadicea leaped on Thayne's back and urged him through the woods. The sounds of battle were just ahead. Never had she heard so many men scream in agony. Dust rose and fell as warriors danced and slashed their way through enemy lines. Where was her father? There—he rode up and down the front lines shouting orders and encouragement.

Thayne snorted, but didn't bolt as Boadicea urged him forward. She rode along the side of the melee keeping to the shadows until she was closer to her father. A young Iceni warrior who clung to his horse like a burr followed him.

"Rhys, oh Rhys," she whispered. He fought alongside her father, his sword cut through one enemy, then two. If anything happened to either of them she would want to die, too.

The Brigantes surged forward and broke through the Iceni ranks. Boadicea sucked in her breath and instinctively her hand went to the slingshot. She kicked Thayne and he bolted toward the left flank of the Iceni front lines that bowed back in the middle. Her father rode out from among the Iceni and into the middle of the enemy.

Boadicea wanted to scream at him, but she knew he could not hear her. "Rhys, Rhys, save him!" But Rhys slashed right and left to save the foot soldiers near him. He had no time for her father.

She stared through the dust in time to see her father surrounded by the Brigantes. "No!"

Boadicea slapped Thayne on the rump with the rawhide sling-shot and as he leaped forward, she pulled four stones from her pouch. She loaded the slingshot, wound it up and let it fly. The stone struck one Brigantes in the forehead dead center and dropped him like an oak. "I hope your brains ooze out."

In quick succession, Boadicea let fly the second, third, and fourth rock. Each met a bare headed soldier and each split open their heads like a ripe melon, and each enemy dropped to the blood soaked ground. Her father was safe.

He glanced her way once, the startled look on his face replaced by a thunder cloud. Boadicea grabbed four more rocks from her pouch, loaded her sling, and prayed that her father would not be too severe with her. But she had saved his life! She didn't care what punishment she'd receive.

She only had a chance to let fly one more stone before the Brigantes pulled back, slashed their way to the rear, and fled.

Garik halted the pursuers. "No need!" he shouted. "It'll be a long time before they bother the Iceni again!" He smiled as cheers enveloped him.

Boadicea tucked her slingshot in the holder tied around her waist and rode home to tell her mother about the victory. She was so elated that she wondered only briefly what her punishment would be. And there would be punishment.

Thayne would have to remain saddled and tied outside while she hurried in to see what duties she needed to attend to. The wounded would be coming soon.

Durina glanced at her disheveled hair, her dusty tunic, and the slingshot. "You picked an interesting time to practice."

"Mother! The Brigantes have fled! Father comes home at the front of a victorious army."

"I had no doubts," Durina said.

"He was wonderful."

"Did you kill anyone with that apparatus?"

"I think I wounded four or five." Boadicea's face felt hot as the red crept up from her neck. She'd been trapped so easily.

"After you've helped with the wounded, we'll discuss your punishment for disobeying your father."

"Yes. I am ready for that. But Mother, it was wonderful! Father is a great warrior. I can learn so much from him!"

"Enough, Boadicea. The wounded have come." Durina turned and stirred dark green powder into a pot of boiling water. "Whatever are we to do with you, child?"

"I don't know, Mother." Boadicea tried to be contrite, but the excitement of battle overrode any guilt. "I love to fight."

"Yes." Durina's lips clamped together, a sign that there would be no more discussion until after the wounded were cared for.

Boadicea sighed. She wished she could have obeyed her parents, but if she had . . .

CHAPTER

II

SUETONIUS PAULINUS rushed through the garden gate and ran toward the villa. He barely had time to change his stained toga before joining friends for a night of long-awaited fun. There were more than enough places in Rome a soldier in training could relieve his aches and pains.

A smile decorated his handsome face as he remembered the ladies of his favorite house. They appreciated young, healthy soldiers. Maybe Phoebe would attend to him this evening. His smile broadened as he recalled her long, dark hair and dark skin. She knew how to please him.

Suetonius walked quickly past flowering hedges and through the grape arbor. He touched the marble bust of Tiberius, a habit he had developed as soon as the statue had been placed in the garden by his father. Tiberius had been emperor for a little more than three years, and the statue had been there almost as long. Suetonius wondered how much money his father had paid for it and if the statue would prevent Tiberius from wrongly suspecting the family of treason.

There were executions on a daily basis with some of the hapless ones killed along with their children and spouses. Suetonius shivered as he thought about the screams from Tarpeian Rock as the unfortunates were thrown to their deaths. Tiberius himself was as cold as the marble bust.

Suetonius pushed these thoughts from his mind lest they contaminate his family and bring them grief. Shivering, he hurried around the corner of the small building used by his family for worship and smacked into a girl, knocking her backwards. Suetonius was momentarily confused by the flash of white-blonde hair and the bouncing of peach-colored fruit flying in every direction from a basket that rolled across the grass. He stared down at the pale pink stola that was not covering the lovely legs of their owner.

Her eyes were the palest blue, almost as if the color had been forgotten by the gods. Hair floated about her shoulders like a thousand spider webs in the sunshine, and Suetonius wondered why this young girl, who was so beautiful, looked so unhappy.

He held his hand out. "Please. I am sorry." He stood and waited for the girl to take his hand. "Come on, let me help you."

She flushed and looked down. "I don't know if it is proper."

"Proper? Why not?"

"I am a slave." She pulled her stola down, covering her legs.

"Of course it's proper that I help you." Suetonius reached down and pulled her to her feet. "Are you new to this house?"

She nodded, tears sliding from the corner of her eyes. Suetonius, still holding her hands, asked, "Does the lady of the house beat you?"

"I don't know. I've just been brought here." She pulled her hands away. "Look at this mess. I was told to be most careful and bring in the best peaches, for the lady's son is coming home from the army's training. I suppose now I will be beaten." The tears flowed faster now, dripping off her cheeks and spotting the front of her stola, deepening the pink where they fell.

"The lady of this house does not beat her slaves. In fact, she treats them well." Suetonius walked the few steps to the peach basket and righted it. He bent over, picked up the fruit, and placed each one carefully in the basket. "There seems to be no harm done to the peaches." He finished and looked up to see the slave girl staring at him. "What is the matter?"

She started crying, again.

Suetonius' mouth gaped. "Now what is wrong? I have never seen one person produce so many tears." He waited for an explanation, but receiving none he stepped closer to her. "Would you explain yourself? Do it quickly before I lose my temper."

She stared at him, her eyes larger. Sniffling, she controlled herself long enough to blurt out, "I have never been a slave before, and I'm afraid I'll do something wrong and be executed." With that dreadful word flung from her mouth, she wept bitterly.

Suetonius almost laughed, then stopped himself. Her speech was hesitant, and she had an accent. Perhaps she had heard terrible stories about the Romans and, in her youthful ignorance, believed them. Well, why not? Did not their own Emperor, Tiberius, have a passion for execution? It must seem like a barbaric place to an outsider in spite of Rome's advanced civilization.

Suetonius lifted the full basket. "Come on, I'll walk you to the kitchen and explain the mishap to your mistress. She will forgive you, but probably not me." He walked a few paces and turned. "Why do you not walk with me?"

"Is it allowed?"

"You do not have to follow behind, but you may walk next to me." Suetonius sighed. "By the gods, you're timid. What is your name?"

"The mistress who purchased me has called me Trista, which I am told means 'melancholy', but that is not the name that my mother gave me." She wiped her eyes with the corner of her stola. "My mother named me Aloisia after her mother. The name fits me."

"I think I'll have to call you Trista for two reasons. The first is that I can't get my tongue to say your birth name." Suetonius moved down the path and stopped to wait for Trista.

She caught up with him and looking at him directly for the first time asked, "What is the second reason?"

"Trista fits you better since you are so sad."

"You would be, too, if you were taken from your family by a marauding band of soldiers."

"Roman soldiers? I don't remember any campaigns in the north. I assume from your light hair that you're from the north, am I right?"

"I am from a place that your people call Batavi." Trista held her chin higher. "Its proper name is Germany."

Suetonius chuckled. "Are you not afraid that your arrogance will get you executed?"

"Sometimes I don't care."

Suetonius walked in silence. "How old are you?"

"Old enough to feel the anger over the separation from my family, and too young to fight back. I'm sixteen." Trista glanced at the young man beside her. "How old are you?"

Suetonius straightened his shoulders. "I'm nearly eighteen. I've been in training for the army for two years. Someday I will be famous. The oracles have said that my name will be associated with victory, and it will live on in history for thousands of years."

Trista giggled.

"Why do you laugh? If you laugh, then we'll have to change your name."

"Now who is arrogant? I was always taught that arrogance could lead to a downfall."

Suetonius shifted the basket of peaches to his other arm. "Come along. I'm certain that you'll be missed if we don't hurry. We slave owners are still leery of slave revolts even a hundred years after Spartacus led slaves against their masters."

"And what happened? Did Spartacus win?" Trista trotted along beside Suetonius.

"You ask too many questions."

"Spartacus won, didn't he?"

"No, he didn't." Suetonius stopped at the back of the villa, holding open the wooden door that led to the kitchen. He waited, but Trista wouldn't enter. "You may enter before me if I say so, and I say so. You're too worried about protocol. Romans are a civilized society."

Trista opened her mouth to say something, then closed it. She walked through the door and stopped when she spied the lady of the house talking with the cook.

The lady turned when she heard the door close. "Son! You look wonderful!" She moved across the kitchen, her stola flowing, and kissed Suetonius on the cheek.

Suetonius put the basket on a table near the door. "I haven't been gone that long, Mother." He smiled at the mirror image of himself, although a softer version. The two of them shared shiny black hair, a patrician face that was delicate, yet powerful, and eyes that were such a dark brown they appeared black.

Suetonius noted that his mother had not aged as her friends had. Her figure was still youthful, and he knew that if she chose to be unfaithful to his father, she could have many suitors. Suetonius kissed her on the forehead, for one of their differences was that he was taller than she by six inches.

"I have prepared a special dinner for your return from training. Your father will be along after a while. I suppose you'll be spending a quiet evening at home with your family?" She tried to keep the smile from her lips and the twinkle from her eyes, but it didn't fool Suetonius.

He laughed. "Did you really expect me to spend a night at home?"

"I have to be realistic. As a woman who understands men, no. As your mother, I was hoping," Vivianne said. She stepped back from Suetonius and looked him over. "I suppose my son has departed and left a handsome soldier in his place. Go on and get rested for dinner. It'll be ready in hour." Vivianne turned toward Trista. "You, my dear, must go and tend to the two girls. They have been asking for the 'new one'. I believe they like you already. I trust you won't let them get into trouble."

Suetonius watched Trista as she almost ran from the kitchen. "Where did you find her? She isn't much like any of your other finds."

"I really didn't need another mouth to feed, but when I saw her at the sale, I couldn't resist. Suetonius, she was so frightened, and she was weeping. You know I can't stand it when someone cries. Besides, she is very beautiful and fragile. Anyway, she seems to get on well with the girls."

"And," Vivianne waved a spoon at her son, "you are not to treat her as your personal concubine. You know my feelings about that. We need no offspring to feed."

Suetonius frowned. "I know your peculiar beliefs and rules. Whatever did father say to you when you brought home another unnecessary slave?"

Vivianne's laughter was like wind in the laurel leaves. Suetonius listened closely. He was never certain of her mood when her laugh was quiet. "What did he say?"

"Caius shook his head, complained about the cost of so many slaves and went off to the bath. Nothing more will be said. Your father does not like conflict at home. He tells me that as a magistrate he sees enough conflict. I suppose that is true."

Suetonius shook his head. "I am amazed at how many times you get what you want. I'm glad I'm a soldier and will not expect to have a wife. If I did, she would not pull tricks on me."

The laughter that burst from the cook as well as Vivianne startled Suetonius. "What is so humorous?" He frowned at the cook who kept her back to him, but whose shoulders were shaking. Suetonius bristled. Since before he was born she had been his mother's slave, and she was like a second mother to him, but she had no right to laugh.

"My son, forgive us." Vivianne patted Suetonius' hand. "Never mind the domestic wars—you'll have real battles to fight. Let us leave the preparations for our meal to Lena and go to the atrium. It'll be cooler there. You need to tell me all about your training."

Suetonius followed his mother from the hot kitchen, wiping sweat from his forehead with a corner of his toga. "I don't want to remember all those hard hours of training. Suffice it to say that I have blisters in many places and muscles that ache that have never ached before."

The coolness of the hallway felt refreshing to Suetonius as they walked down the marble tiled floor. It felt good to be home, and he glanced into each of the family's sleeping rooms as they passed them. Lilting laughter of his two younger sisters drifted to him from the middle room. They sat on the floor and rolled colored glass marbles across a circle made of yarn. Trista was on the floor with them looking perplexed, but almost smiling.

The atrium was Suetonius' favorite part of their home. He stepped through the archway and moved across the mosaic tiled floor being careful not to step on the porpoises, a habit he had developed in childhood. Suetonius leaned against one of the four columns that framed the opening in the ceiling as well as the fountain and pool in the center of the large room.

A breeze ruffled the leaves of the laurel plants that lined one side of the pool. In the center of the pool a fountain in the shape of Venus spouted water from her hand. The spray sparkled in the light like miniature gems.

Vivianne patted the couch. "Come sit by me. I promise not to talk of the army."

Suetonius laughed. "I would appreciate that." He sank into the cushion. "Is this a new couch? I don't remember it." Suetonius ran his fingers over the carved horses' heads that formed the end pieces, their harnesses outlined in silver and copper inlay.

Vivianne swept her arm outward. "I replaced all the furniture in here. It was so old. After all, we do entertain a lot, although I get so tired of it."

Suetonius laughed. "You lead a dreary and difficult life, Mother."

"Don't make fun of me, young man." Vivianne smiled, then became serious. "I want to talk with you, be with you before you leave, but I don't know what to say to you." She paused and looked away. "When you were a child, we had many things in common, but now you've left my world for one of your own."

Suetonius looked at his mother steadily for a moment. "Maybe we don't have much in common anymore, but knowing you're here gives me strength to see myself through the roughest of days."

Vivianne leaned over and kissed her son on the cheek. "Thank you."

The walk through the city to his favorite house of prostitution helped Suetonius' dinner settle. Lena had prepared every dish that she could think of, including some that Suetonius believed she had invented. He might as well enjoy this change from army rations because for the rest of his life, he would be a military man. Only the gods knew where he would go and what he would eat then.

Suetonius looked down at his muscular arms. The rigorous training and the regimentation had given him powers over body and mind he never dreamed he would possess. He grinned as he remembered the many hours of his childhood that he had spent following the army down the broad, paved streets. Suetonius' heart had beat in time to the rhythmic prancing of the cavalry horses and the pounding of the infantry as they marched. Sunlight glared off the silver breast-plates and helmets that caused a knot to form in the pit of his stomach, and he ached with longing. He wanted to shout, to cry, whenever he saw the plumes wave like a rust-colored sea as the soldiers marched past him.

Suetonius laughed aloud and wondered if he would inspire a young boy as he had been inspired. He was glad that his father had promised him the best stallion that could be purchased. Hopefully, the Arabs would have a new shipment in soon. Their horses were the finest in the world, and he would have one, even if it meant more hours of training to teach his own horse what was expected in battle. There were no great riders in Rome, for the army was usually infantry trained, not cavalry, but he would hire an Arab to teach him. Suetonius shook his head. Those Arabs could cling to a horse like a cat on a bird.

The wind in the trees brought him back to the present, and he looked around startled that he stood in front of the place where he had first learned about love. He shivered in anticipation and made up his mind that he would wait for Phoebe. He moved up the few steps to the front door, stopped to listen for the music from the water organ that had made this house most famous. He felt the somber notes from the organ vibrate his breast bone before he actually heard the music. The organ sounded mournful, hardly a proper accompaniment to a night of joy, but none of the customers seemed to mind.

He moved into the atrium where olive-oil lamps cast smoky shadows on the walls. Across from him two young girls danced, castanets clicking in double time as a balding, old man pulled the valves in and out of the organ at a furious rate. His head was pink and shiny, drops of sweat getting bigger and bigger on his pate until they ran down his face pulled by the force of the gods of the underworld.

Suetonius moved to a couch and sat next to two men who looked too drunk to get their money's worth. The one drunk, hair askew, nudged the other one and said, "Do you think it's this one's first time? He hasn't even gotten the razor to shave his cheeks yet."

Suetonius started to speak, but thought better of it. These men weren't worth his time, and the second man was almost asleep anyway. Suetonius waved his hand in front of his face to create fresh air. Both men were in dire need of a bath. He hoped they didn't choose the bath house he and his father frequented.

A tall, red-haired woman smiled and moved quickly across the atrium toward Suetonius. "I see you have survived the army's training. Who would you like tonight? Phoebe, again?"

The wrinkles in her tired face were not skillfully hidden under a bread and cream paste. The oil lanterns did her sagging facial muscles no justice either. Suetonius knew the hair had to be dyed with henna, and it, too, had the look of having lived too long and too hard.

"You must think that I am unimaginative, never having been loved but by one woman."

"I can offer you whatever you want. I don't think about what you want one way or another."

Her smile was practiced. "Tonight I could suggest Phoebe and Patricia. You are young. Two women could make you happy until the light of dawn."

Suetonius hesitated and shook his head. "I want Phoebe."

The madam pursed her creased mouth and cocked her head. "You are not falling in love with my whore, are you? It would be unwise."

Suetonius laughed. "No, I have only lust and a man's need that cannot be fulfilled any other way. Enough talk. Is Phoebe ready for me?"

"Come with me. I will let you spend the night for only a few coins more."

Suetonius rose from the couch, leaving his dual companions to their snoring contest. "I doubt that you have ever offered anyone anything for a few coins."

Her laughter, youthful in contrast to her appearance, rippled from deep within the aging body. She swayed slightly as she crossed the atrium and sauntered down the hallway.

Suetonius felt his strong knees weaken as he drew nearer to the room where memories were made that had carried him through the lonely nights in camp. His stomach betrayed his anxiety with a low rumble, and he coughed to cover the noise. He wondered what Lena had used in the fish sauce, and he vowed to never eat that much again just before love-making.

"Phoebe, your favorite customer has returned from the rigors of camp life. Give him your best. He will stay with you until the sun rises." With a smile, the madam held out her hand and waited as Suetonius dropped in one coin after another.

When he stopped and she still kept her hand out-stretched, Suetonius frowned, but the need to make love was greater than the need to squabble over price, so he paid until the madam got his last coin except for the gold piece he had hidden in his toga. That coin was for Phoebe, for he knew she was not given what she was worth.

He waited until the madam had turned her back and withdrawn to the atrium before he looked at Phoebe. He wanted to give her all his attention in order to build on the memories he already had. She looked more beautiful than the last time he had seen her. Her black hair curled close against her head and dropped in tight, fuzzy ringlets down her back. She smiled at him with her almond-shaped eyes and held out her hand.

Suetonius pulled the curtain across the doorway and took the soft hand. He let himself be led toward the pallet on the floor, not daring to imagine what new tricks Phoebe had for him tonight.

She unpinned his toga, letting it drop to the floor. "You are my most handsome lover. For me, there is pleasure with you." She pushed him down on the pallet and standing above him, dropped her own garment.

Suetonius watched the shadows from the oil lamps darken her already dark skin and pulled her toward him, wanting to feel her warmth. He almost groaned aloud. Tonight would be perfect.

The noise from his younger sisters awakened him, and Suetonius rolled over to look out the doorway to the hall. The shadows told him that it was late afternoon. He didn't care. He pulled the covers over his head and tried to shut out the noise. It was the subsequent screams followed by crying that caused him to bolt off the couch. He grabbed the cover, wrapped it around himself, tripped over his hobnailed marching sandals, and howled in pain. He hopped around, edging his way toward the door and then strode to his sisters' room as the crying became louder. He put his head in their doorway and blinking sleep from his eyes, bellowed.

His roaring never frightened Zia, the older of his two sisters. She giggled, which made her reddish-brown ringlets bob up and down. Her gray eyes sparkled, and her face had a look that told Suetonius she was causing trouble, as usual. She stood there, rocking back and forth on her bare feet holding her hands behind her back.

Suetonius looked across the room. Trista was cowering in the corner, hiding her face with her hands. Elysia, his youngest sister, was clinging to Trista and had her face buried in the folds of the slave girl's stola.

Suetonius frowned at Zia. "What have you done now? How can there be any peace in this house with you around?" He looked at his impish sister. "You're hiding something behind your back. Let me see it."

Zia shook her head and stepped back.

Suetonius moved quickly, but not in time to catch the evasive urchin. She stuck her tongue out and ran toward the door. Suetonius blocked the doorway and swept the child into his arms. In the process of capturing her, he almost lost the sheet he had wrapped around himself. He held Zia and grabbed the sheet with one hand which wasn't enough to keep his backside covered. Zia reached around and twisted a piece of his flesh between her fingers until Suetonius let go of her.

"You child of the underworld! Give me whatever you have hidden behind your back." Suetonius swatted at Zia.

Zia pulled back her right arm and let fly with the object of terror. It hit Suetonius in his mid-section and he caught it without thinking about the consequences. The over-sized rat bit him on the thumb and refused to let go. Suetonius swung his hand against the plaster door frame and snapped the rat's neck. It dropped to the floor, eyes staring at nothing; its long front teeth hanging out of thin lips.

Suetonius kicked the rat toward the fleeing Zia. "I will see to it that a curse is put on you, you child of the demons." He turned and looked at the two girls huddled in the corner. They stared at him, their eyes wide and their faces salt-streaked from tears.

"I'm sorry she scared you. She has always been mischievous." Suetonius' faced reddened as he felt a breeze cool his backside. He pulled the sheet around him and not knowing what else to do, stood there.

"I think Zia's the meanest thing there is," Elysia said. Her chin trembled.

Suetonius forgot his embarrassment and moved across the room toward his sister. He knelt in front of her and pulled her into his arms. He nuzzled her plaited hair, the darkest of black like his own. "You know that if you could overcome your fear of her, she would no longer be able to control you as she does."

Elysia sniffled. "Why is she mean to me? I don't do anything to her."

"I don't know." Suetonius hugged the little girl. "I have an idea. Let's go swimming."

Elysia looked up at her brother. "I don't know how to swim."

"I had to learn while I was in training. I'll show you, and you'll be able to swim away from Zia," Suetonius said.

"What am I supposed to do? I was told to watch both the girls, and I can't be in two places at once," Trista said.

Suetonius studied the round face, the tear streaks cutting across her cheeks like scars. "You come with us. I think you've had enough of Zia for the time being. I'll tell Mother what happened." Suetonius stood and walked toward the doorway, stooping to pick up the dead rat.

He turned, one hand holding his bed sheet and in the other hand dangled the rat. "Wear a short stola for swimming so the material won't wrap around your legs. Be ready in half the hour and wait in the garden." He frowned as he realized Trista was giggling, but he chose to ignore her. He backed from the room and walked swiftly toward his own sleeping quarters.

The booming voice of his father stopped him at the door. Suetonius turned. "Yes, Father?"

"Are you just now getting out of bed? I thought military training would have you up at sunrise." The silver haired man chuckled. "I heard some commotion down the hall coming from your sisters' room. Has Zia been behaving badly again?"

Suetonius pointed to the dead rat he had placed in a potted fern. "That rat was alive when Zia scared the new slave and your younger daughter."

Caius ran his fingers through his hair, pushing back the strand that always fell across his forehead. He squinted a little, age making his eyesight blurry when he looked at things close-up. "She should have been a boy. She's always doing things that I expected from you. Of course, you were nearly ten when Zia was born and you didn't have the benefit of sisters to tease when you were at the teasing stage. You did torment the children in the neighborhood, though." Caius squinted, almost hiding his gray eyes, to study Suetonius' face. "Do you want to eat dinner? Or should we call it breakfast?"

Suetonius shook his head. "I promised Elysia that I would teach her to swim to help her forget the bad time that Zia gave her. I wish I could make Zia change."

Caius laughed. "You can never make women change, no matter what age they are. I learned that the first time I was married." Caius looked past Suetonius. "Even though I have been fortunate both times I've been married, I learned a long time ago that women cannot be changed. My advice to you is to be happy you're in the army."

"I am content, but I'll be more so when I am promoted."

Caius grinned and slapped Suetonius on the back. "You have ambition. You'll go far."

"It has been said by the oracles."

Caius looked steadily at his son. "You have been given word that you'll be famous. Opportunity is presented to you, but it is not a guarantee. You must do your own work."

"I know that, Father."

The sun sparkled off aqua water that was now calm. It hadn't been so smooth while Suetonius and Elysia had been splashing around. Suetonius watched Elysia and Trista through half-closed eyes as he lay back, his head pillowed in his arms. Both were laughing and smiling, as they played a game with knuckle bones, their experience with Zia forgotten.

Suetonius sat up. "Where did you learn to swim, Trista?"

Trista hesitated, frowned, and shook her head. "I don't know. I think we were taught swimming at a very young age. The water here is much warmer. The water where I came from is so cold that we could keep food in it, and it wouldn't spoil." She rolled two knuckle bones around in her left hand. "I can't remember learning to swim. I have always known how." Trista giggled. "Where did you learn to swim?"

"You made fun of my swimming."

"No! I just wondered about the style of it."

"You made fun of my swimming." Suetonius leaned toward her.

"I wouldn't make fun of the son of my mistress. I'm not anxious to be beaten."

"You keep expecting my mother to have you beaten. Don't be absurd. Our slaves are too valuable to be beaten. Besides, we couldn't stand your crying." Suetonius smiled at her. "So tell me the truth. Weren't you making fun of my swimming?"

Trista laughed. "I tried not to, but you looked so funny with your arms flailing about and water going everywhere."

"My commanding officer wouldn't be happy to learn that you don't like the way he taught me to swim." Suetonius leaned back on his elbows.

"What kinds of things did you learn to do in the army? I hope you do better in other things than you did in swimming." Trista bit her lower lip to keep from smiling.

"Your words are barbed. I may bleed from them."

"How did you get in the army? Does everyone have to be in it?" Trista moved over and sat beside Suetonius. She glanced back at Elysia who had fallen asleep on the blanket spread across thick grass.

"Not just anyone is allowed in the army. You have to have a letter of recommendation from someone who has been in the army or is well-known. My father had a friend who agreed to write a letter for me. I did have a little trouble getting in because I was more than a year younger than most recruits. The interview was difficult, but I convinced them that I wanted to spend my life in the army."

"Where will you go?"

Suetonius shrugged. "Anywhere in the world, since we control most of it."

"Aren't you afraid? I was afraid when I came here."

"We are so highly trained that we can conquer any army, any place, any time." Suetonius saw a look of pain wash across Trista's face. Without thinking about her feelings, he continued. "We are trained to be the best. When we train with swords, we start with wooden ones that are double weighted. Soon we're stronger than we need to be. We have to make our shields of heavy branches woven together and those are twice as heavy." Suetonius sat up and bent his arm. "See these muscles? No enemy can conquer a Roman army because we're all strong and well-trained."

Trista touched his muscular arm. "I would still be afraid."

"Hmmmph. All women are born afraid."

"May you have cause to regret those words." Trista's voice was bitter. "My mother was not afraid. She saved my life and gave her own." Trista turned away and stared at the water.

"I'm sorry."

"I don't want to think about it. Tell me more about your training."

"I don't want to spend my life marching, so I'm in the cavalry. You get promoted faster if you're in the cavalry." Suetonius watched the clouds as they swirled across the sky. He hadn't had time to look at the sky while he was in training. He sighed. Lazy days like this would be limited. "I had to learn to vault onto a horse with and without my armor. I had to learn to use a slingshot from the back of a horse, and I had to learn to use my sword from a galloping horse. We trained for months for every possibility in battle."

Trista wrinkled her nose. "I'm glad I don't have to learn all that. It sounds dangerous."

Suetonius chuckled. "No more dangerous than trying to take care of Zia."

"I wish I weren't so afraid of her." Trista looked down at her hands. They were larger than the hands of the Roman women, and she tried to fold them together. The result was awkward.

"If she knows you're afraid of what she does, she'll try it again. I told you that this morning. She won't bother me because I'm not afraid of anything." Suetonius reached for his sandals. "Come on, let's go home and see if Lena has anything for us to eat. I'm hungry."

"Shall I awaken Elysia?" Trista looked at the younger child. "She is so pretty."

"Go ahead. She's slept long enough." Suetonius tied his sandals and stood up. "Bring the blanket and let's go." He took one last look at the pond and turned toward his family's villa.

The walk back would take longer than usual for him since he couldn't practice his double time march with a five year old tagging along.

Elysia skipped up beside him and slipped her hand in his. She looked up at her brother. "Do you like Trista?"

"Why do you ask?" Suetonius looked down at her. Her hand seemed so frail inside his.

"I thought she was nice. Maybe you could marry her, and she wouldn't have to be a slave anymore, and she could still be in the family to play with me. She knows a lot of games."

Suetonius smiled at the simple solution to Elysia's concerns. "A soldier is not allowed to ever get married."

Elysia walked along in silence for a moment. "How long will you be a soldier?"

"I'll be a soldier long after you're married and have children. I'll be a soldier all my life."

"Then how will you ever have children?" Elysia looked up at him, her face brown from the afternoon in the sun.

"I guess I won't; at least none that I will be able to acknowledge." Suetonius was surprised at the sadness that enveloped him. He had never really thought of children and marriage, but it would be impossible to have a family and be in the military.

He glanced at Trista. She had the beginnings of a smile and looked prettier than usual. The water had swept her hair away from her face, and she had let it dry that way. For the first time, Suetonius thought she was pretty. She must have noticed him staring because her color changed from alabaster to rose, rising from beneath her stola and traveling up her face to the edge of her white-blonde hair. Suetonius chuckled.

Trista looked sideways, then back down at the ground. "Why do you stare at me? It is rude in my country to do that."

"Sorry." Suetonius walked along without speaking. For the first time he felt awkward around a slave. Most of the slaves had been with the house for so long they were like family. There were some new ones, of course, but most of them worked in the gardens and didn't speak Latin well enough to have a stimulating conversation.

Suetonius looked at Trista again. "You're still red in the face."

Trista quickly turned and faced Suetonius. "If you don't stop staring at me, I'll punch you in the nose." She stamped her foot, raising a small cloud of dust from the powdery dirt.

"Impudent for a slave, aren't you? We flog slaves who talk to their masters that way."

Trista gasped and dropped to her knees in front of Suetonius. "I forgot. Please forgive me. Today was the best day I've had since being taken from my home. You made me feel as if I were with my older brother again, and Elysia reminded me of my sister. Please, I will never forget I'm a slave, I promise."

Suetonius rolled his eyes skyward. "You stupid girl. Get up from there. I was only teasing you." Suetonius bent down and grabbed Trista by the elbows and pulled her to her feet.

Trista jerked her arms away from Suetonius. "You dare to tease me about slavery? What kind of cruel joke is it that you play? Don't you ever do that again. Never!" She grabbed Elysia's hand and the two of them ran from Suetonius.

"Wait! What did I do? Why are you so angry?" Suetonius ran after them.

"Don't talk to me unless you have an order for a slave. I find you offensive." Trista yanked the wooden garden gate open so hard that it banged against the stone wall. Elysia had to skip to keep up with her.

Suetonius grabbed Trista by the shoulder and turned her around. "I could say the same thing about you. Instead of telling me what I did wrong, you run away like a spoiled child."

Trista's eyes flashed and the light blue turned darker. "I am a slave. I was the daughter of the chief and now I am no one. I find that depressing and degrading. I do not think it amusing to talk of beatings."

"Now that I think about it, my joke was not a very intelligent one. I hope you will accept my apology."

"Oh, really? Is it often that a master apologizes to a slave?" Trista spit the words out with the force of a catapult.

"We are not monsters. We are civilized. My favorite teacher was our slave."

"I think I prefer the so-called barbarism of my people to your civilization. We only killed men, we didn't enslave them. I find your slavery a slow and painful death." Trista turned and marched through the garden.

Elysia looked at him and at Trista. She finally ran after the slave and both disappeared amongst the peach trees. He walked after them at his military double pace and was soon right behind them. "Trista, you're being stubborn. Let me talk with you. I can do no more than apologize to you. It is not within my power to free you."

Trista faced Suetonius. She shook her head. "Freedom will do me no good. I would have no family and no home. I have no idea whether or not my family lives or where they are. I couldn't even find my way to my homeland."

Suetonius took her hands in his. "Let's not fight. Let's make a pact that we will always try to understand each other without getting angry."

"Why?"

"I don't know, but it bothers me when you're angry." Suetonius watched Trista's expression. It didn't change. "I will teach you to read and write Latin."

Trista laughed. "Why? I never could read and write in my own language."

Relieved, Suetonius talked faster. "It would make you more valuable, and you could help with the house accounts and even the business accounts later. If you were ever freed, then you would have a skill. You wouldn't starve."

Trista's lower lip struck out. "I don't want to learn to read your language. It's ugly to the ears, and I'm sure it's ugly to the eyes."

"Trista, be reasonable."

She shook her head.

Suetonius threw his hands up. "Fine. Let's at least be friends."

"I could use a friend." Trista walked through the trees with Elysia hopping along beside her.

"I didn't know I needed a friend until today. The swim made me think of home. We had fun, didn't we? I mean, I did."

"So did I. We can swim again tomorrow if you like." Without breaking stride, Suetonius reached up and plucked a peach from a tree. "Here, try this. We grow the best peaches in Rome."

Vivianne looked in the polished mirror and frowned. The white cosmetic made her look ill. She didn't care what the style was, she didn't like the sticky bread and cream mixture. It made her face feel stiff. She wouldn't smear her face with this grease. She turned to Trista. "Get me a basin of hot water, olive oil and the set of strigils."

Vivianne sighed. Tonight she didn't want to look pretty anyway. She hated being invited to the palace. Tiberius always leered at her. Fortunately, most of the time he seized one of the other women for his consort, or he passed out before he got to her. She shuddered. If Tiberius wanted to make love to her, she would have to comply or possibly risk the death of her entire family. No family had ever been thrown off Tarpeian Rock for the wife's having refused the emperor's advances, but then no woman had had the courage to say no.

She had already refused to have her hair curled, but it still flowed down her back in natural waves. Perhaps if she cut it off and wore a style similar to her son, Tiberius would find her ugly.

She laid down the mirror and picked up a dark blue jar with swirling wide gold bands. Gold sparkled from light that filtered through the skylight. She removed the lid and rubbed cream into her elbows.

Vivianne looked up as Trista returned carrying an orange clay bowl. Looped over one arm was an oval handle that held the copper oil pot and two strigils.

Vivianne pushed her flasks and jars aside. "Put the bowl here with the olive oil next to it." Frowning, she took the smaller of the two strigils and began to scrape the bread and cream mixture from her face and wiped the excess on the edge of the bowl. She glanced into the large square of shiny silver metal and was glad to see pink skin. Her eyes caught Trista's perplexed look. "It is supposed to make one beautiful, but I think it makes me look foolish. What do you think?"

Trista blushed. "I don't know what to think."

Vivianne laughed as she wiped the last of the mixture off the stirgil onto the edge of the bowl. She washed her face with warm water and a sponge. She looked into the mirror satisfied that she had all traces of the awful stuff off her face and reached for the olive oil. She sniffed the contents and satisfied that it had not gone rancid, carefully poured a few drops on her finger tips.

Vivianne smoothed it expertly on her face and made circular motions until it was absorbed. She glanced at Trista who studied her intently. "Do you wonder what I am doing?"

Trista nodded. "I have never observed such rituals before."

"We Roman women believe that olive oil keeps us young and attractive to our husbands. Didn't the women in your country do this?"

Trista chewed her lower lip and narrowed her eyes. Frowning, she shook her head. "I don't remember any woman going through this."

"Sometimes I hate the time I spend in front of a mirror, but then, I'm too much a prisoner of tradition to stop what I learned at my mother's knee." Vivianne wiped her fingers on a linen cloth and surveyed herself in the mirror, turning her head left and right. Her beige under-stola was not a flattering color because of the golden hue of her skin. "Get me that dark brown stola, Trista. Do you think the color is good for me?"

Trista's face reddened as she handed the stola to her mistress. "I don't know style very well."

"Don't be silly. The look on your face tells me that you find the color horrible. I had it dyed specially. It was blue once." She wrapped the stola around her, fastening it at her right shoulder with a gold brooch in the shape of a fish. She looked at herself in the mirror. "I do think it makes my skin look quite muddy. The effect is wonderful." Vivianne chuckled as she sat down in front of the vanity. She picked up an ivory comb. "Trista, just comb my hair straight down my back. I want no curls and no jewels."

When Caius entered, Vivianne opened her eyes, almost from a sleep. She smiled at her husband and with a wave of her hand, dismissed Trista. Vivianne took one last look in the mirror before turning toward Caius. She made an effort to steady her voice before speaking. "I'm almost ready."

Caius put his hands on her shoulders, bent down, and kissed the top of her head. "You look lovely."

Vivianne's eyes widened. "I look lovely!" She jumped up from the vanity stool, almost knocking it over. "You don't know anything. Look at me. I'm a mess."

"I . . . uh . . . I don't . . ." Caius rubbed his forehead. "Tell me what's wrong with how you look."

"I'm going to Tiberius' banquet with uncoiffed hair, no make-up, and my stola is all wrong in color and style." Vivianne could see the perplexed look on Caius' face. "I am afraid of Tiberius' roving eyes and pawing hands."

Caius put his index finger against Vivianne's lips. "Hush, the walls have ears." He leaned closer and whispered, "What are you trying to do?"

Her cheeks suddenly felt hot. "I'm trying to be as unattractive as possible so Tiberius will choose another woman for his evening's entertainment."

"I don't know why you're concerned. You've looked beautiful on other occasions, and Tiberius has not bothered you."

"He was drunk." Vivianne shuddered. She lowered her eyes to block out the steady gaze of her husband. "I don't want him touching me."

"Why are you so worried tonight? Why now?" Caius enfolded her within his arms and rested his chin on her head. Vivianne felt safe for the moment. She loved for Caius to hold her this way.

"I heard that he had a list made of those whom he had not bedded. I'm on that list, of course."

Caius held her closer. "It's a fact of life that our emperor takes women. It won't change us."

Vivianne's head snapped up, and she pushed Caius away. "A lot you know! It will change me. If he wants to . . . to rape me I have to let him, or he will have our family thrown off Tarpeian Rock." Tears blurred her vision of Caius.

"Stop that." Caius shook her. "You're a strong woman. It's not as if you were being tortured to death."

"Caius, I thought I could be clever and could use deceit, but now I'm frightened. The man is repulsive. It would be a living death for me."

"It would be all right if he were handsome and kind?"

"You always try to be mirthful when I'm serious. Maybe it is nothing to you." Vivianne felt like crying. "To me it would be like having him rip away part of my soul."

Caius pulled her back into his arms. "Then you must refuse him."

Vivianne's voice was muffled. "I will not put my family in danger, but will grind my teeth together and endure. Savina has said that a woman must not commit adultery, but if I do, it will be without pleasure."

Caius groaned. "Savina? Has your sister been filling you with that religious rubbish again? What does she call herself? Christian?"

Vivianne felt the color in her cheeks rising. "I believe so. She believes that someone called Jesus of Nazareth was the son of a supreme god."

"I don't think it's wise for you to discuss Savina's religion. Tiberius does not look kindly on the new religious ideas. Christians refuse to sacrifice to our gods, and you know what will happen to us if people are allowed to raise the wrath of the gods." Caius snorted. "A son of a supreme god. Ridiculous."

"No more so than the gods we have, and the Greek gods are even more peculiar." Vivianne plunged forward. "It makes more sense to me that there should be one god. If other gods have had mortal wives and half mortal children, then it seems that for this Jesus . . ."

"Who?"

Vivianne put her hand on Caius' lips. "Jesus is the man whom Pontius Pilate had crucified in Judea the year Suetonius was born."

Caius took her wrist and pulled her hand away. "That wasn't unusual. All enemies of the state were executed in that fashion. How am I supposed to remember what happened seventeen years ago in a country on the other side of the sea?"

"As I started to say, it makes sense to me that Jesus was born of mortal woman and one supreme god." Vivianne looked at Caius' face. She was disturbed to see two spots of color on his cheeks, and she knew a storm billowed inside him.

"You are spending too much time with Savina. She isn't normal, Vivianne, and if you continue to talk and listen to her, then Tiberius will throw us off Tarpeian Rock for certain. I'll listen to no more talk of this new religion from Jesus the Jew." Caius let out a long breath that he'd been holding. It ruffled her hair. "Let's not talk about this ridiculous idea anymore. It's time to go. Tiberius' banquet starts at sundown, and the sun is close to setting."

Music from the atrium drifted across the gardens toward Vivianne and Caius and enveloped them like a mist coming in from the sea. Vivianne hesitated, pulling at Caius' arm. They stopped near an olive tree, and Vivianne watched the shiny leaves flutter in the wind flashing silver underbellies like fish shining in a pond.

Caius looked at her and she smiled. "I just wanted to enjoy this moment before . . ." She stood on tiptoe and kissed her husband. "Now I can face Tiberius."

"I'm not sure I can. I don't want to share you. Let's go home."

Vivianne giggled and let it die with the flicker of hope. "We cannot incur his wrath." She motioned toward the atrium. "We must follow the music."

"Let's follow it to the sky and the clouds. We can rest on the wind."

"Please spare my ears with your words. You give me hope where there is none." Vivianne took Caius' arm. As they continued down the path, Vivianne was aware of the pebbles snapping beneath her sandaled feet, some stones sharp enough to feel through the thin, leather soles.

Music swelled from many musicians. The aroma of spicy meats drifted toward them along with the music. Flashes of color could be seen between the columns of the atrium.

The two of them slipped unobtrusively into the throng. Caius gave Vivianne's hand a squeeze then left her as he was hailed by a colleague. She glanced around at the various couches placed next to the banquet tables laden with food. Vivianne saw the perfect place and moved toward a couch that was already occupied by two young women, coiffed and bejeweled, the lovely daughters of a friend. She waited until Tiberius looked away from her, then she sat on the couch and leaned forward on her elbows.

"I hope you don't mind my joining you."

One of the girls turned, and Vivianne noticed the surprise in her almond-colored eyes. She blinked, long lashes shiny and dark from olive oil.

Her voice was soft, but not submissive. "Mother was going to join us . . ." She waved her hand toward Tiberius. "She wanted to be near him. I'm glad you're here."

Vivianne could not be certain whether or not there was scorn in Leandra's voice, so she simply nodded. "Thank you."

The other girl leaned forward and peered at Vivianne. She was an older version of her sister in coloring, but although she had the same features, they were not arranged as well. She was pretty but not beautiful. Perhaps her eyes were too close or her nose too long, Vivianne couldn't decide. She still had the lovely, pale skin, natural and unadorned by the white cosmetic favored by so many of the less well-endowed ladies. Highlights in her black hair looked like blue-black silk. She and her sister wore fashionable tight curls piled on top of their heads with ringlets framing their faces. They looked young and innocent.

Candra touched Vivianne's hand. "Mother says if Tiberius chooses us tonight, we'll be rewarded with gold," she whispered. "I hope so, for these stolas cost a great deal."

Leandra broke in. "The silk is from the Orient."

Vivianne raised her eyebrows, hoping it conveyed awe. Leandra and Candra were so young. Tiberius would see their youth and beauty, and she would fade into the background like a sparrow among parrots.

She turned her attention toward the musicians and dancers. Vivianne recognized the flute players, and she let her head rest against the bolster as the music carried her away. The notes were clear and each one hung in the air like a kestrel, then swooped down and snatched one's soul.

The clacking of castanets preceded a loud cheer and Vivianne opened her eyes and stared at Tiberius' favorite slave. A swirl of gold against copper-colored skin made her heart race. She had heard that Tiberius took Kesia with him on campaigns. Kesia's movements matched the music note for note and her body glistened in the lamp light, muscles taut and smooth. The dancer whirled faster and faster, the castanets clicking almost as one long sound until the gold costume separated and flew across the room landing in small heaps at the feet of the men. The music and Kesia stopped in the middle of a note and she stood, nude, before Tiberius. When he reached for her, she moved nimbly away from him and smiled. A final click of her castanets, and she disappeared from the atrium.

Tiberius groaned, then laughed. "She alone can refuse me and live. Who, I ask you, is the ruler of this land—me or the woman who rules me?" The guests waited. When he laughed, they laughed.

Tiberius was almost handsome, but his features had a hardness about them brought on, Vivianne decided, by too many banquets and too much intrigue in his fifty-eight years. She studied him closely. Tiberius' eyes were his best feature. They were large and dark with brows that arched suggestively. A straight nose did not detract from his cleft chin which made Vivianne smile. A cleft chin was supposed to be a sign of virility. Perhaps he couldn't help his passion for women. His ears were close to his well-shaped head and not large. Vivianne hated it when a handsome man had large ears that ruined the proportion. Tiberius still had the build of a soldier, and her face felt hot as she realized that he did intrigue her.

Her stomach growled, whether it was from hunger or nerves Vivianne didn't know. When it growled again, she looked toward the table. Perhaps if she concentrated on the food, she would not think so much about Tiberius.

Gold platters piled high with fruit and sweets. Breads lay on the white table cloth side by side like soldiers on march. In the center of the table, a roast boar, and already pieces of meat had been ripped from its side. Four stuffed lambs were on either side of the boar, sentry-like, and next to them were a profusion of colored glass bowls filled with various sauces.

Vivianne sipped wine slowly as she looked over the rim of the goblet and tried to find Caius. She caught Tiberius scrutinizing her. Her heart thumped, and she hoped it would stay within her rib cage. She wanted to look away from him, but she was afraid to do so. She continued sipping her wine aware that the goblet hid most of her face. Maybe he would not recognize her and thus could not call for her.

He would not look away and in nervousness, she felt her eyelids flutter. She hoped he would not take that as an invitation. Aware that the wine was chilling her upper lip, she couldn't keep it there any longer or she would arouse suspicion. She replaced the silver goblet and reached for an olive, never breaking eye contact.

Finally Tiberius' gaze shifted to the two girls next to her. Vivianne let out a long slow breath, then took a deep breath to calm herself. She was aware of a seething argument between Leandra and Candra.

"He looks at me, you fool," Candra hissed under her breath.

Leandra smiled at Tiberius and spoke without moving her lips. "I hardly think so. You have the face of a cow and the body of a pig."

Vivianne clapped a hand to her mouth to keep from giggling. It seemed incongruous that the two pretty girls behaved so rudely toward each other. She glanced back at Tiberius and their eyes met again. Inwardly, she cringed. She watched him as he leaned toward a slave, whispered directions, and handed something to him. The tall, mahogany-skinned man slipped among the revelers until he was near the couch where Vivianne and the two girls lounged. Vivianne watched to see which of the young ladies would be presented with the famous Tiberian ring that summoned a woman to his quarters after the banquet. It would probably be Leandra. She must have thought so, too, for Vivianne noticed that her hands flew up to her hair to make certain it was in place. Next Leandra's finger traced the gold necklace at her throat and she smiled as she watched the panther-like movements of Tiberius' messenger.

Vivianne had leaned back so as to give the slave easier access to Leandra. She watched as his dark paw dropped down, the ring held between his thumb and index finger. The ring was large, but looked small as he held it. When his hand stopped in front of her face, she looked up and stared into his eyes that matched the color of his skin. She was momentarily distracted by his slender nose that ended with flared nostrils. Full lips protruded above a strong jaw.

When she realized that the ring was being held out to her, she stared at its green stone wrapped in laurel leaves of gold. She looked at Tiberius. He smiled and acknowledged her with a slight tilt of his head. A lock of silver hair slipped down his forehead, making him look impish. Vivianne held back a gasp.

The slave moved the ring closer to her, and she reached out slowly, extending her first finger upwards. The ring slipped on easily.

She waited until Tiberius broke eye contact with her, then glanced around the crowded room in search of Caius. She found him laughing and slapping one of his friends on the back. Her anger surfaced quickly. Men were insensitive. Was her husband any better than Tiberius? Her lips pressed together in a tight line. She was aware that the two girls studied her. Their incredulous thoughts bounced off her wall of reserve, and she fought to keep it from cracking. She could not look at them, so she looked down at Tiberius' ring. It was smaller than hers, but was of a much finer quality. The three raised red stones of her ring formed a triangle nestled in gold. With a flick of a finger, she could open the ring. Inside she had placed a very strong sleeping powder, so strong that too much and the recipient would never awaken. She rubbed the red stones with her index finger. She would have to be very careful.

Vivianne whispered in Candra's ear. "I wish it had been you rather than me. I don't understand his desires either." She almost laughed aloud as Candra blushed. It was as if Candra believed Vivianne could read her mind.

Time moved hauntingly slow and terrifyingly fast for Vivainne. She watched Tiberius drink goblet after goblet of wine, sometimes in one long gulp. She lost count at six because the girls with whom she shared the couch constantly bickered and called each other names. Her head ached.

She stared across the room to search out Caius. No matter how long she glared at him, he would not look her way or at Tiberius. He continued to laugh and joke with his cronies. She felt tears rush forth, and it took all of her strength to push them back. It wasn't the fear of Tiberius that caused her to cry. Casius' nonchalance left her empty.

Vivianne sat on the edge of a couch in Tiberius' chambers and waited. She twisted the ring that Tiberius had sent her around and around her finger. She wished Caius had done something. When she told him she could not go home with him, he had merely nodded. Why hadn't Caius done something! She sighed. Men were no help at all. It seemed as if they had a secret society, and women were the victims of their idiosyncracies. Vivianne frowned. She would make Caius pay for his desertion of her. He could have done something.

Her fingers trailed along the edge of the deep purple silk cushion on which she sat. She preferred the bright wall paintings to the foreboding cushion even if it would buy a dozen slaves. Opposite her, a mural depicted a formal garden and had been done in such realistic detail that the narrow room seemed to open into a perfect garden and made the room seem larger.

Vivianne popped open her own ring and looked at the white powder. Perhaps she could use it to get out of the situation at hand gracefully. She snapped the ring shut. The loud sound startled her. She looked at the doorway, half in trepidation, half in anticipation, but Tiberius still had not come. Perhaps she would not use the powder to induce Tiberius to sleep. Maybe that would fix her husband who didn't seem to care about what happened to her.

She shifted about on the cushion. Its softness was deceiving and after having sat there for a short time, the hardness of the wooden couch made itself felt. Vivianne stood and walked to the window to view the private gardens, where she had heard that wild game was kept.

A full moon hung above the olive trees, making it seem like day. Vivianne looked through the trees for a sign of deer or lions or whatever Tiberius had populating the garden. Seeing none, she turned from the window and leaned against the frame watching the doorway at the other side of the chamber. She studied the mosaic tile floor—a scene of Tiberius and a stag. Of course, he was victorious, and the speared stag lay at the feet of the muscular emperor.

Footsteps caused her to jump. Her breath caught. Tiberius smiled at her from the doorway and crossed the room slowly as if she were the prey. He stopped too close to her, and she had no choice but to curtsy. However, it was difficult to do without accidently touching him. She straightened and looked directly into his eyes. They were a surprisingly light blue, like the sky at mid-morning. His silver hair was truly silver. It wasn't white like the hair of most old men, but shone in the lamp light as if it had been mined from the earth. He returned her stare, and she noticed fine lines around his eyes. His face was flushed, probably from the enormous consumption of wine. She had watched him the remainder of the banquet, hoping that he would fall back into a drunken stupor, and she would be free to go.

Vivianne thought she would fear him more because of his temper, but here in his chamber with its peaceful decor, she wondered if the stories were true.

Softly, without a trace of slurred speech, Tiberius said, "Please, we will be more comfortable on the couch."

She shivered when he placed his hand lightly on her arm and led her to the same couch she had just left a few minutes before. She sat and watched Tiberius move toward a low table that held a silver decanter of wine and two silver goblets. He poured wine for both of them. Vivianne rubbed her finger across the ring he had given her, then across her own. It was an honor to spend the night with Tiberius, and there were hundreds of women who would have done anything to be here. Maybe she should feel honored.

He handed a goblet of wine to Vivianne. His fingers were long and slender, the nails perfectly shaped and manicured.

"This wine is the best that gold can buy. It has come from the north, and I am the only one who is allowed to possess it. I want to share it with you." Tiberius smiled. "You are quiet. Do I frighten you?"

"Only your reputation." Vivianne's voice sounded strained, and she hated the sound of its weakness. She cleared her throat. "I find you more charming than I expected." She grimaced at the way the sentence escaped her lips without time to form the thought.

Tiberius laughter rolled out like the sound of a distant marching army. He seated himself next to her. "Do you know why I chose you from all the women who were at the feast?"

Vivianne shook her head. She was afraid to speak for fear she would sound stupid again.

"You are a natural beauty. You did not smear your face with that ghastly white cream that so many of our women think makes them desirable. I want a woman who looks warm and alive, not pale like death."

Vivianne trembled as Tiberius ran his index finger down her arm. He leaned close enough so that she could smell wine on his breath—like a sweet bouquet of flowers.

"I do not like those ridiculous curls the women pile all over their heads. I like to see natural waves. I find it more alluring to see the silkiness fall down the back."

Tiberius wound his fingers through Vivianne's hair. A shiver raced down her spine. She felt youthful—a feeling she hadn't had since before Suetonius was born. She smiled at Tiberius.

Tiberius returned the smile. "You do not speak. I know that you can, for I have often been entertained by your stories."

Vivianne's mouth dropped opened. "I was unaware of your having listened to my stories. When did you listen to me?"

"Your voice carries across the room and is like music on the wind. I have pretended to be listening to one of my generals tell of his exploits when in reality I was listening to you. I could not resist the laughter of your audience."

Vivianne stared at her hands. She twisted the ring Tiberius had given her around and around.

When she realized what she was doing, she stopped. She wished she weren't so nervous. If she could only be like most women and take an affair in stride. Such things had never bothered her until her sister had started telling her about the new religion that forbade so many things. Savina had changed with the new religion. She was content, almost peaceful.

Vivianne chewed her lower lip while she tried to sort things out. Was it wrong to let a man who was not her husband make love to her? Or was it wrong to refuse her emperor who was also considered a god? Why couldn't she just enjoy Tiberius? It was an honor, after all. She leaned closer to her emperor. The heat from his body enveloped her, and she rested her head on his shoulder.

"Are you going to tell me the same witty stories that kept your lady friends laughing?" Tiberius slipped his hand down her back.

Vivianne giggled. "I am sorry, but my stories are only to amuse women. We discuss the shortcomings of men."

Tiberius chuckled. "I am surprised. I didn't think men had any shortcomings."

"There are too many to count," Vivianne whispered. "Each man has a unique set of annoying habits." How could she decide what was right? Was it true what her sister said that there was only one god? If that were true, then how could Tiberius be a god? She closed her eyes to clear her thoughts, but that didn't help. She rubbed the ring that held the sleeping powder. She had heard that the emperor often slept after drinking wine. She twisted the ring around her finger. No one would suspect her.

"Nervous?" Tiberius said.

Vivianne nodded. "I'd like some wine." She tried to remember exactly how much powder she had put in the ring. It would never do to poison the emperor. She took her head from Tiberius' shoulder lest he feel her shudder. The thought of being his murderer, even if accidently, made her heart beat faster and her breath short.

Tiberius stood and refilled the two goblets, smiled, and drank his immediately.

Vivianne sipped hers slowly. She watched as he poured another goblet for himself and placed it on the table in front of her. She leaned forward. "I should like a piece of the delicious fruit. Would it be too much trouble for you to bring that bowl of fruit over there?"

"No trouble for such a beautiful woman." For the first time, Tiberius wavered as he stood. He took higher than normal steps, as if he were wading across a stream, and steered himself toward the bowl of fruit on the other side of the room. "I would conquer the rest of the world for a beautiful woman like you."

Vivianne looked at him with a tinge of disgust. He reminded her of the drunken beast her mother had married. Vivianne had been only ten, but she remembered his sour breath and roving hands. She looked down at her ring filled with the powder of freedom. It would take only a second, and Tiberius would never know.

He tottered back with the bowl of fruit, tripped, and spilled grapes at her feet. A peach rolled across the tile and came to rest on the mosaic of Tiberius, just above his head, making a whimsical hat. Vivianne almost laughed.

She was startled when he sat down heavily next to her and took a long drink from his goblet. She watched his eyes. The lids drooped. Tiberius pulled at her stola. It tore away from the brooch, exposing her under-stola. He pulled at her again, tearing the under-stola away from her until her breast was exposed. She held her breath. His roughness repelled her. His head slumped forward against her naked breast, and she had to grab him to keep him from falling on the floor. Gently she helped his heavy, lax body slide to the floor. He snored.

What is expected of me? Am I supposed to stay the night or go home? She looked at the emperor slumped at her feet. He didn't look as handsome as he had before his drunkenness. He looked like an old, worn-out man, no longer a warrior, no longer a leader, and now, no longer a lover. A wave of sorrow swept over her. How could he know who really liked him or merely was excited by his power? Women would bed him just because he was the emperor. At least with Caius, he knew she loved him. Poor Tiberius.

He groaned when she pulled her foot from under him. Vivianne pinned the brooch to her stola, re-arranging it so that her breast was covered. Holding her skirts away from Tiberius, she walked across the room to the window. She heard movement behind her, and her breath caught in her throat. She whirled around.

The huge Nubian slave stood in the doorway. She removed the ring from her finger and held it toward him. He walked over to the slumbering emperor, picked him up like a small child, and laid him on the sleeping couch.

"The ring is yours to keep. The emperor would not like to have it back, for that would indicate failure. You are to keep the ring and never reveal his . . . his condition. You are to be driven home in the morning."

Vivianne wrapped her fingers about the ring, letting its hard edges gouge her palm.

"You must lie next to Tiberius until morning."

She nodded and moved across the room to the couch. She waited next to the couch until the slave had gone, then eased herself down onto the cushions and lay back. Tiberius snored softly.

He did not stir even as Vivianne pulled up a light covering of linen over them. She did not want to sleep, yet her eyes felt heavy. Soon the sounds of the wind in the trees faded until sleep did steal away her consciousness.

Suetonius flopped down on the grass. It stuck to his sweaty arms and legs and pricked his skin, but he was too tired to care. His leg muscles ached more than they ever had, even while in the infantry. He was aware of a rush of wind and a whumping sound to his right. He turned his head slowly and took in the lanky form of his friend and partner in training.

Suetonius groaned. "Do you hurt as if you've been beaten?"

"I do. I never want to see a horse again. I may never be able to make love again." Lucian yawned. "I will never understand why the army has to get up at sunrise. It puts a strain on my love life."

"You are not handsome enough for a love life," Suetonius said.

"Jealousy makes you speak in such a manner. I am the one who has to give you my extra women, remember?"

"If I didn't hurt so badly, I would laugh. The only woman I took from you was appalled at your lack of culture. She preferred my refined manners to yours. She also told me you were ugly, and it frightened her."

"I think your memory is faulty. She told me that you were so ugly, she felt sorry for you. Sympathy was her reason for love." Lucian stretched his arms. "Every muscle aches from overuse. I thought the cavalry would be easier than marching across the entire world. I didn't know we would leap on and off horses endlessly. Tomorrow we get to do it with weapons. I may stab myself, if I don't die first."

"If you do, I will provide the music for your funeral if I am still alive." Suetonius closed his eyes. "I wish the horse I own was not so large. I thought he was beautiful, but now I admire smallness to bulk."

"You are lucky to have such a fine animal. My father could not afford a steed from the Arabs."

"Come now, your horse is a good animal," Suetonius said.

"Yours has the fine lines of a thoroughbred and the temperament of an animal meant to go into battle. Did you decide to name him Victory, as you said?"

"I did."

"Is it because of what the oracles said about your being associated with victory?"

Suetonius frowned. "Perhaps. I think I did it more to assure my success, however. It's sort of a prayer to the gods."

"I want to be with you for all your victories, Suetonius. We'll have many great adventures together."

"We have been together since infancy, so I believe it only fitting that we serve together." Suetonius sat up, leaning on his elbows. "Do you ever think how odd it is that the same sun that shines on us now also shines on lands that are far away and on people who are so different?"

Lucian turned toward his friend. "I never think about anything more than food, wine, and women."

"I think about faraway places everyday. I wonder why people haven't made the same advancements that we have, and I wonder what those faraway places look like. I wonder if the people are really human, or if they're some form of animal.

"I think of Trista who is aloof with me, but wonderful to my sisters. I never thought of slaves as having feelings or longings, but she has made me think of that. Yet in spite of her, I want to help Rome rule the world. It is her destiny to conquer."

CHAPTER
III

OADICEA LEANED OVER the rose-red bowl and stared into the deep red wine. Flecks of light shivered in the wine from candles on the altar. She hoped the poison would do its deed quickly—not for herself, although that would be acceptable, but for her daughters. She looked at Neila, totally submissive to her for the first time in the young girl's life. She had been born in the spring under the sign of the Willow and was known for her energy and toughness—true willow traits. Boadicea's lips turned upward in the semblance of a smile. Her Druid prayers had been answered. Neila would obey her mother without argument, but the gods had played a sardonic trick on Boadicea. Death was the reward for her daughter's obedience.

Candlelight, mixed with light from the fireplace, highlighted Sydelle's hair, making the red even redder. It flowed down her back like a river of wine. Boadicea was filled with so much love at the sight of her daughters kneeling before her that for the first time in her life she wondered what she could have done differently.

She laughed at Rhys. Mud covered his blonde hair and the tunic that clung to his legs. Thayne pawed the ground and tossed his head. Boadicea was forced to look away from Rhys momentarily until she had the four-year-old calmed. Rhys' horse had stopped a few feet away, nickering softly. It sounded like laughter to Boadicea.

She put her hand to her mouth to stifle her giggles, but they slipped out in snorts.

"Rhys, I don't want to win a race by default. Get back on your horse, and let's try once more." Boadicea tried to smother her laughter again.

"I can't get back on my horse." Rhys flopped back into the mud puddle splashing droplets of water on Boadicea.

"A faint heart from my hero? You, who taught me to ride like a burr attached to wool, have given up? How can you become father to my children with such a timid soul?"

"My soul is not timid. It is my body that is timid. It hurts with timidity." Rhys closed his eyes. "Your laughter cuts my soul like a knife cuts flesh."

Boadicea slid off Thayne and stood next to the supine young man. She nudged him with her foot. "Up, you lazy man, or I shall be forced to drag you home at the end of a rope."

Rhys opened one eye. "I shall never be able to ride again, but if I don't try, I shall never live down your scorn." He sat up and surveyed the damage to himself.

"I don't think you're hurt on the outside, Rhys." Boadicea held out her hand. When Rhys reached up and took it, she pulled him to a standing position. "You are a mess." She wiped freckles of mud from his face. "Ugh, look at your tunic. For two years we've ridden together, and I've never seen such a performance as this one. Whatever happened?"

Rhys sighed. "I don't know. That's the wonder of riding. Never be complacent with horses. I broke one of my own rules and let down my guard. No harm done. I named that horse after the elves, and I am paying for it. See, Ella waits for me just a few feet away, her head down as if she is ashamed, but I know that she laughs at me." Rhys walked to his horse holding out his hand. She nuzzled the outstretched hand.

"She's asking your forgiveness," Boadicea said.

"Reminds me of you. First you throw me around, laugh at me, and then want to make up." Rhys scratched Ella's nose. She nickered softly.

Boadicea walked over to Rhys and put her hand on his shoulder. "I think we girls just love to make up." She leaned over and kissed Rhys on the cheek.

"Come on. Let's get back." Rhys threw the reins over Ella's neck, grabbed her mane and leaped on her back. He gripped her mid-section with his legs and kicked with his heels. She moved forward slowly, picking her way carefully around puddles.

Rhys leaned over and whispered in Ella's ear. "That's right, don't get yourself dirty." Her ear flicked back and forth.

Boadicea leaped nimbly from the ground onto Thayne's back and nudged him forward, matching pace with Rhys. "Do you want to race? I could win today."

Rhys grinned. "You mean you think that I'll get thrown off again, and this time you won't wait. All right. Let's go!" Rhys kicked his horse in the ribs with great force, and she took off like an arrow.

Boadicea was ready, and she kicked Thayne with her heels. She felt his muscles bunch beneath her, then stretch out as he extended his legs to their maximum length. The wind blew her hair out behind her as she urged the horse forward. His mane whipped into her face and it stung, but she liked the feel of it. It made her more alive.

Rhys was in front of her by a length, and she knew Ella would be hard to catch even though Thayne had a longer stride. Ella had the heart of a racer and unmatched stamina. Boadicea kicked Thayne again. She wouldn't catch Rhys, but she could not give up.

Thayne slipped on the muddy road, and Boadicea's heart flew to her throat. She instinctively tightened her grip on the reins, then let them loose so that the bit wouldn't cut into the horse's mouth. She gave him his head again and he righted himself, but she slid off. She screamed as she went down and quickly rolled away from the slashing hooves. Thayne jumped sideways to keep from stepping on her, pulled up short, and stood with sides heaving a few feet away. He put his head down and snorted, his hot breath blowing on the back of Boadicea's neck. She rolled over, sat up, and patted Thayne on the side of his great jaw.

Boadicea looked up in reaction to a shout from Rhys. He looked over his shoulder at her, reined his horse around too quickly, and Ella fell, rolling over him. Boadicea heard herself scream as she scrambled to her feet. It seemed to take too long to get to Rhys where she found him face down and motionless. Rhys' mare nudged her and nickered softly. Boadicea pushed the nosing horse away from the prone figure and dropped to the ground next to Rhys.

His eyes were closed, and Boadicea could detect no life's breath. A trickle of blood cut across his chin from the corner of his mouth. She watched as one drop and another splashed into the mud.

"Please hear me, all the gods of my people, let this man live that he may serve you. He is good and kind. He is to be my protector, my husband, and the father of our children. Do not change my future by taking away my past. Rhys has always been with me. Please, please." Boadicea wiped a smear of beige mud from Rhys' cheek. Even though the earth was light in color, it looked so dark against the whiteness of his face. She licked her fingers and placed them beneath Rhys' nostrils and felt a faint breath of life. Only then did she let tears slip from her eyes.

Boadicea reached out to roll Rhys over then remembered that her mother had told her that often when the living were turned, the death rattle sounded immediately and the person died. She jerked her hand back as if the thought had burned her.

Boadicea sat back and looked around. She was too far to ride home and return quickly. She couldn't leave Rhys to the ever-present danger of wolves, especially the sick ones. They were known to have no fear of humans, and their bite brought certain, agonizing death. Even as she peered into the woods, she imagined their great golden eyes watched them.

Thayne pawed the ground and snorted. Boadicea jumped up, tied the reins over his neck, and turned him toward the village. "It's up to you, Baby. Get help." She slapped him hard on the rump. He jumped forward, snorted, and thundered down the path toward the village at a trot that quickly became a gallop.

Boadicea turned back to Rhys. She could see his shoulders rising and lowering in shallow movements. His mare nudged him again. Boadicea was afraid that Ella would injure her master so she seized the bridle and pulled the horse away. She tied her to a nearby tree with loose reins so the mare could graze even though she knew that a horse with a bit shouldn't be allowed to eat.

She hurried back to Rhys and knelt next to him. In a few hours, it would be dark, and she would have to have a fire, more to keep away the wildlife than to keep warm. She felt Rhys' forehead; it was cold and clammy. She unpinned a gold brooch from her shoulder and let her outer tunic fall free. She looked at the brooch in her hand. She loved the round gold pin with its spiral of colored stones that ended in the center and pinned the brooch to her under-tunic. She shook her outer-tunic, the snapping sound startled her. She spread it across Rhys, tucked the edges beneath him, then rose. She jerked her twisted under-tunic into place and looked at the sky.

Clouds, gray and cumbrous, were close to the ground. A cool wind whipped across the tops of the trees rustling leaves with a sound like the voices of the gods. She hoped it wasn't an epitaph.

Boadicea felt Rhys' neck for life's beat. It was rapid and light. He needed to be kept warm, so she lay down beside him, gently so as not to hurt him. Soon she would have to gather wood and tinder to start a fire. She was glad that her father had taught her to always carry flint, and she reached down to touch the pouch that held a few items for such an emergency.

She held her breath, hoping to hear Rhys' breathing. The sound of silence frightened her, but not as much as the snapping of a twig, then another. She sat up and stared into the woods. The mare reared, pulled at her reins, pawed the air and trampled the sparse grass beneath her. Boadicea sprang up, ran to Ella and pulled her down. The wolves were braver. Perhaps they smelled death. Boadicea shivered. She untied Ella and re-tied her reins loosely across her neck as she had done with Thayne.

"You'll be safer on the run, Ella. That leaves me without a way home, but I don't care." She glanced at Rhys, then slapped the mare on her rump. Ella needed no further prompting. She shot forward and galloped up the road toward the village.

Boadicea didn't wait for the horse to disappear from view before she bent down and gathered twigs and leaves. She pulled open the leather pouch she had attached to her belt, and took out the flint.

The sound of rustling behind her spurred her to kindle a fire as quickly as possible. She stared at the edge of the woods. She saw one lone wolf and sucked in her breath. His coat was sparse. Ribs threatened to poke through his hide. He was alone, a sure sign that his pack had forced him out. There had been more sickness than usual among the animals this year. Boadicea's father had required everyone to keep their animals closer to the village because of it. She chewed on her lower lip. The sickness could kill a man, too.

Boadicea's hands were shaking so badly that she needed a half dozen tries before the spark caught the leaves. They flamed briefly, then went out. Boadicea groaned, but the noises behind her forced her to strike the flint pieces against each other again and again until at last she had a small flame. She dropped the flint to the ground and bent over, blowing on the flames carefully. The twigs glowed, caught, and flamed.

"Thank you, thank you, thank you." Boadicea jumped up and ran to the edge of the woods to gather small branches. She rushed back to the fire and laid the branches one by one on it, knowing that if she put them on too quickly, the entire fire would die out. She looked across the fire at Rhys who had not moved since he had fallen. Boadicea trembled both at the prospect of death for Rhys and the idea of spending the night fending off a sick wolf. She retrieved the flint, stuffed it back in the pouch, and got to her feet. Staying within close range of Rhys and the fire, she gathered larger branches and piled them close to him to break the cool evening breezes. She looked down the road, hoping that help was on the way, but she knew it was too soon. Even if the horses ran to the corral, it might take someone a long time to realize they were back. There was always the chance that it would be assumed that the two riders had returned unnoticed. Boadicea hoped that someone would realize the horses weren't groomed. Her father would start to look for her at dusk when it was past time for her to be home.

Boadicea gathered more wood, more twigs, and more leaves until she had enough to last through the night. Both their lives depended on the fire. She worked for more than an hour, and when she stopped to rest and look at her handiwork, she was pleased. She had built a low wall of branches on three sides of Rhys, with the fire making the fourth side. She looked at the sky crisscrossed with wispy clouds like flax before it had been spun. The sky had turned from the blue of summer to the gray of winter, and matched her changed mood.

Boadicea heard a growl and whirled toward the sound. She could see the outline of the lone wolf between the trees, his slanted, golden eyes challenging her. She picked up a small log and hurled it into the woods. It landed where the wolf had been. "You'll not find me much comfort so you may as well take your leave. I will set what's left of your fur on fire!"

To make certain the wolf understood her, she stuck the end of a slender oak branch in the fire. It was dry and caught rapidly. Boadicea waited until she saw his gleaming eyes again. This time the wolf was closer, and she could see his tongue hanging out. She ran toward him, waved the flaming stick, and stopped short of the dense woods. The shadow disappeared, but she knew he wasn't gone. Something brushed her legs, and she jumped back onto the road. Ferns! It was only plants. She chuckled, not with the throaty sound she was used to, but a strained, high-pitched twang. She took several deep breaths, trying to calm herself.

She looked back at Rhys. "I have two problems, but I can do it. I can do it." She wished she sounded more confident.

A groan issued from Rhys, and Boadicea was at his side in a flash, her hands hovering, afraid to touch him. He moved, and she dropped her fingers lightly on his shoulder to keep him from moving.

"What's wrong?" His voice sounded weak and far away.

"You had a bad fall, but you'll be all right. I sent the horses back to the village for help."

Rhys tried to raise himself, but lay back down. "I don't feel well."

"Don't move." Boadicea's joy was uncontained, and again she had boundless energy. "I'll keep the fire going." Boadicea took two logs from her wooden wall and threw them on the fire. Hundreds of tiny sparks danced and whirled their way above the tops of the trees that lined the road. Their brightness was lost against the colorless sky. Boadicea sat next to Rhys as the evening chill crept about them. Rhys closed his eyes and was still.

She pushed a strand of hair away from Rhys' forehead. He was wet with sweat and chilled. "Rhys, can you hear me?" Boadicea leaned down. She heard nothing. When she felt his forearm, it too, was clammy in spite of the warmth from the fire. She rearranged the tunic that covered him, then lay down between the piled up logs and Rhys, her arms behind her head so that she could stare at the sky.

The sky darkened to the west and clouds formed thick swirls, the lace replaced by the ominous possibility of more rain. The road was muddied from rain of the night before although the warmth of sun had dried the high ground.

"Please don't send rain." Boadicea shuddered at the dual problems of trying to keep the fire going and protecting Rhys from further chills. She wondered, momentarily, why the gods were punishing her, and dismissed the thought as an ungrateful one. Surely they were preparing her for the future through testing, and she would prove to them that she could pass the test.

Boadicea heard a sound like far-off thunder, and her first thought was of rain. She sat up to look for ways to shelter Rhys when she realized the sound was the rumble of horses' hooves. She could barely see the riders. She jumped up, waved her arms, and shouted, and tears tumbled from her eyes. She didn't care. It didn't matter whether or not anyone thought she was weak. It only mattered that Rhys had been found.

She continued to jump, wave, and shout until the front rider signaled to her by returning the wave. She was filled with relief, for it was her father astride Thayne. Her mother sat behind her father and held his waist tightly.

Garik pulled Thayne up short in front of the fire, and Boadicea heard her mother gasp. The other riders waited a short distance away.

Durina let go of her husband and slid to the ground. She pulled her medicine pouch back into place. "What has happened?"

"A fall, Mother. He was conscious only once. I've not moved him, and I've kept him warm, but he is damp and chilled in spite of the fire. There is no red clover here for his chills."

Durina patted Boadicea's shoulder as she pushed past her. "You've learned your lessons well. Garik, ride back and tell the litter bearers to hurry. We must get him home."

Garik turned Thayne around and looked over his shoulder at Boadicea. "Do you want to ride with me?"

Boadicea shook her head. "No, Father. I must stay with Rhys."

Garik nodded, nudged the horse with his heels and grimaced as Thayne lurched forward. "I can't ride this animal as well as you." His final words were lost on the wind as he clattered down the road, two other riders in his wake.

At any other time, Boadicea would have found her father's ungainly ride amusing, but today it made her uneasy. Her mother knelt next to Rhys, the medicine pouch open. The vials, less mysterious now that Boadicea had learned about them, were placed in a neat row next to the wounded boy. Boadicea sat next to her mother, oblivious of the cold ground, and waited for instructions.

Durina held a clay jar in her hand. She pulled the stopper from the narrow neck and held it under Rhys' nostrils. He stirred. "This should revive him. I need to medicate him for the trip back. It's made from the leaves that we gathered along the river bank last spring." Durina waved the jar under Rhys' nose again. When his eyelids fluttered, Durina held it still, allowing him to breath in the pungent aroma until his eyes opened.

"It will be painful to move you, Rhys," Durina said. "We must turn you over. I'll be careful."

Rhys licked his lips. "All right." His voice rasped as it croaked out the two words.

Durina placed her hands behind Rhys' neck and lower back. "Boadicea, you turn his legs when I move him. Do not let them fall."

Boadicea nodded and positioned herself with her hands around Rhys' legs and watched her mother.

"Ready? Turn him now." Durina moved with assurance and swiftly had Rhys turned on his back.

Boadicea grimaced at the long, low moan that issued from between Rhys' parched lips. She fought tears, telling herself Rhys should not see her thus. She could cry later.

"Mother, is there nothing we can do?"

"We can give him mandrake to deaden the pain. Here, try to get him to drink this." Durina pulled a stopper from a small blue bottle and held it toward Boadicea. The fluted top was suited to pouring the thin liquid easily.

"Swirl it around so that it's mixed well," Durina said.

The liquid slapped against the sides of the bottle as Boadicea twirled it and, hesitating no longer, held the bottle to Rhys' lips while at the same time gently elevating his head. "Rhys, you must drink this. It will stop the pain." His eyes fluttered open. She forced herself to ignore the pain she saw and tipped the bottle.

Rhys shuddered and his eyes shut.

"Mother!"

Durina placed her fingers against Rhys' neck. "He's just sleeping. His body is exhausted. The medicine will keep him asleep for the ride back to our home. Do not expect him to awaken for two or three days."

"Will he live?"

Durina stared at her daughter before answering. "He may die no matter how many medicines I prepare for him. If his internal organs are damaged, we will depend on the gods to guide us, for there is little I can do. You know I will do everything to preserve his life. I'll treat Rhys as I would a member of my family." Durina smiled. "He is to be my son-in-law, is that not so?"

"Yes."

Durina took Boadicea's hand in her own. "I will do all I know to help him, but the gods may not grant my prayers or even yours. Please do not expect a miracle from me."

Both women were silent for there were no more words that would help Rhys or them.

Boadicea was the first to hear hoof beats, and she jumped up. Thayne was in the forefront, her father's grim face testifying to his desire to be on any horse but this one.

Garik pulled on the reins and stopped just short of Boadicea, splashing droplets of muddy water on his daughter's already soiled under-tunic, new mud blending with old.

Four other horsemen stopped behind Garik, and slid quickly to the ground. Two of the men untied a litter of two sturdy oak branches with a sling of heavy linen and laid it next to Rhys.

Garik swung off Thayne and carried two rolled-up blankets to Durina. "Where do you want these?" He glanced at Rhys. "How is he?"

Durina shook her head. "Not good. I fear there are terrible injuries to his organs. The ones I can't see are the ones I have most difficulty healing." She motioned toward the litter. "Two of you lift him carefully and lay him on the carrier."

Boadicea winced when Rhys moaned as he was being moved. She held her breath lest Rhys' breath leave his body and take life with it.

Durina took the blankets from Garik and covered the unconscious boy. "Lift him slowly and don't jostle him as you walk back to the village." Boadicea walked beside the litter, one hand laid gently on Rhys' shoulder and the other carried a torch. She was barely aware of her parents' conversation.

Garik put his arm around Durina. "I hope that the boy lives. I've never seen two people more suited."

Durina leaned into her husband. "I can think of at least two others."

"I am a fortunate man. You go with Rhys and Boadicea. I'll take the wood off the road and make certain the fire is out. She must have thought she'd be here all night."

"Hurry. I have enough to worry about without having to wonder about you." Durina kissed him on cheek.

Boadicea sighed as she watched Rhys breathe. He'd been the same for hours. She wrung out a cloth in warm water tinted brown by juniper berries. She laid it across Rhys' chest and reached in the bowl for a second cloth to wash his face and neck. When the cloth cooled, Boadicea rinsed it in the warm water and repeated the process.

Boadicea took the clay bowl from the bedside stand and stood in the doorway looking at Rhys.

Kali, her black and white kitten, rose from the end of the bed, yawned, and jumped to the earthen floor and followed her mistress through the rooms. In the kitchen, she sat next to the hearth, mewing pitifully.

Boadicea stopped stirring medicine into hot water and looked at Kali. "I know you're not starving to death. You were just fed." She scratched the kitten behind her ear. "I have work to do."

She hurried back to her room, sat on a wooden stool next to Rhys, and watched his shallow breathing. Already there were beads of perspiration on his upper lip. Boadicea reached for the cloth, but stopped when she saw Rhys' eyelids flutter. She held her breath until he opened his eyes and focused on her.

"Welcome back."

"I feel terrible."

"Are you in pain?"

"I don't think so. I feel as if I'm looking down from a tall tree, and everything that you say to me sounds as if it comes through the sea." Rhys closed his eyes again.

"Rhys?"

"I'm so tired."

"You've been asleep for three days. Mother says that it's a good sign. Your father was here this morning. Every evening just before dusk your mother comes and spends the night with you. We take turns keeping your fever down." Boadicea reached for a cloth soaked with blessed thistle, squeezed it almost dry and placed it across Rhys' forehead.

He reached up, slowly, and pushed the cloth away. "That hurts."

Boadicea picked up the cloth. "It hurts?"

"So do the covers."

Boadicea pulled the covers down to Rhys' hips. "Does that feel better?"

"No. I feel as if there is a great weight; tons of rocks piled upon my chest and stomach."

Boadicea felt his forehead and cheek. "You have very little fever. I don't understand, but maybe Mother will. She should return soon. She is midwife for Robinia. Mother says that it will be a boy this time. Robinia says if it's a boy, she won't mind the six girls she's already had." Boadicea brushed Rhys' hair away from his forehead. She wished she could wash it. She knew Rhys had never let his hair get so dirty and wouldn't like it now. He was asleep. Maybe the next time he awakened, he could eat.

A sound from the kitchen indicated that her mother was home. Boadicea listened for her footsteps and was not disappointed when she heard her mother came into the bedroom.

Durina smiled. "It was another girl, but Robinia is very happy. This baby was the biggest one of all her children and the most hungry. She is also the most beautiful baby I have seen since you were born."

Boadicea returned her mother's smile. She loved it when her mother came home from delivering a child, for Durina seemed more peaceful and more beautiful at these times. "I have good news. Rhys talked to me. I think he's going to live, Mother."

"Really?" Durina crossed the room and looked down at Rhys. "What did he say?"

"He said he was tired."

"Was he in pain?"

"Yes. He said he felt that there were heavy rocks piled on top of him. He asked me to take the covers down, for they were too heavy."

Durina pursed her lips and placed her hand on Rhys' abdomen. She withdrew her hand when Rhys flinched and moaned. "There is internal swelling. His organs are pushing against one another."

"Isn't that dangerous?"

Durina looked at Boadicea. "It is very dangerous. I have medicines for swelling, but it may not work." Durina moved away from the bed and paused at the doorway. "I want nothing solid given to Rhys. If he awakens, come get some broth."

"Yes, Mother." Boadicea's eyes filled with tears as she looked at her life-long companion. His form wavered before her. Tears splashed down, wetting the front of her tunic.

Rhys moaned and Boadicea collapsed on the stool. It was such a familiar place, even more so now that Rhys had been brought here. It was her room, but she had taken only a slight interest in its walls and furniture, since she spent most of her time outside. Now she knew every crack and heard every creak. With Rhys in her bed, Boadicea rested on a pallet near him. Every night Rhys' mother claimed the stool, to wait for him to awaken.

Boadicea took Rhys' swollen hand. She traced the blue veins across the back of his hand and tried to make it seem as if Rhys were still a familiar part of the life she had known. She was afraid he would never wake up. His hand felt cold, but he had complained of the covers feeling heavy, and she didn't want to make him feel worse. Boadicea felt his upper arm. It was too cold, and she reluctantly pulled the blankets up to his chin, wincing as Rhys tried to push them away.

A rustling sound from the doorway caused her to turn. The blonde-haired woman standing there was the feminine version of Rhys. She was older, but her age in years did not match her face. She seemed more a sister to Rhys than his mother. The only concession to age was a slight heaviness through the middle, perhaps brought on more by having had five children than by the years.

"Good evening, Boadicea. How is Rhys?" Gwyneth stood by the bed and gazed down at her son. Boadicea stood.

"He . . . he was conscious for just a few moments." Boadicea heard the intake of Gwyneth's breath, and she suddenly felt as if she had taken something from her. She looked away and stared at the floor. "He complained of a great weight on his chest. Mother made him a new medicine." Boadicea stepped aside so that Rhys' mother could claim the stool and her place beside her son. "I'll get you a cup of broth."

"He is my first born and so special. He came into the world screaming, red-faced, but healthy. The first child always claims a corner of a mother's heart." Gwyneth took hold of Boadicea's hand. "I am glad that you were here when he awakened. He needs you so much."

"He'll awaken again. Perhaps when you tell him stories of his childhood."

"You heard? Do I keep you awake?"

"No. I like to hear your stories. Your voice soothes me." Boadicea smiled. "I'll be able to tease Rhys when he's better."

"Should I tell more?"

"Please do." Boadicea squeezed her hand.

"I fear. . . ."

"Don't say it lest the gods hear." Boadicea knocked on the wooden night stand.

"Do you fear for Rhys?"

"Every second of every minute of every hour." Boadicea looked away. "I don't know how I could survive, if I'd want to survive, without Rhys."

"My dear, you must not think that. If . . . if Rhys dies, then it is as the gods wish. You cannot change the gods' plans for yourself." Gwyneth used a corner of her tunic to wipe tears from her eyes. "Promise me that you'll live no matter what happens to Rhys."

Boadicea nodded. "I promise. Allow me to get you some broth." She turned at the door. "Have you eaten?"

Gwyneth shook her head. "I have no appetite."

"I'll get you something to eat with your broth. You must stay well." Boadicea walked quickly to the kitchen where her mother mixed various medicines with the help of their cook, Epona. "I've come to get Gwyneth a cup of broth and some bread."

Durina nodded. "Yes, she needs to eat." She continued to stare at her daughter. "Boadicea, you must understand that Rhys may not live."

Epona shook her head. "I prayed for him, Boadicea."

"Thank you, Epona."

Durina placed a hand on Boadicea's sleeve. "Do not expect miracles, although sometimes they occur. We don't know what the gods have planned for us. Everyone's lives are linked to our own. Rhys' destiny is tightly linked to yours. I feel that as surely as I feel my heart beating."

Boadicea smiled. "I believe that, too, Mother. I believe that Rhys and I were meant to be married and have a lot of children. We are to rule our tribe together. That's how I know you'll make him well."

"Boadicea, do not lay such a heavy burden on me. What if Rhys does . . . doesn't live? Will you blame me? Will you hate me for failing?" Durina's chin quivered.

Boadicea put her arms around her mother. It frightened her to see Durina so close to tears. Her mother never wept. "Do not utter such nonsense, Mother. I know that you love Rhys as much as I do. I could never blame you for what the gods decree. I could never blame you for anything because you are my pattern. I want to be like you and in being like you, I could no more blame you for Rhys' condition than I could blame myself. Actually, I blame myself more, for if I hadn't been trying to show off he wouldn't have . . ." Boadicea's voice faltered and a tear slid down her cheek.

Durina held Boadicea close. "It happened. It happened to test our strength. It was no one's fault. Do not harbor such thoughts, for it is destructive." She pulled back and looked into her daughter's eyes. "Wipe the tears away so that Gwyneth doesn't see them."

"Yes, Mother."

The sky through the small window was streaked with rose-colored paths that crisscrossed each other, but led nowhere. Boadicea, still wrapped in blankets and on a pallet on the floor, reached out for Kali and absent-mindedly ran her fingers through the kitten's soft fur. Kali wasn't supposed to sleep in the house, but she had done so ever since she'd been found mewing and nuzzling a long-dead mother cat. Boadicea had the help of her mother in nurturing the tiny kitten, and it had survived.

The day would be sunny. Maybe after five days of rain and gray clouds hovering just above the earth, the sunshine would bring good luck. Boadicea watched the sky lighten further. It was blue at last. She glanced over to Gwyneth who sat quietly, holding Rhys' hand.

Gwyneth must have sensed that she was being watched. "Good morning. Did you sleep well? Rhys has had his best night yet. He seems better."

Boadicea placed Kali on the earthen floor and threw back the covers. Ignoring the morning chill, she scurried barefoot across the floor, and looked at Rhys. "His coloring does look better. He seems more alive. . . ." Boadicea chewed on her lower lip, but it was too late to stop the poor choice of words. She hoped that Gwyneth hadn't noticed. "He . . . he is breathing better."

"I think so, too. I may have slept a little. I thought he spoke to me, but it could have been a mother's dream." Gwyneth yawned, patting her mouth. "I might have been hoping for too much."

"If that is true, then I have hoped for more. How can anything we wish for be too much?" Boadicea bent down and hugged Gwyneth.

Gwyneth leaned into Boadicea, the heat from her body blending with Boadicea's. They remained encased in each other's warmth, taking comfort in a shared sorrow and a shared hope.

Gwyneth looked at Boadicea. "I remember the day when Weylyn and I sat down with your parents to arrange a marriage between you and Rhys. I was proud of him. I was honored that our family was thought worthy enough for a priestess."

"I was not a priestess then, and I'm still not. Perhaps I'll never pass the final tests."

"That would not have mattered to us. We have always loved you, Boadicea." Gwyneth chuckled. "I remember when the two of you had your first argument. You were only seven summers old. You stamped your foot and raged at him, your red curls danced and your eyes snapped. I knew that you would be good for Rhys because you could match his strong will. You will make him happy."

Gwyneth stood. "I must go and break fast for the other children. If he awakens, please send for me."

"Of course." Boadicea walked with Gwyneth to the door of her room. There were fine lines around Gwyneth's eyes, and her face drooped. Gwyneth had grown older in just a few days. Boadicea felt a cold chill of warning race down her spine. If Rhys died, how would Gwyneth live? It would drain her of everything, including perhaps, her will to live. Boadicea kissed Gwyneth's cheek as they parted. Neither said a word.

Reality swept through Boadicea's heart like a sword. Rhys wasted away, arms and legs thinner than she had ever seen them and made all the more slender because of the contrast with his swollen abdomen. She sat on the stool next to him. The sun shone in the window, highlighting Rhys' already sun-bleached hair and making it the same color as sand at the water's edge.

"Sun on such a grievous day fills my soul with abhorrence. The sky should be gray to match my mood. The sun does not bring comfort, but mocks me. It tries to fool the mind into thinking all will be well when it will not." Boadicea blinked rapidly, trying to push the tears back. She didn't care about her blasphemy.

She didn't know how long she had been sitting there when Rhys opened his eyes. At first she was so startled that she didn't react. She fought with her senses until at last she understood.

She gently touched Rhys' hand. "Good morning."

Rhys turned toward her voice. "Have I been asleep very long?"

"Only days. You have become a lazy person."

"I am a very tired person. I can't seem to remember why I am here. I hurt a great deal in my stomach. Was I injured perhaps?"

"You don't remember?" Boadicea placed her hand on his forehead. It was as hot and dry as sun-baked grass. She half expected the skin to split, it felt so thin. She pulled her hand away. "You and Ella tumbled down together. You turned her, she slipped in the mud, and she rolled over you."

Rhys ran his tongue across parched lips. "I can't remember."

"Don't worry. When you're better, you'll remember."

"Is the mare all right? I think she might be with Thayne's foal."

"I've checked on her every day. She's fine. And you're right—she will foal next summer. Now that you're awake, your mother will want to see you. She just left. I'm going to send for her."

Rhys put his hand on Boadicea's arm. "Don't go yet. I want you here."

"I'll stay as long as you want." Boadicea was shocked at the amount of heat radiating from Rhys' hand. She wanted to pull her arm away, but would not. Instead, feeling guilty for thinking such a thing, she placed her own hand over his. "You must drink some liquid, Rhys. All we've been able to do is get you to suck on a rag like a baby." Boadicea reached for a clay jug that kept the spring water cold.

Rhys shook his head. "I cannot. My stomach is too full."

Boadicea gently placed his hand back on the bed and reached for a mug. She splashed water on the covers in her haste to pour. "You must drink." She held the cup close to Rhys' lips.

He turned his head away. "You don't understand. I am too full. If I drink, I shall split open." He stared at Boadicea; his eyes showed the fright that he felt. "I'm going to die, aren't I?"

Boadicea pulled the cup back from his lips and knocked three times on the wooden slat of the bed. "Hush, or the gods of death will hear you and think you are bidding them to come." She knocked three more times.

"Your rapping won't keep the gods from hearing."

"I cannot take that chance. You mean everything to me."

Rhys reached for her hand. "You mean everything to me. I willingly suffer this pain so that you will sit constantly by my side."

"Even now you tease me. Have I not had a lifetime of your teasing?" Boadicea held the cup to his lips again. "Please take this. It is good for you. I don't care how full you feel."

"You still order me around. Must I remind you that you've ordered me around all your life?"

"You need it. Drink."

Rhys lifted his head and drank. He pulled back after a few sips. "Do not drown me."

"That wasn't enough." The expression on his face made her smile. "Why the serious look that rides across your continence? You are like an old Druid priest about to foretell the end of the world."

"The end of the world? I hope it will be just the beginning for us. Boadicea, would you marry me as soon as I am well?"

"Oh."

"You were already promised to my clan." Rhys reached for her hand.

Boadicea put the cup on the table and took his hand in both of hers. "I am honored to be accepted into your family and your clan, but, I wonder if I'm worthy of you. I do tend to be imperious."

"It is what I admire most about you. You aren't afraid to be strong. I know you'll be a good wife for me, and I want to help you keep the Romans at bay. We've been companions since you toddled after me." Rhys stopped talking and closed his eyes.

"Do you want to sleep?"

"I'm tired, but I want you to keep talking to me. It's getting dark, and I don't want night to come."

Boadicea jerked her head toward the window, confused by Rhys' statement. Had she not been aware of the passing of the day or that a storm was brewing? Sunshine scattered across the room and replaced her confusion with fright. She stared into Rhys' eyes. They had the look of death. Her heart thumped angrily against her ribs. She wanted to scream to the death gods to make them go away, but instead she rose slowly.

"Where are you going?" His voice rattled.

"I must get Mother. I'll be right back."

"Don't leave me in the dark. I can't explain, but it frightens me."

"I'll just call her from the doorway." She moved across the small chamber and shouted, "Mother! Mother, come quickly!!"

Rhys called out. "Boadicea, I need a light! Get a candle."

Boadicea was next to Rhys instantly. "I . . . I can't get a candle until later. This one is used up and the wick won't catch." She looked at the pattern of sunlight and shadow on the bed. Her mother had told her of how people who were dying often lost their sight.

As if to keep the death gods away by talking, she chattered to Rhys. "I never answered you about marriage. I will marry you, Rhys. I've always wanted to marry you. We are suited to each other. I'm sure no one else would want to take on my stubborn personage. Rhys? Can you hear me?"

"Yes."

Boadicea leaned down to hear. He was barely whispering. "I will marry you, Rhys. We'll have many happy children."

"Tomorrow."

"Tomorrow?"

"Marry me tomorrow."

Boadicea tried to blink back her tears, but they streamed down her face anyway. She wiped them away with her fingertips and placed the wet fingers on Rhys' dry cheek. "All right. Tomorrow will be perfect." Boadicea held her still damp fingers below Rhys' nostrils. She felt the faint breath of life easing itself out of Rhys' body, and she knew in her mind that he would not live through the day, although her heart denied it.

She was not aware of anything in the room; not the sunshine, not the kitten chasing its tail, not the sound of her weeping. She was not even aware that her mother stood next to her until a hand reached out and clasped her shoulder. Boadicea looked at her mother and was frightened by the look on her face.

"Mother, tell me what to do, and I'll do it. Tell me how to save him."

"It is too late, daughter. See, the death pallor has come over him. All you can do is hold his hand to help lead him to the other world. I've sent for Gwyneth."

As if waiting for her name to be said, Gwyneth appeared in the doorway. It took her no time to guess that the death gods were hovering near. She sobbed and rushed to the side of Rhys' bed.

Boadicea started to get up from the stool when Gwyneth shook her head and gently pushed her down. She sat on the edge of the bed and lightly laid her hand on Rhys' leg. "He is as much yours as mine." Gwyneth looked up at Durina. "His father is in the fields. I have sent for him. Did I do the right thing?" She began to sob, quietly at first.

Durina bit her lower lip and nodded. "Yes." She stared at her daughter. "Why is it that we nurture them, help them to know the ways of good, love them, and scold them and just when we can enjoy the fruits of all the years, the death gods remove them from our care and our reach?"

Gwyneth sobbed. "I cannot answer that. You're the priestess. You tell me why Rhys will not be a part of Boadicea's future."

Boadicea half screamed, half sobbed. "Don't talk as if he is already gone. Don't tempt the gods with his life. Give him something, Mother. Give him medicine. Give him life."

Durina leaned over, placed her fingers in the cup of water on the table, and placed them under Rhys' nostrils. "There is no medicine that can help Rhys now. Our only comfort is that there is no longer pain for him."

"No pain for Rhys? No, the pain is all for us. I feel as if my soul has been shredded." Boadicea laid her head against Rhys' chest. It was strangely quiet; the thumping of life gone. She cried harder, remembering all the times they had lain thus, with her head against his chest and his heart beating steadily.

Boadicea pushed Ella away from her as she walked between Thayne and the mare. Ella would not be ignored, and she nosed Boadicea again, her moist nose breathing steam against Boadicea's arm. Boadicea shivered and pulled her woolen cape tighter about her. Ella nibbled on the edge of the cloth.

"Please, you're making me hot and wet, and I'll be cold on the way home. Just let me give you the extra hay that you need. I have to get back." She spread the hay across the ground in front of the mare, but Ella ignored the food and pushed against Boadicea with her head. Boadicea scratched the persistent horse on her forehead, running her fingers through the forelock. "I can't hate you, you know. I tried. I guess it's because Rhys loved you so much." Boadicea buried her face in the horse's neck.

The memory of Ella and Thayne carrying the funeral bier between them should have caused the tears to come, but they did not. Her tears had dried up a long time ago, and now all she had was a continuous ache. She also had no direction, no purpose in life. The daily care of the horses and a solitary walk through the countryside was the only routine she had. The rest of the time was spent staring at the sky where the death gods had taken Rhys. In the evenings she sat and watched flames in the fireplace and relived her life with him. No matter how she tried, she could not conjure a future.

Boadicea patted Ella on her rump and she scampered off, her snorting making small, frost-colored clouds. She slapped Thayne on his rump as well, but he moved away slowly as if to say that he was too dignified to romp. Boadicea walked away from them, glancing once over her shoulder to make certain they were all right. Thayne had stopped close to Ella, and they stood nickering softly to each other.

The horses had their mates, and she had no one. She looked at the sky—gray and getting darker as night quickened its hold on the earth and her creatures. The sky matched her mood, and she was anxious to get home. The far-off howling of a wolf didn't cheer her. She had always hated wolves, but since the day of Rhys' accident, she had wanted to kill every one she heard. They personified death for her, and death was what she wanted to give them.

The temperature had dropped steadily throughout the day, foretelling a light snow. She pursed her lips and blew through them. Her breath was white like that of the horses. She saw smoke rising from the chimney of her house, smelled cooking meat, and realized that she was hungry. She was surprised at the return of her appetite.

She pushed open the wooden door and was enveloped by the heat from the fireplace. Epona poured milk into mugs while Durina stirred a delicious-smelling soup in a large kettle that hung over the fire. The long-handled spoon was not quite straight, and Boadicea smiled at the memory of having worked for hours trying to make the perfect gift. In her eight-year-old mind, she had thought it beautiful, and so had her mother.

Durina turned and smiled at the spoon maker. "Close the door quickly. I thought hot soup would be good. Wash up. Your father is bringing in wood and will be here soon." She nodded toward the sound of footsteps on the wooden stairs. "There he is. Go quickly."

Epona rushed to open the door, letting Garik in along with the north wind. She slammed the door shut and hurried across the kitchen to stamp out the embers that had blown across the floor from the firepit. They wouldn't have burnt the dirt floor, but might have caught the broom on fire or the timbers that framed the room. Boadicea left the kitchen, but stood in the hall that led past her room to the wash room. She always had to force herself to think of something besides Rhys before she entered her room. She watched her parents.

"Epona, whatever you're cooking smells delicious. It takes a cold night to make a person appreciate hot food."

"Thank you, my lord." Epona grinned.

Garik dropped the wood to the floor next to the firepit, ignoring the banging of the logs against each other. "Durina, how is our daughter today?"

"It is difficult to tell. She visited the horses again, but did not ride either one. I think you should make her ride. She cannot continue this way. Her world grows smaller instead of larger. She takes on the ways of an old woman. She won't even go with her friends anywhere, though they ask her each day to do something with them."

Garik sat down on a stool at the table. "She is in mourning, Durina. Give her time."

Durina stood behind her husband and put her arms about his neck. She whispered in his ear. "More than four full moons have passed. Garik, she is to be the leader of this tribe. She is an Iceni and cannot forget that."

"What you say is true." Garik placed his hands on her arms. "But I don't know what to say to her, Durina."

"Sit with her. You're as strong as the oak tree for which you were named. You have the wisdom of your father and grandfather, and the words will come. I will pray for the gods to guide you."

Garik leaned his head against Durina's breast. "I'll go talk with her." He rose and left the kitchen.

Boadicea had not meant to eavesdrop, and she was uneasy at being the center of the conversation. She heard her father's approach and ran to her room. She crossed to the bed and touched the blanket. She dropped to her knees and gathered the wool blanket to her. Did she imagine that she could smell Rhys' presence? Or was he still there? She had not allowed the blankets to be washed. At night she cried herself to sleep with the blankets wrapped tightly about her.

She turned when her father entered the room.

The look on his face was one of pain and uncertainty. She wanted to run to him, to cry, and have him tell her the hurt would go away. Reality prevented her. There were no more tears anyway. There wasn't really any more pain although that would've been preferable to the empty ache that refused to go away. She felt as if she were a wooden person with no life left in her body.

She knew she should make it easier for her father by asking what he wanted, but she wanted to strike out at something, to punish someone for her hurt, and he was close by. What had she done that was so wrong that the gods punished her daily and taunted her with memories of Rhys? Why did she look at the stables and think of him? The sacred pool where they swam? The woods where they walked and kissed? If only she could go back in time and be a better person. Perhaps she hadn't prayed enough or taken the priestess training seriously enough.

She stood in the room that was getting dark and refused to acknowledge her father's presence.

"Would you like a candle?"

"Why? To brighten my life?"

"Please. It is difficult enough for me to talk with you. I don't know how to explain the gods' choice. All I know is that I've never experienced the pain of losing someone I was to marry. I can't imagine it. I can remember feeling sorrow when my parents died, but it was natural and expected, for they were very old. For them, death was a blessed relief from pain brought on by a body that was no longer useful." Garik reached out for Boadicea, but she was too far away. He dropped his hand. "I don't understand why young men have to die this way. In battle, yes, that would have a purpose, but for Rhys, I can see no purpose and thus I find myself doubting our gods and their reasoning. If someone had to die, it should've been me."

"Oh no, Father. It is not your time. Mother and I could not live without . . ." Boadicea whirled around to stare at the darkened form in the doorway. The light from the kitchen haloed his entire frame, making him seem more than her father at this moment.

"Ah, but you could. It is possible to go on living no matter how painful." Garik stared at the floor. "Life travels daily toward destiny. Your life has a purpose. Your mother and I have always known that. Greatness is your future. Each day that you live past Rhys is a day shaped just for you. Your paths were not meant to be entwined. I don't know why the gods have chosen to send you to the future alone. I think they've made an error."

"I can't imagine you doubting the gods. You've always taught me that they knew and guided our destiny for a greater purpose than we could ever know."

She was shocked to see her father's shoulders slump as if he had been beaten. Boadicea's hand went to her mouth. He shook his head and turned away.

"Father, don't. I did not mean to be so cruel. If you, who are so strong, have doubts, what am I to do? How can I believe in the future? Tell me. What is there for me?" Boadicea ran to her father, slipped under his arm and snuggled against him. "Tell me how to believe in goodness again."

"I am not the one to ask. I have so many doubts. Come, let's join your mother. The one who studies the gods can help us." Garik wrapped his arm around Boadicea, and together they walked to the kitchen.

"She has already told me that this adversity was meant to strengthen me for a greater challenge later in life." Boadicea blinked as the light from the kitchen shone in her eyes. She hugged her father and sat down in front of a steaming bowl of soup. "I can't imagine anything more challenging than losing Rhys."

"I can." Durina sat down across from her husband. She looked from him to Boadicea.

"What could be worse, Mother?"

"Losing a child. The worst fear for a woman and a man is the loss of a child, for when a child dies the future of the parent dies, too. In each child is a piece of the parents and in each grandchild is a piece of the grandparent and so on into the future. The loss of a child closes the door forever to immortality." Durina blinked rapidly.

"I won't pretend to understand that, Mother. I can't imagine having children with any one other than Rhys. My entire life was spent following Rhys, arguing with him, and tormenting him." Boadicea sighed. "My life is gone without the one who was the center of my attention. I don't know what to do, where to go. He's seems to be everywhere, but nowhere. And I am lost."

Garik cleared his throat. "As difficult as it is to say, your destiny did not include Rhys. Whatever the gods have planned for you must be important."

Boadicea gasped at the words that her father said aloud, for these were the thoughts that she had pushed to the back of her mind every time they threatened to surface. She looked to her mother for confirmation of what her father had said, and seeing the look on Durina's face, she knew that the words were true.

Several minutes passed before Boadicea spoke. "Father, you are right. I can't understand the gods' plans for me, but I will no longer question them. I'll visit Rhys' grave tomorrow and explain it to him. And I will say good-bye."

CHAPTER

IV

SUETONIUS LEANED AGAINST THE TRUNK of a peach tree and laced the fingers of both hands behind his head. He should have gone to the house first to see his mother, but he was more interested in the slave girl. He didn't feel guilty about ignoring his mother, but he knew he should. He had been gone for over a year after his few months of cavalry training and while he had been gone, Trista had been transformed.

Suetonius was in a good position to watch as she clambered about the branches in the tree across from him. Her long legs were exposed since she held the ends of her stola together to form a basket for the peaches that she was quickly gathering.

Her legs were extraordinary, beautifully shaped, slender and smooth, with taut muscles. Suetonius smiled. She had grown from a timid and scrawny girl into a beautiful one on the edge of becoming a woman. He had noticed that Trista had men, slaves and freemen alike, making fools of themselves around her. She was unaware of her power over men and it added to her control over their silly antics. He was one of those men, too, which explained why he had sneaked into the orchard to spy on her.

Slavery did not suit her. She was haughty and had the bearing of a queen. Her father had been a chief, but a savage. It was her dignity that fascinated him. He had never thought about a savage having dignity. Perhaps that's why his mother forbid any of the men to be alone with Trista. His own mother protected all her slaves, but she especially protected Trista.

He watched as she moved carefully from one branch to another, oblivious of his presence, and hitching her skirts higher. His breath caught as she exposed a firm buttock. She turned and the sight of her caused him to moan. He wanted her and he wanted her before anyone else had a chance to ruin her. He wanted her more than he had ever wanted any other woman.

Trista leaned forward to get the perfect peach and slipped, but caught herself before she fell. Suetonius yelled out, "Be careful!" and jumped up.

Trista wrapped her toes around the branch on which she was standing, and with an arm hugging another branch, took the time to stare at Suetonius.

"Suetonius? Whatever are you doing here? I thought you were still off in some strange country." Trista smiled, her face reflecting the joy in her heart. "Don't go away. Please wait until I get down. Here, get that basket over there and help me with these peaches."

Suetonius grabbed the basket and rushed to stand under the peach tree. He held the basket up, not daring to look at her. "You see how easily the slave orders the master around?" He tried to keep his voice light.

Trista laughed. "You do not fool me, Suetonius. I will be a slave forever." She took the basket from his hands and carelessly dumped the carefully picked peaches from her stola into it. She handed the basket back to Suetonius and swung down from the tree, dropping gracefully to the ground in front of him.

Suetonius grinned at her antics. "Do you always climb around in trees? It isn't very lady-like."

"I don't have to be a lady, thank goodness. I couldn't stand all that bread and cream they put on their faces, anyway."

"Aren't you glad to see me?"

Trista's cheeks turned pink. "I am always glad to see you."

"So you can argue with me and tease me?"

"Do I do that? I can't believe that I do."

Suetonius stepped closer and looked into her eyes. He had remembered those eyes whenever he saw the silvery-blue lakes in the north. He took a strand of her hair and rolled it between his fingers. The pale golden grasses of the northern plains had reminded him of her beautiful hair. He drew closer, and she stepped back. She had the tree trunk behind her and no place to go. "Did you miss me, Trista?"

"No."

Suetonius saw that she was breathing fast. "You lie."

Trista's cheeks grew pink, and she lowered her eyes. "I do not lie. I scarcely realized that you were gone for a year, two months, and three days."

Suetonius laughed. "Didn't you count the hours, too?"

"Don't be absurd. I wasn't thinking of you that much."

"How often did I enter your thoughts?" Suetonius ran his hand down her arm, letting it rest on her elbow.

"No more than there are drops of water in the sea. No more than there are leaves on the trees. No more than there are tears for the lonely." Trista shivered as Suetonius rested his hand on her waist.

Suetonius slipped his hand around her and pulled her to him. "Do you tell me this because it is what I want to hear, or do you mean what you say?"

Trista leaned into him. "I did not know that I wanted to be near you all the time until after you had gone, and I was left alone. My only thoughts were of you. Even your mother noticed that I was not here in mind, but far away. She must have known it was you who had captured my thoughts."

"I have thought of you, too." Suetonius leaned over and whispered in her ear. "Did you know that you are the subject of many conversations? Men have spoken so much of your beauty that I had to rush home to protect you."

Trista pushed Suetonius away. "Don't tease me. I hate it when you do that. Can't you be serious for more than a hundred heart beats?"

"I am being serious. As soon as I returned to Rome I heard your name mentioned over and over. I will have to warn my mother to keep you from any midnight wanderings. You don't believe me, do you?"

"I'd like to, but who would want a slave girl?"

"You know that you could have any man and anything you want, slave or not." Suetonius picked up the basket of peaches. "Let's go see mother, for I have missed my family. Is Zia still such a mean child?"

"I'm afraid Elysia and I have a lot of trouble with her, but we can sometimes sneak away for a swim. I like to swim, for my fondest memories of you are when we spent time swimming together."

"I would prefer that you remember me as handsome in my uniform and on the back of my beautiful horse rather than flinging my arms about in the water. If I remember correctly, you made fun of my swimming."

Trista laughed and skipped along beside Suetonius, fighting to keep up with his long stride. "I treasure that picture of you."

"I shall treasure the picture of you in the peach tree until such times as a different picture is presented to me."

"What do you mean?"

"I have plans for you."

Trista stopped, placed her hands on her hips and stared at Suetonius' back as he continued toward the villa.

He turned when he noticed her absence. "Come on. I haven't time to waste. Why do you stand there, glowering at me?"

Trista stamped her bare foot. "I am your mother's slave, and she may plan my future, but I resent any mention of 'plans' for me from you. I don't know much, but I know that I belong to no one but Vivianne."

Suetonius' eyes narrowed. "I have enough money to buy you."

"What would that prove? That you could buy a mate? That might get you my body, but never my soul."

Suetonius marched down the path—double time. "I will never understand women, whether they be slaves or whores." He glanced over his shoulder. Trista stood in the path, her hands on her hips. He continued toward the house. "Women are a different species altogether. They should be whipped on a regular basis just to keep them from believing they can control men."

"I have tried, son, but believe me, no one has ever successfully understood or controlled any woman."

Suetonius whirled toward the sound of his father's voice. His father's silver hair sparkled in the sunlight, a reminder to Suetonius of time passing. "Sir, you surprise me." He looked at his father's face and saw lips twitching to repress a smile. "You want to laugh at me, Father."

Caius moved over, making room on a stone bench. "Come, sit with me, and I'll try to instruct you in the ways of women. Perhaps it's something I should have done a long time ago."

Suetonius sat down, pulling at his toga so as to be more comfortable. "I have a feeling that there is no instruction, only advice on survival." When Suetonius heard his father's deep, rumbling laughter, he realized how much he had missed the older man's companionship. In the northern territories, the adventure of war had kept him occupied, but there had always been the thoughts of home and family tucked away in the cupboard of his mind. "You laugh, Father, but have you been able to understand your own woman?"

"Your mother? By the gods, no, my son. The more intelligent they are, the more difficult to control. Often I have wished for an ignorant wench who would question nothing, but give all." Caius let out a long breath. "Unfortunately, when I tried that, I was bored with the poor thing in two short nights. There was no . . . no joy in receiving a gift with no anticipation."

"If that is the case, then I should be overjoyed with Trista, but I am not. Her actions delude me and confound me. I compliment her, and she hates me. Have you ever had problems with Mother?"

"Nothing but problems. Last year, for example, I displeased her, and she did not speak to me for weeks. It took much stumbling on my part to make her come around." Caius ran his fingers through his thick hair. "To this day I don't know what I did to finally win her back to me. One day she was her old self again and that night . . ." Caius laughed. "Never mind."

Suetonius peered at his father, his curiosity piqued. "Perhaps if you told me what happened, we could figure it out together."

"I'll tell you, but don't think you can figure out your mother when I, who have lived with her for twenty years, cannot." Caius glanced toward the back of the house where the ever present sounds of cooking drifted across the porch toward them. "Just before you left for cavalry training, Tiberius invited your mother and me to a banquet. As you know, our emperor has the habit of . . . " Caius lowered his voice. "Of entertaining chosen women. Your mother was concerned that she would be chosen, so that night she wore an ugly stola. It looked all right to me, and I only found out later during our argument that the stola was ugly. But she looked different that night, almost young and vulnerable. She let her hair hang loose, and it flowed down her back like the ocean waves at night. She wore no makeup, and she reminded me of the young girl I had first seen when she was only fourteen. I must confess that I could have bedded her at that moment. She looked so beguiling and different from the other women. The evening started out well, but your mother was worried about being chosen by Tiberius. I was, of course, extremely jealous, but I dared not let her know. If anyone had overheard my words and reported to the emperor I'm certain that all of us would have been thrown off Tarpeian Rock."

"Of course, Father."

Caius nodded. "We often must clamp our teeth together to prevent our tongues from revealing our minds. I knew as soon as Tiberius saw your mother in all her natural beauty that he would send for her to join him."

Suetonius frowned. "Did he?"

"Yes. I could not watch the exchange of glances. He looked like a prowling animal, and she looked like an unlucky hare. I pretended to be in deep conversation with an old friend."

"I would have done the same, Father."

"To say it more economically, I had to go home that evening alone. I could not sleep and spent the night cursing the moon and stars that shone over Tiberius' chambers. If I thought the night was difficult, the next day was doubly, nay ten times worse." Caius plucked at his toga, trying to remove a nub of thread with no success.

Suetonius lost his patience. "Why was the next day more difficult? Was Mother in hysterics?"

Caius continued to pick at the thread. "I wish that she had been. She had a sly smile on her face the entire day, but would not tell me what happened when I questioned her. I was deathly afraid she had fallen under Tiberius' spell . . . that he had proven to be a better . . ." Caius coughed.

Suetonius swallowed hard. "Father," he croaked. "Pretend that I am not your son, but a confidante. Who else can you confide in without fear of losing your life? If it would make it easier, I will never speak of this moment again after today."

"It is not you, but my own inadequacies that stop me." Caius plunged forward. "I tried to compete with Tiberius. It was stupid of me. She became angry when I offered her a ring. She threw it at me and asked if she had ceased to be my wife and was now considered a whore. I only wanted to please her ... to show her I was not angry with her."

Suetonius shook his head. "She's always liked jewelry before. I certainly don't understand her reaction. You gave what should have been considered a most gracious gift, not to mention the gesture of forgiveness."

"I only wanted her to love me and not him. She did not speak to me after that and actually slept in the room with your sisters and Trista." Caius scratched his head.

"You said that all has been forgiven. How?"

"I wish I knew. One day I tripped over one of your mother's cats and went sprawling. I happened to land at her feet, and when I looked up she was laughing. I was angry at that cat until I saw your mother's eyes. I took that moment to grab her and pull her down. I kissed her." Caius looked into the past. "It was the sweetest kiss; even better than our first kiss."

"My father, the poet?"

"No, your father the frustrated."

"She forgave you? Why?"

"If I knew, I would try it more often." Caius smiled. "I've loved that cat ever since."

Suetonius frowned as he tried to understand his mother's actions. "If women were trained in warfare, and would approach problems with a logical solution, maybe they would behave more rationally."

"They aren't and won't be. They are not fit in temperament for battle. They would faint at the sight of blood, especially their own." Caius' eyes sparkled. "They would faint at the sight of a dirty stola, and the gods help the ladies if they had to fight instead of doing their hair."

"If women went into battle, they would be up all night getting their make-up just right. They would spend an exorbitant amount of time trying to decide what armor to wear." Suetonius chuckled, enjoying the picture of an army of indecisive women. "You would never see a woman in battle, Father. They don't have the temperament, strength, or intelligence for it. Women are just weak, in general."

Caius patted his son's arm. "Of course, but they can certainly make life miserable for us."

"I suppose because we are superior in all ways that we will never understand them. They don't think logically as we do," Suetonius said.

"That's true, but I would not underestimate your mother. She seems to me more intelligent than the average. However, she still does not think straight as a man does." Caius stood. "Let's go in and see the women in our life. Your sisters have been asking for you. I'm afraid Zia is still an apparition from the underworld. I don't know where that child gets the ideas for all her naughty tricks."

"She'll lead some poor young man on a merry chase. I pity the one who wins her heart . . . if she has one." Suetonius stood and stretched. "I'm afraid, Father, that all I've learned is what I already know. Women are a puzzle to never to be solved."

"It's a good thing you're in the army where neither wife nor child is allowed. You'll be better off for the single life," Caius said.

"True, Father. I want no woman to ruin my place in history and be my downfall." Suetonius took his father's arm and walked with him toward the villa. It surprised him that he and his father were now the same height. The muscles in his father's arms were still powerful, and that comforted Suetonius.

"Father, I am a normal man and have need of certain outlets. What is a soldier to do?"

"What have you done before?"

"I have a favorite concubine, but it is not enough. My physical needs are met, but . . ."

"You think you want love. Don't be misled by comfort and convenience. You made the choice of giving your life to the army. The other side of the choice is to forego having a wife. If you feel you've made a mistake, then you must drop out of the military and find another way to earn money."

Suetonius was silent as he thought of all the arguments that he had used with himself before joining the cavalry. "I have made the proper decision. It's just that I get tired of prostitutes, even my favorite, Phoebe."

"I thought so. The answer is to buy yourself a slave who will serve you. When you get tired of her, you can buy a younger slave. It works for many of the men in the military." Caius opened the door to the kitchen. "Look who's home," he bellowed at no one in particular.

Trista pushed her way through the crowded, noisy marketplace toward the fishmongers. Vivianne needed oysters for a special dish she wanted prepared for Caius. The young slave switched the basket to her other arm as she skirted around a stray dog and stepped over a pile of fish entrails. She wrinkled her nose at the confusion of odors. In her homeland, she had always liked the smell of fish, but found it overwhelming here.

It took her but a short time to purchase the oysters at a good price; she always enjoyed this part of shopping, for she knew she could bargain well. Trista had flashes of a memory of an old woman showing her how to choose the best oysters by size and smell and how to find the freshest fish, but whenever she tried to picture the woman, the memory slipped beneath the surface of her mind and disappeared in a ripple of confusion.

Trista tucked the wet linen towel tighter about the oyster shells and started toward the villa. She had hoped to catch a glimpse of Suetonius this morning, but he hadn't returned home last night. Trista snorted. Romping with that whore, Phoebe, again, no doubt. If she went past the bath house, perhaps she would see him coming out. After a night with Phoebe, Suetonius always took a much-needed soak.

It was only a few streets out of her way, and no one expected her back this soon anyway. It wouldn't do any harm. She smiled to herself as she turned down one of the narrow streets to take a short-cut past the bathhouse. Although she wasn't sure of the way, she knew the general direction. If she saw Suetonius, she would make him carry the basket. She giggled. She liked making him do things for her.

The buildings were run down and crowded together, making the street seem narrow and gloomy. A pile left from a slop jar momentarily overpowered the smell of decaying buildings. Trista stepped over it and hurried past a building with a screaming baby and a rancid odor. When she turned the corner, she was relieved, but found that her path was blocked by a walled orchard. She walked through the gate and into the orchard a few feet before she decided that there was no gate on the other side.

She frowned and looked around. Confused, she decided to re-trace her steps. Somewhere she must have missed a turn. The sun was getting higher, and she felt the linen towel. She was relieved that it was still damp, but it was drying fast.

Absorbed in watching where she stepped, Trista almost bumped into two men who blocked her way.

"Look here. A lovely young thing." The speaker was short and stocky.

Trista could hardly understand his lisp enshrouded words. She stared at him. Hairy arms protruded from a dirty toga and reminded her of a drawing of an ape that she'd seen in Caius' library. "Excuse me. I'm lost."

"No, pretty thing. You're not lost. You're the answer to our prayers," a second man said. He had a scar that went from his hair-line to his chin, neatly dissecting a puckered eye. He leaned over and looked into the basket. "What have we here?"

"These are for Caius Paulinus. I am from his house. Perhaps you know him?"

"Know him! I've had the pleasure of being fired by him. We used to sail on his ships."

"Excuse me," Trista said. She tried not to let her voice quiver. "I must hurry, for it's getting late. My mistress will worry about me." She stepped to one side, but her way was blocked by the first man. "I have to get these oysters home before they spoil."

The hairy ape laughed. "I've no need of oysters." He grabbed Trista's hand and placed it on his toga. "Feel that?"

Trista jerked her hand away and stepped back, stifling a scream. "I must go." She turned and walked further into the orchard. Her heart was thumping, and she wanted to run.

"You're being rude," the scar-faced man said. He grabbed her, jerked her around, and held her in a powerful grip.

"Let me go!" Trista irrationally clung to the basket of oysters, trying to protect them.

"Kiss her," the hairy ape said. He came up behind Trista and pulled up her stola, then rubbed against her. "You do the front gate, and I'll do the back."

"Nooooo!!!!" Trista twisted away and swung the oyster basket as hard as she could at Scar-face. His grip loosened and Trista ducked down, slipping from his grasp. She threw the basket at Hairy Ape and ran deeper into the orchard, frantically searching for a way out. She came to the wall and ran along it, but she could find no gate.

Scar-face bellowed and Hairy Ape laughed. Trista could hear footsteps behind her. A hand clamped down on her shoulder and she yelped. Scar-face viciously pushed her down. He flipped her over on her back and pushed her stola up. He smelled like rotten meat and cheap ale. Trista squirmed, and heard her stola rip as she slid out from under Scar-face. Holding the pieces of her clothing together, Trista ran straight into the arms of Hairy Ape.

He wrapped his arms around her. When Trista wriggled to get away, the thick hair on his arms and chest dug into her flesh. She stifled a cry because she knew it would do no good.

Trista grabbed his hair above his scarred ears and jerked as hard as she could. His head bobbed to the side, but he laughed as he pushed her to the ground, wrapping arms and legs around her until she felt like a trussed-up lamb ready for slaughter. She had a vision of blood against white.

Hairy Ape pulled her ripped stola away from her body, lying heavily against her.

He pinched her breast until she screeched. She had never experienced that kind of pain, and it was then that she decided she could no longer escape. Trista quit fighting and tears rolled down her cheeks.

Surprised when Hairy Ape was jerked off of her, Trista was quick to pull her stola together and roll away. She scrambled to her feet and ran beside the wall to find the gate.

"You dumb donkey! Look what you done!" bellowed Hairy Ape. "She's getting away!"

"You get the back gate. The front is mine, stupid," Scar-face said.

Trista could see a break in the wall where the gate hung open and with a swift burst of energy, she closed the gap between terror and freedom. Trista heard a noise behind her and looked back to see that Scar-face was right behind her. She had almost reached the gate when she was knocked to the ground. Scar-face dragged her by the hair and one arm further into the orchard. Trista felt every clod of dirt, every rock that she was pulled across. She grabbed a rock and swung at Scar-face's legs.

Scar-face stepped away from her, then doubled up his fist and hit her repeatedly on her stomach, her breasts, and her thighs until she could no longer fight. "That's better. You're a pretty thing. Now just lie back and relax. You'll like it," Scar-face said.

Trista lay still, staring at the sky while Scar-face shoved her torn stola aside. When he tried to kiss her, she turned away. Scar-face's fingers wrapped around her jaws, and he yanked her face toward him. She bit his tongue when he forced her mouth open, and he slapped her. The ringing in her ears shut out all sound. It brought her blessed quiet, and she was glad.

Scar-face grunted as he forced her legs apart. Trista tried to roll to her side, but to no avail. She screamed as Scar-face entered her and tore her virginity away. She closed her eyes so she wouldn't see the beast as he pumped and pumped himself further into her body. She felt as if he filled up her entire being, and she wanted to die. Warm liquid poured down her thighs and matched the tears that cascaded down her face.

When Scar-face rolled off her, panting and grinning, Trista lay still, hoping that he would go away and leave her alone. She yelped when Hairy Ape dropped down next to her and rolled her onto her stomach. Trista didn't know what to expect. She whimpered as she felt the hairy one settled on his knees, straddling her.

"I love the back gate," he whispered.

The pain was worse than any Trista had ever experienced as he spread her buttocks and forced himself into her. She could feel flesh ripping inside, a burning sensation roared through her body. At the same time she was aware of every piece of dirt that pushed into her face and mouth.

"No more, no more," she whimpered.

Hairy Ape kept driving himself deeper and deeper into her. Trista fainted.

When Trista awoke, she was alone. She rolled over, sat up, and winced at the burning pain between her legs that traveled to her waist. Her stola was smeared with blood, dirt, and crusted semen. She was covered with bruises from her knees to her chin. Trista touched her breasts. They were sore, too.

Trista crawled under a berry bush and curled up. She wanted to die. She cried silently and vowed to stay here until she died. She

could never hide her shame from Suetonius. She never wanted to
see him again.

"I'll find her, Mother, don't worry. Maybe she just got to talking. She's only a few hours late." Suetonius trotted out the kitchen
door and through the orchard.

He met Lucian at the edge of the market. "Good, my message
got to you."

"Why all the fuss about one slave, Suetonius?"

Suetonius shrugged. "You know how my mother carries on about
her slaves. This one happens to be a favorite."

"Women," Lucian said. He kicked a pebble out of the street.
"I've already looked through the fish market and the vegetable market."

"Nothing?"

"Not a word. She did buy oysters, but that was early this morning," Lucian said. "But I found one old woman who said she went
up Orchard Street."

"Why would she go that way? That's not the way to the villa."

"Maybe she was meeting a lover."

"Trista? That girl has a hard heart. There's no room in it for
any man," Suetonius said.

"Do I hear regret in your voice, my friend?"

Suetonius punched his friend on the arm. "Not at all. I have
Phoebe, remember?"

"So?"

"So let's walk up Orchard Street."

Trista heard Suetonius calling her. She crawled further into the
berry bush and kept her eyes tightly closed, but tears slipped out
anyway. At times his voice was frightfully close, then mercifully, it
drifted further away. She heard Lucian calling her name, too, but
she didn't want him to see her.

She had almost lapsed into her dream world when she heard
Lucian swear.

"By the gods, Suetonius! Here's an overturned basket of oysters.
She must be here, or she has been here."

"It is ours. See the linen has our mark embroidered on it."
Suetonius looked around the orchard. "You check that side. Look
under each blade of grass and each leaf. I'll check over here."

Trista pulled her legs up tighter and buried her face in the dirt. She clutched her stola.

"She's here!" Suetonius called out. He dropped to his knees and put his hand on her breast. "Lucian! Over here! Her heart still beats!"

Trista pushed his hand away. "Leave me."

"What happened?" Suetonius stared at a myriad of bruises on her legs half hidden by dried blood. He knew what had happened, but he didn't want to believe it.

"By the gods!" Lucien said. "She's been . . ."

"I know what's happened! I will kill him. I will make him die a long and painful death." Suetonius took Trista's hand. She pulled it away. "Leave us, Lucian."

"Shall I get a chariot?"

"No. Just leave." Suetonius pushed Trista's hair away from her face. "Tell me what happened."

Trista listened to just one pair of footsteps fade. She wished there had been two. "Don't talk to me. I want to die."

"No, Trista, I won't let you." Suetonius pulled her to him. "I love you. Whoever did this to you will pay."

Trista pushed Suetonius away. "I won't love you or anyone. I don't want you to touch me."

"We're going home." Suetonius scooped Trista into his arms and carried her from the orchard. When he passed the basket, he kicked it as hard as he could and sent it flying. He crushed the oyster shells with his hobnailed sandals. "I will kill him."

"Son, how is Trista?" Caius clapped his hand on Suetonius' shoulder. "Your mother tells me you found her yesterday."

"Trista won't talk, and I don't want to talk about it."

"I don't know how to tell you this, Suetonius, but she is only a slave. I can understand your mother's concern, for she is that way with injured birds, sick puppies, and her slaves." Caius poked at an ant with a stick. "It isn't seemly for you to act like someone . . . someone took your wife by force."

"I can't explain my reaction. I want to kill the man who did this to her."

"It isn't unusual for a slave to be loved by an owner, but always there is the understanding that it's not permanent." Caius ran his hand through his hair. "I'm not good at this conversation."

"I said that it wasn't open for discussion."

"Ah . . . yes, well, I respect that." Caius toyed with the ant some more.

Suetonius could stand the silence no longer. He pushed a plate of figs toward his father. "You should try these. They're good."

Caius popped a fig into his mouth and chewed. "They are good, but the problem with figs is that there is more seed than fruit." He took another one. "Our trees did very well this year. I hope it is a good omen for other things."

"I do, as well."

"When do you return to your unit, Suetonius?"

"In eight days time. It is a long wait, but we must be ready for another long trek into the northern lands, again."

Caius tapped his index finger against the side of the bowl of figs. "Perhaps you should pray to the god, Mithras, before you go. If you like, I will pray to him as well."

"Thank you. I understand the Gauls are strong again, and it could be a bloody fight." Suetonius heard a rustling noise behind him, and he turned to see his mother in the doorway.

Vivianne moved to Suetonius and placed her hand on his shoulder. "Trista asks that you come to see her. She wonders why you have not visited her yet. She thinks you're angry with her."

Suetonius squirmed. The hand on his shoulder tightened. It reminded him of his childhood when he had done something that caused his mother's disapproval. He wished now, as he had often did, that she would raise her voice like other mothers instead of using the quiet, firm voice and the hand of iron that directed him to do something he did not want to do.

Suetonius spoke to his mother's shadow outlined on the garden wall. "I am not angry with her, Mother. I am saddened by her plight."

"Why do you avoid her?"

"I'm not avoiding her." Suetonius ran his hands through his hair, pushing it back from his face. The sun felt warm on his forehead. "She didn't want to see me. She turned her face to the wall."

Vivianne patted her son on the shoulder. "Go see her. She's in the alcove next to your sisters' room. They have been sent to your Aunt Savina's villa. I did have to bribe her to take Zia. It seems Zia is always putting bruises on Savina's two boys."

Suetonius shook his head. "I can imagine what Zia does to them; no matter that they're bigger than she is." He stood and pushed the stool away from the garden table. "You're right, as usual, Mother. I should have seen her before this whether she wants me to or not. Excuse me, Father."

"Yes, of course." Caius waved his hand in dismissal.

The house was much cooler than the garden and because of its open design, the same breezes that cooled the garden in the evening, cooled the house at night. The heavy walls kept the daytime heat from penetrating.

Because of the tranquility of the villa, Suetonius felt like one of Hannibal's famous elephants as each marching sandal hit the marble floors. The hobnails on the soles sounded like the castanets that the women used in their dances. He stopped and removed his sandals and left them next to the chamber in which he slept. He continued down the hall and felt as if he were an intruder. When he reached his sisters' sleeping room, he cleared his throat.

"Trista? Are you there?" Suetonius stood outside the chamber, waiting for an answer. Hearing none, he ventured inside the room and stepped around scattered toys. He stopped at the door to an alcove that was large enough for a cot, but nothing else. A few pegs on the wall held the stolas that he had seen Trista wear. One peg was empty. He looked at the sleeping Trista. She was curled up just as she had been when he found her; her knees drawn to her chest. Hair fell across her face, hiding the lower half. Long lashes lay against flushed cheeks. A light breeze came through the small window and ruffled the bottom edge of her sleeping stola and revealed the darkening bruises that looked all the more hideous since her dried blood had been washed away.

Suetonius wanted to kill someone for the innocence that had been snatched away. He sat on the cot and pushed hair away from her face. Her breath escaped, and Suetonius was glad that she still had breath to give. He stared at her. As long as he was able, he would be her protector. No one would harm her and nothing would be allowed to hurt her. He had vowed to kill her rapist, and he knew he would.

He was still staring at Trista when she opened her eyes and saw him. He smiled at her.

"Suetonius, you did come to see me. I didn't want you to." Trista pulled her stola over the bruises.

"Why not? We live in the same house. I was bound to see you sometime. Mother said that you asked for me."

"I did, but I changed my mind. It was the yearning of a child for a friend."

"That pleases me."

"I'm so ashamed." Trista turned her head away from him, letting her hair hide her face.

Suetonius took her hand between his two large ones. It felt like a sparrow he had held once—small and warm and delicate. "Why are you ashamed? You did nothing wrong."

"The fault is mine. I should not have been so stupid as to wander around Rome when I didn't know where I was going. It was my own vanity that caused me to play the part of a fool. I wanted to go past the bath house so that you could see me." Trista shivered. "I wanted you to love me. I was jealous that you'd spent the night with Phoebe." She pulled her hand away from Suetonius.

"I spent the night with Phoebe because I knew you wouldn't." Suetonius took back her hand. "Look at me. Does it bother you that I hold your hand?"

Trista's eyelashes fluttered and she blushed. "Yes, it does," she whispered. "It bothers me too much. I am not worthy of you now."

"You are worthy of me. It is I who am not worthy." Suetonius continued to hold her hand, squeezing it gently. "Will you go for a walk with me later? I want to be with you. I'll have to leave in a few days. I need pleasant memories to carry with me into the wild lands of the north." He tried hard to maintain an easy manner in spite of wanting to scream, to slam his fist against the wall, to kill.

"I need more rest. I can't walk without pain," Trista sobbed.

Suetonius controlled his voice with difficulty. He would kill the rapist. "Perhaps tomorrow?"

"Perhaps never."

"You've rested since yesterday. Too much rest and you'll become a lazy, worthless slave." Suetonius smiled to soften the words that he feared Trista would take too seriously.

"Where do you go in the north?" Trista pulled her hand away and tucked it under her cheek.

"I don't know. We are given our orders the day we leave. Sometimes we only know where we're going a day at a time."

Trista looked out the small window. There was distance in her stare. "If you are sent to a place where the water runs cold and is as blue as the sky; where the trees grow tall and dark and have needles instead of leaves; where the grass grows golden and waves in the cooling wind, then you've found my home." Trista looked away from the window at Suetonius. "Bring back a piece of it for me. I miss it so much."

Suetonius was startled by the longing in her voice. He had never thought of Trista as having any home other than the villa. "It must have been difficult for you to leave your home." He colored with embarrassment. How could he have said such a thing?

Trista's lips clamped together, and she shook her head. When she spoke, the words flew past Suetonius like stones from a catapult.

"I miss more than my home. I watched your fellow soldiers kill my friends, my neighbors, and my father. I could never find my brother because there were too many bodies on the battlefield. I watched men, dressed like you, tear the clothes off my father's sister and . . ." Trista pushed Suetonius off the cot with her feet, then flopped back and sobbed.

He hit the floor with a thud. "What are you doing? I didn't do those things to your family."

"But you have done the same things to some other family. You are trained to plunder and take, take and plunder. I am ashamed that I like you. Go away." Trista turned to the wall and curled into a ball.

Suetonius looked up from his place on the cold marble floor. His breathing was fast, and he was confused. He believed that it was the duty of Rome to conquer the world in order to bring them civilization. His father and his teachers had taught him that, and yet here was someone who had been on the receiving end of that philosophy. Had he been taught wrong? Suetonius shook his head. No, it was right that the strong should subdue the weak and rule them.

Suetonius pushed himself to a standing position and looked down at Trista. "You may blame me personally for your troubles if it makes you feel better, but I refuse to accept it. It would be better for you—for all of us—to live for today and tomorrow and not for the past." Suetonius looked at her small shoulders and slender back. The outline of her spine pushed against the sweaty white stola that clung to her. He reached out to touch her, but stopped. She seemed so cold and far away. He pulled his hand back and let it drop to his side.

"Don't you understand that Rome brings your people civilization? Laws? Order? A better life?"

"Whether we want it or not," Trista said.

"How could you not want civilization?"

"It is coupled with slavery and death. Ask yourself what kind of civilization brings destruction?"

Suetonius tugged at his lower lip. How could he explain something as complex as Rome's ideals to this uneducated girl? "If people wouldn't fight us, there would be no destruction."

"That's a stupid argument. Go away." Trista's voice was muffled. "I want to live in the past because it was a most beautiful time for me. Leave me alone."

Suetonius frowned. "As you wish." Turning, he left the room. He wanted to understand her and her pain, but he could not. She seemed the same on the outside, but her heart had changed. Trista couldn't be lost to him.

On the fifth day of Suetonius' vigil in the orchard, he still hadn't seen any sign of the men he sought. He and Lucian had wandered the streets in the area, but saw no one who matched the description Trista had given his mother. Vivianne, of course, knew why Suetonius had broached the subject and had warned him not to do anything rash. Trista's sobs had grieved him, but at least he had a good description of the men from his mother.

Two men! His anger had changed from white hot fury to a red, raw nagging. He hid it under a facade of nonchalance so that his mother would not suspect his plans. Only Lucian knew of his plans, and only Lucian was a true enough friend to help. Except that Lucian didn't know the real plan. His friend had to be protected.

Suetonius' revery was broken by the sound of running footsteps. Lucian ran toward him. "Hail, Lucian. I'm here." Suetonius stepped from behind an olive tree.

"I've found them!" Lucian's dark brown eyes sparkled in triumph. "They are coming this way. I told them we had high stakes gambling and a beautiful slave girl would go to the winner."

"Well done." Suetonius clapped him on the shoulder. "Do your next part."

Lucian flicked a piece of a leaf off his toga. "I don't understand why you're so upset that these men attacked your slave."

Suetonius shrugged. "I'm not sure I understand either, but she is different than most slaves. She is regal, intelligent, and I . . . I don't know. She isn't like other savages that Rome has conquered. I have an overwhelming urge to avenge her."

"I'd rather be here to help." Lucian cocked his head. "You haven't told me the truth. We've been friends long enough for me to know you have something planned other than a beating."

"It is my fight, not yours."

"Since when?"

"You'll be more help on the street to watch for patrols that might happen by. These are scum. I won't go to prison because of them." Suetonius forced himself to smile. "I need you on the streets."

"You're going to kill them."

"No."

"All right." Lucian turned. "They're here. Call me if you need help."

Lucian brushed past two short, stocky men as they came into the orchard. One, indeed, looked like an ape with hairy arms, and the other wouldn't have been handsome even without the scar that traversed his face from top to bottom.

"Are you here to gamble? To see if you can win a slave girl?"

The Hairy Ape chuckled. "That we are."

"This way." Suetonius led them deeper into the orchard. "Have you been here before?"

"It's a good spot for recreation." Scar-face elbowed his companion in the ribs. "If you know what I mean." Both men laughed.

"Like last week?" Suetonius rubbed his hand across the handle of the knife strapped to his waist.

"Oh, we have never had a game here," Hairy Ape said.

"You had a game here," Suetonius said. "You gambled and lost, only you didn't know it."

"You're mistaken. We never gambled here." The man scratched his scar. "If you're going to rob us, it won't do you no good. We ain't got no money to speak of."

Scar-face pulled out his dagger, but Suetonius quickly had his knife to the man's throat. "Drop it." Suetonius saw furtive movements from the corner of his eye. "Tell your friend to do the same."

Hairy Ape lunged at Suetonius, his dagger held too high. This man was not trained in anything more than street fighting. Suetonius forgot about Scar-face and kicked Hairy Ape in the groin, dropping him to his knees. He lay in the dirt groaning.

Suetonius turned just in time to jerk out of the way of Scar-face's thrust with his dagger. He received a cut on his upper arm, but it was nothing. Suetonius aimed his own knife at Scar-face's crotch.

Scar-face jumped back, surprise and fear on his face. "What're you doing? This ain't no fair fight."

"Did I promise you a fair fight? You're here to pay for something vile that you did to a friend of mine." Suetonius rushed at Scar-face who shoved his dagger at him again and again without connecting. It was almost too easy for Suetonius. He slashed under Scar-face's belly, neatly slicing his toga and exposing pubic hair and a flaccid penis.

"What are you doing!" Scar-face stumbled backwards.

"I plan to winnow out rotted flesh." Suetonius was concentrating so hard on Scar-face that he forgot Hairy Ape until the man jumped on his back and wrapped his legs around Suetonius' waist. Suetonius cursed himself for stupidity. He whirled around and bashed his adversary against a tree trunk over and over until the man loosened his grip on Suetonius and fell to the ground.

Suetonius bent over the man and slapped him in the face. "Wake up, you fool. I want you to know what will happen to you." Suetonius slapped him again and again until the man opened his eyes. With one swift movement, Suetonius jerked up the man's toga and sliced through his testicles and penis, severing them neatly from the man's body, and throwing his trophy to the ground in disgust. "That, my friend, is repayment for what you did to Trista." He ignored the screams.

When Suetonius turned toward Scar-face, he saw the man slinking through the trees. Suetonius caught up with him, grabbed him by the greasy hair, and jerked him off his feet.

"No! Please! I didn't do nothing! I tried to stop him, but he kicked me in the head. I couldn't help the girl!" Scar-face screamed.

"That isn't the story I was told." Suetonius said.

Scar-face dropped to his knees and pleaded for mercy, but Suetonius showed none as he performed his second surgery of the day.

Smiling with satisfaction, Suetonius glanced back at the two bloody men as he left the orchard. He wiped his knife on his toga, reveling in the stain it left.

Lucian met Suetonius two alleys away from the orchard. "Come, quickly. I have given the madam and Phoebe two dupondia each to swear that we have been there all night and day dead drunk and over-amorous."

"I don't feel over-amorous."

"You don't look too bad. I guess that you took few blows."

"I gave few blows, but they counted for a lot."

"Come, slip down this alley. It will get us there sooner. There are two patrols between us and the whore house." Lucian grabbed his friend's arm and propelled him into another alley. "You don't seem as jubilant as usual when you win a fight."

"It was no fight, Lucian. It was revenge. Revenge leaves a bitter-sweet taste in the mouth." Suetonius sighed. "I will welcome leaving here three days hence."

The sun shone straight above Suetonius, but the air even cut through his armor and the woolen tunic beneath. His sweat dried until he felt hot and cold at the same time. It amazed him that people chose to live in the north where the sun acted like a capricious ruler, appearing only when necessary and infrequently. The days were too short and the nights too long.

His officer shouted, and Suetonius nudged his horse in order to get in step with the rest of his line. It would never do to be out of step. One more warning, and he would be drawing stable duty. He glanced at the rows of infantry marching double time behind him.

He wondered how many of the armored soldiers would march down this road toward Rome, chosen by the gods to live through battle. Suetonius turned in the saddle, shifted his armor into place with his arms bent and tightened against the metal, noticed the chill of the metal, and wondered about his own mortality.

He had not been in battle yet. The only time he had seen the enemy was when they had captured a few villages south of here. It was disgustingly easy. The men had been away, and the only inhabitants were old men, children, and women. He remembered the look of horror on the faces of the women as the army marched closer to their homes and their children. He watched as the women ran from the army, scooped up their children and shielded them with their unshielded bodies. He watched as the scrawny old men hobbled after the women toward the shelter of their homes which proved to be was no shelter at all from the relentless army.

Suetonius did not remember the skirmish as a whole, but only in bits and pieces and slashes of color. He remembered the color of red that had turned to brown, the white of eyes and the white of teeth as terror widened eyes and opened mouths. He should have heard the screams of the women, the cries of the children, and the curses of the old men, but he didn't. He remembered dust in his nostrils that mixed with the iron odor of blood as he leaned down from his horse and slashed the enemy that had tried to knock him from his horse with a spiked club. He had no remorse. It was his duty to conquer barbarians. If there happened to be a few men who were intelligent, then they would have a place in the local government. The weak would be culled out. Some of the women and children would become slaves. The strong survived, for Rome was meant to rule the world.

Their next target, another village, was supposed to be over the rolling hills ahead. The encampment had purposely been set up twenty miles away. It was an easy march for the army in double time. Suetonius was glad that he had been trained in the cavalry; that was difficult enough, but easier than marching.

He came back to the present as the sound of hundreds of feet marching in rhythm forced its way into his thoughts. Once more he looked behind him and saw a cloud of dust as it was propelled upwards by the thundering of the marchers who drew swiftly near like a deadly wave.

The first sighting of the village was of fields that surrounded the pitifully small, round huts. Boughs from the fir trees of the nearby forest forming the roofs had turned to various shades of yellow and brown. He could not decide whether he imagined children running back and forth in front of the huts or if they were real. Suetonius had no particular fondness for children, but rather he thought it unfortunate that the young had to witness the wars of their parents. He knew that these children had seen skirmishes before, and that often the families followed the warring party.

He was glad that his sisters would never see a battle. That was why it was necessary for Rome to reach out and conquer the world. It would bring peace in the future.

Suetonius looked at the village that seemed out of place in the modern world. The future had no place for the past. He shook his head at the audacity or stupidity of the inhabitants. How could they believe the slender log fences that surrounded their animals and shielded the village would keep the Roman army out any more than the feeble talisman of bone and feathers tacked above the main gate could protect them?

Did they even know that Rome would become their protector, not the simple and ineffective bone and feather amulet. Rome was made of fighting men of flesh, blood, and bone. Living, breathing, thinking, building. Rome had been charged by the gods to build a civilized world. It was the Roman's duty to bring culture to the wild frontier. No matter that Trista argued with him. She had no worldly concept—just the ideas born of being in a small world.

As Suetonius neared, he watched the feathers ripple in the breeze, and he wondered if the wind were from the gods or from the force of the army as it moved closer.

The children stopped, as one, stared at the army, then ran to the huts. Suetonius saw figures in the small doorways. Women, he supposed. He watched as streaks of color left the huts and ran toward the fields beyond to warn the men. It would do no good, of course, for the Roman army was a machine marching as a unit with one commander, one purpose, and with so much momentum that nothing could stop it.

The commander ordered the army to tighten ranks. The cavalry was in place, and Suetonius made himself ready. The screeching from the savages as they ran down the hill toward the well-trained army unnerved him, but he refused to let his momentary dismay turn to terror. He had been taught that terror prevented clear thinking and without clear thinking, one might as well be dead.

The first sounds of an attack made him suck in his breath. After the initial wave of noise rushed over him, he heard no sounds except what his own short sword produced or the clang of his shield as it caught the blows of the enemy. Sometimes he heard nothing but the breathing of his adversary, and he focused on it until he stopped it. He replaced the silence of his enemy's death with his own breathing. He paused before taking up the sword to fight another attacker to breathlessness.

He had killed only four men in his short military career and each time it was the same for him. He had never known fear, as some of his colleagues had confessed to him. He had never become ill, and he had never thought about the widows he created in the space of a moment. It seemed to him that all he learned in his short life and all he loved culminated in this one activity. Undoubtedly, the gods meant him to be a soldier. He longed for a real battle. However, he didn't dwell on the everyday details of where he was going and with whom, but accepted his orders with no more notice than that of a piece of bread put before him at meal time. Likewise, he never thought of himself as doing anything other than the job he was meant to do in spite of his commanding officer's compliments and admiration.

A savage rushed toward Suetonius' mount, ax in hand, going for his horse's legs and ultimately him. Suetonius leaned down, ready, held his breath and instinctively waited for the precise moment to remove the breath of life from his opponent. He dispatched the wild-eyed barbarian without raising so much as a good sweat and rode into the fray. An infantry man was down, but still hacked away with his sword. Suetonius thundered toward the half-naked man who swung a club at the unfortunate soldier. Suetonius needed no more than one well-placed swipe to kill the man.

In the eternity of a half hour, the conflict was over, and the Romans captured the village. Soldiers gathered the surviving women, children, and men. They were to be properly guarded until those who were strong enough to survive the trek back to Rome would be chosen as slaves. The rest were to be destroyed, for in this village they were obviously too barbaric ever to suppose they could govern themselves.

Suetonius hated the screams from the women and the cries of the children after a battle. He had no patience for the weak. A flash of white-blonde hair at the edge of his vision captured his attention, and he turned in the saddle in time to see one of the infantry soldiers chasing a young girl. A soldier tackled her and they rolled together, legs entangled. She never stopped screaming.

His heart banged against his ribs. He knew it wasn't Trista, but yet his emotions cried out for the innocent slave girl robbed of her chastity. The horrible scene he had only imagined was about to be replayed here in front of him.

Suetonius didn't wait to see the soldier tear at her clothing, but spurred his horse forward. The soldier didn't noticed Suetonius until a sword was placed against his throat where the jugular was located. The soldier froze in position still straddling his quarry, his hand clutching a piece of her clothing.

"Get up and leave this girl alone." Suetonius was surprised at the vehemence of his voice.

The soldier let go of the girl's clothing and stood slowly. As soon as Suetonius lowered the sword, the soldier turned toward him. "It is the custom to take the women. Why do you stop me?"

Suetonius was stunned. The question of why had not entered his own thoughts. He had merely reacted. "Get back to the ranks."

The soldier reached down and grabbed the girl's arm. He jerked her to her feet. "Who are you to order me around? We are the same, you and I."

Suetonius could feel his face get hot with rage, and he touched the soldier's cheek with the tip of his sword. "I am called Suetonius. Let go of the girl and return to your commanding officer, or I will slice your face to the bone. We may be the same rank, but I have the upper hand and therefore, you will do as I say."

The soldier's eyes narrowed. He waited just long enough to pretend he wasn't frightened and let go of the girl. He turned and stomped off, but shouted over his shoulder, "Why don't you get your own girl?"

Suetonius looked at the girl. For an instant, Trista's face looked back at him. He shook his head to clear it. She had the coloring of Trista and although she had an interesting face, she was not as pretty. She might have been fourteen or twenty. Suetonius watched her. She never moved. Her eyes flicked back and forth from Suetonius to the forest on her right and back to her village that was in ruins. The flames were reflected in her eyes, and burned them from blue to orange. There was no terror, only despair, and Suetonius wondered how many times in her lifetime she had seen her village destroyed.

She pulled her torn tunic into place as best she could and moved slowly while she watched Suetonius' sword. In answer to her unasked question, Suetonius sheathed it. He motioned toward the forest.

The girl looked toward the woods with a puzzled expression. She moved sideways toward the trees a few inches at a time. Finally she turned and ran.

Suetonius watched her hair stream out behind her like a banner. She disappeared in the woods and the shadows enveloped her, blotting out even her light colored hair.

Suetonius rode back toward his commanding officer and only then did he wonder at his actions. He looked around at the men who were disappearing into huts with the women. It was common for soldiers to relieve their needs with captured women. It was a normal part of war; he had even done it himself. Some women didn't mind being loved by a strong, young soldier. Some women saw it as a way to survive. Some women seemed to enjoy lovemaking.

So why did he stop this soldier? Because she looked like Trista, that's why. Shaking his head at his unexpected sentimentality, he rode forward. If he felt the need of a woman tonight, he would make certain she had dark hair and came to him willingly.

CHAPTER

V

OADICEA SQUEEZED HER EYES SHUT. She didn't want to see her daughters. How much was one supposed to endure in a lifetime? Neila and Sydelle were supposed to be the future, but now they would rest in the ground to become part of the past. Would they be remembered with a line or two in a story told by the wandering tellers of tales, or would they lie forgotten—the end of the family and of a people? Boadicea opened her eyes slowly.

Light from the firepit flickered across her kneeling daughters, highlighting Neila's tight, black curls and making Sydelle's auburn hair a red-gold. A smile appeared on Boadicea's face, then disappeared. After Rhys died, she had vowed never to marry. Ironically the children she had pledged not to have were born after all. In death, she would see her husband, Prasutagus, dead such a short time ago. It seemed to have happened in another lifetime and to some other being. This life would end, but there would be another life to live. She would return, and she hoped that Prasutagus would share the new life with her. Perhaps they would be peasants the next time since she'd failed as a queen.

The wind blew hair away from Boadicea's face, and feeling free, she nudged Thayne forward with a swift kick. She leaned forward and let his mane sting her face. She felt more alive than she had in a long time. It was good to have a break from her Latin and

Greek studies. Her mother had told Boadicea that she, Durina, had never had the passion for languages that her daughter had. Pleased with her mother's compliment, Boadicea replayed the conversation in her mind.

The sun shone above her, bright and hot. It was the month of her birth sixteen hot summers ago. Her mother said it was good to have been born under the sign of the oak, the Druid's most sacred tree. Destiny decreed that she be a leader.

Boadicea loosened the reins and gave Thayne his head. With eyes teared from the wind, she blinked rapidly to see where she was headed. It wasn't far across the field and into the woods. She waited until the trees were too close, then pulled hard on the reins to test her skill and Thayne's. If she hadn't been such an experienced rider, she would have unseated herself. Thayne shook his head, his mane rippling, and pawed the ground. Boadicea nudged him forward into the cool woods. She looked around carefully, mentally marking her way in so that she would find the way out. They were at least five hours ride north of the Thames and three hours west of the Narrow Sea. She was no more than two hours from her village, but she felt as if she were in another world.

Two great oak trees framed the barely perceptible path that was covered with last year's fallen leaves. Already they were dank and part of the forest floor. Boadicea liked the way Thayne's hooves sounded as he carefully put one foot in front of the other. It was as if they were from another world and, ghost-like, they traversed the path without a sound.

It was cool in the forest, and Boadicea inhaled the fresh, moist air. She reached back with one hand and lifted her thick, auburn hair away from her neck. When a ripple of air cooled the perspiration, she shivered and let her hair drop. Rhys had always teased her about her wild hair that, he said, matched her wild ways. His voice speaking to her from the past made Boadicea frown. Memories of Rhys slipped into her mind at peculiar times. She closed her eyes, and his laughing face appeared before her. That image faded, and the pale face of death replaced the laughing one. She opened her eyes. She wished she could cry to rid herself of the demons of pain. It had been more than a year since Rhys had died, and she supposed all the tears were gone. She wanted to remember him, but only when she could choose the time and place.

Boadicea didn't know how long she had been riding through the woods when the sunlight began to filter through the thinning trees. She didn't know this part of the country well. Once, when she had been very small, she and her father had come here to visit the neighboring tribe. Today she chose to ride in a part of the country where she and Rhys had never gone.

Boadicea had forgotten the brightness of the sun and involuntarily squinted as she rode into the field. The grass was a beautiful green, the sun was warm, and the sky was a brilliant blue. It made Boadicea feel like singing, so she did as loudly as she could. Her voice was strong, yet delicate with a haunting clarity. She sang the Druid songs of her priesthood. She was allowed to sing them as often as she wanted to having passed the final test just before the Mother Night on the shortest day of the year last winter.

As she rode farther around the field, memories of Rhys floated into her mind and skirting the edge of the woods, she sang the dark refrains of the funerals.

The last notes drifted across the fields, and she smiled at herself for her melancholia and vowed to sing happier songs. She had just begun when she caught a shadow moving along opposite her. Abruptly she stopped singing and unsheathed her dagger as she turned toward the shadow.

A warrior smiled at her from the back of the biggest war horse that Boadicea had ever seen.

"I mean you no harm. You may put the dagger away."

Boadicea stared at him. His eyes were the unusual reddish-brown that some people with red hair have, but his hair was a very dark brown. In any other light but sunlight, it might have looked black.

Boadicea's hand gripped the dagger tighter. "What makes you think that I believe you?"

He smiled, making small, comfortable wrinkles around his eyes as if he smiled a lot. "Perhaps if I introduced myself you might recognize my name."

"I know very few people from this area." Boadicea looked at his massive build. He sat higher on his horse than she by far. It was unusual since she was almost as tall as most men. He looked as if he knew hard work. Every muscle seemed to want to push out through his tunic. The sun glinted off the hair on his arms, and she wondered about him. He seemed older than she, but younger than her father.

"I am called Prasutagus, ruler of the tribe that is over yonder hill." He pointed across the field. "If memory serves me correctly, there can be no other child with hair that color and that thick, but Boadicea, daughter to Garik and Durina. You have been to my house with your father when a young girl."

"You know my father?"

Prasutagus nodded. He rode closer, slowly. "I also know your mother. She, too, is famous as a priestess. People in my tribe have heard of her skills."

Boadicea nudged Thayne forward. "Tell me your name once more and your lineage, please."

"I am Prasutagus, son of Aila and her mother, Darcy. My father was Kincaid, and his father was Ulric. You are too young to remember them, but your father knew my father and mother."

Boadicea nodded. "I have no reason to doubt you." Prasutagus' sister, she remembered, was the only family he had. No wife, no children.

She turned Thayne slowly toward the direction from which she had come. Prasutagus rode along next to her, but not so close as to be menacing. She liked his thoughtfulness. She sheathed her dagger, she hoped unobtrusively, but when she saw him smile again, she knew he had noticed. Boadicea grinned, but neither spoke of the truce.

"My father has spoken of a Prasutagus who rules. It seems that you and he banded together against the northern tribes who tried to take our lands."

Prasutagus shrugged. "That is somewhat true. It was your father who came to my aid, for the lands that were invaded were mine."

"Ah, yes."

"I suspect you were testing me. I would expect your knowledge of history to be perfect as is necessary for one who is to be a priestess and a leader of her tribe."

Boadicea laughed. "Am I that transparent that I cannot deceive even a new acquaintance?"

"You are very clever. I was impressed by your caution. However, I am curious as to why you are this far from home."

"Just an urge to see our outlying lands and the country beyond. It was a beautiful day for riding." Boadicea looked across the field to the hills. "I have a dreadful curiosity that cannot be quenched. Each hill is a mystery, but once conquered is forgotten in the quest for the next hill." Boadicea stopped next to a path that led through the forest.

Prasutagus stopped his horse as well. "If you are on your way home, I would like to be your escort. I know you need no protection, but I need the company."

Boadicea was startled to hear what sounded like a confession from a man so strong. "Certainly. I would appreciate the company. I have spent a lot of time alone, too." Boadicea nudged Thayne into the woods. The path was too narrow for the two of them to ride side by side, so Prasutagus dropped back. Boadicea loosened the reins, and knowing that Thayne would find his way up the path, sat at an angle on his broad back so she could talk to Prasutagus. "How did you acquire such a large horse?"

"A man in my tribe breeds them. They are strong, fearless in battle, and strike terror in any enemy that we encounter. He crossed the wild ones he found roaming the hills with some Roman horses we captured when we had a skirmish with the Brigantes." Prasutagus patted his horse's neck. "This one is known as Rand. He is a warrior and deserves a warrior's name. What is your horse's name?"

"I named him Thayne. He, too, could be a warrior if I needed him to be." Boadicea patted him. "He has the heart of a soldier."

"Like his owner, no doubt," Prasutagus said.

Boadicea smiled at the compliment. The two rode in silence through the rest of the woods listening as the birds and squirrels announced their presence and appraised their progress. When they came out of the forest near Boadicea's land, she waited for Prasutagus.

"I'm sure you remember that my clan lives two hills over." Boadicea looked at the sun. "There is plenty of daylight left. Would you care to visit my family? My parents would be honored."

"I would also be honored."

Boadicea's heart skipped a beat as Prasutagus smiled at her, and she wondered what Rhys would think of her. She wished that she hadn't invited this near stranger to her home. After today, she vowed she would never see him again.

"Let's race to the top of the next hill," Prasutagus said.

"No!" Boadicea was surprised at the vehement tone of her voice. Her cheeks flamed, and she looked down. "I don't believe in using a horse for sport. It's a good way to ruin an . . . an animal."

Prasutagus looked at her carefully as if judging her words with her reaction. "You are wise. It would be foolish to put good steeds like ours in danger for a few thrills." After a pause, he said, "To be honest, I gave in so easily because I fear that I would lose to you. Thayne has the legs of a runner."

Boadicea looked up at him, her cheeks still flushed. "I don't believe that you would lose. At least not easily."

She studied him again. He asked no penetrating questions, although she could tell that he was astute in his observations. Probably he was curious, but patient. She hesitated. Should she tell him why she had a fear of racing? No. She would not see him again. He was a diversion, nothing more, nothing less.

She tossed her hair away from her face. "Come, I'd like you to see my parents again. We need only to cross those two hills."

Boadicea looked at her mother and shook her head. Her mother smiled as she brought out oat cakes and tea.

Her father clapped Prasutagus on the back. "Old friend, it's been too long."

"Old? Not so, Garik. I am a child compared to you."

"Indeed? Still need a nursemaid to guide you?" Garik laughed. "I swear you haven't eaten since the last time you were here. Sit at my table and have something to fill that flat belly of yours."

"Gladly, for there is no better kitchen than right here." Prasutagus straddled a stool. He leaned his arms on the table and grinned. "Remember the last time we fought the Brigantes?"

"How could I forget? They outnumbered us, and the fighting was brutal. We lost many a good lad that day. We would've lost that battle had you and your people not come to help."

"We just helped finish the fight sooner. You were outnumbered, but the battle was yours to win. You were magnificent." Prasutagus took an oat cake from Durina and smiled his thanks.

"I was not so magnificent after being dumped by my horse. You saved my life." Garik laughed.

"You didn't need me to save your life. If memory serves me correctly, you leaped up and pounded a Brigantes into the next world."

"I have never understood why they keep trying to take our lands," Garik said.

"Your soil is far less rocky than their land. They'll always try to take your land and mine because their stony soil matches their hearts and their heads," Prasutagus said.

Another burst of laughter from her father caused Boadicea to look at her mother. She leaned closer to Durina, elbows on the wooden table and asked, "Does he always laugh like this with Prasutagus?"

"I had forgotten how well they got along in spite of the years of difference in their ages. We have not seen Prasutagus for a long time." Durina pushed a plate of cakes toward the men. "Here, you must have some more."

Prasutagus reached a hand toward the plate and grasped two cakes easily. "I must go. The sun will set in a few hours."

Garik reached for a cake. He took a bite and chewed. "You could stay the night."

"Another time when it has been planned. If I don't return before dark, my tribe will worry. It would not be fair to have them out searching for me instead of spending time with their families." Prasutagus pushed his stool away from the table, stood, and stretched his massive arms toward the low ceiling. "I find that leaving such entertaining company will make my ride home that much lonelier. It is better that I start right away."

Garik stood as well. He brushed crumbs from his chest. "Then I shall walk you to the corral. We will not wait for a chance meeting the next time. In fact, would you like to bring some of your people here for our celebration of the oak?"

"We would be honored." Prasutagus bowed to Durina and Boadicea. "I would hope that Boadicea would be in the ceremony as well."

Boadicea was stunned. Not at the suggestion, that was ordinary enough, but at the idea that this man found her interesting enough to want to see her again. She had enjoyed the afternoon, but more as an onlooker than a participant. He had not been forgetful of her presence, but Prasutagus had not pressured her into conversation. She wondered, for the first time, if he somehow knew about Rhys. Had word of her grieving been carried by the storytellers to other tribes?

Durina nudged her daughter. "Your manners!" she whispered.

Boadicea felt her cheeks flush. She took a deep breath and hoped she wouldn't stumble over her words. "It would be my pleasure to have you and your clan join us in our ceremony to the oak."

Prasutagus' eyes sparkled. "We will be here. Until then, farewell." He turned and strode away, Garik next to him.

Boadicea watched her father's arms wave about as he explained, she guessed, how far their lands went and how many people composed their tribe. "Mother, I have to talk to you."

Durina put her arm around Boadicea's shoulder and squeezed. "Let's go for a walk."

"Yes." Boadicea leaned into her mother as they walked. She was surprised to see that they were the same height. When did that happen? She glanced at her mother again. Were there a few hairs of silver amongst the black? It appeared so, but her face was still youthful. There were none of time's tracks across her mother's face. She was relieved, for she wasn't ready for another death.

Boadicea picked at her bright blue and red striped tunic. She let her eye follow streaks of yellow that crisscrossed the other colors. Finally, she could no longer put off the conversation. "I need to know something."

Durina looked at her daughter. "I'm here for you."

"I find Prasutagus rather interesting. Does that mean that I am being unfair to Rhys? Am I going to forget him?"

"Do you doubt yourself that much? Are you afraid that you're so fickle that you'll throw Rhys aside like an old toy no longer needed?"

"I don't know." Boadicea kicked a pebble out of the road. "I had my life planned. It was neatly bundled and tied like your medicine packets, and I was content. Then the strings came untied, and I was left with nothing."

"You have more than you realize. I agree that a big part of your life is empty because of Rhys' death, but that doesn't mean you have to stop living. Would Rhys want you to give up life's gifts? I don't think so." Durina stopped walking and faced Boadicea. "You have mourned enough. It is time to put away your mantle of gloominess before it becomes a part of you and haunts you permanently."

Boadicea pursed her lips. "You mean like Linelle?"

"Why do you say that?"

"She talks incessantly about her husband who died before I was born. Only when she speaks of him do her eyes have life. It seems that she is a shell."

"Very well put."

"I don't want to be like that."

Durina took both Boadicea's hands in her own. "You don't have to forget Rhys, just place him in a corner of your heart where he can reside without interfering with your life."

Boadicea felt hot tears slide down her cheek. "I don't want to lose him."

"He'll be safe in your heart. You won't lose him."

"Mother, how do you know?"

"Have you heard me talk of your grandfather?"

"Of course, many times."

"Have I forgotten him, though he died a long time ago?"

Boadicea wiped the tears from her face. "No."

"Trust yourself to remember Rhys as a special part of your life, not as the end of your life. It is time to put away the past and think of the future, for within your future lies your father's and mine."

Boadicea started walking again. "If I become like Linelle would I lose the tribe?"

"It wouldn't be fair to them to have a leader who could not lead to the best of her ability," Durina said. "Do you know why everyone wants children?"

"I never thought about it much. I would guess that without children, there would be no increase in the tribe."

"There would be no one to carry the family name into the future. Children have children and the future is assured. Your father and I never wanted to influence you to think of marriage after Rhys' death, but . . ."

"Please don't now. I have had enough trouble today accepting the fact that I enjoyed someone else's company."

"Did you really accept it?"

"Mother, I'm trying to. I want to stop mourning. I love Rhys, but I have to go on. Just let me do it little by little. I would like to start by having Prasutagus as a friend if he will agree to that and nothing more."

Durina took her daughter's hand in hers, and they walked along in silence. Finally, she said, "That's all we can ask of you—to put your life back together piece by piece."

Boadicea slid off Thayne and laughed at Prasutagus as he dropped to the ground, his plaid tunic a reflection of the summer colors. Boadicea dropped the reins and let Thayne wander. She flung herself to the ground near Prasutagus and stretched out full length in the meadow, throwing her arms above her head. Her eyes were closed, but the sun still fought its way through her eyelids. She loved the warmth of the sun on her face. She reached for Prasutagus. He lay close by.

Boadicea sat up and looked at him. "You look like a fallen warrior."

"Do not say such things. The gods may hear."

"I can protect you from angry gods." Boadicea flopped back down. "I can protect you from anyone."

"You have faith in yourself." Prasutagus sat up and leaned back on both elbows.

Boadicea barely opened her eyes, using her dark eyelashes to keep out the sun. "My father has trained me for battle."

Prasutagus rolled over on his side and held his head in one hand. "How long have we been friends? I mean true friends?"

"For me, since the first day we met." Boadicea looked at Prasutagus with his serious eyes. She thought back to all the days they had ridden together, had mock jousting tournaments, had tried to swim in the cold stream that ran through the forest, and had shared ceremonies with each of their tribes.

She wondered how they had become such close friends so suddenly. It was the same kind of feeling she'd had for Rhys except for the arguments. She and Prasutagus never argued. They had so many similar ideas that it was uncanny.

This had been done as friend to friend with no formal statement made by Boadicea. It was as if Prasutagus understood her needs. He was a remarkable man. He was so serious.

"May I ask you a question?"

"You may ask me anything you wish. We are friends."

Prasutagus hesitated, then plunged forward. "I have noticed that there is a sadness about you that underlies all that you do. I would like to know why, but . . ." He held up his hand. "I don't want you to tell me at the expense of our friendship."

Boadicea lay back, her head cradled in her intertwined fingers. "I think we are good enough friends." She looked at the clouds, fluffy and white, that changed shape as they floated along. "More than a year ago, when I was fifteen, I had a good friend who was injured in an accident and later died. I felt that it was my fault." A cloud changed from a hare to a wolf. "We had been together since childhood. We would have been married at the beginning of this summer. We were suited. He was born under the sign of the Rowan Tree. I miss him every day."

"I cannot pretend to understand how deep that grief must be," Prasutagus said. "It must be like the loss of a parent or a brother or sister."

Boadicea sat up and hugged her knees. She traced the broad saffron stripe that ran down the front of her tunic, letting her fingers hop over the blue stripe that crisscrossed the saffron at irregular intervals. "Did you not know about Rhys?"

"I had heard the story through the gossip woman and then again from your father. He wanted me to understand that you were still mourning."

"Didn't you think I was somewhat weak for grieving that length of time?"

Prasutagus sat up and took Boadicea's hands in his own. "I found you loyal; a trait more valuable than gold." He leaned over and kissed her cheek. "If ever you find me worthy, I would like you to be my queen."

Boadicea's heart thumped in spite of her attempt to remain detached. She looked into Prasutagus' eyes and found a near perfect person looking back at her. She did admire him, but there was not the same overwhelming feeling of love that she had had for Rhys.

"I know I am more than ten years older than you, but I feel a kinship I have never felt with another woman." Prasutagus looked down at his hands that still held hers. He cleared his throat. "I know I am not particularly handsome, but I want you to share my power and help rule the tribe. No other woman has been trained as you have for destiny, and I am selfish. I want to share your fate."

Boadicea looked down at the hands that held her own. She felt their warmth and protection, and she was content. "I would like to answer you, Prasutagus, but I cannot. With a little time, I can give you an answer."

"I have time." Prasutagus leaned over to kiss Boadicea, but was startled when she pulled back.

"Look at yonder hill! There is a cloud of dust on the horizon."

"Does your father expect anyone to arrive for a special occasion?"

"No, do you?"

"No."

"Prasutagus! Trouble comes for us." She looked around for the horses that had been allowed to roam free. Thayne was nowhere in sight, but Rand was a few feet away.

Prasutagus leaped to his feet and ran for his horse. He grabbed the reins and vaulted onto Rand. He came for Boadicea, holding his arm down. She seized it, and he swung her up, tunic flying. Boadicea grabbed hold of his waist.

As soon as she could catch her breath, she whistled for Thayne. Looking around frantically, she could still not see the horse. "Stop, please. I can't find Thayne."

Prasutagus pulled Rand up short, causing Boadicea to bang her head against his back. She whistled for Thayne in different directions. They had covered a lot of ground in a short time, and she was worried.

"We can't wait any longer. Those people may have seen us, but I think they are on foot."

"Who are they, for the gods' sake?" Boadicea continued to whistle.

"An old enemy from the north, the Brigantes, usually led by King Venutius. They swoop down on us for no reason with their painted blue bodies and spiked hair. I have to get back to my people and warn them. If my tribe does not stop them, then yours will be in danger." Prasutagus kicked Rand in the ribs, and they flew across the meadow.

Boadicea knew that the right decision had been made, and she hoped that the enemy wouldn't find her beloved horse. She could only hang on and wait until they arrived at Prasutagus' village.

They covered two miles quickly at a full gallop, and Boadicea could see huts scattered across the flat area ahead. Farther up a hill more huts were perched around a huge dwelling. Rand's hooves sounded like thunder before a storm.

They rode to the first hut, Prasutagus shouting all the while. People came running from other dwellings. Farther away, people in the fields became aware of danger and stopped their work.

A loud banging nearly deafened Boadicea as the gong sounded a cadence of warning. Boadicea's breast bone vibrated, but she paid little attention as she dropped off the horse. Picking up the skirts of her tunic, she raced after Prasutagus as he shouted orders to arm.

"I can help," Boadicea said.

"Good. All the women are armed. Follow me—I have extra weapons." Prasutagus led the way, pulling his horse along with him.

Prasutagus' dwelling was more than Boadicea expected. It was a series of five round huts placed in the shape of a pentagon. In order to get to it, they had to clamber over three small bridges and up a steep incline.

The tribe ran with them, wielding spears, clubs, and daggers. It was apparent to Boadicea that they would take their stand here. She looked around and was relieved to see the men and women running from the fields. They were behind the main hut and therefore separated from the army coming toward them. These people never went to the fields unarmed, however, and she could see spears.

It seemed that everything moved in an odd time, as if the gods were mocking man and his pitiful attempts. The people from the fields seemed to be coming at a slower pace than the army from the north. How could the army could be here already? She stared at the horizon, and not for the first time she heard the barbaric yell of the grizzled, half-naked men from the north. She shivered and wished she had her slingshot.

The last man from the field crossed the first bridge and two guards quickly turned the wheel that wound the twisted rope and brought the bridge to a standing position, sentinel-like. The other two bridges were likewise pulled up. Boadicea seized the sword that was handed her and swung it around her head testing its balance and weight. Its handle was carved silver. The swirling design pleased her, and she was happy to think that Prasutagus thought highly enough of her to give her a family sword.

Boadicea looked at the fierce faces on men and women alike. They had spread out and surrounded the huts above the last ditch, that unlike the first two, was dry. She walked to the edge and looked into it. The bottom was filled with sharp boulders. Prasutagus had planned well. She knew it would stop the Brigantes only temporarily, but the advantage of time helped.

She tossed her hair back, startled at its effect on those around her. She was aware that she was taller than most women, even though as a race, her tribe and that of Prasutagus' were taller than average Celt.

Boadicea brushed her thick, auburn hair away from her face again, but it had its own mind. It would never do in battle for her eyesight to be compromised. She grasped her dagger, bent down, and cut a strip of multi-colored material from her tunic. She had tied her hair back before she noticed several women watching her with looks of surprise on their faces, and she shrugged.

"My hair is always in the way."

"Seems like a good idea to me." One of the women bent over, cut a strip of cloth from her tunic and tied back her hair. "I think you've started a new style." She reached her hand out and touched Boadicea on the sleeve. "May the gods favor you. I am Rhianna, sister to Prasutagus. I believe you must be the secret he has kept from us."

"Secret?"

"He would not tell us why he was acting like a young colt, but our seer said that it had to be you. I'm sorry we don't have more time to talk." Rhianna lifted her sword. "I believe we have some heads to sever today. See, the disgusting Brigantes come."

Boadicea, overwhelmed by all the information thrown at her, elected not to worry about any of it at the moment. If the day did not go well, then this first real battle of hers could be her last, and she would join Rhys in the land beyond. She felt frozen in time as the peculiar thought occurred to her that the gods had set this battle up to seal her fate. If she died, she was meant to be with Rhys in the other world beneath the salt sea. The gods would decree who would be her mate. Today. And the Brigantes were to be the deliverer of her destiny.

If she lived, and if Prasutagus lived, of course, then she was meant to be with him in this land and time.

And what if Prasutagus died and she lived? What were the gods saying then? She would think about that at another time.

A peculiar rasping sound brought her back to the present danger. She turned, trying to locate the sound that seemed all around her, only to find that she was viewing the backsides of the women who were bent over, cutting strips of cloth from their tunics with which to tie their hair. She hoped these women had the same determination in battle. A gray-haired woman peered at Boadicea, her head still down at her knees. Boadicea laughed aloud.

The roar from down the hill told her that the Brigantes were close. She pushed through the women in front of her and stood at the edge of the man-made ravine. The enemy splashed through water in the first ravine. A hail of arrows rained down on them from a group of men who had stayed at the second level in spite of the fact they were cut off from the rest of the tribe. Boadicea shivered.

She remembered Prasutagus and turned, looking for him. He wasn't difficult to find, for his voice boomed orders to his followers.

Rhianna grabbed her on the shoulder and turned her back toward the battle scene. "You must watch the battle, but listen to my brother. The Brigantes are very fast and very strong, but we have beaten them back each time. In the past our losses have been heavy."

Boadicea nodded, saving her strength for the task ahead. Her calmness surprised her. She had imagined that in a battle situation her nerves would be screaming, but it was not so. In the battle when she'd used her slingshot, she had also been calm.

She looked below her at the enemy who rushed to the second level in one large mass. A hail of arrows found their mark and some of the Brigantes fell in death, but most rose and continued up the hill toward the spearmen. At that moment, Prasutagus ordered the spears thrown. Some found their mark, but the enemy kept coming.

Boadicea's hand tightened about her sword handle, and she tested its balance once more. Hatred for the Brigantes washed over her—hatred for the stupid destruction they had brought on a peaceful tribe. They had no right to come and take what they had not built, not toiled over, had not fertilized, and had not reaped. She vowed that she would rather die fighting these marauders than to allow them to take anything that belonged to Prasutagus' people. No matter that it was not her tribe. If it were to be her life's work to fight beside Prasutagus, she would know after today. The sound of Prasutagus' voice was near, and she listened intently.

"Spread out and wait until they are close enough to kill before you swing your sword. Keep a good eye and spare no one. May the gods be with you."

Boadicea barely had time to move away to give herself room when three of the enemy flung themselves across the boulders and attacked the bridge ropes, hacking them in two and dropping the bridge with a thud that sent a cloud of dust toward the sky. The rest of the Brigantes rushed across the bridge, and Boadicea was shocked to hear from her throat a guttural sound like a wolf on the prowl. She held the sword above her head with both hands and waited for her first victim. Something inside of her coiled, then sprang forward, and before Boadicea knew what was happening, she charged ahead toward the first of the Brigantes. She never saw his face until she had the sword above his head. She brought the bronze blade crashing down on the top of his skull. It was only then that she saw his ruddy face and the look of hatred in his brown eyes. In the same instant, she watched his eyes spread apart as his skull split with a crack. She jerked the sword out and turned to find another victim. She felt exhilarated, and she wanted the battle to go on forever. Never had she felt so alive. Behind her she heard a shout, and she whirled around bringing the sword about waist-high. Her victim this time had turned away from Rhianna, who had fallen to the ground, but it was too late. His life was cut short by a wild, auburn-haired woman who smiled.

Rhianna clenched her sword and scrambled to her feet. "Thank you," she shouted. "I was stupid and did not watch my back."

Boadicea nodded an acknowledgment, saving her breath and strength for fighting. She picked her next victim because he was huge. His arms looked like the trunks of an oak tree and in the sunlight, the black hair shone. His eyebrows were so heavy that they appeared as one across his forehead. He showed his teeth in the grin of one who expects an easy victim and swung his sword.

Boadicea moved quickly, but not fast enough. His long arms reached out, and he held a broad sword with two huge paws. His broad sword nicked the upper part of her left arm. Instead of slowing her down, her anger raged and made her stronger. The swing of her own broad sword sliced through the Brigantes' right arm. She was as stunned as he was at the crack of bone and sloughing of flesh, and she stepped back. The sounds of battle faded as she focused on his arm. It hesitated as if waiting to see whether or not it was really detached, then fell to the ground, the fist curled as if in anger.

Boadicea could see the killer instinct in his eyes, and she knew he would not let her live. With his good arm, he raised his sword above his head and brought it down, but he miscalculated, and Boadicea easily side-stepped the intended blow. She brought her own sword around and struck him in the armless right side with a backhanded swing, slicing him deeply. He toppled forward, and she danced out of his way as blood splattered onto her tunic, mixing itself with the many colors that were already there. A metallic smell assaulted her, and she turned away.

Quickly Boadicea surveyed the battle scene. In spite of her own personal victory, Prasutagus' tribe was outnumbered and from the bodies on the ground, it was not going well. She glanced at the sun. They had been fighting longer than she realized. She wiped the sweat from her eyes and in doing so, saw a group of men on horses racing toward the battle area. "By the gods, we do not need more Brigantes!"

Rhianna screamed at her and brought her back to the immediate problem. Boadicea whirled around in time to see Rhianna stab an assailant with a dagger between his ribs and directly into his heart. She withdrew the blade swiftly. "Now, we're even," she shouted. "We'll celebrate and brag about this later."

Boadicea had to laugh. Rhianna was rather delicate compared to her own large stature. Boadicea turned and charged toward her next victim. If she were going to die, then she would take as many of the Brigantes with her as possible.

She turned at a clash of swords behind her. Prasutagus dispatched another soul to the land beyond and was working his way toward her, slashing right and left. He had a smile on his face.

He shouted, "Look! Your father comes with help! How did he know? I didn't have time to send a messenger for him." Prasutagus ran up and down the line of battle, cutting down any enemy that happened in his way. "Keep fighting! Keep fighting! Garik comes with help."

Boadicea felt renewed vigor. She rushed forward into a knot of Brigantes who attacked a group of young people. Boadicea hacked away at the outside of the circle and freed the youngsters who fought viciously. She felt warm blood flow freely down her arm, but she ignored the stinging.

She paused to watch her tribe's progress up the hill behind her father. His powerful arms shone with sweat, and he held a mace in his hand. Again and again he brought the spiked ball down on the heads of the hapless enemy, clearing a path for his men. The bridges dropped into place by the Brigantes proved to be their downfall, for Garik and his army were able to cross them and ride up the hill in a short time.

Pride filled Boadicea's heart to see her father and her neighbors dispatch the Brigantes one by one. Caught between the two armies, the enemy had no chance to survive the bloody vise.

It was over in less than an hour. When the last victim had been sent to the other world, there was a moment of silence and then a mighty roar went up as victorious fighters celebrated. Garik pounded Prasutagus on the back and exchanged hugs with the men from both tribes.

"Where's my warrior daughter?" Garik shouted.

Boadicea rushed to her father. "Here, father. I stand before you unharmed and rejoicing!"

Garik grabbed Boadicea's arm and frowned. "Unharmed! You are injured, Daughter."

"I don't care. I have never felt better. I love fighting." She threw herself at her father and flung her arms around his neck. He picked her up and whirled around, then set her down on the earth again. She looked into her father's eyes. "Where's Mother? She wouldn't let you go off to war alone." Boadicea cocked her head to one side and stepped away from Garik. "How did you know we were in trouble?"

"Thayne came home without you again. He was injured and blood was everywhere. . . ."

Boadicea felt her heart twist. "Is he badly hurt? Is he all right?"

"His injury is light, but we were afraid that something terrible had happened to you, and we came as quickly as we could. When we got near, we could hear the battle. Your mother and some of the other women are in the forest gathering mold from the stumps of the sacred oak trees to tend to the wounds. She will be here soon with medicines."

Garik took hold of Boadicea's arm. "This wound is not the worst I've seen, but it could fester easily. It gaps and must be stitched closed."

"Oh, Father. I am a warrior. I don't need anything. Mother and I will tend to the ones who are really injured."

Garik shook his head. "Your mother will never let this alone." Garik turned at the sound of cheers. "There comes your mother riding

Ella. She rides Rhys' horse as if she were born to ride. Ah, what a beautiful woman."

Boadicea held onto her father's arm and leaned against him, so proud of both her parents. "Father, she has brought every woman in the village who could ride."

"That she has. Boadicea, we must set up a hospital. Find a good hut. I'll help your mother because I am sure she has many bags of medicine with her."

"You carry the wounded to us. The women can carry the bags." Boadicea turned to go, but caught her mother's eye and hesitated just a moment to raise her uninjured arm in greeting. She saw the relief on her mother's face, and she had to smile. Boadicea walked across the torn and bloodied earth littered with bodies of enemy and friend, men and women. Her elation began to temper.

"May your souls have the strength of the oak tree and find their way to the other world without difficulty." She felt hot tears slide down her sweaty face. The exhilaration she had felt at the battle's end drained away when she saw the people of both her tribe and Prasutagus' tribe who would not rise again. There would be the pain of living without family and friends for Prasutagus' people.

A closer look at the bodies showed that there were a few families from her tribe that would grieve for the souls of the dead and the souls of the unborn.

Boadicea entered the huts that were placed together, sharing walls. The first was the kitchen. It would be good to be close to the coals and hot water, but it was too small for the number of wounded. She stepped into the next hut and its large size surprised her. There were woven rugs scattered on the floor. Cauldrons stood guard at the edge of a large firepit that took up an entire wall. Along the other walls long benches could be used for the injured and above them were torch holders.

She crossed the room and stood at the door. Boadicea looked up at a shout from her mother who waved at her from across the yard. She started to motion for her to come, then winced when she raised her injured arm. It was beginning to burn and itch. She dropped it to her side and motioned with her good arm, then waited while Durina rode to her.

"Boadicea, take these medicines." Durina turned to the youngsters who followed her. "Run and tell Prasutagus that we will use this hut for the wounded. Show him where to bring the injured." When the children didn't move, she stared at them. "Scat! Or I'll turn you into frogs."

Boadicea giggled as the urchins scampered off. "Mother! What a terrible thing to say."

"Speed is what I need. It worked, didn't it?"

She slid off Ella. "Help get these medicines set up. Is there boiling water? Good heavens! Did you get in the way of someone?" She grabbed Boadicea's arm. "Let me see that. I'll have to stitch that up or you'll have a horrible scar."

"Mother, I don't want . . ."

"No one asked you. I'm telling you. In fact, you can be my first patient and set a good example for the rest of them." Durina handed as many bags to Boadicea as she could carry with one arm, then looked at the people watching her. "Come here, please, and help me. You are Rhianna. We met at the spring oak festival."

Rhianna pushed her thick, chestnut-colored hair away from her face and wiped the perspiration from her neck with a corner of her tunic. "I'm pleased that you remember me."

"You seem strong and uninjured. I'll need you to help."

"Yes, madam."

Durina dumped the vivid red, blue, and saffron colored bags into her arms. "Do you think you could get some water boiling? Could you find the other women from my clan and bring them here?"

Durina and Boadicea entered the hut. Durina walked across the room and placed the bags on the hearth stone. "Boadicea, come here and sit down so that I can stitch that wound."

Boadicea looked at Rhianna and smiled. "Go get the other women."

Rhianna's eyes widened. "Does she sew you like a piece of cloth?"

"I'm afraid so. I've had to help hold down strong men who screamed when she sewed them." Boadicea's voice wavered, and she coughed to cover her nervousness.

Rhianna backed away from Boadicea and ran from the hut, not looking back.

Boadicea was startled to see the walls start to swirl, and she turned to Durina, who arranged bags of medicine in order. "Mother, may I sit down? I feel the world spin."

Durina looked up in time to catch Boadicea and ease her down on one of the rugs that covered the hard-packed earthen floor. "You have lost a lot of blood. Stay still until I have the water boiling."

Boadicea closed her eyes. She could hear women come in, ask questions, and be directed to the kitchen or ordered to stay and help. Soon she heard the moaning, gurgling, and cursing of the injured as they were carried or shuffled in, but these sounds faded as she fainted.

When hot water was applied to the cut in Boadicea's arm, she jerked to the surface of consciousness. She sucked in her breath, but she refused to scream. She turned her head away so that she wouldn't smell her own blood as it was washed away. Someone took her good hand and held it. The hand was strong and rough, and she opened her eyes.

"Prasutagus, what are you doing here?"

"This is my home." He cleared his throat. "I wanted to be here with you. I am worried about your arm. Too many good soldiers die after a battle with the putrid green sickness."

"Mother has learned to keep the festering away." Her curiosity was such that she opened her eyes and looked at her newly cleansed wound. A jagged opening revealed sliced muscle tissue. She watched her mother take out a bone needle and thread it with goat gut. She refused to turn away.

Boadicea felt her breath leave her as the first prick of the needle brought her from her faint state into the world of pain. She drew in her breath and held it, thinking of the men and women she had cut down today. She concentrated on the battle, the noises, the dust, the smell of blood, and how the intestines of the Brigantes looked dragged from their bodies and smeared across the dirt. It was not much help, and now she understood why grown men screamed and cried when her mother sewed them up.

A scream burst out and she jammed her fist in her mouth to stop it, and bit her knuckles until they bled. Mercifully, the piercing pain was replaced by a fiery sting. Her mother sprinkled the wound with the mold from rotted tree trunks. She swallowed hard. She would be bound with clean cloth, and then it would be over.

Prasutagus brushed Boadicea's hair from her face. "You are a great warrior. I wouldn't be able to take the pain you have."

"It will make me a better healer, for I will be more sympathetic to the injuries of others," Boadicea whispered. "Besides, the pain is nothing to the thought of incurring the wrath of Durina had I gone against her wishes."

"Ah, Boadicea still has her barbed wit," Durina said. "She will be all right. Her caustic words will heal her from the inside out." Durina wrapped a bright yellow cloth around Boadicea's wound and tied it. "There. I have many more to care for. If you feel better soon, I could use your help."

Durina looked at Prasutagus. "She is quite good at medicine, you know." Durina kissed her daughter's cheek and rose, looking around the room where the women scurried about helping the injured. "We'll be here all night."

Boadicea sat on the grass outside of Prasutagus's hut, propped against the wall close to the door. All casualties had been treated. Night turned to day. The sun rose above the hills, and fog followed a river, cutting a gray path through dark trees.

"Are you tired?" Prasutagus asked. He settled next to her on the grass.

"No, just weary from all the blood, the pain. I'm always this way after we repair the damage to our people. Thank the gods, it doesn't happen often."

"I fear the world won't be peaceful much longer. More and more I fear that our country will become a permanent battle ground." Prasutagus looked at the horizon.

Boadicea followed his gaze, but could not see the imaginary army that he did. "Why do you say that?"

"I don't know. It's a premonition."

"Have you talked with a seer?"

"I don't want to."

"But if you knew the future, could you not change it?"

"Would you fight harder if you knew the future?"

Boadicea traced a star pattern in the dust. "No. I will always fight as hard as I can for what is right."

"Sometimes we have to compromise in order to . . ."

"Compromise!" Boadicea stared at Prasutagus. "There can never be compromise. There can only be honor and if honor requires death, then so be it."

Prasutagus took Boadicea's good hand. "You were brave in yesterday's battle."

"No more than the other women and men. Even the children of your tribe contributed." Boadicea grinned. "I think a few of them bashed some enemy brains out."

"Yes, they did, but we have had to bury a few of our children." Prasutagus shook his head. "We won the battle, but at what price?"

"It is the same with any battle. The innocent will perish along with the enemy. The gods have a strange sense of justice." Boadicea squeezed Prasutagus' hand. "Do you know what I like about you?"

"No."

"I'm glad you don't pry into my past. I was relieved when you didn't ask about Rhys." Boadicea leaned against Prasutagus. She liked the feeling of strength and warmth she felt from his shoulder. "I was afraid that I was not being true to Rhys' memory, but I cannot live in the past. My mother told me that, and she is right. This little skirmish of ours proved to me that life is precious and must be taken as a gift. I must live in the present and for the future."

Boadicea pulled Prasutagus' hand up to her cheek and held it there. "I find that I want you in my future."

"Together we shall be strong and powerful." Prasutagus kissed her gently on the lips.

Boadicea let his lips linger on hers, then pulled away. "I am frightened of marriage."

The laughter that erupted from Prasutagus' throat was hearty. "The great warrior who is not afraid of death is afraid of marriage?"

Boadicea grinned. "It is true. I don't know why I am afraid. Maybe because I'm not certain how to be a wife, but I've been trained in battle."

"Some say it is the same."

"Oh, I hope not!"

"You would not do me injury by being my wife and queen." Prasutagus put his arm around Boadicea's shoulder. "You would do more harm by refusing me."

"Would I?"

"You would also harm your own tribe. Think of our marriage as a strengthening of our tribes. Together we can keep the northern Brigantes at bay. I can promise you excitement."

"In battle, dear Prasutagus?"

"In battle and elsewhere, dear Boadicea."

"May I talk with my father and mother first?"

"I could not stop you. You are headstrong and stubborn and do what you want. I know enough to see that and will not interfere. I will give you time, for I know that you need it."

Boadicea stared across the field of battle to the low hills that lay beyond. Rhys' image faded, and she could not bring his face to mind. She closed her eyes and willed him to appear to her. He did not. She turned her face away from Prasutagus so that he would not see the farewell tear to Rhys slide down her cheek.

"I will not tease you by taking advantage of time. I'll have an answer for you in seven days."

CHAPTER
VI

UETONIUS HELD A PINE BOUGH behind his back as he paced back and forth in the orchard. All the way from the north, Lucian had chided him about the gifts he'd brought back. Suetonius heard a twig snap and looked up. "Where have you been? I sent for you an hour ago."

Trista stopped as soon as he spoke and put her hands on her hips. "I am not your slave, but your mother's. She told me I didn't have to do anything you told me to do."

"Really? When was that?"

"This morning when you bellowed for me to come and wash your back. I had told your mother I didn't want to be around such a bear. She had said I didn't have to. Not ever."

Suetonius frowned. This was not going as he had thought it would. "It sounds as if my mother has forgotten who is the slave."

"I am too valuable to anger; your mother says so."

"Valuable?" Suetonius pursed his lips. "Why is that? Can you read and do figures? Have you become an exceptional cook? It certainly cannot be your loving temperament."

"I have learned to control that monster sister of yours who seems a lot like you. I have brought peace to the household."

"Zia? You've learned to control her? How did you do it? Did you beat her?"

"Never. Your father would not have allowed it, though there were times when I wanted to." Trista held her long, pale blonde hair away from her neck. "I was so angry when she put a dead mouse in Elysia's bed that I wouldn't speak to her. She hates to be ignored. When she isn't good, Elysia and I won't talk to her. Elysia loves controlling her as much as I do. All she has to say to Zia is, 'I won't speak to you if you do that' and there is peace. Your father is especially appreciative. He says that he always thought the battle-field was in his home."

Trista dropped her hair and looked at Suetonius. "You didn't call me to the orchard to ask about your sisters. Why did you want me here?"

"I have been gone for three years, and you wouldn't do much more than say good morning to me in the house. I thought you would talk to me out here. Why do you avoid me? Have I grown ugly?"

Trista giggled. "You're not any worse than when you left."

Suetonius laid his hand on his chest. "Trista, you wound me mortally with your barbed words."

"Don't be stupid, Suetonius. You care not for me, but only for your own physical needs. You can continue to see your . . . your Phoebe. She is still at the same place and awaits the soldiers. I'm sure that I was not in your thoughts at all until the day you re-turned."

"You speak words like spears. I have thought of you many times. I only want to give you this." Suetonius swept the pine bough from behind his back and held it out to Trista. "I have carried this and more from the regions up north near your homeland. You see, I have thought about you. I have thought about you every day."

Trista looked at the pine bough, then into Suetonius' eyes. "Oh!" She reached for the branch, and when Suetonius let go, she held it to her face, breathing in the forgotten odors of home.

"Are you crying, Trista? I have never seen anyone turn on the tears so quickly and so often. Can I not make you happy? Mother named you well, for you are melancholy. I am afraid to give you the rest of the gifts I have for you."

Trista looked through the dark green needles of the bough. "You have other things for me?"

Suetonius motioned toward the leather pouch at the base of a peach tree. "There. More things to make you cry, I'm sure." He snatched up the pouch. "Here, at the risk of creating a flood of tears, I'll give you these, too." He held the pouch out to her.

Trista skipped over to Suetonius and sat down on the grass, laying the pine bough next to her. "What have you brought me?"

Suetonius sat down with her and placed the pouch in her lap. "You may open this if you promise not to cry."

"I cannot promise anything of the sort. You are as cruel as Zia." Trista's lower lip protruded.

"Forget I tried to force you to do the impossible. Go ahead and open it."

Trista untied the leather thong. The leather piece flattened and revealed a dark brown pine cone and an iridescent, white pebble that was smooth and oval.

"These are from my homeland, also." Trista picked up the rock. "This must have been in the river for years and years to have been worn as smooth as this." She turned the pebble over and over in her hand. "It's beautiful."

"That pebble reminded me of your hair."

"My hair?"

"It is nearly the same color." Suetonius felt his face get hot. "It's just a rock. It's not worth much."

"Suetonius, it's not just a rock. It's a piece of home. I will never forget that you cared enough about me to think of me and bring me a part of my homeland." Trista leaned over and kissed Suetonius on the cheek.

"If I'd given you the rock last night, would you have washed my back this morning?"

"Suetonius! Are you trying to bribe me?"

Suetonius laughed. "I will do anything that works."

"I don't want you as a lover. It would make my life miserable. If I loved you, then I would be happy only when you were here and that would be seldom. You are a soldier. I'd cry when you were gone and worry that you wouldn't come back. Then I'd cry when you were here and worry about when you were leaving. I don't want to love someone that way."

Suetonius leaned toward her. Her hair and skin smelled of roses, and he knew he wanted her more than he had ever wanted anyone. "Is there a chance that I could make you love me?"

Trista pushed him away. "No."

Suetonius sighed. "You are difficult and obstinate for a slave."

"Tell me about my home. Did you like the snow? It's so beautiful, isn't it? It shines in the moonlight as if the stars have fallen to the earth. Wasn't it wonderful?"

"It was not wonderful. It was painful. I had to wrap my feet in wool cloth and then jam them into my sandals. When marching in the snow, one's toes became cold, and when warming them by the camp fire, they hurt like a thousand pins. I found all that white ice blinding during the day and colorless at night. I hated walking in it, for it was like being a baby again. I fell many times before I learned how to walk."

Trista laughed until the tears rolled down her cheeks. "I wish I could have seen you fall. Where was your wonderful horse?"

"I couldn't ride him. He slipped so many times that I was afraid I would fall off and break a leg. See? You have tears of joy and a vicious heart to match. It was more difficult to conquer the snow than the people. I see no reason why anyone would want to live in that terrible place."

"But Suetonius, it has beautiful rivers of blue. The pine trees give off an aroma in the summer and winter that cannot be described. Here." Trista thrust the pine bough under Suetonius' nose. "Smell this and imagine a whole forest that smells this wonderful."

"We had to build a wooden fort for the winter. We used those trees. It took months to get the sap off us."

"You are a bear. I love my country and think it more beautiful than this hot place. The trees here are not as tall and majestic as my trees. You don't have a pine forest as dark and dense as ours."

"I have seen trees like these high up in the mountains."

"You don't know the power of a winter storm and the wonder of spring." Trista picked up the pine cone and traced each hard petal with her finger. "I cannot thank you enough for thinking of me. I'll treasure these gifts, for you brought a little of my past back with you and with it, memories of my family. That's worth more than gold or silver to me."

"Or freedom?"

"There is no freedom in my country. I would have no place to go, no one for me." Trista looked into Suetonius' eyes. "Your family has taken the place of the ones I loved. Your country has to take the place of the country I lost, and your home has to be my home."

Suetonius placed his arm around Trista's shoulder. She pulled away from him. "Can't I hold you as a friend?"

"I find it difficult to be a friend to someone who has conquered my people."

"They weren't your people," Suetonius growled.

"Not this time. How many women did you . . ."

"Did I what?"

Trista raised her chin and glared at Suetonius. "How many women did you rape?"

"None! I don't rape women." Suetonius leaped to his feet and paced back and forth. He shook his finger in Trista's face. "I may have a woman or two, but they are willing. It doesn't mean anything."

"You let a woman love you, and you don't love her in return?" Trista shoved his finger away.

"I mean nothing to them. I hurt no one."

"A conquered woman gives herself to you willingly, and you take willingly. It's fair? No. She fears for her life and gives the only thing left after the Romans have destroyed her village, her crops, her animals, her people. You call that fair? I call it surviving." Trista turned away.

"There was one young girl who reminded me of you." Suetonius touched Trista's hair.

"Did she pleasure you?"

"I did not want her that way. I saved her from a soldier who tried to rape her." Suetonius turned Trista's face toward him. "She had hair the color of yours and blue eyes, but she wasn't as pretty."

"You never touched her?"

"I helped her escape to the woods."

"You're not like the other soldiers."

"Because of you." Suetonius sat next to Trista and pulled her to him. "Can we still be friends?"

"I want to, but I feel disloyal to my family."

"If you live in the past, you'll never know happiness." Suetonius kissed her forehead. "I'll never do anything that you don't want me to."

"I know." Trista stared at the pine cone in her lap.

"I missed you."

"I missed you, too. I didn't want to, but I did." Trista took Suetonius' hand and kissed his fingers. "I love you, Suetonius."

Suetonius was surprised when she lay against his chest. He put his cheek against the top of her head. Her hair was soft. "I need you."

"Does it matter to you that I'm not . . . that those men . . ."

"Don't think about that. It happened years ago."

"I have demon dreams. Sometimes I scream in my sleep."

Suetonius kissed her temple, her eyelids, and her cheek. She did not resist him, but did not respond. "I am here to keep the demon dreams away." He pushed her back gently on the grass and kissed her soft mouth carefully. His heart thumped faster when she responded by pulling him closer and kissing him in return.

"Suetonius, I don't want any babies."

"There are ways to prevent babies." He was nervous and fumbled at the brooch on her stola. He had never had this kind of trouble with Phoebe. He leaned on his elbows and tried to unpin the damnable brooch with both hands.

Trista giggled. "It's a gift from your mother. There's a trick to it." She reached up, unpinned the brooch and laid it aside. Her stola slid from her shoulders and fell open.

Suetonius waited while she untied the girdle at her waist and let the stola fall completely away. He was taken aback at her pale skin that was almost translucent. He traced a pale blue vein across her breast. She shivered at his touch. He kissed her neck, her shoulders, both breasts. He felt her rise and push against him. He kissed her temple.

"Suetonius, I have never loved a man as much as I love you."

"I have loved you longer than you've loved me."

"I didn't want to love you, but I always have. Please make love to me."

Caius burst through the doorway to the kitchen. "Vivianne! Have you seen that errant son of ours? He was to meet me and go visiting this afternoon. We are late, and I don't want to be late. Where is that boy?"

Vivianne turned from a large kettle that sat at the edge of the kitchen firepit. She stopped stirring. Her husband was still a handsome man, and the unexpected sight of him caused her heart to race.

"He is too young to want to spend time with a bunch of old men. He has his own friends to entertain him. Why don't you go along and see him later."

"I told my colleagues that he would be with me. They want to hear about his three years up north." Caius stood behind his wife and put his arms around her. He leaned his chin on her shoulder and looked into the big kettle.

"Smells good. Where's Lena? Why isn't she cooking? What is it?"

Vivianne chuckled. "It's laundry."

"Laundry? Why are you doing laundry? We have slaves for that."

"There is a sickness amongst the slaves, and they are lying like dead flies on their cots. Only Trista and I have escaped the illness. I had to wash these horrible blankets because they smelled of the sickness. Besides, the physicians from Greece tell us that clean bedding helps to cut the sickness short. I have told the servants to stay in their quarters to rest."

"Rubbish. What do the Greeks know that our own doctors don't? You put too much faith in those foreigners." Caius kissed Vivianne on the neck. "With all the servants gone, perhaps I should stay home. We could take to our beds."

Vivianne stared at him. "What is wrong with you? Are you ill, too?"

Caius pulled her toward him. "You wound my intentions. I feel romantic."

"Perhaps I should play the slave and wash the sheets more often. Alas, I have learned the way to your heart too late to do anything about it now." Vivianne sighed loudly and turned back to the large kettle. A strand of hair slipped down across her forehead. The thought that Caius could still be excited by the sight of her made her smile. She had been lucky to have such a good marriage, and she silently thanked her long-dead mother for seeing the wisdom in this choice.

Vivianne remembered seeing Caius up close for the first time outside the market square when she and her mother shopped. She had seen him at a distance when they had gone to plays and to the games, but she had never hoped to meet him. He had been the talk of all her friends, for he was handsome and had a good income. Incredibly he had had the audacity to approach her mother and speak to her without an older gentlemen initiating the conversation first. Because of his effrontery, she had been speechless, but fortunately, her mother had not.

In fact, her mother had seemed to enjoy his boldness. Caius was the son of an acquaintance, she explained later, and for that reason she broke all taboos by actually introducing her to Caius.

It was his rashness that still appealed to her, and remembering this, Vivianne dropped the stirring rod and turned to Caius. "Perhaps it is not too late for me to take advantage of you." Vivianne kissed him.

"It would be a question of who is taking advantage of whom, Vivianne." Caius took her hand. "Let's leave quietly and spend a few hours hidden away in our apartments."

Vivianne giggled. Sneaking away reminded her of the days in the past when they had contrived to meet alone. She blushed at the memory that Suetonius had been one of the love children born before he was due. She looked at her husband. He still caused her heart to beat more quickly than normal. "Take me away, sir, and do what you will."

The light of dawn slid through the small window above Suetonius. In another moment, a ray of the sun struck him in the eye and he awoke. He heard a rustling next to him and turning over, he could see Trista smiling at him as she fastened her stola with the gold brooch he had given her.

He stretched and yawned. "Where are you going so early in the morning?"

Trista stopped, her hand still on the brooch. "I must not be seen in your bed chamber."

"Why not? It won't hurt my reputation one bit." Suetonius sat up and grabbed for her, but Trista eluded him. "Do not tease me, Trista, for now that I know the sweetness of you, I cannot be parted from you."

Trista's pale blue eyes clouded and turned to gray. "You're a soldier. You'll be called back to your regiment. You will forget about me as you go rampaging through other people's countries and ruining their lives." She turned and ran through the door.

Suetonius sat up in bed and shouted, "If you hate me so much then why do you share my bed?" Her footsteps faded down the hall. He pounded his fist against the thin mattress, then regretted it as he shook his hand to relieve the pain. "I will never understand her." He lay down and rolled over, his back to the door. He closed his eyes, but sleep wouldn't come. He sat up, turned his pillow over so the cool side was up and lay facing the door. Sleep still did not come.

"By Jupiter! I might as well get up." Suetonius bounced out of bed and poured water in the porcelain basin. It wasn't fresh, for the slaves were still ill, but it would have to do. He washed away the sweat from the night and resolved that later this morning, he would go to the bath with his friends. Suetonius leaned toward the shiny metal mirror nailed above the wash basin and rubbed his fingers across his chin. He picked up his shaving blade and started the detestable act of shaving, wishing that facial hair were in style. He winced as he cut himself, reached for a scrap of linen and stuck it on the cut.

He was ready for more adventure, even though staying at home with Trista these last three weeks had held a certain appeal for him. Suetonius thought about finding a career at home and leaving the army, but that idea left him almost as fast as it had come.

Suetonius picked up his oil flask and two strigils and attached them to a handle. Instead of letting the metal tools hang down, he held them so they wouldn't rattle. He scooped his pocket toilet set off the table where he had thrown them a few days ago. The silver tools flashed in the light of the rising sun.

Suetonius slipped out the kitchen door and strode across the garden. As he lifted the gate handle, it squealed and he winced, for the sound assaulted his ears so early in the morning. He glanced eastward and saw that the streaks of pink and orange were giving way to the golden light of the full sun as it rose. Suetonius could smell the freshness of the morning, and he was glad that he awakened so early. The trees seemed greener in the morning and the sky bluer. Even the man-made buildings looked newborn and unblemished by life.

As he neared the bath building, he could smell the heat from the fires under the floors of the heated pool. He doubted that his friends would be here this soon, but it wouldn't matter. The peace would be welcome before the boisterous crowd arrived.

His bath finished, Suetonius lay on a slab of marble on his stomach and fell asleep during his massage. He was pleasantly warm, which was a change from the cold swim after his bath.

Suetonius didn't know how long he'd slept. He was awakened by someone roaring with laughter. He opened one eye and saw Lucian standing next to him. "What have you done now?" Suetonius looked around and then groaned when he saw that Lucian had stolen his toga. It was rolled up and under Lucian's arm. "Give me the toga. I swear by the gods, Lucian, you have never aged past childhood."

"It will cost you to get this back." Lucian stepped back from the massage table.

"What is it to cost me?"

Lucian laughed. "You'll volunteer for hazardous duty."

"To what purpose?" Suetonius raised up and grabbed for his toga. He grimaced when Lucian stepped out of reach. "I cannot discuss our future if you don't let me dress properly." Suetonius threw back the sheet that covered his lower body and stood, stretching his arms. He turned to the slave who was massaging him and nodded, dismissing him.

Suetonius stood with his arms folded across his chest and glared at Lucian. "Please explain this hazardous duty. Why should I be interested in any scheme of yours?"

Lucian threw Suetonius his clothes. "There is a call for volunteers to form a unit to go eastward. Rumor has it that we are to take more lands from Adiabeni, especially the territory north of the Tigris River. We would sail to Judea, then ride northeast for ten days. It would take us more than five years before we would see home again, but the pay is fantastic, especially for those of us in the cavalry. Are you interested?"

Suetonius picked up his under-toga from the floor and put it on, all the while digesting what his friend had told him. The prospect of a new adventure excited him, but the thought of leaving his new-found mistress saddened him. He wanted to be a general or even earn his own governorship. He didn't care where he went, he just wanted to prove he was an excellent soldier.

Suetonius wrapped his outer toga around himself, making certain the folds were in proper proportion before turning toward Lucian, whose dark brown eyes that usually laughed at him were serious now. "Lucian, do you want to go?"

Lucian nodded. "I want to advance, and this is the quickest way to do it. Come with me. You're destined for greatness. Didn't you tell me that the seers cast your fortune and told you that victory was in your future?"

"Yes."

"Then I believe that wherever you go, I should go. I want to be in the light of the shining star."

Suetonius took his friend's arm, and they walked from the chamber. "Why do you put so much faith in a seer? I might get both of us killed."

"What better way to die than in the uniform of the greatest country on earth?"

Suetonius looked at his friend to see if he were joking. He was not. "I'll go with you to sign up. I share your belief that to die in Roman uniform is an honor, however, I prefer it to be an old honor, and I hope it is not until we are old men."

"Agreed. Shall we go?" Lucian pushed the outside door open and the two soldiers strode into the street.

Suetonius walked faster. "Yes! It'll be good to get back into a battle or two. I haven't had breakfast. Let's eat first, for it may take hours."

"One of our last chances for decent food." Lucian laughed. "At least Adiabeni is warm part of the time."

Suetonius shrugged his shoulders. "Until we get into the mountains. I think I'll prefer it to the cold areas of the northern lands where we've spent so much time." He spread his arms to take in the bustling city. "It's time to leave all this behind."

Vivianne leaned forward and wrung the cold water out of a cotton cloth. She folded it and laid it across Trista's forehead and glanced down at her swollen belly. It looked like it couldn't possibly stretch any further without ripping. Vivianne was angry with her son, but unfortunately, he had no idea that he had left behind a pregnant mistress. She grimaced when Trista screamed. She held Trista's hand and was amazed at the bone-crushing strength the girl had. Another scream burst forth, and Vivianne shuddered. Why didn't the midwife would do something besides lay out her instruments?

"Milena, how soon is her time? She has been this way for more than a day and loses strength more rapidly now." Vivianne continued to wash Trista's face with cool water.

"She is not like our women. She is narrow through the hips. I cannot get this baby to move down. I have prepared a medicine to let her sleep." Milena leaned close to Vivianne and whispered, "She has to rest or she will not live through the day."

"Then by all means give it to her." Vivianne slipped her arm under Trista's shoulders and held her up. Milena squeezed medicine from a cloth into the girl's mouth. She was almost too weak to swallow, and Vivianne laid her gently down. She waited until Trista's eyes closed and her breathing became deep and regular.

Vivianne stood, moving her shoulders to restore circulation. It didn't work, for she was still stiff. She walked to the window and looked out. The sun was rising, sending fingers of pink, orange, and rose red across the heavens that grasped the aqua-colored sky. She looked around the room—Suetonius' chamber, and she thought it ironic that his child would be born here. When Trista had gone into labor, she had been brought here because her room was too cramped, and the girls were always underfoot.

A small altar that Caius had built for Suetonius when he went into military training stood in the corner. Vivianne went to it and stroked the cold marble where the god of soldiers straddled a downed bull in order to slit its throat. Vivianne ran her hand down the bulging muscles of the bull.

There was no other indication that her son had ever occupied this room except for a dish of colored glass marbles and a toy chariot pulled by two horses that Vivianne had insisted be placed on a table to the left of the doorway. She picked up the tiny model. It was still intact. The molded bronze horses tossed their heads upwards and their eyes rolled wild as legs stretched out in a never-ending race. The small wooden chariot, attached to the horses by a red leather harness, imitated the racing tack of the adult world. Vivianne put the chariot down, touched her finger to the back of the toy, and pushed it forward. The wheels moved. Tiny spokes had always enchanted her.

Sounds of a little boy's voice came back to her, and memories of pretend races that had taken place all over the villa made her smile. She shook her head in disbelief as she remembered she had given the racehorses and chariot to Suetonius so many years ago, and yet it was not so long ago. Where was the child of her past?

She looked at Trista. Maybe if Trista had a son, the toy would be in use once more and the sounds of childhood would fill their home with joy. Vivianne sat by the window and stared outside.

Vivianne must have fallen asleep. She blinked and saw that Trista's eyes had opened. "How are you?"

"I never knew that having a baby was so difficult. Is the baby going to be born alive?"

"The baby still lives." Vivianne sat on the stool next to Trista. She picked up a water glass and held it to Trista's lips. "Drink."

The peacefulness of the last few minutes was interrupted by a scream from Trista. "No more, no more."

Milena leaned over her. "Push, push. You must push." She looked at Vivianne and shook her head. "Trista, you must help this baby." Sweat dripped down Milena's face as she rubbed Trista's stomach with oil. "Vivianne, the baby just dropped further. It won't be long now."

"Thank the goddess Juno." Vivianne looked up at the statue of the enthroned figure with her arm around a peacock. She had ordered that it be brought to Suetonius' room to help Trista's labor. She looked back just as Trista groaned again. Vivianne grabbed her hand and once more felt the crushing of her bones as Trista squeezed. A cry of joy from Milena announced the birth at last.

Trista looked at the squalling, blood-covered child, then closed her eyes. "Is it a boy or a girl?"

Milena laid the baby on Trista's stomach. "It's a boy. A beautiful baby boy." Vivianne leaned over and kissed Trista on the cheek.

Milena cut and tied the umbilical cord, then set about washing the little boy. She was quick and had him wrapped warmly and placed in Trista's arms in a few minutes.

Trista smiled. "He has my hair and eyes."

Milena laughed. "He indeed has your hair, but all babies are born with blue eyes. Their true color comes in about six weeks."

"I would not be surprised to see your eyes in this child's countenance," Vivianne said. "My own grandmother had blue eyes."

Milena leaned down. She shook her head. "This will never do. We are not done yet. Push once more for the afterbirth. We need it to give to the goddess. Push!"

Vivianne massaged Trista's abdomen until the afterbirth was delivered into a silver bowl. "A good offering for Juno. Now you sleep. The child will rest, too, and in a few hours, he will want to eat." Vivianne leaned down and brushed Trista's hair away from her face. "Do you have a name for this child?"

"Perhaps. First I have to know if he will be a slave or a freeman." Trista watched Vivianne.

"My son's son cannot be a slave. I will also draw up the papers to free you. You'll live here as long as you and the child wish." Vivianne relaxed when she saw Trista nod. She nearly cried when a tear escaped from Trista's eyes and rolled down her cheek.

"If he is free, then I would like to call him Derek. In my homeland it means 'ruler of the people'. He could not have that name if he were a slave."

"I like that name, although I have never heard it before." Vivianne said it over and over in her mind. Each time it seemed less foreign. "I'll have it put in the family records." She looked down at the weakened girl. "You rest now. Milena will stay to watch over you and the baby." Vivianne leaned down and kissed the mother, then the child. She left the room quickly and went to her own chambers, almost as tired as if she had given birth herself. She worried about Trista. The girl had lost a lot of blood—too much.

And the baby wasn't thriving. His weak cry and listlessness worried Vivianne. She prayed to Juno just before she dropped off to sleep.

It seemed she had slept but a few minutes when one of the slave girls shook her awake. When Vivianne opened her eyes, she could see that it was dark outside, and the slave held a bronze oil lamp. Vivianne sat up. "What is wrong?"

"Please, Milena asks that you come quickly." The girl stepped away as Vivianne threw back the covers and leaped from her bed.

Vivianne's heart beat faster as she followed the girl down the hallway to her son's room. As soon as she saw Trista, her heart pounded against her ribs.

"What is wrong, Milena?" Vivianne touched Trista's cheek.

"She continues to lose blood. I cannot stop it." Milena's eyes were cast down. "I don't think she'll live through the night. She has bled too much. I have already sent for a wet nurse. The child won't suckle because he is weak, but no matter—there is no milk."

"The child must be saved even if Trista cannot be." Vivianne turned at a rustling behind her. A young girl with a baby stood in the doorway. Vivianne bent down and picked up her grandson. He lay in her arms like a child's rag doll. She almost cried. Poor babe. He was about to lose his mother. "I'm afraid I have not held such a beautiful baby boy for over twenty years." She kissed him on top of his head and enjoyed his fine hair against her lips, then walked quietly across the room and slipped the baby into the wet nurse's free arm. "He needs you. His mother is very ill and cannot nurse him."

Motioning to the slave who had accompanied her to her son's room, Vivianne pointed to the woman holding the two babes. "Take the wet nurse to Trista's room and stay with her until she is ready to sleep, then you are to watch both babies. The girls will be sleeping. I don't think they'll bother you. Do watch the one called Zia, though. She is a terror. Elysia will love both babies and can be a great help. You are to be nursemaid."

Vivianne was pleased when the slave girl smiled as she motioned for the wet nurse to follow her. Black smoke from the oil lamp rose toward the ceiling as the quartet made their way down the hall to the nursery. The smoke trailed behind them and marked their progress. Life would be exciting with a new baby in the house. Vivianne had already made up her mind that she would spoil the boy, but not so much as to make him difficult. She turned back toward the bed.

Milena caught her eye and shook her head. Vivianne rushed over to the bedside and sat on a stool. She took Trista's hand in her own. It felt hot and dry like dead leaves. Vivianne was rewarded with a wan smile.

Trista opened her eyes. "I am going to die, aren't I?"

"I cannot speak as a goddess and tell you. I will tell you that you're very weak. I would like for you to rest so that you will get strong." Vivianne squeezed her hand.

"If I die, what will happen to my baby?" Trista stared at Vivianne.

"He will be brought up by me as my grandson. He'll have all the opportunities that his father had, and he'll be treated the same as Suetonius." Vivianne leaned over and whispered to Trista. "I already love him and cannot wait to hold him again. He is a beautiful baby."

"Do not tell him his mother was a slave. It shames me so much." A tear slid down Trista's cheek and dropped onto her sweat-soaked stola.

Vivianne's eyebrow raised. She was astonished at this confession. She had never thought of slavery or slaves in any particular way except that she had a duty to protect them. To hear that Trista had any feelings at all about slavery was something new to her. "Why would serving others be abhorrent to you?"

"Please don't misunderstand. I love Elysia and Zia as if they were my own sisters, and I have been fortunate to be in this family, but . . ." Trista stopped talking as if she had run totally out of energy.

Vivianne was alarmed at the brightness of Trista's eyes. They were the same fevered eyes that she remembered when her father had died. Her throat felt tight and she swallowed. "I think I understand. Since my grandson should not have any shadow of slavery about him, then I declare you a free person. You are no longer a slave. I will have the papers drawn up, but all it really takes is one witness. Milena can be the witness." Vivianne looked around and motioned to Milena as she prepared more medicine.

Milena nodded. "I will be your witness." She brought the medicine over to Trista, held the sick girl's head up, and forced the warm liquid down her throat. Milena, ignoring Trista's resistance, left not one drop in the cup.

"If I am no longer a slave, then what is my name?"

Vivianne pulled a strand of Trista's hair away from her face. It felt hot and limp like the rest of her. Vivianne shook her head. It was only a matter of minutes before her grandson would be motherless. "I don't think I understand."

"I was given my grandmother's name by my mother. I would like to be remembered by that name." Trista's cheeks were flushed, and she pushed weakly against the thin covering that was over her. "I'm so hot."

"I will call you by your given name since you are no longer a slave, but first you must tell it to me."

Trista smiled. "It is Aloisia."

Vivianne leaned down. "Tell me again."

"Aloisia."

"Aloisia?"

"Perfect. You sound like my mother calling me." Trista closed her eyes and heaved a sigh.

Vivianne smiled. "You should sleep now, and when you're stronger, I'll bring your son to see you."

Trista's eyelids fluttered and she began to babble.

"Trista, I don't understand your speech. Milena, do you understand her tongue?"

Milena shook her head. "I think she calls on her gods in her own language. It sounds harsh to me."

"She has quit talking," Vivianne said.

Milena leaned over Trista and listened. "She sleeps the permanent sleep."

Vivianne's eyes widened. "Please don't tell me that."

"It is true." Milena reached up and touched Trista's pale cheek. "She has no more blood, no more life. She should be cremated soon. Poor motherless baby."

"Of whom do you speak? Trista or her son?" Vivianne stroked Trista's hair.

Milena shrugged. "I don't know. Perhaps both."

"Call the undertaker for me. I will sit with her until she comes. I want her to have the same funeral that any member of my family would have, for she was family."

Vivianne felt the shock of Trista's death replaced by sorrow as the tears began to flow down her own cheeks. She stuck her tongue out the side of her mouth and caught her tears. They tasted hot and salty. "Tell the undertaker that her name is Aloisia."

"Yes, I will." Milena scurried from the room.

Vivianne laid her head down on the bed. She felt as if her life's breath also wanted to leave her.

"Mistress, you have a guest," Milena said.

"I don't want to see anyone." Vivianne wouldn't raise her head.

"It is your sister, Savina."

"I don't care. I don't want to see anyone."

"That is too bad, Vivianne, for I am already here." Savina swept into the room, her ample figure still graceful after the bearing of two large baby boys in just fourteen months.

"I'm sorry, Savina." Vivianne sat up and pulled her stola into place.

"We can pray to God for her soul," Savina said. "She was a good person. I'm sure he'll take her into heaven."

"Oh, Savina. She was not a Christian."

"No matter."

"No!"

"Why not? Heaven is a beautiful place." Savina motioned for Milena to bring her a stool.

"How do you know? Have you been there?"

"I know that heaven exists the same way that you know about the River Styx and all the Roman gods." Savina sat and put her arms around Vivianne.

Vivianne nestled into her sister's arms. "She can't go to heaven. None of her people would be there."

"She would be so happy that it wouldn't matter."

"Savina, as much as I love you, I can't let you dictate how I'm to bury my daughter-in-law. She will be buried according to our traditions. She had learned about our gods and goddesses. Juno is . . . was her favorite. She prayed to our gods for Suetonius' safety."

"Her soul would be better off in our Christian heaven."

"No. We'll not discuss it further. The trouble with you Christians is that you won't let any of the rest of us alone."

"It's because we know the truth."

"Don't be ridiculous. How can one god create all this, protect all people, and create our destiny? That takes many gods." Vivianne pulled away from Savina.

"You won't consider even a tiny Christian ceremony after yours?"

"No. Trista was not Christian. Remember, we've talked several times about your new found religion, and I've always told you that I could not believe in it. You promised me that you wouldn't discuss it anymore."

"I just wanted to comfort you with the promise of everlasting life for Trista. I know how much she meant to you." Savina hugged her sister. "I'll not talk about it any more. I'll go see the baby, then see myself to the door."

"The baby is weak."

"I'll pray for him. You need to rest."

"You are kind, Savina." Vivianne tilted her cheek toward her sister who kissed her quickly, then departed her stola swaying.

Vivianne awoke from a series of good and bad dreams and looked up, sensing she was not alone. Her fingers rested on Trista's arm. Caius was standing at the end of the bed his hands clasped behind him. He looked older, wiser, and sadder. Vivianne sat up and pushed strands of hair back into place as best she could. "She gave birth to a beautiful boy, and then she died like so many of the women do."

"I am sorry." Caius rocked back and forth on the balls of his feet. "Does the boy look like Suetonius?"

Vivianne smiled. "No, he is like his mother. He might have the blue eyes of Trista as does my sister, Savina. You should go see him. I know, I know. Babies make you nervous, but this is our first grandchild. Put aside your fears and go down to the girls' room. It has been quickly made into a nursery."

"Babies make me nervous," Caius said.

"Don't be absurd. Go see him while he lives."

"While he lives?"

"Caius, he is weak." Vivianne tried to hold back tears.

"All babies seem weak to me. I'm sure that he'll be all right." Caius walked around the bed, leaned over, and kissed Vivianne's cheek. "I'll go see our heir. I needed to know how you were feeling. In the last few months you and Trista became like mother and daughter."

"Her name is Aloisia."

"What?"

"Her mother named her for her grandmother. Her real name is Aloisia." Vivianne blinked back her tears that threatened to flow again. "I think that her name sounds like the wind whispering through the leaves of an olive tree." Vivianne took a deep breath. "I shall plant an olive tree for her in the orchard. She loved the orchard."

"I remember," Caius said.

"Do you have a gold coin?"

Caius nodded and pulled the coin from a leather pouch that hung from his belt. He handed it to Vivianne. "She is very beautiful, isn't she? I can see why Suetonius loved her."

"Unfortunate for a soldier." Vivianne pulled the dead girls chin down to open her mouth. She studied the gold coin with Tiberius' likeness for a moment, then placed it on Trista's tongue and closed her mouth. "That is your fare for the ferryman so that you may cross the River Styx to Hades. May the underworld treat you well, my daughter."

The day of the funeral was sunny and comfortably cool, and Vivianne believed the gods were mocking her sorrow. She was also frustrated because she couldn't contact her son to tell him of the double-edged sword of joy and grief.

She shifted the child from her right arm to her left as she walked behind the bier, and little Derek settled down. He had only eaten a short time, but Vivianne was hopeful. He sucked honey off her finger. His eyes, closed in the slumber of the innocent, were sunken as were his cheeks. He felt lighter in weight than he had at birth.

The slow and solemn drumbeat set the pace for the small procession to the crematorium. Vivianne was numb, and she walked without feeling or seeing. The hours flew and crawled at the same time, and she didn't realize that they had arrived at the crematorium until Caius nudged her.

"Do you want to see her one last time?"

Vivianne could not speak, so she nodded and moved to the bier. The little slave, now free, wore a pale blue stola in memory of her eyes. Her hair had been left unbound as was her custom, and her hands were folded across her breasts. A dried pine bough and cone lay next to her on the bier. Vivianne had made certain that the small, smooth stone had been placed in a pouch that hung from her neck. These were Trista's treasures. Someday Vivianne would ask Suetonius about them.

Trista was beautiful and looked peaceful. Vivianne was glad that Trista's suffering was over. She held up little Derek and shook him so that he would awaken. He opened his eyes and looked toward his mother, and closed them again immediately. There was no way to know whether or not he saw her. Vivianne clasped him back to her breast, her sorrow enveloping him. She nodded and the bier was taken into the crematorium.

Vivianne handed the baby to the wet nurse. "Take little Derek home, try to get him to eat, and put him to bed. We will be home later in the evening."

It was near sunset when the Vivianne heard the door open. Iron against iron grated as the rusty hinges resisted the force from within. The darkness from inside contrasted to the bright sun that was low in the sky and outlined the building. Vivianne's nose wrinkled with distaste at the odor that wafted toward her.

The funeral director walked toward her holding an urn. Vivianne stared at the alabaster container that she had paid as much for as she would have for an urn for a family member. Leaves and flowers twisted themselves around each other, the color changing from white to cream as the thickness of the alabaster changed. Carved amongst the flowers was *'Dismanibus Aloisia Paulinus, Matri Miserrim'*. Vivianne shook her head. Aloisia was, indeed, an unfortunate mother. Not knowing Aloisia's true family name, she had given her their own last name, for she was a member of the family in every sense of the word.

Vivianne traced the dome-shaped lid of the urn. Peach leaves were carved on the lid like a canopy and the handle was a perfectly shaped peach, complete with stem and one lone leaf attached to the stem.

Tears slipped from Vivianne's eyes, making dual tracks down her cheeks. She would never again be able to see the orchard without remembering Trista, nay Aloisia. Vivianne took a deep breath and reached for the urn. She was startled by the rattling inside until she remembered the pebble, and another tear slid down her cheek. Vivianne had no idea why the pebble was so important to Trista, but the girl had worn it in a pouch around her neck every day in life, and now she and the pebble would rest together forever. Vivianne hated the thought of the beautiful young girl reduced to ashes. The gods could be cruel. She immediately said a prayer of forgiveness to the gods so as to not anger them.

The marble felt cool in her hands, except for the bottom that still held the warmth from the newly created ashes. She held it against her breast as she walked home. Streaks of color raced across the sky and colored the buildings and streets. Usually Vivianne liked sunsets, but tonight she had no joy at the rainbow of color presented to her. Although she couldn't accept the gifts from the gods, she hoped they would understand and not punish her for her disinterest. Vivianne was unaware of anything but the urn that cooled in her arms, except for Caius who walked silently next to her.

"No!" Vivianne screamed and threw herself at the physician. "No! The gods would not be so cruel. What have I done to anger them?"

"Hush, Wife. Hush. You have done nothing wrong." Caius pulled her away from the physician who hovered over the infant.

"He was getting better. He felt heavier. Stronger. Just this morning little Derek smiled at me." Vivianne pulled away from her husband and pushed the physician aside. She picked up the limp form of the baby.

"He lives. See there is movement." Vivianne hugged the child to her breast.

"He has crossed over, Vivianne. He needed to be with his mother." Caius put his arms around his wife.

"He wanted to be with me." Vivianne's tears dropped onto the baby's swaddling cloth. "By Juno, he wanted to stay with me."

"You have a son. She has none."

"I have no grandson. Oh, Caius, I told him stories. I told him of the medals that his father won for bravery, I told him that his father couldn't wait to see him, I told him his mother was a wonderful artist and painted murals for this house." Vivianne held the baby tighter.

The physician pulled Caius aside. "I've seen this before. It's best to force her to give up the baby."

"Force her?" Caius shook his head. "I won't do that. Can't you see the pain that has torn her heart asunder? Can't you see that she needs to hold this child?"

"For how long?" The physician frowned.

"For as long as it takes her to give up the baby to the inevitable." Caius closed his eyes and took a deep breath.

"You need to be strong. Take the child from her. It's the best way."

"Stop it!" Vivianne shouted. "I can hear you."

Caius grabbed hold of the physician's elbow and led him to the door. "Leave. It'll be better for you."

"For me?"

"Yes, because if you stay, one of us will double up a fist and scatter your teeth across these marble floors." If Caius hadn't been so angry, he would've laughed at the physician's hurried exit.

Vivianne crooned a lullaby and rocked the dead baby. "I think his eyes will be blue like his mother's."

"Probably. I don't know anything about babies." Caius put his arm around Vivianne's shoulder. "I do know that you're a wise and practical woman. I know you've tended the slaves' children when they've had sickness. I know you've helped bury their babies, and you've comforted the mothers."

"I've done all that. It is the duty of all Romans to care for the less fortunate." Vivianne kissed the top of Derek's head. "I love the feel of his hair. It's like the finest silk thread."

"Do you know why he grows cool?"

"He needs another blanket."

"Do you believe a blanket will help this baby?"

Vivanne shook her head. "No."

"Do you know why?"

"Yes," she whispered.

"I'll walk with you to the crematorium to make arrangements," Caius said. "Do you want to carry him or shall I?"

"I will take the child myself. He can share his mother's urn. He would've liked the peach orchard. He would've climbed trees and stolen peaches and eaten them green like his father did. And I would've had to help him get well." Vivianne choked out a sob. "He is a beautiful boy."

"Come, it's time to put him with his mother." Caius kissed his wife.

"I know." Vivianne leaned against Caius. "I'm ready."

CHAPTER
VII

BOADICEA HESITATED. She was ready for the inevitable, but she wanted to relive the past a few moments more. She ran her hand along the stone slab that had served as an altar for generations, and she wondered what would happen to it. Would it lose its powers if it were lost and became just another slab of rock?

The rock was worn smooth in the front where she had spent countless hours leaning against it to mix potions and weave spells. Minute pieces had worn away like bits of her life that had been lived a moment at a time. Now her life was over, and she was to become nothing more than ordinary bones in an ordinary grave.

She traced the smooth, rounded edge of the stone. What did it matter anyway? All was lost, as her body and the bodies of her daughters would be. Boadicea turned and looked at the sun shining through the tiny window. It was the last light she and her daughters would see before they were reborn from everlasting darkness. The sun would set soon and light would be replaced by darkness as it was meant to be. She took a deep breath. It was meant to be, but for what reason she could not say.

A happy moment. She wanted to think about a happy moment. A bittersweet smile graced her face. She almost laughed at the incongruity of her calmness at death when she remembered the day of her wedding to Prasutagus. She had been in front of this same altar, pacing because her nerves were on fire. She was the most frightened she had ever been in her life.

Boadicea paced back and forth in front of the altar, tripping on her long tunic. She grasped the skirt impatiently and jerked it up around her calves. She wondered why in the world women were hampered by their ridiculous clothing that became even more asinine for special occasions. She liked the tunic only for the bright slashes of blue, red, and saffron.

She whirled around and marched back across the room. "I would rather be in battle than go through this." She turned at the sound of laughter and saw her mother standing in the doorway to the kitchen. Boadicea stopped pacing and dropped her skirts to put her hands on her hips. "Pray tell me, Mother, what is so amusing?"

Durina crossed the room to her daughter and hugged her. "I find it amusing that you could go through battle in a joyous state and approach your marriage with trepidation."

"Don't tease me, Mother. I cannot help myself." Boadicea laid her head on her mother's shoulder and was surprised to find that she was taller than Durina by a hand's span. She pulled back and studied her mother for the first time. The tiny lines at the corners of her mother's eyes, shocked her, but she was relieved to see the eyes still bright and inquisitive. Her mother was beautiful, and a pang of home-sickness struck quickly. Boadicea kissed her mother on the cheek.

Durina smiled. "Why a kiss?"

"I'm going to miss you. How did you leave your mother?"

"With great difficulty, but you must remember that my mother was part of this tribe and therefore only a few huts away. We two will be separated a half day's journey by horse." Durina took her daughter's hands in her own. "I promise that once every seven moons we will see each other. I will visit you one week, and you shall visit me the next."

Boadicea shook her head. "But I am used to having you with me every day."

"You will be busy helping Prasutagus lead the tribe. And you'll also have the second duty of priestess. These responsibilities will keep you busy, and the weeks will fly by as do the winds. As time goes by people will ask you for advice, prayer, and healing."

"I cannot imagine that time will go quickly." Boadicea looked toward the altar where for most of her life she had meditated and learned.

"You were wise in choosing Prasutagus as your husband. His people are wise in choosing you to help them. It is the way of things and the desire of the gods, or they would not have molded your life in such a manner." Durina dropped Boadicea's hands. "Come, it is time to see your father before we begin the ceremony. You should not be before the altar until your future husband is there to wait for you."

"Take me to Father. Does he pray for me?" Boadicea took her mother's arm, and they crossed the altar room, the kitchen, and into a tiny room where Garik knelt before an altar. There were no windows in this room and the burning candles threw a larger than life shadow of her father against the far wall. Durina and Boadicea knelt next to him on either side and waited for his prayer to end. Garik finished, then took a hand of each of the women and placed them on a smooth stone colored with red powder. "May this red powder, symbol of the blood of life, protect you for eternity in this life and the afterlife." Garik and the two women stood. "Let's begin. I'm certain that Prasutagus is as nervous as you are, Boadicea."

"How could he be?"

Garik smiled. "I remember my own marriage day. I have never since been as nervous as that."

Boadicea had to prevent her mouth from dropping open. She could not imagine her father, stoic and unshakable, being apprehensive. "You were nervous? Why?"

"I was marrying the most beautiful and sought-after woman in the tribe—indeed, in several tribes. After I convinced her to marry me, I was afraid that I would not be worthy of her." Garik shook his head. "I was right."

"You were not!" Durina leaned her head on his shoulder as they walked into the great altar room. "You were perfect, and I was afraid that I would not be a good wife to a warrior tribal king."

Boadicea stopped pacing and folded her arms. "Your attempt to calm my nerves with your stories is not working. I have learned only that I'm not the first case of a nervous bride. Perhaps I will live through this ceremony, but I have doubts."

"She is difficult, Garik."

Garik nodded in agreement. "An errant daughter, but better than no daughter. Stay here by the door until it is time to call you forth." Garik leaned down and kissed Boadicea's cheek.

Boadicea blinked back the tears that threatened to flow. Not usually given to tears, today she didn't want to ruin her usual stoic reputation. She watched her parents as they moved into the altar room, and waited for her turn to cross from one life to another. More than anything she wanted to see if Prasutagus were there, but it was forbidden, and she didn't want to anger the gods. Life would be difficult enough without having the gods angry.

Boadicea put her hands to her face, covering her nose and mouth to keep from screaming. Then she giggled when she thought of how the people would react to such a noise coming through the walls behind the altar. The mental picture of the guests climbing all over themselves to escape the 'demon' caused her to double over. She grabbed the skirts of her tunic and held them over her mouth to muffle her laughter. She was still in this position when she heard the words of her father and mother in chorus. She dropped her skirts and clamping her lips tightly together, tried with some success to compose herself.

Boadicea stepped through the doorway. She barely noticed the crowd of people from both tribes as she looked from her mother to her father and then to Rhys' mother who stood in the front row of the guests. Boadicea caught Gwyneth watching her, and remembered Gwyneth's simple advice that Rhys was a part of her past, and Prasutagus was to be a part of her future. It was the wish of the gods, of course. Still she felt relieved when Gwyneth smiled at her, and Boadicea smiled in return.

Boadicea let her gaze slide from Gwyneth to her bridegroom. Prasutagus looked more handsome than she had ever seen him. He returned her look, and she noticed that his eyes twinkled. Although he seemed relaxed, she hoped he wasn't, then she chastised herself for such unkind thoughts. Her mind drifted back in time to their brief, but intense courtship. When she had told Prasutagus that she would marry him, he had sent gifts every day to her parents, to her tribe, and to her. Today's gift was the tunic that she was wearing for her wedding. Yesterday he presented his gift—new bridles for Thayne and Ella, the leather worked until it was smooth and soft, and carved by an artist with swirls and curves. Boadicea loved that gift even more than the gold ring, now on her right hand, to show her love for Prasutagus would be forever and unbroken.

She stepped from the doorway trimmed with oak branches from the tree planted at her birth, stopping to take an acorn from the bowl at the edge of the altar. She approached Prasutagus and stood next to him waiting for the words from her mother that would bind them to each other and to the gods. Her father would speak the ceremonial words to bind the two tribes together.

Durina raised her arms and held them above Boadicea and Prasutagus. She held an oak branch in her right hand. "Let the gods make the two as one and to be as strong as three. Let them have many children to take the families into the unknown future. Let a piece of each, Prasutagus and Boadicea, travel to the future through their children and grandchildren and great-grandchildren. May the seeds they sow cover many lands. Let them stand side by side, never to be cast asunder by any man." Durina dropped her arms and laid the oak branch on the altar. She stepped aside, and Garik took her place. He held a large golden bowl without any type of ornamentation. It was smooth and shiny and pieces of sunlight bounced from it to dance on the walls. It had been filled with small, brown cakes.

"Let our two tribes be joined today as a cohesive unit to become one to protect each other and to multiply just as Boadicea and Prasutagus are bound by the gods to do. Let us become as strong as three. Let no other tribe or any other nation split our tribes." Garik turned and held the bowl to Durina. She took a cake. Garik turned to Boadicea and Prasutagus and waited until they had each taken a cake, then he handed the bowl to Gwyneth, who took one and passed it to the person next to her. When everyone had taken a cake, Garik nodded and each person consumed it.

A shout went up and the crowd, no longer quiet, roared their approval and rushed to the tables outside laden with wine for further celebration.

Boadicea smiled at the wild rainbow rushing toward the door. It would be three days before the wine was gone and the people would wander off to their homes. She and Prasutagus were to hide for three days in a special hut that had been built for them. A likeness of the goddess of fertility was drawn on either side of the doorway, and as soon as they entered the windowless building, the door would be barred from the outside. She had not been allowed to see the inside, and the only clue she had as to what was in there was that a steady stream of women with pots of food had entered the hut all morning.

Boadicea's father cleared his throat, and Boadicea was brought back to the present. She turned to Garik and kissed his cheek, then kissed her mother. She took Prasutagus' hand and led him past the shouting guests. Boadicea pulled her new husband down the path to the fertility hut, followed by her father and two other men. She hesitated by the doorway and looked at Prasutagus. He smiled at her and placed her fingers to his lips. Heartened, she stepped through the doorway into the candle-lit hut. The shaft of sunlight from the doorway was suddenly snuffed out as the door was shut. Even though she expected it, the first hammer blow caused her to start.

Prasutagus put his arms around her and pulled her to him. "Within you I find strength. Together we'll rule. Together we'll have two strong countries."

Boadicea leaned against him and closed her eyes. She felt serene for the first time in many days, and she could feel the tension leave her muscles. She opened her eyes to see a table laden with roast boar, wild rice, vegetables, dozens of special sweet dishes, and several kinds of wine. She stood back and looked across the hut. The marriage bed was made of oak and had been decorated with the sacred leaves and acorns. She stood on her toes and kissed Prasutagus.

Prasutagus' laid his head against hers, and the breath from his soft laughter ruffled her hair. "You're very calm for one who dreaded this day."

"I didn't dread this day. I welcomed it and you, but it was peculiar and did make me nervous. I have made the right choice. I know it both in my head and in my heart." Boadicea sighed, feeling content and protected. It was the same feeling she had as a child whenever she needed to be held and one of her parents had been there.

Prasutagus took hold of her hair and let it ripple through his fingers. "I have a confession."

"You?" Boadicea inhaled, savoring the odor of Prasutagus' skin, still pink from having been scrubbed in the purification rite. "I have the curiosity of a dozen cats, so tell me your hideous confession."

Prasutagus remained silent for a moment, then he cleared his throat. "I'm afraid . . . afraid of this. I'm no longer calm, but ready to run and hide."

Boadicea laid her head against his chest. "I love you. Your presence makes me soar to magnificent heights. The trees whisper your name, and I become sick with desire." She stepped back and smiled at Prasutagus. "Perhaps that is the real reason for locking the door . . . to keep in the frightened bridegroom." She kissed Prasutagus. "I can't imagine any warrior king being nervous. Why are you in such a state?"

"You've seen eighteen summers, and I have seen nearly thirty. You're beautiful and I'm ugly. I don't know why you want an old dog like me. I worry that I won't be able to . . . to make you happy." Prasutagus stuttered to a stop.

Boadicea smiled. "If that is all that bothers you, then you have nothing to worry about. I find you handsome. You have made my heart beat faster, my palms sweaty, and my desires overwhelm me since the day we met. I was always afraid I would not be good enough for you." She took his hand and pulled him toward the bed, stopping next to it. She plucked a holly leaf from a wreath and twirled it between her fingers. "This is your birth tree and means that you are affectionate and trustworthy. I love you for both qualities. Remember, we are in this fertility hut but for one reason. We are to have a child before this season comes again. Do we dare disappoint the gods?"

"Not at all," Prasutagus whispered.

The gray sky spit gray scraps of snow. Boadicea pulled her cape tighter across her bulging stomach and shivered. If only Spring got over its indecisiveness and let the flowers grow. She kicked at the pebbles that peeked through the dusting of snow that obscured the ground, and welcomed the soft earth under the pebbles. Maybe Spring was on her way. Sometimes Boadicea believed Spring liked to be contrary so that when she did arrive, no one would take her for granted. True Spring would gladden her heart, for that meant that her own time had come. She wondered about the baby that nestled within her. If a boy, would he be strong and intelligent? If the baby were a girl-child, would she be able to follow in the wake of Durina and herself and become a priestess?

Boadicea looked up when she heard the soft neighing of Thayne. He tossed his head and his mane rippled, then pawed the ground and snorted, more insistently this time. "You are spoiled," Boadicea shouted. She watched Thayne flick his tail, then trot over to Ella and nuzzle her flank. Ella raised her head slowly and looked at Boadicea with her big, dark eyes. Boadicea laughed. "You know I could never resist you, Ella." Boadicea walked across the snowy ground to the corral, ignoring the cold that seeped through her thin-soled shoes. Ella, Thayne, and Boadicea reached the fence at the same time. Ella reached over the fence and laid her head against Boadicea's shoulder. Boadicea scratched the top of Ella's head while trying to fend off Thayne who was as demanding as a spoiled child. Boadicea bent over as far as she could, given her circumstance, and ran her hand along Ella's side. "Well, my girl, you're going to make Thayne a father again." The sound of hoof beats lightly tapping across the pasture caused her to look up. She had to smile at the yearling's gangly run. Rhys would have been pleased with Ella's offspring. Her smile disappeared as she thought of Rhys. It seemed like another lifetime, and so long ago. She tried to remember his face, but all she could remember was his hair forming a halo of sunshine around his features. She couldn't get his face to form, and she closed her eyes tightly, trying to force his blue eyes into her mind. She fought back the tears. Which was worse: to still grieve for an old love or to forget his face?

The yearling stood beside his mother and tried to suckle, but she moved away from him each time he nosed her. "You're too old, you silly thing. Your mother has another foal to concern herself with now." Boadicea leaned across the fence, then chuckled at the thought of how strange her swollen stomach must look against the rails. "How does it feel, Ella, to get a fat stomach and shorter legs at the same time? How does it feel to have a baby?" Boadicea stood, put her hands in the curve of her back and arched backwards. "How does it feel not to have a backache?"

She straightened and rubbed Thayne's nose, soft as the moss by the stream. She felt the baby kick, and she put her fingers on the place, tracing the movement. "You must have gotten some powerful kicks, Ella."

The wind whipped around and tore at Boadicea's cape, forcing her to grab it and hold it with both hands. Her eyes teared from the cold, and the same gale sent the three horses across the field to the shelter of the trees. Boadicea watched them go, tails streaming behind them and sparkling in the gray light. She had accepted Ella as a wedding gift from Rhys' mother, even though it was painful for both of them. Boadicea had hugged Gwyneth, knowing that the time had come for their lives to separate like a braid that had come undone.

Boadicea shook the memories from her mind and walked back toward the complex of five buildings, each round and each attached to the other, that had been her home since her marriage to Prasutagus. Memories of Rhys rushed into her mind. She saw his face clearly and heard his laughter. What kind of home would she and Rhys have had? Then seeing Prasutagus waving and smiling at her, felt guilty for still loving a dead lover.

She smiled and waved back, more exuberant than usual, then tried to run. She hooked her fingers together in a basket weave under her protruding stomach, but gave up and slowed to a walk. She stopped before Prasutagus and put her hands on her hips.

"What is so funny, Husband?"

Prasutagus' grin was wide. "I find it peculiar to watch you trying to run. I think you should roll instead, like a round rock."

"What an ungracious husband you have become since you did this to me." Boadicea tapped her foot to feign anger.

"Come inside and let's argue. It's too cold outside."

Prasutagus put his arm around Boadicea and led her through the doorway. "I want to know how you feel. Do you want to eat? I fear you have grown thin."

"Thin! With my stomach so far out? How could you call this body thin?"

"Did you eat?"

"I haven't been hungry today. I've felt strange since the moon rose last evening."

Prasutagus' face showed alarm, and he stopped still to look at Boadicea closely. "Should I send for my sister? Do you have the pain that comes with birth?"

Boadicea shook her head while trying not to smile at her warrior husband's distress. "I haven't had the pain that the goddess sends to tell us to make ready. When it does, I will tell you." She put her hand to her mouth to hide the smile that would not go away. "Please, let's . . ." Boadicea gasped and grabbed her stomach with both hands. "I cannot believe this! Get Rhianna quickly. No, wait. The pain is gone." Boadicea stood quietly, breathing heavily. "Perhaps it would be best to send for my mother. I would like for her to be here."

"I will go for your mother myself, but I won't leave until Rhianna has come." Prasutagus paced back and forth. "I will get Rhianna right now. Will you be all right while I'm gone?"

Boadicea grinned at him. "My husband, she is in the hut within a stone's throw. You can't be gone long."

"Promise me you'll sit down and not move while I'm gone. You are sure you'll be all right?"

"Many women have had babies before without trouble. I am wide of hip and should have my children drop out like ripe acorns." She shook her head as she finished her sentence to the empty hut, for Prasutagus had already gone.

Perspiration slid into Boadicea's eyes and mixed with the tears of joy. She kissed the baby on top of the head, savoring the softness of the depression in her tiny skull and the silkiness of her hair. She placed a finger near the perfect little hand, and diminutive fingers grasped hers. The bond was complete, and Boadicea felt an overwhelming urge to protect and care for the beautiful child whom the gods had entrusted to her. She reached for her own mother with her other hand and the two women intertwined fingers, bridging three generations.

"Mother, she is like a princess. She is very beautiful, don't you think so?"

Durina peered at the infant. "She is very beautiful. She has your coloring. Her hair seems a little darker, but it is still red. See how peaceful she is? She is born under the sign of the Ash Tree and thus should make a great medicine woman. She will be a docile child and should give you no trouble in spite of her auburn hair."

Boadicea raised one eyebrow in mock horror. "Are you saying that girls with red hair are usually difficult?"

Durina laughed, the sound rippling across the small hut. "I have had some moments of difficulty with you."

"How can you tell that this child will not be difficult? She is only a few hours old!" Boadicea stroked the baby's soft skin and marveled at the miracle that snuggled next to her.

"She does not scream and wriggle about, throwing her arms out and getting red in the face."

"I did not do that," Boadicea said.

"Oh, my daughter, but you did. You always fought everything. You had questions about rules, about the world, about the heavens, about the gods, about all living and non-living things. The list is endless." Durina hesitated as her mind traveled back in time. "You were not a bad child, though. You brought me years of pleasure, and you still do. You will hear men talk of having sons, but there is nothing better for a mother than a daughter.

"Sons grow away from mothers and when they marry, usually they live with their wife's family, but daughters stay in their mother's tribe, and their lives continue to intertwine. The weave of life between mother and daughter is just like the making of a basket. As time goes by, the interlacing takes shape and becomes stronger."

Boadicea held her mother's hand to her lips and kissed it. "I miss you a great deal. I wish our tribes were closer."

"I miss you, too, but it was necessary for you to come to Prasutagus' tribe to learn about his people. Someday you will rule in your father's stead, and our tribes will be one. There will be a large area for you to rule, but you will have a strong nation." Durina sighed. "It saddens me to see that your father grows older and slower. His hair has turned from the color of the sun to the silver of the moon. In time, he will need to cross to the other world."

Boadicea looked down at her own daughter and she realized that each joyous birth was tainted with the passage of time. This child would become living proof of the days dwindling and her parents aging. "Don't talk of that, Mother. I cannot bear the thought."

"You should not despair. Each child carries a part of all of us." Durina stroked the baby's hair. "See, her hair is the color of your father's and of yours. There is proof that she is of all of us." Durina continued rubbing her hand across the baby's hair. "Have you thought of a name for her?"

Boadicea nodded. "I have talked with the bards who travel a great deal and they told me of many names. I wanted a different name. I was told of one from Judaea. I'm naming her Sydelle. It means princess in Hebrew. She is a princess in many ways, and I want her to remember it every time she hears her name."

Durina spoke the name over several times. "It sounds strange at first, but does roll off the tongue after practice. I like it."

"When will we have the naming ceremony?"

"In five days. She will be strong then." Durina turned at a rustling sound in the doorway. Rhianna entered with a jug of water and a basket of flat bread. "It is good that you were here to help care for my daughter. She gave birth so quickly I barely got here in time."

Rhianna placed the bread and water on a low table next to Boadicea's birthing bed. "It was an easy birth. Usually first babies are reluctant to leave the warmth of the womb." She poured water in a silver cup and held it out to Boadicea. "Here, drink this."

Boadicea sat up. The cup felt cool against her lips. She drank the entire cup without stopping and was surprised to find she was thirstier than she had thought. "Thank you, Rhianna. You have been wonderful. It was a good thing that you were here, for your brother was worthless."

Durina and Rhianna burst out laughing. Rhianna's eyes twinkled, and she shook her head. "It seems men are confounded by the simple things like birth and women, but a little war is taken in stride. I have never seen Prasutagus so pale."

"Who speaks my name in jest?" Prasutagus filled the doorway with his large frame.

Boadicea reached out for him. "Come and see our beautiful daughter once more. She is perfect."

"Is it safe for me amongst all you strong-willed women?"

"We are no worse than the barbarians from the north who make war on us from time to time."

Prasutagus tip-toed across the room and looked down at his offspring. He placed a finger against her tiny chest. "She has the heartbeat of a warrior. She will be a strong soldier." He kissed Boadicea on her forehead. "I am pleased that she looks like you. She is pretty. I will have to think about a suitable husband for her already, for the boy children will flock about her. This I predict. I remember Rhianna's suitors, but she would have no one."

Rhianna snorted. "I don't want an ordinary man, brother. Bring me someone who is handsome, strong, and will ride a horse like the wind. There is no good that comes of a strong line weakened by a soft link." Rhianna was interrupted by a soft cry from the newly named Sydelle. "It is time for you to leave so that the child can be nursed." She pushed Prasutagus toward the door. "Leave us in peace so that your daughter can get a good start in life."

Prasutagus seemed willing to be pushed out of the unfamiliarity of the world of women. He turned at the door and waved to Boadicea. "Tell me, did you name her after the foreign princess?"

"Yes. She is to be called Sydelle." Boadicea unpinned her tunic and pulled a breast out, heavy with milk. She placed the nipple on the baby's cheek. The child turned instinctively toward it and began to suckle, making happy noises of contentment. Boadicea watched the tiny lips working against her swollen breast, and she was filled with love for the helpless infant. "Sydelle, you're very beautiful. Do you like it here, little one?"

Boadicea slid off Thayne while holding Sydelle carefully in her left arm. She adjusted her tunic, and smiled at the baby who appeared to be content wherever she was. In the last few months since Sydelle's birth, there seemed to be no time when the child had been unhappy. The baby gurgled and smiled, but rarely cried. Boadicea handed the reins to a young boy that she didn't recognize. There was no time to wonder whose child it was.

"Put him in the corral where the other horses are. Be careful of the bit. He has a tender mouth." Boadicea hesitated outside the door of her parents' home and turned to look at the once familiar view. The trees seemed taller, especially the oak tree that had been planted close to the house the day she was born.

In the distance she heard the river as it rushed across the stones. Farther away the birds were cawing over the newly-planted fields, and Boadicea heard the voices of her tribal friends shouting across the plowed furrows at each other and the hated crows. A breeze ruffled the new leaves in the trees and the buzzing of flies reminded her that her favorite season was approaching. She loved summer when the heat pressed down on the wind and caused it to cease. She wondered how many summers her father had seen and if he would see any more.

Boadicea kissed Sydelle to affirm life, then stepped through the door to the altar room. Her eyes needed a few minutes to adjust to the darkness. She could hear only ragged breathing coming from across the room. She stepped toward the sound even before she could see because she knew the room better than any other, and she recognized the breathing. The smell of impending death hovered in the room.

Boadicea knelt by the low bed that had been placed in front of the altar. She saw his hair, the former deep auburn white with age and unkempt. She touched his hair lightly, alarmed to find that it was wet with perspiration. Her hand moved to his shoulder. When he groaned, she started and withdrew her hand.

"Father," Boadicea whispered. "I have come to visit you." She leaned as close as she could without crushing her baby. "Can you hear me?"

"He may awaken later, Daughter." Durina stood in the doorway with a large metal bowl in her arms. Steam floated upwards and obscured her face. Across her arm was a linen cloth. "I am sorry I did not hear you arrive. I was getting hot water to help your father breathe."

Boadicea caught her lower lip in her teeth to keep from crying out. Her mother looked old and worn. Her hair had not been combed for days. Never had Boadicea seen her with a dirty tunic, but she was as deteriorated as her father. It was then that Boadicea realized her mother had kept the illness of her father from her as long as possible. The poor woman must have cared for him endlessly for days and nights without help from servants.

Boadicea stood, but her mother waved her back down. "How long has he been ill?" Her mother placed the bowl on the altar and dropped in a handful of yew needles. The odor was pungent, but refreshing. Durina dipped a cloth in a second bowl that held cold water. Her mother seemed to be in a trance. Both her parents were in a state of distress she had never seen before. She felt betrayed by time and realized that in only a few years, she would be the elder generation. She didn't want to be the elder generation, for that meant that she would be on the edge of the abyss of destruction and no longer protected by her parents. In her imagination she peered down into the other world beneath the great sea and saw the faces of ancestors past, all the while being dragged closer to them. She shuddered.

"Mother, please talk to me. How long has he been like this?"

Durina placed the cold cloth on Garik's face and washed him carefully, then wiped his arms. The pungent odor of the herbs masked, momentarily, the odor of death. "He has been ill for awhile. I don't remember when I noticed that he was ill. Day by day he became frailer, and I feel it is my fault that I did not notice until it was too late."

"It cannot be your fault. I know you have done all you could." Boadicea looked down at the sleeping child in her arms.

"Would you let me take care of my father? You could take Sydelle. She is sleeping, and you could sleep." Boadicea waited for her mother to answer, but she did not. "Mother, you will kill yourself. Why did you not get help from one of the women in the village?"

"I did not want to let anyone know. Your father said that it was not advisable in case there is an attempt to take over during this time of weakness. Gryffyth suspects, however."

"Gryffyth? That old childhood maker of trouble? The one who tormented me all my life?"

"The very one. Your father asked that I send for you secretly." Durina continued to wash her husband, pulling aside his tunic.

"Have we ever had to worry about anyone within our own tribe?" Boadicea studied her mother closely. There were dark circles under her mother's eyes and her cheeks were sunken. Boadicea glanced at the hands working with the cloth and herbal water. They were thinner than usual, and she realized that her mother had lost a great deal of weight. She looked almost as ill as her father, but it was fatigue rather than illness. Boadicea hoped that the fatigue had not advanced to the point of no return. "Mother, do we have to worry about someone taking the tribe away from our care?"

"I have suspicions, but nothing that I can say for certain. We sent for you so that if. . . when your father goes to the other world, you can step in and lead us."

"That has always been the plan. What is the problem?"

Durina brushed a strand of hair away from her face. "I don't know. I am so tired."

"Here. Take the baby and let me work with Father. I know how. I've been taught medicine by the best teacher."

Durina shook her head. "I cannot leave him."

"Mother, you will die before him if you do not get some rest. Please, take Sydelle and go sleep. I will do fine. If he awakens, I'll come to get you. It will do Father no good if you collapse on the floor from lack of sleep."

Boadicea took her mother's hand from the water and kissed it. "This hand is only good if your mind is alert enough to tell it what to do."

Durina dropped the cloth in the bowl and placed that hand on Boadicea's. "I suppose that if you trust me with your first-born child, then I should trust you with my husband."

"You can, Mother." Boadicea handed the baby across her father to Durina.

"Wash him often with cold water to keep the fever down. If he awakens, make him drink the broth that's in the red glass bowl. If he will, have him take the cup of medicine that is there." She pointed to a metal cup etched with a flourish of leafy patterns.

"I understand, Mother. Please go to the next room and rest. I will call you when he awakens."

Her mother took the baby. As she was leaving, she looked back, and Boadicea was struck by the fact that her mother must have thought she might be taking her last look at the living Garik. She was relieved when her mother disappeared, but troubled by her own fear that she could not help her father. She took the cloth and began to wipe perspiration from her father's face. His breathing was shallow and irregular. She wrung the cloth out in the bowl again and wiped his arms, clamping her lips together to keep from crying out at the wasted limbs of the once oak-strong Garik.

Perhaps that would be preferable to a weakening of the mind that she remembered her mother's father suffered before he died.

She believed the taking of the mind was worse, and if she were to die, she prayed that it would be before she were robbed of her faculties. Death would be preferable to loss of control—a welcome relief if one could not command one's destiny.

She stared out the window, trying to determine the time of day, when a guttural sound from her father caused her to look down at him. His eyes were open, but shining with fever. "Yes, Father?"

"Boadicea, I have much to tell you." His voice was weak.

"It's all right. I know."

"You must watch for a faction who will try to take the tribe from you." Garik closed his eyes.

Boadicea frowned. Her mother had mentioned Gryffth, but she couldn't imagine that he'd have the gall or power to try anything. She sighed. Although he had always harassed her, she had never taken his threats seriously. What had he said over and over again? She closed her eyes and let her mind wander back across time. He always said . . . Boadicea's eyes popped open. Gryffyth always said that he would be the next chief of the Iceni.

"Boadicea."

It was a command and Boadicea was surprised at the strength of Garik's voice. "I'm here."

"Gryffyth has gathered his friends."

"Don't talk, Father. Save your strength."

"For what? I need to help you and the tribe."

He raised his fingers, for he did not have the energy to raise his hand. Boadicea took his hand between both of hers. It was cold. She leaned closer to hear his words. "I promised Mother I would get her when you awoke."

"Not yet." Garik coughed. "I want to talk to you alone first."

Boadicea stayed quiet, for she could barely hear him. "I'm listening."

"There are friends of Gryffyth who would follow him in a war to gain this tribe." Garik squeezed her hand lightly. "You cannot let that happen, for it would weaken the unity between this tribe and your husband's. It is only through unity that there will be strength enough to resist any enemy who comes. The Romans grow brave. Their eyes have seen our land and our gold."

Although Boadicea was concerned about the Romans, she was angrier at the audacity of Gryffyth's traitorous ways. She resolved that he would not get away with an overthrow even if she had to kill him. They had been enemies from childhood, and she should've expected this, but to hear her father put into words her mother's fears alarmed her. Gryffyth could be a formidable foe as he had been schooled by her father in the art of combat. She hoped that he hadn't learned his lessons as well as she had.

"I understand, Father. I will fight to the death if that is what it takes to rebuke Gryffyth's attempt at overthrow. I wish I had time to send for Prasutagus."

"The messenger would never get through. Gryffyth's spies are everywhere."

"Is he powerful?"

"I know not. The sickness causes sleep to overcome me whenever I try to listen to my own spies." Garik's eyes opened suddenly. "You must win."

"I know I have many who will fight by my side, but I have a plan that may save a civil war," Boadicea said. "I shall talk to Gryffyth first."

"He won't listen, but others might."

"I hope so."

"I fear that before the night is through, I shall see the mysterious other world." Garik's bright eyes closed and his fingers loosened their grip.

Boadicea was seized with fear that he had already gone to the other world, and she leaned forward, but was relieved to find he was still breathing. He felt cold to her touch. She pulled the covers up to his chin and tucked them about him. It would be a long and dreary night. Who could she trust to take a note to Prasutagus? No one. She needed every one of the men who had come with her. Besides, she needed to fight this battle alone. If she sent a note and it was intercepted, her plan of surprise would be useless.

Her head ached as it always seemed to do when she had a problem. She squeezed her eyes shut. In the distance she heard a horse neighing. Her eyes popped open. It was a sign from the gods. The answer was given to her—she would write a note and Thayne would take it. Boadicea went to the kitchen cupboard where the writing materials were kept. The sun had dropped almost below the horizon. She lit a candle, placed it on the wooden table, and removed a small piece of vellum that had writing on one side.

Determining it was a formula well known to both her and her mother and turned it over. She wrote the words carefully. She wasn't used to writing much, but the Greek her father had insisted she learn was still at the front of her memory. Fortunately, Prasutagus had also been forced by his father to learn the language used for household accounts.

She signed her name, rolled the vellum, and secured it with a piece of rawhide. She took the candle and went back to check on her father. She felt guilty for not waking her mother, but decided that the walk to the corral wouldn't take long. It was almost dark, and it wouldn't appear unusual for her to check on her horse at this time. However, anyone watching her would think it odd if they were to see her turn the horse out.

Thayne saw her, tossed his head back, circled the corral once before he approached the gate. Boadicea scratched him under his forelock. "You must go quickly to Prasutagus as my messenger." Boadicea tied the small rolled-up vellum securely to Thayne's halter with rawhide.

Holding the halter, she pulled the gate open and led the horse through it. "Don't circle back for me." Boadicea slapped him on the rump, and Thayne trotted forward. He stopped once and looked back as if to see if she were really serious. Boadicea waved him onward and he snorted, then cantered down the road toward Prasutagus' village. She watched him until he disappeared.

Boadicea walked as quickly as she could in the newly darkened night. There was no moon, and it seemed clouds might bring rain. Her thoughts returned to her father, and she ran the rest of the way to the hut. She slipped through the doorway and was relieved to hear her father's ragged breathing. She crossed the room and settled herself beside him, laying her cool hand on his hot one and fell asleep.

Boadicea was awakened by a hand on her hair. She sat up slowly, and stared at her father.

"Boadicea, it is my time. I have seen the other world in my dreams, and I am not afraid. It is a beautiful place full of streams, oak trees, and singing birds. It is peopled with my family, and they wait for me with arms outstretched. You should have no fear of death, either, for I will be waiting for you in that same place, then we will live again on this earth."

"I only fear for my loneliness between the times you leave me and when I join you." Boadicea felt a tear slide down her face.

"Stay and help your mother." Garik closed his eyes. When next he spoke, it was in a whisper. "Have you thought about Gryffyth? What do you plan to do to the traitor?"

Boadicea leaned down. "I shall stop him any way that I can. If I win a battle of words, then Gryffyth will be banished. If he wages war against me and I don't kill him in battle, I shall execute him as a warning to others. You have taught me that one should never let the enemy live, for to do so would be like a wound that is left to fester and erupt at a later time with more pestilence. I shall not weaken. I shall not think of the times we spent together as children, for the child in me no longer exists, and the child no longer exists in Gryffyth."

"You are a good warrior, my daughter. You deserve to be chief." Garik pushed himself into a sitting position.

"Father! You are to rest." Boadicea couldn't believe he had a surge of energy. His color looked better, his eyes less fevered.

"Summon your mother and bring my granddaughter to me. My time has come."

"It does not seem so."

"Do what I ask."

Boadicea hastened to the room where her mother slept. The sleeping baby was between her mother and the wall. She thought she would have trouble waking her exhausted mother, but to her surprise, Durina opened her eyes as soon as Boadicea leaned over her.

"Has he awakened?"

"He asks for you. He seems better. Perhaps . . ."

"Shhhh. Don't tempt the gods." Durina pushed back the cover and sat up, glancing back at the baby, then left the room. Boadicea picked up Sydelle and followed her mother.

Boadicea stood aside while Durina whispered to her husband. A moment later, Durina motioned for her. Boadicea held Sydelle so that her father could see her.

He smiled. "She is getting prettier by the day. She looks like you did when you were an infant. Let me hold her."

Boadicea laid the child next to her father. He put his wasted hand on her chest and watched her breathe. The baby opened her eyes and, squirming around, looked up at her grandfather. She gurgled and he chuckled. Boadicea's heart was filled with wonder at this exchange between the generations.

"I'm tired, Durina. I need the permanent rest that belongs to the elderly and sick. I don't want to fight this sickness any longer. Help me to lie down."

Durina blinked rapidly to hold back tears as she helped her husband.

"Boadicea, fight Gryffyth the way that I taught you. First with words, then with a sword if you must. Use the speaking stone in the center of the village. I have prayed. The gods tell me that you will be victorious."

"I will do as you command, Father." He closed his eyes. His hand, the one that lay across Sydelle, became limp, and his head fell to the side. Durina gasped, then dropped to her knees and said the prayers that would help Garik cross to the other world.

Boadicea picked up her child and left the hut to tell her people of their leader's death. She walked proud and tall, for at the moment of Garik's death, she had become the chief. These were her people, and the meaning of her life became clear. She wondered how long it would take Gryffyth to act against her.

Garik's funeral was barely finished when Boadicea noticed signs of unrest. People averted her gaze or pretended not to see her as she came toward them. She had spent a lot of time walking about the village, getting the feel for the mood of the people. It wasn't good. She knew they trusted her ability, so that was not the problem. More than likely Gryffyth was at fault.

Dyer's Alley lay ahead of Boadicea, and she scanned the scene. Only Gwendolyn continued to work in the dye vats. Would she tell Boadicea anything?

"Peace be with you, Gwendolyn."

"Oh." Gwendolyn whirled around; colors dripped from the cloth she held.

"I didn't mean to startle you."

"I didn't hear you."

"Where are your children? Usually you have at least one knee-baby clinging to your skirts," Boadicea said.

"At my mother's hut. She is in a safer . . ." Gwendolyn's face turned scarlet.

"Safe from what?"

Gwendolyn shook her head. Tears cascaded down her cheeks.

"If you are loyal to me, then you'll speak plainly."

"I can't."

"Can't?"

"Gryffyth threatened . . ." Gwendolyn's hand flew to her mouth. Streaks of color dripped down her arm.

"Who has he threatened?" When Gwendolyn didn't answer, she said, "you can tell me."

Gwendolyn wiped her hands on her tunic and sniffled. "I can't."

"Do you want me as your chief?"

"Oh, yes! Gryffyth would be cruel."

"I can fight him better if I know what scheme he has concocted," Boadicea said.

Gwendolyn's silence irritated her, and she knew she didn't have time to cajole information from the dyer's wife. "Would you and your children be better served by Gryffyth?"

"No!"

"Then talk to me! I have need of information!" Boadicea was aware that she had commanded Gwendolyn, but no matter. She was her chief.

"He has threatened everyone in the village. If we help you, he will torture our children before our eyes. We are frightened and so do nothing."

"Am I so weak that people fear Gryffyth more than me?" Boadicea stormed away from Gwendolyn and charged up the road towards her parents' hut.

As the time went on, Boadicea noticed that some twenty or thirty young men would disappear for hours. They weren't working in the fields, so they must be practicing war games somewhere. Boadicea jaws clenched as she worked to control her anger. Always death brought confrontation and a struggle for power. If she could prevent bloodshed, she would. Except for Gryffyth's blood. She knew he was her enemy. Gwendolyn had provided the proof. He would die for his treachery.

She looked around the village. She could win the war with words, but would Gryffyth allow it? She was not from a long line of chiefs without reason. The determination to win had been taught to her until it was as natural as breathing.

The wind was strong and the day gray as ashes. Boadicea walked to the corral to see if Thayne had returned. She frowned when she saw that he had not. She couldn't whistle for him. Too many people knew her great horse and too many people would wonder where he was.

On her way back through the village, she saw Gryffyth and a band of men armed with spears. If they had planned to go hunting, they would have had bows. Boadicea regarded them carefully. These were men who as boys had been the village trouble-makers. Only Gryffyth had been brave enough to torment her when they were children. She smiled to herself. They were long on talk, but too cowardly to be long on action. It was almost unfair.

Five of them stood in the center of the village in the clearing. She knew several more would be hovering out of sight. During good weather, this clearing was used for open air meetings. She stopped, her eyes narrowing. Except for a knife that was fastened to her left arm and within easy reach, she was unarmed. She looked around. The villagers watched from doorways, their children sequestered out of harm's way. She had no desire to level the village. These people were innocent for the most part. The villagers were her family and friends, and they only wanted to view her ability to lead them.

She stopped at the edge of the clearing. Gryffyth stared at her, and for the first time she realized his jealousy had turned to hatred. She remembered all the wicked tricks he had played on her as a child, and her own malice bubbled up, forgotten transgressions by Gryffyth remembered.

Boadicea stepped on the speaking stone. This was the first time she had ever done so. She was two feet above the audience. She turned slowly on the huge boulder and stared at the crowd. In the past, her father had stood here. She chose this place on purpose to emphasize the fact that she belonged, and Gryffyth was the usurper. She waited for more people to gather. They came hesitantly, slowly, but with a great deal of curiosity.

"I stand alone to face you. I stand here as your chief. I have been chief for four days." Boadicea looked at one of the men who stood next to Gryffyth. He could not hold her gaze, and he looked down. "I stand here as the daughter of Garik, your chief. He expected me to be your leader when he died, and he trained me to that end. Who can lead you better?"

Gryffyth put one foot on the speaking stone and held his sword high. "I can. I have been trained by the same man as Boadicea. I am stronger and have fought the Brigantes. I am fierce and will let no one take these lands."

"Ah, Gryffyth. That is no more than any of the men in this village. For shame. Do you not remember your promise to Garik that you would be my lieutenant, to ride beside me, not before me? Who trained you to this end? Garik did."

"None of that matters." Gryffyth put the tip of his sword under Boadicea's chin.

She smiled. "Go ahead and slice my throat. I don't stand alone."

Gryffyth laughed. "But you do stand alone." He motioned with his free hand. "Bring the horse."

Two men led Thayne forward, but stopped twenty feet away. Boadicea held her facial expression stone-like. The horse appeared to be unharmed. He had a muddy flank where it seemed he'd fallen— no doubt brought down by ropes. His nostrils flared and he tossed his head.

"Am I supposed to be frightened of my own horse?"

"I have something better with which to frighten you." Gryffyth held up the vellum that she thought had been sent to Prasutagus.

"That is nothing."

"It is a note asking your husband to come to your aid if needed." Gryffyth spat on the ground. "I have companions who watched everything that you did. We captured the horse as soon as he had ridden from the corral. Did you think we wouldn't know that animal?"

Boadicea felt the prick of the sword on her neck and the warm blood that trickled down her tunic. "Gryffyth, you are no leader. You take on an unarmed woman. Who among you dares to question the wisdom of a chief who led you in victory and later in peace? Who is stupid enough to follow a coward? The gods make certain that cowards die a cowardly death."

"Quiet!" Gryffyth leaped on the stone.

Boadicea countered his movement with a foot to his stomach. She shoved him off the speaking stone. She laughed when he hit the ground with a thud. "Who dares go against Boadicea whose name means 'Victory'?" Boadicea tossed her hair back. "Who will throw the first spear? Who will strike the first blow? Who will be the first to die by Boadicea's hand?"

Gryffyth scrambled up the stone at the same time one of his accomplices grabbed Boadicea's hand that held the knife she'd pulled from its hiding place. She turned from Gryffyth and pushed the man's face with her left hand. He slipped aside and tumbled to the ground. She tossed the knife up, caught the tip of the blade with her right hand, and sent it into the man's chest.

She took advantage of Gryffyth's hesitation and kicked him off the speaking stone again. Boadicea held her arm up, letting the sleeve of the tunic fall, revealing a long gash turned from red to silver with time. "Who has forgotten the joy I had in killing the enemy when they attacked Prasutagus' tribe?" She glared at each of the men who stood before her in turn, then she smiled, baring her teeth. "Who will make my happiness complete by letting me kill the other traitors among us? Who is willing to go to the other world with Gryffyth? Who remembers that I am also a priestess and can call the gods to me?"

Boadicea observed as the people on the edge of the crowd began to disperse. They walked away without saying a word, but in not saying anything, re-affirmed their loyalty to Garik's daughter. The knot of men around Gryffyth began to shrink. She couldn't help smiling as she saw the hatred in his eyes turn to astonishment and then fear. He would go kicking and screaming to the other world. She would dispatch him quickly even weaponless. She could kill him with her bare hands.

Boadicea felt a presence next to her, and she looked down. "Mother, what are you doing here? It could be dangerous."

"Not for us, Boadicea, but it is for Gryffyth. I have brought you your father's legacy." Durina held a sword hilt upwards for Boadicea.

Boadicea took the sword and turned toward Gryffyth. He moved quickly and picked up his sword from the ground.

"An unfair fight, Gryffyth, for my father's sword has been blessed by the gods!" Boadicea leaped from the stone and advanced.

"Not so. You will die by my hand." Gryffyth met her sword thrust with one of his own followed by a backhanded swing meant to slice into her arm.

Boadicea danced backwards and drew him away from the crowd who had stopped to watch. She countered his next thrust with one that was so powerful both swords rang out. She noted with anger that Gryffyth wore leather padding.

She went on the defensive to preserve her strength and her vital organs since she had no armor. "Show me what my father taught you! Let's see if you were man enough to learn the lessons."

"I am more the man than you," Gryffyth swung his sword, and Boadicea leaped back.

"No matter, Coward." Boadicea moved around in a tight circle, drawing Gryffyth around her in an arc. She parried and thrust as she forced Gryffyth to take three steps to her one. His sword arced toward her over and over, but each time she deflected the blow meant to kill her. Gryffyth's temper hindered his thinking, and as soon as Boadicea realized it, she had the advantage. Cooly she maneuvered the enemy until fatigue showed in his slowed movements.

It was time to end the skirmish. Boadicea was ready for the fatal thrust, for she saw that Gryffyth faltered once.

"Look out!" Durina shouted.

Her warning came too late and Boadicea tripped over a branch that must've been thrown by Gryffyth's friend. She rolled as she hit the ground, but too late. Her sword flew from her hand and as Boadicea crawled toward it, Orthe kicked it out of reach. Gryffyth grinned as he advanced toward her.

"The pride of the Iceni has fallen," Gryffyth said. He kicked her in the ribs and knocked her on her back. He placed his sword on Boadicea's breast. "No husband comes to your aid."

"I don't need aid. I am not yet finished." Boadicea smiled and whistled a shrill blast that split the air.

The look on Gryffyth's face showed puzzlement that turned to fear when he heard Thayne's thundering hooves. He turned his head and stared at the beast who bore down on him. Thayne roared. Boadicea grabbed the blade with both hands and shoved the hilt into Gryffyth's belly. He fell backwards and the Iceni Chief sprinted to her feet. She ignored her stinging hands and the blood that cascaded down her fingers. In one smooth motion, she switched the sword around and thrust it through Gryffyth's abdomen with so much strength from the gods that the sword cut through leather, skin, guts, and bone. She kept pushing until he fell to the ground where she pinned him neatly to the earth.

Boadicea looked down at the man who had once been a boy, stoning her cats and teasing her horses. His eyes glazed over and blood gurgled from his mouth. He had been without conscience even though his round face had deemed otherwise. His brown hair was cut straight across his forehead, and it was with some amusement that Boadicea noticed his stomach rose higher than his chest. He had eaten too much in his lifetime to be a good warrior. He had been as flabby in life as he was in death.

Boadicea looked at two of his comrades. "If you wish the same fate, then stay in this village past sunrise tomorrow." She bent down and yanked Gryffyth's sword from the circle of blood and viscera.

"Leave at once and take Gryffyth with you. If you are still here at sunset, it will be your last." Boadicea kicked Gryffyth with her foot as she left the clearing. She deliberately turned her back on Gryffyth's companions to show her contempt. She had no fear of them. Their strength had come with empty phrases and promises from Gryffyth.

Boadicea walked through the streets of her village with her head held high and disdain still visible on her features. She was the chief, and she had proven herself. Now it was time to thank the gods for her victory, then she would be ready to see Prasutagus. Together they would rule the vast lands of her father and his father. Together they would be strong and their people would prosper.

CHAPTER

VIII

SUETONIUS PACED BACK AND FORTH in the atrium. He felt like a stranger in his birth place he left over two decades ago. He glanced across the room at his mother who sat in the sun, her hair caught up with jeweled pins in one of the latest styles. She threaded a needle, started to sew, but glanced at Suetonius.

"Mother, what keeps my father? Is he not at least curious about my next assignment?"

Vivianne shrugged her shoulders. "I do not know." She put her sewing in her lap and looked at him. "Your father has been wary of late. Another assassination attempt has been made against Emperor Claudius. Your father fears reprisal."

"Why? Father has nothing to do with these attempts." Suetonius whirled around. "Has he?"

"Of course not. He would do nothing to hinder your climb to a governorship." Vivianne waved her hand. "He suspects that one of his business acquaintances has talked about doing away with our demented emperor, and your father doesn't want the circle of investigation to include him. Caius is working with a group of men to decide how best to show their allegiance."

"Do I hear my name?"

"Ah, Father. There you are." Suetonius clasped his father's hand. "I have an announcement."

"Caius, do sit next to me." Vivianne moved over, gathered her sewing, and patted the couch.

"What is this announcement?" Caius kissed his wife on the cheek and sat.

"Our beloved Emperor Claudius has seen fit to send me to Mauretania to quell the rebellion."

"That's what you wanted to tell us?" Vivianne asked. She frowned. "Isn't that across the Mediterranean?"

"Precisely. Northern Africa, to be even more exact," Suetonius said.

"A good opportunity for you," Caius said.

"I don't think you have to worry about the emperor doubting your loyalty, Father. Else he wouldn't have appointed me. I may call the governorship of Mauretania my own after I conquer the rebellious natives."

"Suetonius, I had just become used to you being near me in my old age," Vivianne said.

"You're not old, Mother. Your eyesight is perfect, you look young, and you survived the rearing of Zia." Suetonius grinned.

"Zia is difficult still. She is in love at last, but the poor man cannot understand her. He often yells at her!" Vivianne said.

"Cannot abide her intolerable temper you mean," Caius said.

"Don't talk so. She's had a difficult life adjusting to . . . to everything. Why she still grieves for Aloisia."

"Who?" Suetonius asked.

"Trista."

Suetonius felt his face get hot. He always forgot Trista's birth name although he'd seen it on the urn often enough. He wished, as he often did, that Trista and the baby had not died. He would've liked a son and a wife. Would the boy have been fiery-tempered like his mother? Or sweet as honey as Trista could often be?

"Son, you haven't answered me," Caius said. "When do you leave?"

"In a week or two. Lucian has assembled most of the army and supplies. He works to get us ships. That is always the most difficult."

Screams echoed down the hall from the bed chambers. "Ah, Zia is home," Suetonius said.

The screams preceded Zia as she charged through the atrium followed by a man who bellowed as she stormed into the atrium.

"Don't you dare leave me in the middle of an argument!" Pax stopped as soon as he saw Vivianne. "Forgive me," he stammered.

"My daughter brings out the best in you, I see," Vivianne said.

"Mother!" Zia glared at Pax. "He doesn't understand why I won't marry him."

"Why won't you marry him? Have you grown a soft heart in your old age? You don't want to torture him as you have always tortured us?" Suetonius flinched as Zia landed a blow on his chest.

"Zia!" Caius shouted. "Your manners."

"I care not one fig for manners. This oaf wants to marry me so we can have children. By the gods, that is the last thing I need."

"What? To be married or to have children?" Suetonius asked. "Is it that you're afraid you'll have brats?"

"Suetonius, I expect better of you," Vivianne said.

"Sorry, Mother." He sighed at the look his mother gave him. "I'm sorry, Zia. I should never talk to you that way, especially in front of Pax."

"She'll marry me," Pax said.

"No, I won't."

"You love me."

"Never."

Vivianne stood and tried to shoo them from the atrium. "Your brother is about to go to Mauretania, and I need to talk. . . ."

"Mauretania?" Zia whirled around. "Isn't that in Africa?"

"Yes," Suetonius said.

"Will you be safe?"

"As safe as always." Suetonius gathered the tearful woman into his arms. "Don't worry about me, Zia. I have Lucian who guards me always. There is no better friend."

"Can you not retire? I miss you so. You're gone for months and months."

"It's my life." Suetonius hugged his sister. "Who will protect you while I'm gone?"

"I need no protection."

"Zia, you aren't telling the truth. Who do you need?"

Zia looked at Pax and smiled. "I need someone who will love me for my temper."

"I love you for your temper," Pax said.

"I expect to attend a wedding before I go to Mauretania. It would give me peace of mind," Suetonius said.

"I, too, would like to have peace of mind," Caius said.

Pax grinned. "We shall oblige. Hush, Zia. You have nothing to say."

Vivianne laughed as her daughter clamped her mouth shut. "Come, Zia. We have many plans to make and a short time to do it."

Suetonius pulled back the flap and looked across the sea of leather tents that stretched out before him in strict order. His men stepped out of their tents, one and two at a time, stretched, looked at the sky, then wandered off toward the latrines. He blinked at the sun that peered back at him from between peaks of the mountain range that stretched as far as he could see. He inhaled, noticed that the air was humid, and licked his lips. There was no longer a salty taste. They were far enough inland from the Mediterranean that the air carried no trace of the sea.

Suetonius felt his chin. The stubble was there. It was time to shave before getting ready to move out. He let the tent flap drop and turned toward the pitcher of hot water brought to him by an infantryman. He wondered why the army regulations required one to shave. It was a waste of time, inconvenient, and uncomfortable most of the time. Ah, well. He was not to question these things; he was to fight the battles and bring home the victories. Someday he wanted to have his own governorship. It would be profitable and nearly trouble-free. It would be good to live the last years of his life doing nothing more than giving dinners and parties and checking with his lieutenants to see how his corner of the world fared. He wanted to go out with grace and ease. His biggest worry would be whether or not the taxes had been collected.

Suetonius dipped the shaving blade in the water and leaned forward to see himself in the shiny metal mirror. The first scrape was always the hardest because of the sound it made. That first stroke always caused Suetonius to shudder, but by the third stroke, he'd forgotten the sound as he reviewed the day to come. He always went to sleep at night after planning the following day, and he always started his day by going over the plan to look for flaws.

The sounds of camp coming to life drifted through his tent as he rinsed the cut whiskers from his face with cold water to close the pores. He grabbed a towel and wiped his face. Now only a few moments to dress.

Today would be a difficult march in terrain that would sap the strength of his men. The day would begin to cool, then get hot. By evening, the air would be cool again. The farther up the mountains the army climbed, the colder the air felt, until it would seem that winter had arrived out of season.

Suetonius checked his clothing for ease of movement, then went to the map case that hung on a tent pole. He pulled out a map and unrolled it across his cot to study the mountain range, satisfied with the audacity of this move against the enemy from an unexpected direction. Like Alexander the Great, whose military exploits he'd studied, Suetonius planned to cross the impossible mountains behind the enemy and smash them flat.

The surprise to the enemy would be worth the ten or twelve day march. The enemy would learn the wrath of Rome and its army. Suetonius snorted. The Mauretanians would learn the hard way what happened to traitorous nations that gave up the relative freedom and safety they enjoyed under Roman rule for so-called "independence." They had chosen to align themselves with a weak neighbor, and they would pay the price for their stupidity and deception. Instead of being protected by the army of Rome, they would be annihilated. The weak and the foolish needed to be culled.

Soon the command to strike the tents would be given, and Suetonius rolled up the map. His favorite map maker had prepared it for him after spending hours doing research. There were places that were sketched in with charcoal instead of color. The map maker had explained to Suetonius that he could only find one reference for those places. He asked that Suetonius to fill in the gaps.

The lifting of the tent flap and the subsequent entry of his second in command reminded Suetonius that it was time to mount up and begin the climb. "Good morning, Lucian, old friend. How goes the morning?"

"The men have eaten and are packed. I am ready to leave whenever you're ready. I could have spent another four or five hours in bed. I think age is catching up with me."

"Never admit that in front of the ladies, Lucian. Come, let's mount up."

Suetonius looked around the tent to make certain his trunks were fastened. "Remember when we had to break down the tents and carry all the things that belonged to our leaders?"

Lucian chuckled. "We hated it."

"And now we get to walk away and have our underlings do the work we always hated." Suetonius slapped Lucian on the back. "Let's mount up and lead. After all, we are the leaders."

Suetonius pointed to the town laid out below them. "There is no activity, Lucian. We are not expected from this direction."

"Your plan worked, Suetonius. We have the element of surprise. Tomorrow we shall strike."

"Yes." Suetonius turned and clambered over the rocks that separated him from the outcropping of granite where he had left his knapsack. He was proud of the fact that he hadn't even become short of breath from the climb. He stood high and looked down at the men below him, in various states of rest. Some were flat out on the ground, sleeping while others leaned against trees and talked. A few groups of men played games. "Gambling, no doubt, but no harm," Suetonius thought.

The sun glinted off the shields propped up near the men, and if Suetonius listened carefully, he could hear laughter drifting towards him. His men were relaxed, secure in the knowledge that they were the best-trained army in the world. Tomorrow would be yet another test of the well-trained machine that had marched across the world and conquered it.

"Come, Lucian. We need to discuss some last minute details, and then we rest." Suetonius turned to the men who stood behind him. "You are to maintain a watch on the town. Report any unusual activity immediately to me. Light no fires tonight. Tomorrow before dawn we will slip through the pass and surprise them." Suetonius returned the salute given him, turned on his heel, and climbed down the trail toward the campsite.

Suetonius was ready for the battle, the most important one in his life so far. He was calm. He was always calm on the day before a battle, and he often wondered if his heart stopped beating and his blood stopped flowing. It seemed as if he were capable of suspending all thoughts of anything but the battle ahead. He was the perfect fighting machine at this point and would remain so until long after the last casualty had died.

Suetonius rode up and down the front lines urging his men to move forward, oblivious to the noise of shields clashing and men grunting. He hoped they would destroy the hapless Mauretanians without many losses. The enemy was not weak. A soldier ran at him to attack. Suetonius raised his shield with his left hand and speared him with his right. He felt the warmth of the man's blood as it splattered across his thigh, and he rode on. His voice rasped as it usually did, but he shouted orders, knowing that his men had faith in him. They followed his orders without hesitation, and he noted with pride that the army he had built was strong and true to the Roman philosophy of each man as a part of something better.

His horse stumbled, and Suetonius gripped his knees tightly against the heaving sides of the beast. He wished he had a place for his feet. He hated having to hold his thighs so tightly against the sides of his horse, for at the end of a battle, it took a good massage to get the cramps out of them. Older generals told him that the cramps got worse as one got older, but it would be almost certain death to be unseated. Suetonius knew he would not be able to get back on his horse without help. He looked down to see what had made his horse trip, and he saw the body. It was not in Roman armor, and he rode on, glad of one less notation to make in the loss book.

Shouting behind him caused him to pull his horse around just in time to raise his shield and deflect an arrow. He nodded his thanks to Lucian and cantered off down the line to give the order for the battering rams to be brought forward. The defenses outside the walls were essentially depleted, and now the citizens and soldiers inside the walls would pay for their treachery. Suetonius watched as the teams of men, six to a ram with three battering rams in each set, lined up outside the southern gates. Sweat glistened off the soldiers, outlining their ox-like muscles as they moved the battering rams forward. They moved in a rhythm learned from months of working together in tandem. It was like a dance done by the women he'd seen in the east. The wheels reflected the movement of the men, first by rolling forward, then backward, bouncing off the heavy wooden gates until, with a splintering crash, the huge logs broke through.

"Wood against wood and man against man," Suetonius thought. He winced as arrows flew through the splintered gates, felling some of his men. It was painful to lose good men. After months of leading them, living with them, and training them, he felt the loss keenly.

He ordered a small force to push through the cracks in the gate and then ordered the second and third battering rams into place. At his signal, they finished tearing the gates off their hinges. Another signal from him, and the army poured into the town. He kicked his horse and hurried to join Lucian. It would be a matter of minutes before they had the town under control.

Suetonius and Lucian rode through the gates in the middle of the army, threading their way between the men who no longer had to fight. The two leaders made their way to the edge of the marching army and watched as the men flowed through the gates and spread out like water that had spilled from a pitcher.

Suetonius looked over his shoulder to check the height of the sun when he felt a blow to his chest, and he was knocked from his horse. The sound of his armor hitting the ground rang in his ears, and he instinctively tightened his grasp on his shield while pulling it over his chest. He looked around frantically trying to locate the enemy who had done this to him. His ears still rang and his chest stung, but that was the least of his worries. He whipped his head around at the thud next to him and was surprised to see Lucian on the ground next to him. Suetonius sat up and reached out to his friend who was covered with blood.

"Fear not, Suetonius. It is not my blood."

"Praise to Mithras. You saved me."

"From a battle ax."

Suetonius leaned closer to his friend. "You knocked me from my horse, didn't you? You did it to save me."

Lucian smiled. He tightened his grip on Suetonius' hand. "It is my duty."

"And duty calls me. Let us fight." Suetonius leaped up and pulled Lucian to his feet.

Lucian nodded and turned toward a ruckus. "This one is for me!" He brandished his sword and charged into a group of Mauretanians who had two Romans surrounded.

Suetonius laughed as his friend's voice drifted to him. He thought Lucian hollered, "Victory! Victory! Victory!" He laughed further when his own horse trotted toward Lucian. "You ungrateful animal! I'm your owner."

"Excuse me, General."

Suetonius turned. "Yes?"

"The capitol has been taken. Mauretania is yours, sir."

Suetonius nodded to show he understood. The governorship would soon follow.

Suetonius leaned against the frame of the window and looked out toward the sea that bordered Mauretania. The sails were like pieces of white mosaic tile against the sapphire blue of the Mediterranean. The breeze from the sea carried salt with it, and when Suetonius licked his lips he could taste it. Below him the soldiers marched in small units to keep order and prevent an uprising. The sun glinted off armor and sparkled like the sun on the sea. His emotions reeled between despair for his fallen men and ecstasy at his victory.

He left the window and walked to the table where the rolled parchment lay. He picked it up, pulled the roll down from the top, and looked at the words that gave him the governorship of Mauretania. The seal that graced the document was that of Emperor Claudius. He had had but two conversations with the Emperor before his invasion of this country. Some said the Emperor was stupid, but Suetonius could not believe that. Claudius was shrewd beneath a show of obtuseness. It was a clever ruse to fool one's enemies and make them complacent.

Suetonius let the scroll roll up and held it against his chest. He had gotten what he wanted. Life would be easier now.

Suetonius turned back to the window and looked at the ships. One of these days a ship would arrive with his favorite map maker aboard. The new governor of Mauretania required a map maker. The reply had been swift. Suetonius had read the letter over and had decided that it was full of excitement. The old man, Rodas, was indeed happy to be coming, although he had expressed a certain sadness at leaving his grandchildren.

A note from Suetonius' mother expressed her excitement at Zia's pregnancy that seemed to have improved her disposition. His father was pleased with his appointment of the governorship and admitted that he bragged about it at the baths.

Suetonius looked at the blue sky and the blue sea. A happy color for a happy day. He had earned the easy life after years of being a soldier.

Blue. He looked at the sea again. It had changed to a paler color—the color of Trista's eyes. Suetonius saw her face clearly in spite of the chasm of time that separated him from the living Trista. Had he known about her pregnancy . . . Suetonius shook his head to rid himself of thoughts of what couldn't be changed. He would follow the plan of the gods.

Vivianne laughed and whirled about. "Caius, this news is too good to be true!"

"All right. The letter from Suetonius is a forgery. He is not coming home after five years overseas."

"I must tell Zia and Elysia. They are both so busy with their children and husbands that they rarely come home. But they will to see Suetonius."

"We should plan a banquet," Caius said.

"Not until he's been home awhile. I don't want to share my son with anyone but family."

"You have to have a banquet. People expect it."

"I'll have a banquet, but not until he's home a week or two." Vivianne whirled around again. "I'll have to have his room done over."

"Don't paint over the mural. He loves the mural that Trista painted."

"Never would I do that."

Tears filled Vivianne's eyes and made Caius shimmer. She pushed her chair back, not hearing the scraping sound that usually irritated her, and went to the window. The orchard was fresh and green with spots of peach color peeking through the leaves. It had rained in the morning leaving every leaf, every peach dewy. This was a favorite time of year for her, and the peaches were her time-keeper for the seasons. Her favorite season would always be tinged with the sadness of Trista's death.

A hot tear skimmed across her cheek and dropped on her stola. She turned so that Caius would not see her. She felt his arm around her shoulders, and instinctively nestled in his arms.

Caius cleared his throat. "I haven't seen you like this since Elysia was married."

Vivianne blushed. "How did you know about that?"

"I know you better than you think I do." He kissed her cheek. "I would be worried if you did not cry for your children. You have always been an excellent mother to them."

Vivianne shook her head. "I used to think I had failed with Zia, but she seems to thrive with Pax. I tried so hard with her, and the more I tried, the worse she became."

"My mother was just as contrary. There is nothing you can do to take the meanness out of her soul."

"Don't say such things, Caius. The gods will hear you and punish you."

"Nonsense. The gods understand Zia. I often wonder if she weren't sent back from the other world so that they could have peace." Caius laughed. "Even with my mother's awful way, she was married finally. My father loved her angry manner. Pax seems to be the same with Zia."

Vivianne pushed away from Caius. With her hands on her hips and her eyes narrowed, she glared at him. "What a terrible thing to say about your mother and your daughter. Two blows in one sentence. For shame, Caius."

Caius laughed. "You're a hypocrite, Wife. You've thought the same things about your darling daughter and my wonderful mother."

"So I have, but I had the good grace to keep those thoughts to myself." Vivianne turned toward the orchard. "I think of Trista every time I look at a peach tree."

"It was so many years ago, and yet you still grieve?" Caius asked.

"I suppose I'll always wonder what our life would've been like had Trista and the baby lived. She was special to me."

Vivianne turned to Caius and kissed him. She pulled back and smiled. "It'll be noisy and busy with Suetonius here. All his friends and your friends will want to hear his stories. We don't have much time to be alone."

"Is there a promise of things to come in that statement?"

"Yes." Vivianne kissed her husband again.

"The gods are cruel." Vivianne sat next to the bier of her husband. Her hand rested on his chest. "They took him from me when I needed someone the most. Remember when you were appointed governor of Mauretania? You came home and we partied until dawn?"

"How long ago has that been?" Suetonius asked.

"I think about six summers or so. I've never seen your father so proud as he was at that moment."

"He bragged too much. I was embarrassed."

Vivianne chuckled. "You were strutting through the villa pounding everyone on the back. You were not embarrassed."

"I am sorry, Mother, that I was not here when he died." Suetonius looked at his father's face. He seemed at peace and youthful-looking in spite of the illness that had taken his body away pound by pound the last year. Twice Suetonius had been recalled from Mauretania, but twice his father had rallied. This time he could not.

"He knew you were coming home again. He knew." Vivianne sighed. "It's time. Look at all the people who came to say good-bye." She kissed Caius on the cheek, nodded to the funeral director, and turned to Suetonius.

"Take me home. I cannot watch." Vivianne allowed herself to be sheltered by Suetonius as they left the crematorium through a crowd of people.

The walk to the villa was eerily quiet. Suetonius was used to the sounds of soldiers patrolling all hours of the day outside his headquarters. He was used to voices as his men shouted at each other. Now all he heard was the quiet sobbing of his mother. How was he going to tell her that he had been appointed to another governorship farther away? He might have to ask for retirement from the military. An unpleasant thought, indeed.

The servants helped Vivianne to her bed. It was odd to see his mother without energy and content to be put to bed during the day. Suetonius entered his own sleeping quarters. He had much to do.

He looked in the mirror above the wash basin. Gray mixed through the dark hair in both his beard and his hair reminded him how many years he'd been in service to Rome. Maybe it was time to quit.

He turned at the sound of scratching on the door jamb. "Lucian! Good to see you."

"I followed you and your mother home, but didn't want to disturb you."

"Come, sit. We must talk," Suetonius said.

"You want to retire and stay close to your mother."

"How did you know?"

"I know you very well." Lucian plopped down on the bed. "Would she want you to give up Britannia?"

"Would I want him to give up what?" Vivianne appeared in the doorway. "I heard your wonderful voice, Lucian, and I had to see you."

Lucian leaped from the bed, extended his hands to Vivianne, and kissed her on the cheek.

"Did I disturb you?"

"Not at all. I found it boring to be in bed during the day." Vivianne stared at her son. "What have you not told me?"

"I wanted to spare you." Suetonius glanced at his half-packed trunk. Or was it half-unpacked? How could he know?

"Lucian, tell me about this assignment? Is it important?"

"It is very important. Emperor Nero has appointed your son to the governorship of Britannia. It is a great honor."

"Not so great, Lucian. It is the most barbaric place that we've ever tried to conquer." Suetonius frowned. "Who would want to go there?"

"Is it more prestigious than Mauretania?" Vivianne asked.

"I think so." Suetonius shrugged. "But at my age, why should I want to leave the comforts of Rome?"

"What do you want?" Vivianne asked.

"I don't know."

"Suetonius, I am your mother. I know you. What do you want?"

"I want the governorship of Britannia, but not if it means leaving you alone." Suetonius ran his hand through his hair.

"I am not alone. I have Zia and her sweet little girls. Pax is a great help and comfort to me. I have Elysia, her husband, and sons. I sometimes have too many people around me."

"I don't know what to do."

"Suetonius, I am proud of you, but it saddens me at the same time." Vivianne threw her frail arms around his neck. "First Emperor Claudius makes you governor of Mauretania, then Emperor Nero makes you governor. This new governorship. Is it far away? Where is this place called Britannia?"

"Farther than Mauretania and in the opposite direction. I was cold in Gaul, but I'll be colder in Britannia. It has white flakes of frozen water that rain down." Suetonius took his mother's arms from around his neck and held her hands. He squeezed her fingers. "Imagine being so cold that your fingers and toes are in pain. In the highest of mountains in Mauretania I was not as cold as I will be in Britannia."

Vivianne's eyes clouded over. "How can you know that which is in the future?"

"I have been told this by the officers who have returned from that far-away place. It is quite barbaric. I'll have primitive quarters until I get a proper villa built. Lucian will be good at helping me. The people aren't ready to rule themselves, so Rome has to do it for them. We're to collect taxes and keep peace."

"Will that be dangerous?"

"I don't think so. They haven't an organized army as we have. You needn't worry. It will be so peaceful that I'll be bored." Suetonius sighed as he looked at the soft bed. "That is one comfort I shall miss." He dropped Vivianne's hands and returned to his trunk. He picked up a toga and folded it neatly. He was so accustomed to the military life and its rules that he did his packing automatically.

"So I should pack, too?" Lucian asked.

Suetonius looked into his mother's eyes. "Yes."

"That is the right answer," Vivianne said.

Suetonius pulled his woolen cape tighter about his shoulders. He thought that the governorship of Britannia would be easy. Freezing to death in a foreign country would not be easy. He drew his chair closer to the fire built in a pit in the center of the room. He shivered as the wind forced its way through a hole in the ceiling and whipped the ashes and flames into a frenzied dance. A knock on the door made him shiver again in anticipation of the blast of cold air. "Enter and do so quickly." He didn't even look as the door opened and shut. Swirls of snow came in with the Roman soldier who stepped close to the fire. The soldier saluted and waited for his superior's acknowledgment.

Suetonius looked at the youthful face, unlined as yet by age or worry. He reached up and felt his own face, then dropped his hand quickly and pulled his cape tighter once more. "I will be quite content when my villa is finished. Cursed be this weather that has halted construction. I long for the fires that are built beneath the floors to warm one's feet. This land is worse than primitive. If the Britons were more intelligent, they would have central heating for these frigid houses just as we have." Suetonius shifted in his chair to ease the stiffness of his joints. "What news have you?"

The soldier opened a leather pouch. "I have a lengthy letter from your family and this."

"This?"

"A message from Poenius Postumus of Legio II."

"Give it here." Suetonius reached for the parchment that was held out to him. He ripped it open and skimmed the meticulous writing quickly. "He begs like a slave and cries like a woman. The weak pig. He wants to bring his Legion here. He fears that they are too few to properly defend Exeter from the Druids." Suetonius threw the parchment to the floor. "They are almost at the southern tip of this blasted island, and he doesn't feel safe. Safe from what? A pack of wild-eyed and crazy religious fanatics who live in the northern part and are probably mad?"

"Sir, the Druids seem to be everywhere. Some appear to be spies."

"Get out of here. Don't bother me with gossip. Come back tomorrow to take a letter to Postumus."

"Yes, sir. Here is your mail from your family, sir. Good night, sir."

"Good night." Suetonius watched the youth depart, closing the door quickly behind him, but not fast enough to keep out the invading snow. Suetonius willed himself not to shiver, but he failed. Laying the scroll on the small table next to his chair, he crossed the room and took a good sized log from the pile next to the door. The flames wrapped themselves around the log, and the sudden warmth made Suetonius' cheeks burn.

He moved back to the chair and looked at the parchment in the delicate handwriting of his mother. It must have cost her a fair amount of money to send such a large letter this far. Suetonius hoped it contained no bad news. He ran his finger over the seal of the house of Paulinus, then hesitated before he popped it open. He sat and unrolled the scroll. The first sentence told of the birth of his third nephew. It was a large baby and Zia had a difficult time, but she was fine. Vivianne thought each grandchild that was born was more beautiful than the last one. She was one of the oldest women he knew, her life having been long and rich because she was still full of vitality.

Suetonius stretched his feet toward the fire and unrolled the letter again. He chuckled at his mother's description of the antics of Elysia's oldest child. He was glad that his mother had many heirs to keep her busy. She had been lost for a while after his father had died. He remembered the empty feeling that he had carried with him for months and wondered how his mother fared.

He felt the heat through the leather of his boots. He sat near the fire there and enjoyed the relief from the cold that had plagued him since his arrival last month. Finally, Suetonius realized his back was cold, and he faced away from the firepit. The woolen cape warmed quickly, and he was thankful that the Britons knew how to make the most of their sheep.

A frantic knocking at the door interrupted Suetonius' thoughts, and he frowned at the unseen intruder. "Come in."

The snow impolitely blew in before the officer of the Hispana IX entered. He closed the door and saluted. "Governor, we have a problem with the barbarians."

Suetonius locked his fingers together behind his back and rocked back and forth. "General Petilius Cerialis, your first mistake is to call these people barbarians. Even though their religion seems barbaric and their civilization unlike ours, still it is advanced in many ways. If you underestimate them, it could cost you in battle." It was unfortunate that Suetonius had inherited the inept soldier from the hapless third governor of Britannia.

General Cerialis' right eye twitched. He stood rigid. "The . . . natives are gathering in the central part of this island, according to my scouts. I believe there will be an uprising within the next two weeks. Also, the Druids have traveled great distances and have converged on Anglesey Island to the west."

Suetonius stared at his silver-haired general with the blue-gray eyes. The general's right eye twitched. It always did when he had to deal with Suetonius. The hatred hung like a heavy fog between them; neither wanted to see the other's point of view.

"I want to know the details, of course." The general shifted from one foot to another, but Suetonius would not ask him to sit. A small insult was better than no insult. "Who saw the Britons gathering? Why are they gathering?"

"One of my most trusted men, Cassius, has led a small detachment forth and has seen the gathering to the west of here." Cerialis stood as straight as a javelin, his hands at his side. "Five days march from this fort."

Suetonius turned his back to the general and warmed his hands above the fire. He spoke to him over his shoulder and tried to hide his contempt for the general. "Did he find out why the Britons were there? Could it be one of their religious ceremonies? Were they near a forest? I understand they worship the trees."

"They were armed. My scouts consider them dangerous. If I may make a suggestion . . ."

Suetonius stared at Cerialis, then waved a hand as if warding off an insect. "Go ahead."

"I suggest that you send an army after the rebellious natives to stop them before the uprising becomes larger." Cerialis clenched his fists.

Suetonius turned away from his general and watched the flames destroy the log. "It bears looking into further."

"With the respect I give to you as a former general and now a governor, I must protest these thoughts of yours. We don't have time to watch them further. They have arms, although their fighting skills are not as good as ours. They wear no armor and fight half-naked."

Suetonius turned his back to the fire and again faced the general. "Who would lead this attack against the Britons?"

Cerialis' chest swelled. "Why, I would lead my men. It isn't a task that can be left to underlings."

Suetonius held back a snort with difficulty. "Do we intend to sweep into a victory?"

"Certainly."

"If you fail, your career will suffer." Suetonius watched for a sign of fear.

Cerialis' face contorted and turned gray as the color left it. His thin lips turned downward, emphasizing his nose that had given him the nickname of The Hawk.

Suetonius sensed a weakness in his general and continued. "I have heard of generals who failed in a small mission and were given a second chance only to fail in a larger mission. I do not believe in failures. One such act and I consider it treason. If you agree to these conditions, then you may proceed against this so-called uprising."

Suetonius saw a flash of fear in the blue-gray eyes of the general. "Of course, you must make certain first that the Britons have plans to run us through with their long swords."

General Petilius Cerialis saluted. "I will report to you just before we leave. These barbarians . . . natives will learn that Rome is invincible."

Suetonius' lips curved upward in an attempt at a smile. "I certainly hope you are right. You may go."

The general whirled around, opened the door, and left in a flurry of snow and wind. The door slammed behind him, the rush of air blowing embers across the packed earthen floor.

"Stupid fool," Suetonius said to the door. "I don't know how he became a general. He cannot be depended on to do what is necessary." Suetonius returned to his chair and sat. The torch on the wall was smoking badly—almost out—but he didn't want to move yet. He had to separate his dislike for the general from what he had been told.

It was indeed possible that the Britons were planning to try to take back lands from the Romans. Suetonius shivered. They could have it. There was nothing endearing about this godless land with its cold winds, thin soil, and primitive conditions.

The torch sputtered, and Suetonius heaved himself out of the chair, took the old torch from the wall bracket, and threw it into the fire. Taking a torch lighter, he pushed it into the fire until it caught, and lit a new torch. Warm at last, he sat and picked up the letter from his mother. He reread it again, smiling at his mother's sense of humor that pervaded the letter. He held the letter to his chest.

"The life of a governor is as lonely as the life of a soldier." Suetonius, startled at hearing his own voice, was overwhelmed with homesickness that engulfed him. He reached for a pitcher of wine and drank without pouring it into a mug. He drank quickly, consuming as much as possible in a short time. It was a shame to rush the good Roman wine past his tongue so quickly, but he needed to numb his brain. He wanted a big hangover.

Suetonius glanced at the bed in the corner of the room piled high with furs. He hoped the servants would be able to help him find his bed in the darkest hours of night. No one would find his heart.

The day was sunny and deceptively cold. Suetonius stood on the platform that had been built for him and watched the rising sun reflect off row after row of metal armor. The men marched in perfect unison, heads held high, for they were the best army in the world. The powerful sound of feet hitting the hard packed earth at the same time sent shivers down Suetonius' spine. He sucked in his stomach. Suetonius was pleased that he could still get into his uniform and on these occasions, he wore it.

Squad leaders saluted him as they passed, and Suetonius stood straight with his arm held at a perfect forty-five degree angle in a return salute. He was still strong, in spite of being nearly half a century, and he held the salute from the time the review began until the last man had passed. Suetonius' fingers tingled when at last he dropped his arm. As he turned to leave the platform, he saw General Cerialis ride toward him. Suetonius waited for the salute before he returned his own and stood silently while The Hawk stared up at him.

General Cerialis cleared his throat. "I have chosen to lead the men myself into this most important battle. They stand prepared and have been ready since before the review."

Suetonius nodded and dropped his salute. "All battles are important to Rome, but I think you have over-estimated this one. May the gods be with your men." Suetonius grimaced when he thought of the anger he had for this particular general. Cerialis had slithered to the top rank by political means. How had he managed to ingratiate himself to not one, but two emperors? Flattery and gifts, no doubt. Suetonius would like to be rid of him, but at what cost?

Suetonius climbed down from the platform and kicked a pebble. It hurt his cold toes, and he cursed the gods. He turned to watch the army as General Cerialis marched them toward a far away battle. "General, I hope that you won't fail me when I need you the most. The future may prove to be difficult with you in command." He turned away from the sun that had risen higher in the sky and walked toward his hut across the road from his partially built villa. He pushed his way through the door to shut out the sight of the unfinished building. It was going too slowly to suit him.

The pounding of horses' hooves on the road in his dream became the pounding on the door in reality. Suetonius sat up in bed and frowned. The idiot who beat upon the door when it wasn't daylight had better have a good story.

Suetonius looked around for the servant, who was nowhere to be seen. "Worthless peasant." He threw back the covers and climbed out of bed, wishing he hadn't drunk so much wine. It made his head hurt.

The noise was unrelenting. "I am coming. Stop that infernal pounding or you'll wake up Nero in Rome." Suetonius jerked open the door and glared at the young messenger who stood before him. "What is it that drags me out of bed? This had better be important. What time is it?"

The soldier saluted. "'Tis but three hours until the cock crows, sir." The young soldier shifted from one foot to another.

Suetonius glared at the soldier. "What news then brings me out of bed at this hour?"

"I have distressing word from General Cerialis, sir. He has found the barbarians most difficult. He said to tell you that the barbarians outnumber him ten to one."

"That idiot general has allowed his inflated arrogance to deflate his brain! Will he never learn?" Suetonius bellowed. "You!" He shouted at the quaking soldier. "Get the remainder of the Legio IX as well as my guards. Find General Lucian! Prepare to depart at first light. That idiot was too stupid to take enough men. Where is the servant who tends me? Get the lazy boy in here." Suetonius whirled away from the door and stomped across the floor in his bare feet. "Where is that servant?"

The door banged shut and Suetonius turned. "There you are. Where do you hide at night? Are you frolicking with the local women or do you steal from my men?"

The servant shook his head. Neither servant nor master could understand one another's language.

Suetonius stared at the quaking youth. "Anger must be universal since you seem to understand my wrath." Suetonius pointed to the armor. "Get me into my fighting gear. I must rescue a simpleton who fights no better than a woman could."

Suetonius shifted in the saddle to relieve the stiffness in his right leg. His knee had ached continuously since he had come to this frozen land, and it made him grouchy. The sun was a quarter of the way across the sky, and Suetonius had yet to see any sign of Cerialis' men. He leaned over and patted his horse, named Victory after a long line of other horses named the same, and whispered, "Settle yourself. It is not always a battle that we ride to."

Suetonius looked at the soldier beside him. "Are you certain this is the right way? How far afield did the general have to go to put down an uprising? Where is the scout I sent ahead?"

"I know not, Governor."

Suetonius stared into the woods to his right. "Soldier, how long have you been in this country?"

"Two years, sir."

"Have you noticed that nature is the same no matter what country a person is in?"

"I don't understand, sir."

Suetonius raised his arm and halted the company. He waited until all was quiet. "Do the birds sing in this country in the winter?"

"Yes, sir. Toward spring, sir."

Suetonius pointed to the woods. "Shouldn't they be singing now?"

"Yes, sir, unless . . ." The soldier's face showed his alarm as he understood what Suetonius meant.

"Unless there is an enemy lurking about." Suetonius looked toward the woods, again. "We seem to have walked into a trap. I wonder at the stupidity of Cerialis! Or is he a traitor?"

"No traitor, sir, to my knowledge. I have told you true. When I left him, he was engaged in battle and had planned to stop when it was dark. That is the norm."

Suetonius felt the cold wind blow through his cape. It blew against the sweat that trickled down his back as it always did when instinct told him all was not right. He turned his horse and cantered back to his lieutenants. "See the woods ahead? I believe an ambush awaits us." Suetonius looked at the plains beside him. "We will have to ride as if we don't know about the Britons in the trees. Let them think they can surprise us. Pass the word that we will ride down the middle of the field. The ground is frozen and will hold our horses. Make the Britons leave the sanctity of their woods so that we can fight them." Suetonius whirled his horse around and trotted off at an angle toward the middle of the field. The army followed him.

They had ridden a short way across the field when the shouts of men reached Suetonius' ears. He smiled as he looked over to see more than a hundred half-naked men rushing from the woods, brandishing scythes, axes, pitchforks, and large sticks.

Suetonius gave the signal to the trumpet player to announce that his soldiers were to assume the battle stance.

The notes of the trumpet stopped the Britons in mid-stride as the Roman shields came up, the spear carriers were in place, and the cavalry moved to the rear. Suetonius ordered a group of men to follow him, and the army split rank.

The attacking Britons yelled and began their charge. Suetonius was amazed that the bare-chested men came at his armored soldiers with no thought of injury or death. His men momentarily halted, apparently taken by surprise.

Suetonius drew his sword and charged to the front lines, yelling, "Charge forward, men! Do not let their tactics fool you! Charge!"

Suetonius was relieved to see his men come to their senses and surge forward.

The sounds of swords hitting thick wood, of axes hitting armor, and metal against metal swirled around Suetonius. He felt invigorated as he always did in battle. He turned and loudly gave the order for the splinter group to follow him.

Suetonius and his men whirled around the half-naked Britons like leaves in a storm, effectively charging them from the rear. Like a vise, the Roman army closed in on the hapless men and crushed them. Suetonius' horse slipped time and time again in the bloody field. Suetonius drew his sword above his head and let it fly downwards. It cut through the unarmored men as if it were guided by the gods. He heard the sound of flesh being sliced and bones being broken until he could hear no more. His horse danced around the fallen victims, at times sliding in the gore and at other times jarring the rider because of the frozen ground.

Suetonius first noticed the quiet. He knew the battle was over, but he always hated the time between the battle's end and the time he could leave the battlefield. The iron-smell of blood assaulted his nostrils and reminded Suetonius of his own mortality. In less time than it took the sun to reach its zenith, the Roman army had sent every native to his heaven. Victory was his.

Carefully, Suetonius guided his horse through the disemboweled bodies, treating the fallen victims as he would have his own soldiers. He respected the man, if not the reason, for the fight. He rode to a knoll and waited for the burial detail to report to him the losses in his own ranks. He did not expect many Roman casualties. A pair of scouts rode forth to see if they could find the village from which the men had come in order to tell the women they would have to bury their dead.

Suetonius frowned. He thought he saw a cloud of dust, then realized it couldn't be, given the frozen ground. It took him a moment to see that it was snow being thrown up by a group of riders. He strained his eyes to see. The sun was shining off the snow the same as it did off the waters of the Mediterranean in summer. He raised his hand to his forehead to shade his eyes, then sighed with relief when he saw that it was a Roman cavalry unit and not another group of Britons attacking.

When they got closer, Suetonius saw that it was the rest of the IX Hispana. General Petilius Cerialis would be leading them, no doubt. Suetonius settled back against the saddle to wait. His knee ached from hanging down for so long, and he pulled it up to hook it over the pommel. He signaled his lieutenant forward with a wave of his arm.

Suetonius waited until his aide was next to him. "Do you see General Cerialis in front?" Suetonius studied the lieutenant as he stared at the advancing troops. The man was past his youth, but not yet old. His curly, blonde hair was without any signs of gray, unlike Suetonius' that was streaked with silver.

Suetonius looked back to the horizon. "Is it General Cerialis?"

Lieutenant Marcellus nodded. "Yes, it is he. He comes with the other half of the IX Hispana."

Suetonius squinted, then gave up when he couldn't see the details and cursed his age. "Does he look as if he has been in battle?"

"I cannot tell, sir."

"Let us go to meet him." Suetonius dropped his leg and spurred his horse forward, instinctively tightening his legs around the horse's middle as it bolted. With a grip on the reins, he held the horse to a slow trot.

Suetonius stopped a short distance from General Cerialis and waited.

General Cerialis pulled back on the reins and saluted. "Hail, Governor. With your help, we were saved from a second wave of barbarians attacking us."

Suetonius returned the salute, briefly. "How did the battle go in which you were engaged?"

"We easily defeated them." General Cerialis' eyebrows were raised in surprise. "I will never understand why those warriors choose to go into battle with no armor. We cut through their lines with ease. I left all the men dead who attacked us."

"Could you not have cut through the lines of the men that came from the woods? Or did you not know they were there?" Suetonius tried to hide his contempt. "Did you not have scouts to give you an accurate report?"

"The scouts told us that we were nearly surrounded. I felt it best not to risk the lives of the men since we were outnumbered." The general broke eye contact and stared at the ground.

"We have an entire legion of five thousand men at our disposal. Why did you take so few soldiers?" Suetonius glared at the general. "I believe that you didn't expect to do more than terrorize a small, unarmed village, but were taken by surprise. In panic, you sent for reinforcements. As a general, you cause much more trouble than your rank warrants."

Suetonius pulled hard on the reins and kicked his horse. He rode toward home, his anger causing him to forget about the cold, the ache in his knee, and the smell of death on the battlefield.

CHAPTER

IX

OADICEA WAS CALM. She had said her Druid prayers and had given gifts to her Druid gods. Water hemlock that had been gathered from the swamp waited for her, and she was ready. Death would be another adventure in which she and her daughters would travel together as they had in the war against the Romans. Boadicea swirled the poisoned wine in the bowl. It captured the last pieces of sunlight, broke it into many colors, and then flung the sun-colors across the wine, casting them aside like an old tunic.

Very much like her life. Boadicea swirled the wine again. The colors stumbled, then curled like a broken rainbow. If she had to do it again, would she do the same things? Boadicea looked at her two daughters. Neila, with her black ringlets, and Sydelle, with her auburn hair, were like the two sides of the earth. The top side was sunny and bright and the other side was dark and shiny. Both were necessary for life and balance. Boadicea would not have changed anything. She would still have married Prasutagus, and she would still have her beautiful daughters. She would still fight the battles— all of them. She smiled at the memories.

Boadicea clapped her hands together as the spear thudded into the ground inside the circle she had drawn. "Good, Sydelle. You've learned to throw the spear well. You have a natural arm."

"Am I as good as Neila?" Sydelle danced around her mother, pulling her toward the circle in order to retrieve the spear. "Have I beaten her yet?"

"It isn't a contest, Sydelle. Each of you has different talents. Neila is competent at spear throwing, but you're good with the bow and arrow." Sydelle struggled to pull the spear from the edge of the circle made from stones, and Boadicea chuckled to herself. In spite of Sydelle's gentle nature, she had thrown herself into learning the techniques of fighting. Boadicea suspected that it was competition with her sister, Neila, that had caught her enthusiasm for spears and arrows.

Neila stood off to one side, her hand resting easily on a spear held upright that was taller than she. Although she was almost two years younger than her sister, she was already a few inches taller—taller even than other twelve year olds. Black hair tumbled down her back in tight curls, each curl going its own way. Neila's eyes were the color of the sea on a stormy day and seemed capable of changing color to match her mood. Neila tapped her fingers against the shaft of the spear as she watched her older sister struggle to pull the spear from the ground. "I'm certain you didn't throw the spear so hard that you are unable to pull it from the earth. You must be weak."

Sydelle glanced at her sister, then jerked the spear from the ground, spraying dirt on her tunic as she did so. She turned and stared at Neila one hand on her hip. "I won't get into an argument with you about who is better. I simply wish to challenge you with the bow." Sydelle smiled. "Of course, if you're certain that I would beat you, then you could concede."

"Dear sister, I would never concede to defeat without trying. Get your bow and arrows. We'll have a contest with Mother as the judge. I'll make it as difficult for you as possible." Neila tossed her head back, trying to get her hair out of her eyes. "Mother, you will be the judge won't you?"

Boadicea looked from one daughter to another. "It's always good to have a competition as long as it's friendly. Remember, won't you, that we're the same clan?"

Sydelle leaned her spear against a tree, ran over to Neila, and put her arms around her. "We are sisters and by being sisters have sworn to protect each other in the worst of times. Isn't that right, Neila?"

Neila leaned against her older sister. "That's right, but don't think that I'll let sisterly love stand in the way of trying to beat you."

Boadicea enjoyed their banter, always pleasant, but competitive. "The rules are to be the same as always. You must name your target beforehand. Get your weapons and prepare for a tough match. The first one with twenty-one strikes wins."

Boadicea winced as the girls' excited high-pitched squeals assaulted her ears. They raced to the trees and grabbed their bows and arrows propped against the small trunks. The trees, an ash for Sydelle and an alder for Neila, had been transplanted from the sacred grove a few hours after the birth of each of her daughters. Both trees had grown straight and were strong. It had become a habit for the girls to place anything they owned under their personal tree for protection. When they were younger, it had been dolls; now it was weapons. If ever there were another conflict with a northern tribe, all hands would be needed for protection.

Her daughters were not the only girls trained in weaponry, but because of their status as princesses, they would someday inherit the responsibility of caring for their people. They had to be well-trained. The entire tribe would depend on them just as the tribe depended on Prasutagus and Boadicea to protect them from the Brigantes who roared down from the north like the winter winds. Boadicea looked south. How much longer would the Romans be content to stay south of the Thames? In the two years they'd been here, the Romans had built roads across lands that weren't theirs, fought with the southern tribes, and then had the audacity to ask for taxes to protect the tribes they'd conquered from an unnamed enemy across the Narrow Sea! She hated the Romans. Boadicea forced thoughts of the invaders from her mind and turned her attention back to her daughters.

Neila held her bow tightly in her hand while she slung the shaft of arrows across her back. "I will let my older sister go first."

"You may go first if you like. The advantage should be with the less able."

Sydelle grinned. "I always beat you at this."

Neila frowned. "I always beat you at spear throwing."

"You first, then."

Neila put an arrow in place. "I shall shoot the middle of the cloth that is still in place from yesterday. My arrow will be found in the center on the red spot." Neila raised the bow and aimed. The twang of the bowstring and the swish of the arrow as it sliced through the air held everyone's attention. The arrow landed to the left edge of the bull's-eye. "It counts, it counts."

"Barely." Sydelle raised her bow. "I'll shoot closer than you."

Boadicea placed her hand on Sydelle's arm. "Aim carefully, for braggarts often miss."

"Mother, I am merely stating facts. I'm not bragging."

Boadicea laughed and took her hand away from Sydelle's arm. "If that is the case, then you had better make certain the facts do not lie."

Sydelle took careful, but quick aim and let fly the arrow. The whistling sound was followed by a thud as the arrow hit the target. It was dead center. Boadicea could not help but be proud of Sydelle. She would make a good leader.

"See, Mother? I can make the arrow do what I wish." Sydelle turned at the sound behind her, then smiled as her father came toward her. "Father! Did you see? I beat Neila with the bow."

Prasutagus frowned as he walked toward his daughter, his long strides closing the distance between them in a flash. He stood quietly and looked at the smiling face turned upwards toward him. He placed a hand on her shoulder. "Sydelle, you must not be the braggart at the expense of someone else, especially a member of your own clan or tribe."

Sydelle hung her head down, staring at her bare feet. "I am sorry, Father."

"It is not I who have been offended." Prasutagus stared at her, frowning.

Sydelle turned to Neila who stood close by. "I shan't be happy to have beaten you anymore, Neila. I shall only be glad that I'm better than I was the last time." Sydelle kissed her sister on the cheek. "I was glad that I did better than you because you always seem to do the best at most everything."

Neila shrugged and pushed her hair away from her face. The perspiration glistened on her forehead. "I spend more time practicing because I'm not good at the other things you do." She looked away. "I'm not good at being a priestess although Mother teaches me the same as you. I don't think I'll ever be able to remember all the secrets. I will just have to be the hunter and warrior, and you'll have to be my protector with your priesthood."

Boadicea pursed her lips and glanced at Prasutagus to see if he were listening. He smiled at her and cocked his head toward the girls, so deep in conversation that they didn't notice either parent. Boadicea was both pleased and surprised that Neila had the insight to recognize the strengths and weaknesses of not only herself, but of Sydelle as well. It could be that to force Neila into the priesthood would be unwise. Of course, she should know the practical parts like the medicinal spells, but was it really necessary for both girls to study the same thing? Shouldn't she help each develop her natural talents? She would talk with Prasutagus after the girls were in bed.

Prasutagus placed a large hand on the top of each of his daughters' heads. They looked up at him, seemingly surprised at this display. "I think we should go hunting. Your mother is going to make some visits to the old people who are ill. Wouldn't you like to try your powers against a real target, one that doesn't stand still?"

Neila clapped her hands together and jumped up and down. "With my spear? Could we hunt the big, old boar that has injured so many of our hunters?"

Boadicea gasped. "No! The boar is too dangerous. Even our most skilled hunters have come to harm from him. No, the boar is not to be hunted. He is cantankerous like our old, worn-out hunters who can no longer hunt."

"What then?" Neila looked at her mother. "It can't be anything too easy."

Prasutagus laughed. "Nothing is too easy in hunting animals except the old and sick. Hunting won't be easy, believe me."

"We could hunt birds," Sydelle said.

Neila snorted. "I can't shoot down a bird with a spear."

"Use a bow and arrow. You can't hunt the old boar, Father and Mother just said so."

Neila stamped her foot. "You just want to bring home more than . . ."

Boadicea tugged at the sleeve of Neila's tunic. She spoke to her quietly, for she knew that to be too obvious would make her second child stubborn and difficult. "Neila, didn't you hear what your father said to Sydelle about arguing over who was best at what? That works for both of you."

Neila looked down at her toes making round marks in the gray-brown dust of summer as she wriggled them. She mumbled, "Yes, I heard," and continued to stare at the ground.

Prasutagus dropped his hand from the top of Neila's curly hair and slid it around until he cupped her chin. He tilted her face upward. "We will hunt with both the spear and the bow. We will hunt anything we choose so long as it's not that boar. Even our men won't hunt that crabby old thing."

Boadicea smiled at her husband. He was always good at arbitration, sometimes to the detriment of his own person. It was a quality that she had grown accustomed to and had admired in the cases of judgement that he had to oversee. He had settled a two-year argument over payment of a bride price. One of the sheep had died en route to the bride's home, and her father wanted a replacement. The groom's family said that since her brother had come for the flock of sheep, that it already belonged to them. Neither side would relent. Prasutagus solved the problem by giving the bride's family a sheep from his own flock.

She placed her arm under his and stood closer to him. She liked the warmth that radiated from him and the strength that had kept the tribe prosperous and free from war. He was known as a fierce warrior when attacked, but a peaceful man when left alone. "That's an excellent idea," Boadicea said. "When you return from the hunt, I shall be home, too. We'll celebrate your hunt with a special dinner. Tomorrow we'll eat what you catch today."

Prasutagus groaned. "If we count on that, we may starve tomorrow."

Sydelle's eyes widened, and she pushed him with her free hand. "Father!"

The silence of the woods was broken by the twittering of birds that fell mute as the hunters walked beneath them. Prasutagus walked quietly in front of his daughters, trying to show them by example how to avoid the snapping twigs. He liked the smell of the damp earth where the sun never shone and the odor of the pine trees. As a boy he had liked to walk in the pine groves so that he could feel the soft needles under his feet.

Prasutagus had told his daughters about the wounded animal and its temper. He hoped they would remember all he had told them all the while knowing, however, that the best lessons were taught through experience.

He glanced over his shoulder at Sydelle. Her bright hair shone like copper whenever the sun sneaked through the branches and danced off her head. By contrast, Neila was almost totally hidden even when she stepped into a sunny spot. Her dark hair absorbed the sun rather than intensified it. Prasutagus smiled to himself as he watched Neila tuck her hair behind her ears again.

Prasutagus heard splashing water before he saw the creek. He held up his hand to stop the girls. Prasutagus looked up and down the creek, but all he saw and heard was the water as it made its way from the woods on a long journey across his lands to the ocean.

The girls stopped next to him, one on each side, imitated his stance, and mimicked his way of checking the stream for animals. Prasutagus had to force himself not to laugh, for they would never forgive him. For a fleeting moment, he wondered what it would be like to have a son. The thought left as quickly as it had come, leaving no path to show it had ever entered his mind.

Prasutagus pointed to the tracks in the mud at the edge of the creek. "You can tell the wolves have been here. The large tracks are of the leader. He is bigger and he was allowed to drink first."

Sydelle bent down and ran her fingers over the prints as if to memorize them. "How can you tell he was allowed to drink first?"

Prasutagus pointed to the dozens of tracks at the edge of the creek. "His prints are under the smaller ones."

"I see that! It's as plain as anything." Neila scampered off to her left. "And see here? This is where the deer came to drink. Their tracks aren't as plain."

"That's because they came earlier. I imagine their scent brought the wolves, too." Prasutagus moved up the creek away from the girls. "Up here are tracks of other creatures who depend on the water. We even have the track of the wild boar." He knelt down. "He has been here recently, so I want you girls to be especially wary. The wild boar is more dangerous than the wolf."

"Why is that, Father?" Sydelle asked.

"The wolf is predictable. He will run when afraid, and he will drop dead when struck by an arrow or a spear, but the boar is mad. He will attack for no reason. He is not intelligent enough to know fear, and he doesn't have the sense to know when he is wounded. He refuses to drop when hit by a spear. Don't try to kill the boar. He has gored many a good hunter with his tusks."

Sydelle's eyes were wide, and she listened intently whereas Neila seemed to be calculating his every word, but not believing what he said. She was difficult to convince, and often she had to try everything for herself. Prasutagus waited until he had eye contact with Neila. "The boar is too dangerous for us. It takes many hunters to bring him in. Do you understand?"

Neila nodded. "Yes, Father."

He was not convinced. He bent down and examined the boar's tracks again. It had not been here since yesterday. Its range was great, so it was probably far enough away that they didn't need to worry. Prasutagus straightened and wiped sweat from his brow with his sleeve. "Let's go. Our best hunting ground is not far from here."

He followed the creek through the woods until the trees thinned and a meadow glistened in sunlight. They stopped at the edge of the meadow and watched the grass ripple as the wind blew across it. The sun and clouds played tag across the field, making irregular patterns of dark gray and green. Prasutagus took in a deep breath. He liked the smell of the grass and wild flowers. He listened to the buzzing of the bees and other insects until he sensed the impatience of the youthful hunters beside him. "It is best that we stay together for a while. The first person to see a deer, signal the others. That way the animal is yours."

The girls nodded, quiet for a change, but Prasutagus could see the excitement in their faces. Neila danced up and down, shifting from one foot to another while Sydelle stared across the meadow into the darkness of the woods. Prasutagus stepped from the shadow of the trees into the sunlight. The grass was tall enough to brush his knees, and it tugged at his tunic. As he continued through the meadow, he could smell the fresh grass. The odor became stronger because of the broken blades that he had trampled.

Prasutagus turned to the girls. "We will never find game by walking in a single file. I'll walk on ahead and flush some game toward you. I think a hare will probably break cover. Remember what I told you about the hare?"

Sydelle leaned on her spear and shooed a bug away with her bow. "It switches directions many times while running."

Prasutagus smiled. "That's right. What of the pheasant? What does he do?"

"They burst forth from the bush very quickly. One needs to aim the arrow in their path of flight." Neila scratched her nose with the tip of her bow.

"You have practiced a lot with targets, but live animals are different. Stay here and watch. Do not shoot toward me. Remember the safety rules."

Prasutagus raised his arm and pointed across the meadow. "I will go around by the edge of the woods and walk toward you to scare the hares from their nests. You'll have to be quick with the bow. If you're good, then tomorrow we'll have a hare for dinner."

He moved away from them and never looking back, walked quietly along the edge of the woods. He was in place a few minutes later, his long legs having taken the meadow in great strides. Prasutagus was about to wave when he saw the grass parting as an animal ran through it. He was ready to point out the creature to the girls when he realized that the path it made was much too big for a hare. He heard the grunting and snorting, and his blood chilled.

The wild boar had scented him and had chosen to run rather than fight, but the animal's flight was toward the girls. His only hope was to distract the animal. With a glance at his daughters to see whether they understood the danger, Prasutagus ran across the meadow. This time the grass smelled sour as he broke the blades while running through them. He shouted and ran faster. He ignored the pain that burned under his ribs. The grass was shorter in the middle of the meadow, and he could see the boar. It seemed much larger than any of the other boars. By contrast, his daughters seemed ridiculously tiny.

Prasutagus stopped running and doubled over to ease the pain and catch his breath, but then straightened up and shouted. He swore at the boar again and again, but it wouldn't turn and chase him. Prasutagus looked across the meadow at his daughters and stopped dead. Neila stood poised with her spear, legs slightly apart with her unruly hair tucked behind her ears. Sydelle had an arrow aimed at the boar. She stood in front of her sister and off to the side, arms steady, hair shining like the sun. She waited, steadfast and seemingly unafraid.

Prasutagus let out long held breath. Of course she was unafraid, for she had never seen the damage done to a human by the tusks of a boar. Prasutagus had seen men ripped to pieces, and now the gap between his daughters and the animal was closing ever faster and faster as the boar made his way in a straight line.

Prasutagus started to run again, but realized that Sydelle wouldn't shoot her arrow because he was close to her line of sight. He threw his weight to his right foot and pushed off toward the left. He saw the arrow leave the bow, then shifted his eyes to the boar. Its scream of fury at being hit sent a chill down his spine. He didn't want to distract Neila and Sydelle by shouting at them. Prasutagus was too far away to shoot the boar with his own arrow, and he felt helpless.

The wounded boar streaked toward Sydelle. Prasutagus watched as she calmly placed a second arrow. Prasutagus knew she wouldn't have time to get off another shot, but she didn't know that. To have the boar drop dead was her only hope. The animal trailed a stream of blood from the wound in its chest, but the arrow must not have hit the heart directly.

Prasutagus hadn't been watching Neila. He heard the thud before he realized what the girl had done. Her spear was imbedded deep in the boar's chest, and it was able to take only a few steps before dropping near the girls like a gift from the gods. The sigh that issued from Prasutagus' mouth was so audible it surprised him. He stood like a tree, his feet rooted to the ground. When he tried to talk, no sound came. Prasutagus looked at the boar to make certain it was no longer running. There was no movement . Only then did he glance at his daughters and was relieved to see them dancing up and down congratulating each other on the kill. At last he found his voice and shouted at them, his hands cupped around his mouth to help his voice carry across the field.

"Do not touch him until I make certain he is really dead." Prasutagus trotted through the grass, and stopped near the boar to examine it carefully. No air seemed to escape from its nostrils. He kicked it so hard in the ribs that the head flopped and the tusks moved. It was dead.

"Sydelle and Neila, you may come and look at him now." Prasutagus grinned as his daughters skipped toward the boar.

Sydelle stared at the boar. "He has a homely face."

"It was uglier in life," Neila said. "Look at his tusks. One is chipped. His body is almost hairless, and what's there is coarse. His eyes are small and ugly. He is really a pitiful creature. I feel sorry for him. Is he too old to be good to eat?"

Prasutagus laughed at his daughter's pragmatic outlook. "He is still very good to eat. I have memories of a roasted boar that make my mouth water. He will make a fine meal for our tribe."

"I'm glad he will taste better than he looks." Sydelle put her foot against the animal's chest between the spear and her arrow, grasped the arrow with both hands, and pulled. The arrow made a sucking sound followed by a snap as the barb was freed from the flesh of the boar. She shook the blood from the tip, wiped it on the grass, and shoved it in the quiver. She stepped out of Neila's way.

Neila pulled at her spear, then wriggled it back and forth. "It feels stuck."

"It's imbedded deep. Perhaps it's caught between his ribs. Keep trying." Prasutagus stepped back to show her he would not help her.

Neila nodded and pulled at the spear once more. Her upper lip was covered with perspiration, and she frowned as she concentrated on retrieving her weapon. Neila tugged again on the spear, and it gave way. She tumbled backwards and landed on the ground with a thud. Her eyes widened, then she started to giggle. Sydelle giggled with her. The giggles turned to laughter and Sydelle fell to the ground, weakened from the uncontrollable relief that surged through both of them.

Prasutagus grabbed a hand from each of his daughters and pulled them to their feet. "You must learn to gut this creature properly so as to not ruin the meat. The intestines are especially foul and must not be ruptured." Prasutagus pulled a long bladed knife from the sheath attached to the belt around his tunic. "It is difficult for me to decide which hunter should have the honor of the first cut."

Both girls said, "Let my sister have the honor, it was her weapon that killed him." They stared at each other and were reduced to a fit of giggles again, ignoring their father's exasperated countenance.

Prasutagus handed the knife to Neila. "I can see only one way to satisfy the god of the hunt. Both of you shall have the honor by holding the knife together." Each of the girls solemnly wrapped her fingers around the handle.

Neila glanced at her father. "What do we do now?"

"You and Sydelle need to cut open his chest and belly. Make one long, deep cut, but not too deep. You must leave the intestines uncut."

Neila groaned. "How deep is too deep, Father?"

"It's difficult to explain. You start and I will help you. Don't hesitate or you will think too much. You have helped your mother and grandmother prepare enough food that you should have some idea."

Sydelle nudged her sister and whispered, "He doesn't know."

"Cut the beast!"

"Yes, Father." Sydelle guided her sister's hand and together they laid the knife against the boar's lower chest and pressed through the flesh, the muscle tissue, and into the cavity.

For a while the only sounds were an occasional grunt from the girls and the sounds of the splintering of wood as their father made a pole on which to carry the boar back to the village.

Neila sat back on her heels and called to her father. "What do we do now?"

"You remove the viscera. Throw away the intestines, but save the other organs and replace them. These will be saved for an offering to the gods and goddesses of the hunt. When that is done, I'll help you attach this creature to the pole so that we can carry him back."

The first to notice their arrival back in the village were the children and the dogs. Prasutagus had both girls at the front, holding the pole at shoulder height between them, for they were the killers of the boar. He walked behind them, carrying the pole chest high to keep it even. He enjoyed the swaying of the boar that was so heavy it bowed the pole in the middle. He kicked at the yapping dogs who leaped and nipped at the beast, and he shouted for the boys to corral their pets before the meat was ripped.

Prasutagus couldn't see the faces of Sydelle and Neila, but he could tell from the way they walked that they were pleased with the attention paid them. As they penetrated the village further, people came to the doors of their huts and stared at the small parade of hunters with children who tagged along and dogs that jumped and barked. Curiosity showed on the faces of everyone who viewed the spectacle of their chief who followed the sun-haired child and the night-haired child as they carried a most dangerous animal between them.

The men could not contain their curiosity and walked along with Prasutagus, silent at first, and then full of questions.

"How did you kill a boar alone?"

"Are you not injured?"

"Did he charge you straight on or did he swerve?"

Prasutagus shook his head, enjoying the attention until he could no longer contain his pride. "I cannot take credit for this kill. It belongs to my daughters who together brought this animal to its death." He smiled at the disbelieving looks and the shaking of heads. He knew the villagers would have to hear the story. Tonight would be special. "Get the pit ready for a roast. We will have an extraordinary meal by the light of the moon to celebrate the finest kill my daughters have ever made. They shall tell the story of their hunt."

Prasutagus shifted the pole from his right side to his left as he and the girls carried the boar up the ramparts to their home. He was glad when Boadicea, obviously curious about the commotion in the village, stepped through the doorway. The look on her face, a mixture of awe, fear, and shock, was worth all the worry he had gone through when the boar was charging the girls. "Boadicea, congratulate your daughters on their fine kill."

"Their kill!?" Boadicea's hand came up to her mouth as she gasped. "What do you mean, 'their kill'?"

"They will be great hunters. They are already better than you or me. Together they will be able to rule our combined tribes and build a great kingdom for the Iceni."

Prasutagus helped the girls place the pole with their new treasure in the forks of two trees that had been used for this purpose for as long as Prasutagus could remember. He had often wondered if the slow-growing oaks had been planted by an ancestor for this purpose or whether the gods had done it for them.

Prasutagus flexed his hands. The joints of his fingers were often swollen in the mornings from the old person's disease, and when he carried something heavy for a long time his hands grew stiff. He inspected his fingers. Three joints on his right hand were affected, and it brought back memories of his grandfather's hands. He wiped his hands on his tunic, then placed his arms around his daughters' shoulders as he led them toward their mother. "Have they a story to tell you, but you will have to wait until tonight when we tell the story to the village. We're having a roast before we have a secret ceremony to make them true hunters."

Neila stopped abruptly and pulled away from her father. She turned to face him. "What secret ceremony to make us hunters?" She cocked her head and eyed him with one eye, as if to see whether or not he were lying. "What ceremony?"

"You'll see," Prasutagus said.

"Mother!" Neila howled. "Tell me what ceremony?"

Boadicea placed her fingers against Neila's lips to quiet her. "If I tell you, then it won't be secret." She kissed Neila on the top of her head, then turned to Sydelle and kissed her as well. "We have brave children, Prasutagus."

Prasutagus smiled at the trio in front of him. He felt full of pride, for they had brought him much honor. "It is a good thing to have brave children. They would not have learned to be brave if it weren't for their mother."

The embers glowed red; a contrast to the blackness of night. Boadicea looked at the sky. The moon was a sliver of light and stars scattered across the sky like droplets of dew. The boar was a memory of seared meat. Only the bones and small scraps were left. She pulled her legs up and planted her elbows on her knees in order to prop up her chin. She was tired, but she didn't want the evening to end although it had for Sydelle and Neila. She watched the gentle rising and falling of the girls' rib cages as they slept stretched out next to what remained of the roasted boar in the pit. They had not wanted to leave the scene of their triumph. It was definitely a triumph for a pair of young girls to kill a boar when a group of skilled hunters had trouble doing the same. She remembered the tribal people were in awe as the story was told first by Sydelle, who spoke more freely than ever before in her life, and then by Neila, whose natural storytelling ability was at its height and consequently held her audience spellbound.

"You're deep in thought, Prasutagus," Boadicea said.

"I am dazzled by the unusual events of the day. Do you suppose the gods have wonderful plans for our daughters and through them our tribes? Do you think the Iceni is destined for greatness?" Prasutagus poked a stick into the embers.

Boadicea looked up at the sky with its countless stars and fragile moon. She felt insignificant. "I don't know if I can answer that. If it were fated that you and I meet and marry, then perhaps it is for a cause. We are seeing the best traits of both of us in our children. Do the gods want them for something special? I don't know."

Prasutagus leaned against Boadicea and kissed her cheek. "We could change bad things to good if we knew the future. We might be able to save the village from drought, from war, from disasters. I would like to know the future, so it could be changed."

"The future is set. It can't be changed."

"How do you know that?"

"I have studied the teachings of the ancients. I believe them when they say that to know the future is to know pain. To prevent pain, one must not know the future and therefore, the future cannot be changed." Boadicea took Prasutagus' hand in hers. "Let's not talk of this any more. Let's stay here until the sun rises."

Boadicea began to notice a subtle shift in the attitude of the people toward her and her daughters. The ceremony that acknowledged her daughters as hunters had been an important step for them, but apparently for her as well. Always Prasutagus' people had been pleasant to her. Some of the women were her closest friends, especially her sister-in-law, Rhianna, but now she seemed to have the respect of the men as well. Probably because she had given birth to two fierce hunters, and she was basking in their glory. She heard the whispers of the women quiet as she came close to them, and they smiled and waved at her. She took special pains to stop and chat with them, asking about their health, their families, and their needs. It was a time to acknowledge her daughters' skills with disclaimers of luck so as to not appear arrogant. Boadicea remembered what her father had always said to her. "To lead without followers is to not be a leader at all." Her mother had taught her to always care for the people who depended on her leadership.

Boadicea unexpectedly felt a rush of homesickness. She wanted to visit her mother. It would be best if Sydelle and Neila could tell their grandmother about the boar themselves.

Her step had a new lightness to it as she finished walking about the village. Tomorrow at first light they would start the short journey to her own village. The people there should know how strong their future leaders would be. She smiled at the antics of a pair of puppies pulling at a piece of old hide. The future looked bright.

Boadicea hugged her mother and nestled her face in Durina's hair. She stepped back to let Sydelle and Neila clasp their grandmother in a double hug. Boadicea was struck by the amount of silver that was threaded through her mother's black hair. Her face was youthful with very few lines of age that crisscrossed the faces of most of Durina's contemporaries. The bronze freckles that were scattered across her nose and cheeks that Boadicea loved were faded much like color that vanishes from cloth over time.

Durina peered over the heads of her granddaughters, her eyes bright with unreleased tears. "To what do I owe the honor of a visit from the Queen of the Iceni and her lovely daughters?"

Boadicea heard the giggles of the girls and smiled at them. They were never impressed with her titles. "I have come to see my mother, not a subject. You shall always be the queen. I am merely a protector of your people."

"You are the queen. I am merely the mother and grandmother of rulers and rulers to be. Please, come into the house." Durina waved at three young men who stared at the horses that pawed the ground. "Boys! Come here and take care of these horses. Do a good job for Queen Boadicea." Durina watched the three boys as each led a horse toward the corral. "Those are fine animals. You've done well with the breeding program."

Boadicea turned and looked at the horses. Their coats were glossy and shone in the sunlight. "I learned a lot of what I know from Rhys." She stared at the meadow where she and Rhys used to ride. "That was a long time ago and yet it seems . . ."

"I understand. It is the same when I think of your father. It seems as if he were here yesterday, and then I remember that Sydelle was only an infant when he died. Come, let's sit under the grove of oak trees, and you can tell me why you've come."

"Must I have a reason?"

Durina took Boadicea's hand and led her around the corner of the hut to the back yard. "You have that look in your eye that says you need to be mothered."

"I must wear my thoughts on my face." Boadicea laughed. "I could never fool you."

"Boadicea, you look as if you're with child. Are you?"

"What?" Boadicea stared at her mother. "I think not. I would not mind, but . . ."

"Never mind. Maybe it is just a grandmother's fancy," Durina said.

"It would pleasure me to have another child, but it has been years since the girls were born." Boadicea looked at a grove of oak trees in the back yard. Benches had been made from the wood of a fallen oak. They were gray with age, like people, but still sturdy. The girls danced around them, and spying a black and white kitten ran after it, squealing with delight. "Which generation of Kali's kittens is that?"

Durina shook her head as she sat on the bench. "Indeed, I don't know."

Sydelle's laughter floated toward them, and Boadicea turned to watch the copper-haired child running across the grass toward them. A black and white kitten clung to Sydelle's shoulder. Neila was close behind with a second black and white kitten held upside down in her arms.

"See what we caught?" Neila flopped down on the grass at her grandmother's feet. "He really likes to be petted."

Durina watched the struggling kitten. "It seems to like being held very much."

Sydelle dropped down next to her sister, her hands full of a similar kitten struggling to get free. "This one is tame already."

Boadicea chuckled. "I know that compared to a boar these creatures seem tame. Tell your grandmother about the other animal you met before the new moon."

Neila held the kitten's four feet in her hands. "Oh, yes, Grandmother. Sydelle and I killed a boar."

Durina gasped. "What were you doing on such a hunt?"

Sydelle squeezed her kitten to her chest. "Father took us hunting because we were both good with our weapons."

Durina frowned and glanced at Boadicea. "Don't you think that hunting boars was a little extreme?"

"We didn't go looking for the boar. He found us," Neila said. "But Sydelle shot him with an arrow, and I got him with my spear. Father was too far away to help us."

"Who killed him?"

"Both of us did. He dropped dead at our feet." Neila sucked the blood from her finger where the kitten had scratched her.

Durina leaned forward. "Weren't you afraid?"

Sydelle pursed her lips and frowned. "I wasn't scared until after we got back to the village, and I saw the fright on the men's faces."

Neila pulled her scratched finger from her mouth. "I wasn't scared either until I saw Sydelle get scared. I really thought that since she's the oldest, she knew more than I did."

Boadicea and Durina burst into laughter. Durina shook her head and looked at Neila. "I don't suppose I should worry about you girls. I think the hunted should worry." She leaned against a tree trunk and was silent while she watched the girls play with the duplicate black and white kittens. After awhile she turned to Boadicea. "Have you been teaching the ways of the priesthood on a regular basis?"

"Yes, every day." Boadicea looked down at her two daughters. "Sydelle has the patience to learn whatever it is I am teaching her. Neila is as quick to learn, but she does not like to sit very long."

Neila looked up at her mother. "I enjoy hearing about what needs to be done and how it's done, but I don't like to remember all those details. I'd rather hunt."

"I like the ceremonies." Sydelle's eyes met her mother's. "I want to be a priestess. I want to be able to talk with the gods and goddesses. I like to hunt, but I liked the sacrifices to the gods of the hunt afterwards much more."

Durina glanced at Boadicea, then at Sydelle. "You were the same as Sydelle when you were her age. Perhaps the gods have chosen your successor for you."

"It matters not which of them want to carry on the tradition of our family. I thought perhaps both would want to be part of our tradition, but I suppose the task is better kept by one."

Durina looked out across the meadow. "Would you like to go for a walk before we prepare the evening meal? How long are you staying?"

"We'll stay until day after tomorrow." Boadicea leaned down and petted the purring kitten that was lying still in Neila's arms. "I cannot stay away from Prasutagus very long, for I miss him too much."

"I understand that very well." Durina stood. "Come, let's walk. I'd like to see the river this morning. It speaks to me of the past. I find that it has a calming effect."

Boadicea stood by a small window and looked at the stars. She was restless and didn't know why. The ride back from her old village had been uneventful. She looked at the sky where the stars danced against a backdrop of deepest blue. The breeze that lifted strands of hair away from her face was warm. She listened to Prasutagus' even breathing. He was asleep after a hard day in the fields with his men and had not even known when his family had come home. Boadicea crossed the small room and lay on the bed next to him, then rolled over and placed her hand on his chest. She liked to feel the rise and fall of it to confirm that he still breathed. She had always feared his death even though he was robust and healthy. She assumed it was because Rhys had been snatched from her with no warning. Giving oneself in love meant accepting the pain of loss. She wished she could live without this fear that was worse at night.

Prasutagus' hand clasped hers. "How was your mother?"

"I didn't mean to awaken you."

"I tried to stay awake, but I couldn't. I'm not very good at welcoming home my women. We had to move many rocks to get the new fields cleared. I expected trouble from the enemy up north, but we didn't see them. We're building a wall with the stones."

"Isn't it too late to be clearing fields?" Boadicea moved closer to her husband and laid her head against his chest. His heartbeat was steady.

"Everything has gone so well this year that some of the men and I are getting ready for next year. We have increased our numbers. . . ."

Boadicea chuckled. "That's a cold way to discuss the young ones that have been born the last two years."

"I suppose it is." Prasutagus laid his chin against the top of Boadicea's head. "Did you enjoy the time at your mother's?"

"I did, but . . ."

"But what?"

"I saw her for the first time."

"What do you mean?"

"I didn't realize until I saw her that time is flying faster than our arrows do. Her hair is ever more silver, and I know she's seen a good many summers. She is still agile, but she walks more slowly than she used to."

"It is difficult to watch parents age." Prasutagus wrapped his strong arm around his wife.

Boadicea snuggled closer. "I think it would be more difficult to watch one's children die. To have life cut short would be more tragic. I don't want to think any more of death."

"Then I will tell you something that will make you happy. Our daughters are the talk of the village. The men say that they are natural leaders like their mother. They say the gods favor our daughters. They say that they could follow the daughters into battle because their mother has given them her strength and wisdom and bravery."

"Do they really say that?"

"Yes. It is true."

"Good. For when we have departed for the other world, then this world should be left in good hands. The gods have been good to us to give us such fine daughters."

Prasutagus yawned. "It is more difficult to stay awake."

Boadicea giggled. "Go to sleep. I will try to follow."

"Father! Mother!" Neila burst into the sleeping room. "Sydelle is gone!"

Boadicea pushed the blankets aside and leaped out of bed. Neila was a shadowy figure in the gloom just before dawn. "Gone? What do you mean?"

"She didn't want to wake you. She said she could take care of the problem."

"What problem?" Prasutagus was already out of bed and pulling on his tunic.

"It was Keir's watch last night. His horse brought him here half-dead. He had an arrow in his back. He called for Sydelle outside our windows. She told me to tend to him, so I did. I didn't realize what she was doing." Neila burst into tears. "I'm so sorry, Mother."

"Pray tell quickly what Sydelle is doing," Boadicea said. Her heart did double time as she pulled on her clothes.

"Sydelle raced from the room after whispering to me that I was to get help after I tended to Keir. I fear she has gone to gather a few of her friends to avenge Keir's injury. He told me a small band of Brigantes have crossed our northern border and are just over the hill from our farthest pasture."

"By all the gods! She means to fight them!" Prasutagus grabbed his sword and ran toward the door. "I'll sound the call to arms. Neila! Help the stable boys saddle our horses. We have a battle!"

"I want to fight, too," Neila said.

"I don't think you should," Boadicea said.

"She's my sister!"

"No!"

Prasutagus stopped at the doorway. "Neila is trained for battle. She needs to go. It is her place to go."

"I can't. . . ."

"Other mothers will send their children."

Boadicea knew that her husband was right, but she didn't want him to be. Suddenly she understood her own mother's fears. She buckled her sword-belt about her waist, rubbing the pommel with her thumb for good luck. She nodded, not wanting to voice her approval. "Take spears and your bow and arrows. Don't forget your shield."

Neila turned and raced from the room right behind her father. "I'll be with you on the battlefield."

The sun was almost ready to pop over the horizon as Boadicea, Prasutagus, and Neila rode through the wooded area to the west of their farthest piece of land. Men and women from their tribe followed them; some were on horseback, others walked, carrying weapons that ranged from excellent swords to farm implements.

The shriek of wounded horses, the screams of dying men, and the clash of sword against shield assaulted Boadicea's ears before she saw the skirmish. "May the gods protect my headstrong Sydelle." Boadicea urged Thayne into a canter to the top of a hill. The battle was below them. At first Boadicea couldn't see Sydelle or her friends.

"There she is!" Prasutagus pointed. "See, she leads a half dozen through the middle of the enemy's lines. She means to split them in two. Well done!"

"Aye, Husband. She hacks away at them with a fury I didn't know she possessed."

"They've angered her, Mother. The Brigantes should never have attacked someone so important to her!" Neila leaned forward in the saddle. "Let's tear out their left flank. It appears to be faltering."

Boadicea was startled at Neila's suggestion. The girl had learned her lessons so well. She reached over and grasped Neila's arm. "You lead. Your father and I will follow."

Neila grinned, pulled a spear from its holder, spurred her horse and tore down the hill, screeching at the top of her lungs.

"By the gods, she's vicious!" Prasutagus said. He followed his daughter into the fray.

Boadicea was pleased to see Neila rip into the enemy. She had time to watch Neila run her spear through a blue-tattooed Brigantes before she herself was confronted by a grizzled opponent.

The old man was clever and went after Thayne's front legs, trying to cut them out from under him with a double-bladed ax. Boadicea loosened the reins as she drew her sword. Neatly running the old man through didn't give her as much satisfaction as the look of surprise on his face. He had been a tough old bird; even his blood smelled ancient.

Boadicea had no time to check on Neila or Sydelle before a group of men and women came rushing toward her, maces swinging. Of all the weapons, Boadicea hated the mace the most. She pulled back her arm and slashed through the air holding her sword with its sharp edge horizontal to the ground. It served to momentarily confuse the woman who led the group toward her, and Boadicea was able to slice off her head as Thayne raced past. Boadicea pulled hard on the reins, and Thayne responded by rearing up, turning around on his hind feet, and slashing out with his hooves. This gave her the advantage of a few seconds to choose her next victim. She severed his sword arm and left him drowning in his own blood as he fell forward.

A lull in the fighting allowed Boadicea to search for Sydelle. She smiled as she spied her daughter covered with gore, but seemingly unharmed. Sydelle had managed to lead her small band of followers through the lines of the enemy, and she was now swinging back around like the tail of a whip. With vigor that Boadicea envied, Sydelle dispatched two more of the enemy in quick succession.

She turned to look for Neila and was alarmed to see Prasutagus kneeling on the ground next to the prone figure of their youngest daughter. She rode toward them, but was hindered by two Brigantes who came at her, maces swinging. Without much thought, Boadicea sliced both their throats with the tip of her sword. The sounds of the battle quieted, which meant that the enemy would retreat soon.

It seemed that Boadicea could not get any closer to Neila to see what had happened. She rode over the next Brigantes who stepped up to her and squashed his head under Thayne's hooves. She stopped in front of a group of her tribal women who were doing a good job of damaging their adversaries with wooden pitchforks, but they needed help. Boadicea disemboweled one man and sent a woman off to her gods.

A shout rose from Boadicea's tribe as she forced her way toward Neila. She glanced around. The Brigantes were in retreat with her tribe pursuing them in order to dispatch a few more.

Her people opened a path for her, and Boadicea rode toward Prasutagus who was holding Neila in his arms. "By the gods, don't take my child. I'll sacrifice anything you want, but spare my daughter!" Prasutagus begged.

Boadicea slid off Thayne and dropped down next to Neila. She glanced at Prasutagus who had tears cascading down his face, and she feared the worst. She looked at Neila, who, thank the gods, was breathing faintly. Boadicea was confused, for she saw no wounds. "What happened to her?"

"A mace to the back of her head."

"Oh, no!" Boadicea gently took her daughter from Prasutagus and laid her on the ground, face down. Blood matted Neila's thick hair turning the black curls to deep maroon. Boadicea forced herself to think as a Druid priestess, not a mother, as she probed Neila's wound with her fingers. "Bring my medicines."

Prasutagus was back in an instant, fumbling with the bags that had been tied to Thayne's saddle. "I'm no good at this." He laid the bags out for her.

"No matter."

"How is she?"

"It's only superficial. The mace barely touched her. It pushed her senses from her, gave her a wound that I must stitch, but she'll be fine. She'll have a headache for a few days and maybe she'll see two of everything, but the gods have answered our prayers." Boadicea threaded goat gut through a heavy needle. "Hold this." She parted Neila's hair and sprinkled myrrh and mold from dead oak trees in the gaping split before taking the needle from Prasutagus and expertly stitching Neila's scalp together. She bit through the gut when she was finished and sat back. "There. She'll be all right."

It wasn't until she was tying her medicinal bags that Boadicea saw Sydelle standing next to her father. In her concern about Neila, she had forgotten Sydelle. She sat back on her haunches and examined Sydelle from head to toe. "You have fared well, Daughter," Boadicea said.

"Better than Neila. What can I do to help?"

"Get a litter ready for her." Boadicea grasped Sydelle's hand and squeezed. "I'm proud of you. You're a fine warrior."

Sydelle blushed and stared at the ground. "Thank you."

Prasutagus shook his head. "We've created a warrior generation with our daughters."

"That we have. I fear we shall need warrior daughters to fend off not only the Brigantes, but the Romans who come closer and closer."

"Rhianna, please come." Boadicea clutched her stomach and bent over, holding onto the door frame. The sun made her head hurt. She called across the yard toward Rhianna's hut again. "Rhianna, please help me." The pain radiated from her stomach down her right leg. She was perspiring and her heart beat faster than normal. She was relieved when she saw Rhianna run toward her.

"You look pale. What happened?" Rhianna put her arms around Boadicea, walked her back to bed, and helped Boadicea slip under the covers.

Boadicea felt the room swirl around her, and she closed her eyes. It didn't help. Pain whipped across her lower abdomen again and she cried out. "It feels like a labor pain."

Rhianna reached for a cloth next to a fresh bowl of water. She washed Boadicea's face with cool water. "By the gods! Are you pregnant?"

"I don't know. I never pay attention to things like that. Why would I be pregnant after so many barren years?" Boadicea groaned. "This is worse than giving birth."

"Let me see." Rhianna took Boadicea's bright-colored tunic and pulled it up above her hips. Her eyes filled with tears as she looked at Boadicea. "It is the loss of a child."

"The gods give, and the gods take away. I did make a bargain with them." Boadicea's last words were lost as new pain took her breath away. "Get my mother. She will prepare the herbs to stop this."

"You can't fool the gods, Boadicea. It's already too late. There is much blood. All we can do is wait for the baby to leave your body." Rhianna picked up the wash cloth again. "I must wash you, but I need water. Will you be all right until I get back?"

"I'll have to be. Prepare tansy to rid my womb of the dead child." Boadicea opened her eyes and watched Rhianna leave the room. She was still dizzy. Her head was hot and she was thirsty, but she felt that if she drank anything it would make her worse. She closed her eyes. She must have slept because it seemed that in no time at all, she felt Rhianna's delicate hand. "Send for my mother."

Rhianna rinsed the cloth in the clear water, turning it pink. "There is no longer a baby to save."

Boadicea felt hot tears sting her eyes and run down her face. "Are you certain?"

"I am certain."

Boadicea let the tears flow. "Why do I feel so sad? It is a child unformed, and yet the loss is the same as if Neila or Sydelle had left for the other world."

"You're the priestess. Tell me why that is."

"I can't. Maybe it's because the child has a soul. I feel that because I did not know of his coming the gods were angry and took him from me." Boadicea looked toward the window. The sky was gray and the clouds tumbled across it as if in anger. "Even the sky is upset that I didn't know about the child that was given to me. I am being punished."

"I can't believe that. You were beside Prasutagus five times when the barbaric tribes from the north have come down and tried to take our villages. You fought as well as any man. You have given us two daughters who will lead after you and Prasutagus have gone. You have been a friend to all of us. Our combined tribes are strong. I cannot believe that a priestess would be punished by the very gods she serves." Rhianna folded a cloth and laid it under her sister-in-law.

"I hope you're right." Boadicea closed her eyes. "When Prasutagus and Sydelle get back from hunting, would you bring them in to see me?"

"Of course."

"Will you tend to Neila? She still has headaches."

"Yes. Don't worry about her. She is quite well today. Right now, you must drink the tansy to clean out your womb. And drink this, too. It'll help you sleep."

"What is it?" Boadicea raised herself on her elbows.

Rhianna held a cup to Boadicea's lips. "It's your famous chamomile and blessed thistle drink to bring down a fever and help you sleep. You're very hot. Whenever a woman has a miscarriage, there is a danger of corruption. I have also put in mold from the cheese you keep for medication. I don't know if it will help, but it can't hurt."

Boadicea took a sip. "This is terrible."

"Drink it. You make everyone else do so." Rhianna held the cup to Boadicea's lips until the last drop was gone. "You must rest. I promise that Prasutagus will come to see you."

"Thank you." Boadicea lay down and felt the real world leave her mind as the dream world entered her thoughts. She heard her mother's soothing voice.

When Boadicea awakened, she saw that the sky had darkened, and she decided that if the sun had been out today, it would be down by now. The sky was a darker gray, and she could no longer see the turbulent clouds. She sniffed the air. It smelled fresh as if it had rained, and she looked at the corner of the window. It was damp in the usual spot.

Boadicea heard familiar footsteps and looked toward the door. "Prasutagus, I'm glad to see you."

"Rhianna told me you were ill, but she wouldn't tell me anything else." Prasutagus sat on the bed next to Boadicea. "You look so very sad."

"I lost our child. I lost a child I didn't even know we were going to have." Boadicea reached for her husband.

He gathered her in his arms. "I am sorry. I am so sorry."

"There is nothing we can do. There were no prayers to help, no herbs to help. Maybe I could have saved the baby if I hadn't been too stupid to know he existed. I may have bargained away his life." Boadicea leaned against his chest and let the tears flow.

"Do not think that. The baby would have been lost no matter what you said or did. I've seen animals lose their young. There seems to be no reason for it. I've often said the gods know more than we do." Prasutagus brushed her dampened hair away from her face.

"I hope you're right, but it does not make the sadness go away." Boadicea blinked so that her husband would not see her cry. She wanted him always to think of her as strong as he was. She was a warrior and would always stand by his side.

Prasutagus smiled. "Go ahead and cry. I'll not think less of your strength as a warrior."

"How did you know?"

"I know you. Are you feeling all right? You seem hot to the touch."

"It's just from crying. I'll be all right in the morning. Tomorrow, I will say a prayer for the child whose soul is on the way to the other world."

Prasutagus squeezed Boadicea's hand. "I will say one with you."

"Sydelle will perform the going away ceremony for the unborn who die."

"I will be there, too."

CHAPTER

X

S UETONIUS PULLED BACK HIS FEET as he sat in the tub and watched as his servant carefully poured in a kettle of steaming water. The return ride had been quick, for the men were anxious to get to the barracks. Suetonius shivered at the memory of the bone-chilling wind that flew down the small hollows and whipped his woolen cape about his body like the furies attacking.

The servant backed away from the tub, refilled the kettle, and placed it on the trivet at the edge of the fire. Suetonius stretched out again and scooted down until the water was up to his chin. He felt confined to the small tub. He would be glad when the bathhouse was finished. It would be difficult to bring civilization to this outpost, but he was determined. Suetonius missed the companionship of the baths. He stared at the ceiling. How long had it been since he'd played a good game of dice? He was governor and had no time for games. It would be constant work to keep this land for Nero. The advantage of being here, however, was that it kept him far away from the ugly little man who ruled the greatest country on earth, but was unfit. Nero's decisions caused wars where there should be none. The emperor changed his mind capriciously and favored incompetents like General Cerialis.

His mother had told him that Nero was insane, and based on what he observed, he was inclined to believe her. Although he had tried to shush her, she had told him she was too old to worry about death.

Nero was not as destructive as Emperor Caligula had been. For three years, the good people of Rome shivered at the name of Caligula. He had been unpredictable, obsessed with bizarre sexual games, and bloodthirsty.

Suetonius shuddered at the memory of the circus of beasts against old men and women who had merely professed a belief in a prophet called Jesus of Nazareth. His mother's own sister had talked about this Jewish prophet. Suetonius barely remembered Savina, but he had liked her. She at least was safe in death from Nero's derangement. She wouldn't lose her life by the claws of a beast. It was a terrible price to pay for one's belief. One god, indeed. There was so much to watch in the world that one god couldn't do it all. Suetonius chuckled at the absurdity of the idea. He would be bored with one god.

He waved his hand to stay the servant who wanted to add more hot water to the tub and rose. The servant wrapped him in a cotton cloth before he moved closer to the fire. He listened to the wind howl about the hut and rattle the door. Tonight it would be difficult to keep warm without the company of a woman. He was too old for women, and he found them too much trouble.

Suetonius had dressed and was chewing a tough piece of meat when he heard a cry. It seemed far away, and he cocked his head to listen. Hearing nothing, he decided it was the howl of a wolf. The sun had set, and the winter night approached like a fast-drawn chariot. The sound came again, and this time Suetonius noted that his servant raised his head from the task at hand and stared toward the door. Suetonius checked the dagger sheathed at his waist, rose quickly, and threw a woolen cloak about his shoulders. He pinned it securely against the evening's wind and stood aside as the servant held the door for him.

The wind pulled at Suetonius' hair, and he cursed himself for not having had the sense to fasten the hood more securely. He was instantly chilled by the wind that lashed him with pellets of hard snow. The sounds of a woman screaming made him forget his own distress, and he raced toward the edge of the village from whence the sound came. There was enough light for him to see a woman huddled against the side of a hut, holding a bundle in her arms. A short distance away was a sight that filled Suetonius with more dread than a legion of the enemy charging. The animal was dirty gray, its shaggy coat bare in places. The wolf's mouth opened and spittle poured forth in a fountain of foam. Its yellow eyes were glazed, and the disease that caused the wolf to be so brazen also prevented it from acting rationally. It staggered in a circle, seeming to forget where its prey was located.

Suetonius cursed himself for his carelessness in leaving his sword behind. He had expected to find a woman being attacked by a man, but not this. He moved closer to the woman only to have the wolf focus on him. It staggered away from the woman toward its new target.

Suetonius shifted his gaze from the wolf to the woman. She had her back to the wolf and him, hovering to protect whatever it was in her arms. She was dirty and clothed in rags. Her matted hair hung down her back. At any other time, Suetonius would have noted the hag with disgust. He whispered loudly enough for the woman to hear him. "The wolf is watching me. Slip carefully around the corner of the hut and be gone."

Suetonius saw no response and wondered if she were crazy or didn't understand his tongue. "Go! Go slowly." He breathed with relief when he saw that she understood. He pulled his dagger and flashed it before the wolf, hoping to hold its attention. The hag looked back once before slipping around the corner of the hut.

With no time to worry about the ignominious manner of his death, Suetonius thought to get on with it. He stepped forward, holding the dagger at an angle so that he could thrust upward through the wolf's heart.

The wolf snarled and shook its head, spraying the air with spittle. Suetonius held himself in check. It would do him no good to avoid the spittle that was known to drive men as well as animals mad. He was to die. It became a simple fact. Suetonius had no fear, only regret that he would be buried in this cold and unforgiving land far away from the flowers of home.

The wolf staggered forward, and Suetonius braced himself for his final battle.

The old woman sped past Suetonius. A glare of light caught his eye, and it took a moment for Suetonius to realize that the glare was from a long sword as it came down on the neck of the wolf, not once but three times. The wolf gurgled and dropped, its head nearly severed from its body. The hag had saved his life. Now he knew she was crazy to attack a mad wolf. He ran over to her and pulled her out of range of any of the juices from the animal. It was a dreaded disease that this wolf carried and mad or not, the hag deserved some consideration. He was responsible for her, too, since he was the governor.

"Come, lay the sword down. Do not touch the blade or any part of the wolf. I will send someone to burn this beast. Is this your hut?" Suetonius added his dagger to the sword she laid down.

The hag nodded.

"And the sword?"

"It was my husband's sword. I hid it from the Iceni after he died. May I have it back?"

Suetonius was startled by the youthfulness of her voice, and he turned her toward him. The face was of a woman, not young, but not as old as he had thought. She was probably no more than twenty and eight. "Why are you in such dire circumstances?"

She shook her head and clamped her mouth in a tight line.

"Come with me. The least I can do is give you some decent food."

She shook her head again.

"Have you suddenly become mute? Or have you exhausted the words of my language?"

"I am grateful to you, sir, but I have other matters that are pressing." She inclined her head toward the cottage.

Suetonius grabbed her arm. "Do you hide someone?" He jerked her toward the front of the hut, and holding her in front of him, kicked open the flimsy door. The room was dark. "Who do you hide here?" Suetonius twisted her thin arm behind her back until she gasped in pain. "Who is here?"

"No one. I swear. No one." The woman tried to pull away.

"You lie. I can always tell a lie." Suetonius held the woman with one hand and pushed her through the door. A sound in the corner of the hut commanded his attention, and he moved toward it, still holding his hostage. He pulled his hidden dagger from his tunic and held it up, straining to see in the dimly lit room.

The woman gasped. "Stay your dagger, sir, it is only a babe. She is my babe. Do not harm her."

Suetonius looked about the hovel and seeing no one else, let the woman's arm drop. She rushed to the bundle of rags and swooped them up in her arms. "Why are you in such a situation? You are obviously well-born with a king's sword and a command of Latin."

"I won't tire you with my tale of woe, sir." She pulled the rags from the face of the child and kissed her.

Suetonius eyed her carefully. She intrigued him. "You can't stay here. Come with me to my hut where it is more attuned to living."

"No thank you, sir."

"Must I keep reminding you that you saved my life? It is degrading to me personally to have been saved by a woman. I insist on repaying you in order to soothe my chagrin."

The woman laughed, her voice like the sound of bells. "I find men the same no matter what their origins."

Suetonius frowned. "Do you know who I am?"

"No, for I have been here but a week." The woman spit on her fingers and rubbed a spot of dirt from the cheek of the baby. "You are well-dressed, so I assume a man of some importance."

Suetonius shivered. "Do you not have wood for a fire?"

"I have nothing."

"Then there is no reason to stay here. I am the Governor of Britannia, Suetonius Paulinus. I order you to bring the child to my home." Suetonius pushed the woman toward the door. "I grow cold. Hurry along." Suetonius smelled the sour odor of unwashed flesh.

The woman pulled her arm away from Suetonius. "I will not be your mistress."

"Don't be an ass, woman. I am too old for thoughts such as those." Suetonius pushed her through the door.

In short time, the woman with her babe was shepherded into Suetonius' quarters. He was pleased to see the tub of water was still full. He pointed to it. "You will scrub yourself clean." The gurgling of the babe reminded Suetonius of its plight. "Clean the child as well." He turned to his servant who stared at the trio. "Get the kettle and warm the water." When his servant looked at him, he turned to the woman. "Do you speak his tongue?"

The woman said something that sounded to Suetonius like dogs barking. The language of this island always sounded that way to him. The servant answered her, and she turned to Suetonius.

"He will do as you bid. Would you like to know his name?"

Suetonius looked at the servant who was scurrying between the fire pit and the tub. "If I say 'no' you will tell me anyway."

"His name is Cullen. He says that you are strange, and you frighten him with your foreign ways. He said the last governor died after only being here nine moons."

Suetonius frowned. "What does he know of Governor Veranius?"

The woman spoke to Cullen, then turned to Suetonius. "He says the other governor didn't act like a bear."

"So I frighten him?"

"Cullen says you growl like a hungry dog each morning. He also says that you snore like the rumbling of thunder in the summer."

Suetonius folded his arms and scowled at his servant. "No more talk of my habits. Lay the child aside and cleanse yourself."

"What of my clothes? I should burn them. I'm afraid that I share them with vermin."

Suetonius shuddered. "Then throw them into the fire."

"Would you like to know my name and the name of my child?"

Suetonius threw up his hands. "Why not be able to call you by a name?"

"My name is Caitlin. I've named my child Darcy, for she was born at a dark time in my life. She will never know her father, for he was killed before her birth." Caitlin's voice cracked, and she busied herself with the child.

"I will send the servant for proper clothing for you and the child. Tell him to do so. Tell him to send someone to burn the diseased wolf."

"Where will you go, sir, so that I may have some privacy?"

"I will go nowhere. I have had a difficult night, and I intend to go to bed. You may sleep by the fire. Have the servant get you a pallet as well." Suetonius stared at her. "Why do you stand there? Tell the servant."

Caitlin spoke to the young servant, and when he nodded in understanding, she dismissed him. "I told you that his name is Cullen. You may call him that."

Suetonius frowned. "Are you giving me lessons in manners?"

"It seems necessary."

"You're very impertinent for someone who is in such dire need." Suetonius stomped to his bed, threw his cloak on it, and sat down. He removed his boots and threw them in a heap on the floor.

Caitlin sighed, laid the now sleeping infant near the fire, and walked to the boots. She picked them up and stood them against the wall. "If you care not for the boots each evening, they will not last." She ran her hand over the leather. "These are fine boots, indeed, and need a fine hand to care for them. I will teach Cullen the proper way to protect them from our harsh winter."

"What do you know of boot tending?" Suetonius looked at Caitlin's hands. "Your hands are not that of the laboring class."

Caitlin held out her hands and looked at the dirty fingernails. "I believe they are now." She blinked back a tear. "It seems my life has changed for the worse. The gods are angry with me, and I am at their mercy. On a whim they took my father, mother, brothers, and husband from me." Caitlin scratched her hip. "In their stead, I have lice. If you'll excuse me, I welcome the bath you've offered."

Suetonius grunted and laid down on the bed, pulling the covers over himself. "I will be asleep in a moment. Never fear about your privacy. I am an old man and beyond any desires."

Caitlin laughed. "You do act older than your appearance. I assume it comes from making heavy decisions, and it has weighted down your soul."

Suetonius rolled toward the wall, shifting around to make the pallet more comfortable. "You are an impertinent wench." He heard her laughter, and a pang of loneliness swept through him.

He heard a whump and the fire spit. Soon a rancid odor wafted across the room from burning clothes. The splashing in the tub irritated him. He pulled the covers about his head to shut out the sound of bathing.

It would not shut out the sound of the baby's crying, however. Suetonius waited for Caitlin to tend to the child, but when she did not, he threw back the covers in disgust. He swung his bare feet to the cold, earthen floor and marched across the room toward the child.

The sight of Caitlin beneath the water in the tub startled him, and he grabbed the drowning woman's hair and pulled her head above the water.

Caitlin sputtered, dug her fingernails into Suetonius' arm, and yelled, "What are you doing? Let go of me!"

Suetonius bellowed and pushed her hands away. "What are you doing, woman? What kind of gratitude do I get for saving you from drowning?" He looked at the scratches on his arm. "You have wounded me."

Caitlin tossed her wet hair away from her face. "I was drowning the vermin in my hair, you fool, not myself."

Suetonius grimaced at the thought of lice and stepped back from the tub. He examined his hand for tiny, moving white spots. Seeing none, he sighed with relief, but still felt like scratching. "Perhaps you should drown more than the lice with all the trouble you've already caused me."

"Perhaps I should not, since my child would surely die from neglect. She is still crying, and you have not had the decency to soothe her." Caitlin slid down into the water until her hair floated around her. "She has no teeth and cannot bite."

"I am a soldier, not a nursemaid. I know nothing of infants." He walked over to the babe, bent down, and patted her stomach. He winced as she screamed louder. Caitlin laughed and he turned toward her. "What am I to do? Do you expect me to pick her up and have her share her vermin with me?"

Caitlin glowered. "She has no lice. I made certain of that."

Suetonius stroked the child's head. "Lice do not discriminate. They accept everyone." He was surprised when the babe stopped its squalling, and he continued stroking her hair.

Caitlin splashed water on her face. "She likes you."

"She has no idea who I am. How can she like whom she doesn't know?" Suetonius looked down at the little girl. Her mother had tried to keep her clean. The child looked undernourished, but in spite of that, she was very pretty. Suetonius continued petting her until her eyes closed, and her breathing was regular. He stood and went back to his bed. "Your daughter sleeps now and so will I." The only answer as he lay down was splashing. He grunted at the noise and squeezed his eyes shut.

The odor of seared meat penetrated Suetonius' dreams, and he sat up, rubbing the sleep from his eyes. His servant was worthless when it came to the culinary arts, so the tempting smells were new to the hut.

Caitlin carried a steaming pot as she moved from the fireplace to the rough wooden table. She glanced at Suetonius. "Good morrow. Pray come and taste the breakfast I have prepared for you."

Suetonius saw that there were two places set at the table. "Are you planning to eat with me?"

"Of course. I will be your housekeeper, but I will not be your servant."

"If I say so, then you will be my slave."

"Nay, only those who allow themselves to be ruled can be made slaves. I have never been ruled by anyone. If my father were alive, or my husband, they would confirm what I say. In fact, my husband often said that I was stubborn." Caitlin bit her lip and blinked rapidly. "Come sit and eat before it gets cold."

Suetonius snarled. "I don't eat breakfast."

"No wonder you're grouchy like Cullen says. Come over here, or I will have to drag the table over there."

Suetonius groaned. This woman was indeed stubborn. He climbed out of bed, pulled the blanket around him, and sat on the stool at the table. He watched Caitlin place a slab of meat on a piece of bread. She put the pewter plate in front of him along with a tankard of ale, and sat across from him.

Caitlin pushed a strand of chestnut-colored hair behind her ear. "Can you not try to eat?" She picked up the piece of bread that held a slab of meat and nibbled carefully at it, and stared at Suetonius all the while.

Suetonius bit into the bread with the meat. He chewed slowly, then smiled at Caitlin. "This is very good. Where did you learn to cook like this?"

"My mother taught me that it was a woman's duty to keep her husband in good form so that when in battle, he may win."

Caitlin's voice cracked, and she bent over her food, letting her hair hide her face.

Suetonius glanced away from her private grief toward the corner where the baby lay on a new pallet. She was gurgling and playing with her toes. The child had the same chestnut brown hair as her mother, and in the light from the window, Suetonius could see that she was as clean as her new clothes. The servant had obeyed his orders well.

Suetonius looked back at Caitlin and saw that she was watching him. "The babe looks cleaner."

Caitlin smiled. "Thank you for your kindness. We are both feeling better although I still don't have enough milk for her."

Suetonius coughed. He wasn't used to women's problems. "Where is your homeland?"

"My family is from the north. Over the last few years we have been in several desperate battles alongside the Brigantes against the Iceni." Caitlin's brown eyes blazed from anger. "A red-haired witch helped her husband defeat my clan. May she go to the other world in pieces."

Suetonius' eyebrows were raised at this outburst. His curiosity overcame his discomfort at Caitlin's anger. "Did your husband die in battle?"

Caitlin nodded. "My brother died in the first battle. I thought there could be no sadness worse until I lost both father and husband in the next one. My mother's pain was so great that she went mad." Caitlin stared at her child who still lay contentedly by the fire. "She died by her own hand after the birth of my daughter."

Suetonius shook his head. "You have had many burdens placed on you."

"Yes, because of the Queen of the Iceni. I will see her soul rot in the underworld before I die. I have cursed her daily. I will kill her."

"Kill her? How?"

"I don't know, but the gods will show me the way."

"You can't kill her."

"I will slice her throat with a dagger."

"You have no dagger."

"I will." Caitlin's lower lip quivered. "I promised my brother, my father, my husband that I would avenge their deaths. Only the death of Boadicea will appease my menfolk."

"You have no family left?"

"None. We are quite alone in this hostile world." Caitlin turned to Suetonius and smiled. "Except for your kindness, I fear that my daughter and I would surely have perished last night."

"But for your valor, I would have perished at the fangs of the wolf at best, or the wolf's disease at the worst. My debt to you is greater, I think."

Caitlin's hand went to her throat. "My sword! It is all I possess of my husband's. What happened to it?"

"Did you not tell Cullen to burn it with the wolf?"

"I did not mention the sword. Burning it would take the disease away, but the hilt could be damaged. Someone could have taken it." Caitlin stared into the fire. "I held my dying husband and promised him I would care for his sword and pass it on to the child. Have I failed him in that?"

"I will locate the sword for you if I have to inspect every hovel in this village." Suetonius crammed a last piece of bread and meat in his mouth and stood. He swallowed the last of the ale in his tankard. "The meal was good."

"Thank you."

Suetonius looked for his woolen cloak from the end of the bed where he had thrown it the night before and was surprised to find it gone. He muttered and knelt to look under the bed. The cloak was not there. He pushed himself up, only to see Caitlin point toward the wall. His cloak hung on a peg in plain sight.

"First you place yourself in charge of my boots, and now you've taken over my wardrobe." Suetonius grabbed the cloak and threw it on.

"If you don't take care of your things . . ."

Suetonius held his hand up to halt her words. "I know what you're going to say, so don't." He marched to the door, then realized his feet were bare. He thought about pretending that it was a regular ritual of his to go barefoot in the morning, but could not bear the thought of his feet touching the frozen ground. He nonchalantly moved back toward the bed and sat down, but not before Caitlin got there before him. She knelt and held one boot. A smile tugged at the corners of her mouth.

"I have put my own boots on my own feet for many years now. I do not need a nursemaid to do it for me. I don't even allow a servant to put my boots on my feet."

"Cullen was right. You are a grouch in the morning. As for a nursemaid, I believe you do need one. How many men do you know who go barefoot into the snow?"

Suetonius continued to grumble as he let Caitlin put the boots on his feet. At last she was finished, and he marched to the door. As he opened it, he called back over his shoulder. "Find that servant and tell him to get a second tub and have it ready by tonight. You'll need daily baths to get rid of the vermin that will continue to hatch for a few days."

Caitlin grimaced as the door slammed. "Ugh! I'll be happy to tell him that."

Suetonius walked slowly through the village toward the place where the wolf had fallen, his thoughts on the new problems he had in his hut. He could imagine the looks his soldiers would give him when they discovered his new guests, especially after he had forbidden them to have women in their quarters.

Suetonius squared his shoulders. Of course, they may believe him still virile. Perhaps it wouldn't be a difficult burden after all. He would find the sword for Caitlin and return to the hut for the noon meal. The bath had helped her looks although she was scrawny. Her eyes, brown like oak leaves, were pretty except when she mocked him. Too many thoughts of a young widow's eyes.

Sunlight dropped down through the branches of a huge tree at the edge of the village and sparkled off the blade of the sword propped against the tree's trunk. Suetonius sniffed. The odor of burnt hair and flesh hung in the air. He saw the remains of the wolf between the hut and the tree. Moving to the sword, Suetonius saw that the blade showed signs of having been fired. He picked it up and tested its balance. It was a well-made weapon. The handle felt comfortable in his hand. Suetonius smiled as he thought about the shine that would be in Caitlin's eyes when he handed her the sword, hilt undamaged. His dagger had been fired as well, and he placed it in its sheath. He looked for the sword's sheath and seeing none, he stopped at the hovel to see if Caitlin had forgotten about it in the excitement of last evening.

Suetonius pushed open the flimsy door and stepped into the darkened hut. He let his eyes adjust to the dimness and looked around. There was nothing to see and therefore, no place for a sheath to hide. He started to leave when he spied the pallet. Except there. A woman like Caitlin would hide the only valuable she had close by. Suetonius moved to the pallet and lifted it with his sword. The sheath lay there. Suetonius picked it up and was careful not to touch the pallet. He walked quickly out of the hut and toward his own place.

The few minutes that it took Suetonius to cover the distance to his home was cold enough to remind him that winter was still upon the village. He marched double time to keep warm and was at his hut quickly. He smiled as he opened the door and held the sword in front of him.

Caitlin was putting wood on the fire when Suetonius came through the door. She squealed, dropped an arm load of wood and ran to Suetonius. "Thank you, sir. Thank you for the sword." She ran her hand across the leather sheath, tracing the curled design that wrapped itself around the sheath from end to end. The same design continued on the handle of the sword.

"It isn't damaged, Caitlin. A polishing will make it the same as new." Suetonius handed the sword to its owner. "It is a beautiful piece of work."

"It is a shame that something so beautiful is for killing. I don't hope for peace for myself, but if we could but have peace for my daughter, then all would be wonderful. My lot in life is to search out the red-haired witch and kill her."

"You are determined, but it is nearly impossible."

"Not for me. I will have peace only when she is dead."

"Peace?" Suetonius nodded. "That is the desire of Rome. We will have peace on this island as long as our army remains here. Your daughter will have a wonderful future with Rome's army to protect her."

CHAPTER
XI

HE BIRDS CHIRPED, and Boadicea frowned. A mere sparrow would live past this day when she and her daughters would not. She turned toward the window where the musical notes of the sparrow sang out with as much gusto as the tiny bird could manage. Prasutagus had loved birds, whether it be a sparrow or a hawk.

Boadicea held up the hemlock-laced wine and sniffed the acrid brew. The bouquet was not to her liking. She put the bowl down and watched the wine ripple. A small drink, then she and her daughters would cross over. Prasutagus would be standing on the other side with arms opened wide for her and their daughters. It would be a swift journey to see Prasutagus and worth the short time in pain. Boadicea stared at her reflection in the wine. Who was this woman that Prasutagus loved? Who was he?

She loved him for his seriousness and for his antics. Perhaps his frivolous moments were the best thoughts to have in her heart at death.

"Mother, Mother, come quickly! Father has brought home a wolf cub." Neila danced back and forth in front of her father as he walked up the ramparts.

Boadicea ran out the door at the first yelp from Neila and stood with her hands on her hips. "What ails you, Daughter?"

"Father and I were hunting when I spied this poor wolf cub next to her dead mother." Neila giggled. "Father had a terrible time getting the cub tied up in his cloak."

Boadicea stared at the wriggling bundle that Prasutagus held at arm's length. She stamped her foot. "Husband, if you bring that foul-smelling animal into this hut, then you'll have to move out. It has already rendered your cloak beyond washing with its stench. See, it has wet itself and thoroughly soaked your cloak."

Prasutagus hesitated and stopped a short way from Boadicea. "I brought you an orphan to mother and mend."

Sydelle burst through the door of the hut, her sewing still in her hand. "What is it, Mother? What have Neila and Father gotten into this time?"

Boadicea shook her head. "Do not speak in such a manner as that about your father." She giggled. "Even if it is true."

Prasutagus grasped the wriggling bundle tighter. "This poor, motherless baby needs some nourishment."

"Do not play with my emotions, Husband. You know how I hate wolves! I hate them with as much passion as I have for the Romans. You think I will be tender of heart."

Neila ran to Boadicea and grabbed her arm. "You should have seen Father trying to catch the cub. He wouldn't let me near in case she was sick, but after we watched her for awhile, Father knew she was all right." Neila glanced back at her father. "The cub bit him often, and Father called on the gods at least ten times."

"Neila, do not tell your mother everything I do."

Boadicea laughed. She felt a sudden rush of love for her husband course through her. "Did the gods respond to your pleas?"

"No." Prasutagus' outstretched arm began to tremble from the weight of the cub. "Take this poor baby and give her nourishment."

Sydelle wrinkled her nose. "Won't she make our home stink?"

"Oh, Sydelle, we can give her a bath." Neila went to her sister. "Think of the fun it will be to have a wolf to play with. She can be tamed, for she isn't weaned yet."

Sydelle looked at her mother. "Father did bring her all the way back here so that we could help her. She is a creature of the forest, and the forest is in your protection. This means that the creatures are in your protection as well. You must help even though you hate wolves."

"Sydelle, your arguments coupled with your father's pained expression at having lost his favorite hunting cloak give me no leave but to become nurse to a furry baby." Boadicea shook her head at the look of relief on Prasutagus' face. She should make him wonder longer at her intentions, but he looked like a small boy with hopeful eyes instead of a warrior and a king. "Bring the cub into the kitchen. I will tend to her needs there. Neila and Sydelle, run ahead and place the table across the doorway. I don't want that animal running and hiding in the rest of the house. Come, Prasutagus. As soon as you've let go of your treasure, you will have to burn that cloak."

Prasutagus followed Sydelle and Neila around the hut and into the back door, all the while holding the squirming, stinking bundle away from him. Boadicea held open the door and waited until her family was inside before she stepped in herself. She made certain the door was shut and the table had been turned on its side to block the other doorway before she allowed the wolf cub to be released.

Boadicea felt a sudden pity for the cub as it scooted across the floor and huddled in a corner, baring it tiny teeth to scare them away. The wolf cub was shivering in terror. "Sydelle, you have always understood animals. Give this one some milk from the jug. Put it in a shallow bowl and let's see if it will lap."

Sydelle hurried across the kitchen and poured the milk in a bowl. "What if she isn't weaned?"

Prasutagus held out hands covered with tiny teeth marks. "I believe she has already learned to eat meat."

Boadicea chuckled. "Obviously she has. You need to let me tend to your hands later." She turned and watched as Sydelle placed the bowl of milk in front of the growling cub. Boadicea winced as the cub snapped at Sydelle, but her daughter was quick and escaped without getting her fingers bitten by the cub's tiny, sharp teeth.

Neila knelt next to Sydelle. "May we pet her?"

Sydelle snorted. "You may if you want to lose a piece of your finger. You have to win her trust—you can't force friendship."

Neila rocked back and forth on her heels. "What can I do? I want to help tame her, too."

Sydelle placed a hand on Neila's shoulder, restraining her. "First you can sit still so that you don't upset the poor thing."

Neila sat back on her heels and was still. "I think we should name her. If we name her, then she'll be ours."

"I'm afraid that is true." Boadicea wrinkled her nose.

"Prasutagus, if you would take yourself and your cloak outside, the kitchen would smell much better. Burn that cloak!"

Prasutagus looked at the offensive garment in his hand and exited quickly, calling back over his shoulder, "I will need a new one."

"Indeed, you will. I will make one for you right away, with the restriction that you cannot use it for any creature but yourself." Boadicea grinned at the sight of her husband disappearing through the door, his face reddening as he held his breath.

Boadicea sat on a stool and watched her two daughters discuss taming the cub. "I hope you plan to clean up after this new responsibility of yours."

Neila chewed on her lower lip. "I think Father already promised that he would make a fence for her so that we could put her out for that sort of thing."

"It will be too dark to make a fence." Boadicea leaned forward. "An animal will not soil its bed, for then its enemies would discover it. If you place the cub in a chest for the night, she will wait until you put her out in the morning."

Sydelle pushed the dish closer to the cowering cub. "She'll run away."

Neila placed her hand on her sister's arm. "I can make her a leash, Sydelle. It won't take long."

"She won't eat," Sydelle said.

"If you back away, she may eat." Boadicea looked at the small bundle of gray fur. Two shining eyes watched every movement. Although the cub was frightened, Boadicea was impressed by her bravery.

Neila and Sydelle moved away from the cub and sat on the floor near their mother. Neila twisted her dark ringlets around her fingers, squirmed, and tapped her foot. Sydelle sat very still and watched the cub.

Boadicea placed a hand on Neila's shoulder to quiet her. "What shall we name her?"

Sydelle looked at the cub intently. "It should be a name that shows she is brave. I would be very frightened if someone took me from my mother." Sydelle looked around at Boadicea. "Even if my mother were dead, I would want to be with her."

Neila sighed. "Oh, Sydelle, there you go being melancholy, again."

Boadicea shivered. She didn't understand why, and she spoke quickly to change the subject. "Let's name this poor cub."

Sydelle whispered, "Let's call her Rosebud because of what she did to Father."

"Sydelle, to give her an unkind name would make her an unkind animal. Give her a noble name, for she is a noble animal."

Neila snapped her fingers. "That's it, Mother. You've just named her. Let's call her 'Noble'."

Sydelle clapped her hands together. "I like it. We'll call her that. Look, she laps the milk."

Boadicea tousled Sydelle's hair. "I think you have a friend. You and Neila take turns giving her a little milk several times through the night and often during the day. She will soon see you both as her mother. When she licks your hand, then that means she has given her heart to you."

Neila cocked her head to one side and looked at her mother. "Can she give her heart to more than one of us?"

"Of course," Boadicea said. "Did I not give my heart to my mother, my father and then to your father? Did I not give my heart to both my beautiful daughters?"

Sydelle studied her mother's words in silence.

Neila nodded. "I guess a heart can stretch a lot."

"Boadicea! Prasutagus! Come quickly!" Rhianna burst through the kitchen door.

Boadicea leaped up from the table, knocking her noon meal to the floor. She pushed Telyn, the cook, aside and grabbed her sword that was always close to her these days. "What is it?"

"Keir and his men have been patrolling the border between us and our friends, the Trinovantes."

"Along the River Stour?" Prasutagus asked.

"Yes. He says a group of twenty to thirty riders are coming this way at a fast pace."

"Did he say who?" Boadicea buckled her sword belt.

"He couldn't tell. He doesn't think it's the Roman fiends." Rhianna leaned against the door jamb and held her side. "I ran from the sheep barn. Listen, there's the gong to bring in our people."

"We go to greet our company," Prasutagus said. He was somber as he adjusted his sword.

"Keir! Where are the riders now?" Boadicea asked.

"They have slowed to a walk and come through the woods quietly." Keir wiped his face with his forearm, making his tunic damp.

"We shall meet them at the edge. Keir, gather your troops and ride around to the south of them. We want them between us." Boadicea whistled for Thayne as she ran toward the corral. A stable boy ran toward her with Thayne's bridle in one hand and Rand's in the other.

Boadicea heard Prasutagus shout at her to slow down as she raced Thayne across the pasture to the edge of the woods, but she couldn't force herself to. She got to the top of the last rise where she expected to find the riders and pulled Thayne to a halt. Prasutagus, Sydelle, Neila, and thirty of their people were close behind with weapons ready.

"Spread out in a half-moon. When they come closer, be they enemy or friend, we will surround them," Prasutagus said.

Her mouth went dry as Boadicea saw men appear suddenly over the rise. She stared at each man and woman in turn, trying to place the faces. They weren't Roman, thank the gods. "Prasutagus, the older man has a familiar countenance. What do you think?"

"I cannot place him, but from their dress, I'd say they are from far to the south."

The riders stopped in front of Boadicea and Prasutagus, ignoring the Iceni who closed around them at a discreet distance. The leader was covered with the grime of several days riding as were the others. He slumped forward, barely raising his arm in a salute. "Forgive me," he rasped, taking great breaths of air. "I need to breathe the air of a free people, for no longer are we free."

"Whatever do you mean? Don't speak in riddles," Boadicea said. Her hand tightened on the hilt of her sword.

"Queen Boadicea, do you not remember me? We first met more than twenty-eight summers ago at your father's court."

"You want me to remember something when I was but five summers on this earth?" Boadicea was torn between being amused and being angry. "I am sorry that my memory is not better suited to this encounter."

"I am Dearg, leader of the Durotriges, south on the far sea coast. We have ridden for ten days to get here."

"Dearg?" Boadicea nodded. "Now my memory serves me. You had come to council to talk about the pending Roman invasion. Did you believe it when my father warned all of you?"

Dearg looked at the ground. "No, we did not have the courage to view the future as your father did." He glanced at Prasutagus, then Boadicea. "The future is here. It comes not with peace, but with the Romans as your father promised."

"Why have you ridden here? Have the Romans attacked your people?" Prasutagus asked.

"A small band of Dobunni, who live three days ride to the north and west of us, was attacked by a Roman general named Cerialis," Dearg said.

"For no reason?" Boadicea asked.

"It depends on who answers the question. The Dobunni have been paying the Romans half of everything they have for *pax Romana*." Dearg shrugged. "They wanted some of their horses back, so they went to get them."

"Roman peace." Boadicea spit out the words. "What do the Romans know of peace? They want to protect us, but from what? A scant five summers ago they invaded this island, and now they spread like a disease."

"What happened after the Dobrunni retrieved their horses?" Prasutagus asked.

"The Romans considered themselves attacked, and they retaliated. At first, they had General Petilius Cerialis in retreat until he was saved by their supreme leader, Governor Suetonius Paulinus. All of the Dobunni were slain save for one woman who feigned death."

"Thank you for the warning, Dearg. Come, you and your people need to eat and rest. Your journey has been difficult." Prasutagus said.

"A word to warn you," Dearg said. "Today the Romans are far from here, but what of tomorrow?"

Prasutagus stared across the hills and valleys of his country. "I do not know."

"One more thing," Dearg said. "We, too, have had to give half of what we grow or own to the Romans. Beware of what the Romans call a client-king relationship. Our stores of grain are gone, for the Romans have no idea what half is. Our children grow hungry, our women grow sad, and our warriors grow weak. We need food."

"You shall have whatever you need." Boadicea's hatred of the Romans multiplied ten-fold. "We have good sheep and goats. A few cows for milk can be spared along with seed for next year's planting."

Boadicea turned Thayne toward home. She felt as if her world had disappeared, as the hills do when fog rolls in from the Narrow Sea. She wondered what the future would bring. *Pax Romana?* She shuddered.

When Neila asked her a question, Boadicea shook her head. She didn't have the strength to deal with Neila's persistent questions when a wall of gray blocked her path to the future.

Boadicea walked along with Prasutagus, slowing her stride to match his. The morning air was no longer chilly, and her tunic dragged the dew off the meadow grass. She looked out across the field to the cluster of horses that stood nose to rump, swishing their tails to ward off the annoying flies. In a field farther away, Boadicea could see the men and women of the village tend the crops. Children ran back and forth on errands from the fields to the wells, the huts, or tended the animals.

Boadicea swatted a gnat that continuously buzzed in front of her face. Annoyed, she finally slapped her hands together, and the gnat ceased to exist. "Prasutagus, I have wanted to talk to you about the invaders, but you seem to have excuses not to do so."

"There is nothing to discuss. I will do what I think is best for the Iceni." Prasutagus clasped his hands behind his back and continued to walk.

"I am half of the throne and therefore, I should be involved in the decision. Whatever affects your village affects my village. Nay, I should not talk of villages, for your people are my people, and my people are yours. We have never disagreed on how to rule until now." Boadicea stepped in front of Prasutagus and stopped him. She placed her hands on his arms and turned him toward the fields. "Look at our people, husband. They work for us, they trust us, and they depend on us. If the Romans offer us a client-king position as they have done south of here, then I think we should go to war, and send them from this land."

Boadicea bent down and scooped up a handful of dirt. She held it in front of Prasutagus. "This is our land. The dirt is made of the bones and flesh and blood of our fathers and mothers. We use this land to grow food for our children. No Roman has the right to march in here and claim this land. No Roman has the right to be on the land built from the deaths of our forefathers."

Prasutagus took the lump of dirt from Boadicea. "This land was given to us by our ancestors to protect. We are to protect it and our people the best that we know how. Tell me, how do we fight an army that has conquered the best warriors in the south?" He let the dirt sift through his fingers. "If we are not careful in our dealings with the Romans, they will destroy us. What happens to everything our ancestors taught us? What happens to our people and what happens to us?"

Boadicea sighed. "Are they as strong as our spies have told us? Do you believe their armies are never-ending and swarm across the sea like vultures above the dying?"

"I don't know what to believe. I only know that we have been told that a man will visit us. He will be here soon, and he will want an answer." Prasutagus brushed the dirt from his hands. "Do not think that I have thought lightly of this problem. I have walked and prayed many days, but the answer will not come. I ask that you use your powers as a priestess to help decide our future."

"I will. I will perform the five-day prayer and fast in the sacred grove. Take care not to tell our people why I have to do this. We must not worry them." In times of trouble, the priesthood always helped her.

The trees formed a canopy above the altar shutting out most of the sunlight. Slender rays sliced through the leaves and illuminated tiny dust motes that seemed to have life. Birds flitted back and forth, rustled leaves, and created whirlwinds among the sunlit specks of dust. The smell of damp earth mixed with rotting wood and decaying vegetation filled Boadicea's nostrils.

Boadicea stood before the stone altar placed at the base of the largest oak tree in the grove. She chanted the ancient prayers of her ancestors. She had crisscrossed her cheeks and nose with blue stripes. Her tunic was white with horizontal stripes of blue broken by vertical bands of red and yellow. With arms upraised toward the canopy of leaves, she called on the ancient gods of her people. The sleeves of her tunic fell toward her shoulders, revealing painted arms of blue.

"My father of gods and my mother of goddesses, please heed my call. Help me to see the future. Give me eyes with which to see truth and a heart with which to know wisdom. Give me your blessings that I may do your will. Our people need you in this time of invasion. This is the fifth day of my fast, and I feel the power of the gods surging through me. I will do as you wish, for I am your daughter." Boadicea felt faint, but still she kept her eyes closed and her arms stretched toward the sky. The dizziness that she had experienced throughout the day was becoming worse, and she stepped away from the stone altar. Boadicea knew she was swaying, but held herself as steady as possible, just as her mother had taught her. The dreams would come soon. It was with expectation, but still a surprise when the ground rose up and hit the full length of her body. She remembered only the songs of the birds before her senses left her completely.

Boadicea saw her husband at the edge of the clearing. She smiled, for he reposed nonchalantly against a tree as if he were merely passing the time of day. He chewed a long piece of meadow grass and lazily shooed insects away from his face.

"Prasutagus!" Boadicea picked up her skirts and ran to her husband. She felt weak, but at peace. She didn't stop running until she fell into his outstretched arms. Only then did she allow her quaking knees to desert her, and she slid to the ground with Prasutagus breaking her fall.

He held out a skin of wine. "Here, drink this. It will bring back some of the color to your cheeks. I have brought you meat and bread."

Boadicea nodded and placed her hand on his to steady the stream of wine. She lay back against Prasutagus' chest. "Thank you."

Prasutagus pulled a sack from his belt and untied the rawhide string. He placed a slab of meat on a chunk of bread, he held it to Boadicea's mouth.

"I can feed myself, now. The wine helped." Boadicea took the food and chewed. She was pleased that Prasutagus knew that she could not yet tell him what the gods wanted them to do. She would need to gain strength, for a five-day fast was the most punishing ordeal a priestess had to endure.

"Our daughters send their love."

"I missed all of you, but mostly I missed my husband." Boadicea pulled Prasutagus' face to her and kissed him.

Prasutagus sighed. "I missed you. Our bed seemed cold and uninviting. I missed feeling your warmth next to me, and I missed feeling the weight of your body next to mine."

"I had the thought of you tucked in the back of my heart the entire time I talked with our gods. I do that so I won't feel alone. Thoughts of you gave me strength. Tell me of the Romans."

"They have raided another country, Atrebates. It is closer to us than Dearg's country by a three days ride."

"Oh, no! Have they killed great numbers?" Boadicea felt like smashing a Roman skull or two. "Atrebates have land that takes many days to cross. If they went after them, will they want our lands? We have four times the land that they have. Our farm lands are richer and our forests thicker. Will the Romans want Iceni?"

"I have no way of knowing. You did the fast." Prasutagus sighed. "Come, let's go home. Our daughters wait." Prasutagus stood and took Boadicea by her hands and pulled her to her feet barely giving her time to snatch the wine skin and sack of food off her lap.

Boadicea leaned against Prasutagus as they walked across the meadow where the wild flowers were splattered as if a dyer had thrown water from his dye vats. Birds flew above them, swooping and gliding in a dance for them. The sun shone brilliantly, and the sky was clear of clouds. A rabbit bounded out in front of them and whipped back and forth through the meadow grass until it disappeared out of sight into its burrow.

"Look, Prasutagus. A hare. 'Tis a good omen from the gods." Boadicea felt at peace. The world was at peace, for the day showed it to be so. The course of action was set for her people by the gods, and she knew that Prasutagus would follow it.

They entered the woods, hand in hand, and walked along the path toward the fields where their people toiled. The woods felt cool, and Boadicea was revived. She touched each oak tree that they passed and said a small prayer of thanks.

The two rulers of the Iceni stopped at the edge of the woods and looked over the pasture where the cattle, sheep, and horses were kept. Prasutagus swept his arm to take in the panoramic view. "Never did I dream that I would rule lands so vast, and never did I dream that you would be beside me to guide both our peoples. We have responsibility for these many lands and to people whom we cannot see from our own home. We have been blessed."

"We are wealthy, that is true, Husband." Boadicea listened to the quiet, broken only by the whisper of the breeze rustling the leaves in the woods they left behind them. She turned her face toward the sun. Boadicea was startled as the shadow of a raven flickered across her face, but she forgot it at the sight of her daughters running toward her. Neila was in front of Sydelle, her skirts hiked up above her knees and feet pounding like a running horse. Sydelle followed, running also, but with a more delicate gait. Her auburn hair flowed behind her like a sail, and the smile on her face warmed Boadicea's heart.

Boadicea held wide her arms and received her offspring one after the other. Nothing would harm her children—she would make certain of that. But she frowned when a flock of ravens flew over them, casting shadows over the four of them.

Boadicea looked skyward at the stars scattered across the sky like thousands of tiny, white flames against black wool. Boadicea lay back on the fur skin Prasutagus had thrown down for them and snuggled against her husband.

Prasutagus whispered in her ear. "The night was made for lovers."

"My husband has become a poet." Boadicea squirmed to get more comfortable. "It is time that I tell you what the gods shared with me about our future."

"Did they tell you what to do?"

"Yes, they did." Boadicea took Prasutagus' hand in her own. "My visions spoke of peace for our people. In order to ensure that our children and the children of our people will not perish, we are to accept whatever the Romans offer us as long as it is offered with dignity and respect for our beliefs. The gods were very emphatic. We are to accept a client-kingship only to preserve our people and our ways. If the Romans treat us badly, then we must dispatch them to their own gods in the land beyond life." Boadicea listened to Prasutagus' breathing. "Have you thoughts on this?"

"I trust in your visions. Your ability to talk with the gods has helped us in the past. When the Roman soldier comes with his message, then we will listen. If he speaks with respect for us, we will do what the gods expect."

"The gods have also shown me something else."

"What?"

"We must call the Council of Elders together and tell them of my visions. They should have a voice in our future," Boadicea said.

"It shall be so. I will call them before us seven days hence."

Boadicea and Prasutagus rarely sat on the thrones in the great hall, and tonight there would be no exception. She explained to Prasutagus that to do so would keep the elders from voicing their true opinions. "We need their wise counsel," she told him.

The night was cold and misty and the dampness settled in Boadicea's bones. She and Prasutagus had huge oak tables placed close to a roaring fire to warm the ancient bodies of the men and women who sat on cushioned benches.

Thirteen in number, they represented the families that made one-fourth of a tribe. Each was the oldest member of their particular clan, and each would speak not for themselves, but for the majority of their tribe.

Faces were somber. The elders were called together infrequently, usually to discuss war. Boadicea hoped that these ancients could come to an agreement with each other and with her and Prasutagus. The gods were all-knowing, so Boadicea would not question this decision, but she had to convey the wishes of the gods to the elders.

The oldest member of the Council called the meeting to order after Boadicea and Prasutagus were seated at the table with them.

In a voice that was still strong even for her more than eighty years, Fallon said, "We have come from the far corners of our land to lend our wisdom to our Queen Boadicea and King Prasutagus. We know that whatever we say will be taken by them as truth. We also know that whatever the reason for being here, the final authority rests with our two leaders.

"I fear that we have come to be told of the Roman problem. No matter where we live, talk of the Romans has reached our ears. It is a serious problem that we discuss tonight. The strictest of Council rules will prevail so that we may part as friends even if we do not agree."

Boadicea waited for Fallon to signal that it was time to talk to the Council. Prasutagus had asked that Boadicea talk with the elders as the priestess of the Iceni. They both thought that the elders should be privy to the gods' advice.

She wanted to smile at Graehme, whose chin rested on his ample chest and, with eyes closed, seemed oblivious to the meeting. Boadicea knew from experience that this was not so. He would know everything.

"My esteemed advisors, your King, Prasutagus, and I have asked you to give us your wise counsel concerning the Romans. They have kept to the south of us, but now they are to the west of our country. In twelve days time, the Roman Governor, Suetonius Paulinus, will come to meet with your King and me."

The gasp from the elders startled Boadicea. Their fear of the Romans was greater than she thought. In spite of the strict Council rules, there was a murmuring amongst them. Boadicea saw Graehme's eyes pop open, and he sat straight up. He was no longer the jovial joker, and it saddened Boadicea to see him so distraught.

"I have talked with the gods to see what should be done about the Romans. I have dreamed of rivers of blood. Now I talk with you."

Stunned silence was finally broken by Fallon. "My queen, I have heard that the Romans take the grain, animals, and cloth that other tribes have worked hard to create. The Romans call this taxes, and it is payment for protection from an enemy across the sea. I have yet to see the enemy from across the sea except for the Romans. I say that we run them from our lands."

The silence was stunning. Expecting to hear arguments and protests, Boadicea was ready to pound the handle of her knife on the table. Instead, she looked at Prasutagus in puzzlement.

He spoke. "I, too, have wondered about an enemy across the sea. I know we have enemies, but we have always been victorious in battle. However, there is change on our island, and we need to change, too. No longer can we ignore the outsiders."

"We won't ignore them. We will push them from our lands," Calhoun said.

Prasutagus paused again and waited for the elders to stop murmuring. "Queen Boadicea was concerned about our future, and so she went to the sacred grove and performed the high fast of five days." This time the elders stared at Boadicea, the wonder evident on their faces.

"I made that sacrifice in order to know the gods' wishes."

"Our gods will talk with you, a priestess, Queen Boadicea, but do they expect us to follow their wishes?"

Boadicea stared at Calhoun, who had placed himself in the front of the room and in the center of the strongest of the elders. "Calhoun, if we call on the gods, they do not expect us to waste their time by not following their advice."

"But our religion says that we are to think freely. We are human, but the gods gave us the ability to decide our fate," Calhoun said. He glared at Boadicea, his belligerent expression reminding her of her childhood enemy, Gryffyth. She shook that thought from her mind. Calhoun was nothing like Gryffyth. This man was concerned for his clan, nothing more.

"Calhoun, the decision about the Romans will affect more than the generations that live today. What we do as Iceni will make our tribe stronger or destroy it forever. If we are destroyed, where will the seed of our heirs be planted? Where will our religion be housed? Who will remember us?"

"Queen Boadicea is right. The Roman army is powerful. They call themselves the most powerful army on earth, and perhaps they are," Fallon said. "I for one believe in the wisdom of the gods. Tell us what was revealed to you."

"The gods have said that we should allow the Romans to protect us, and that we should pay their taxes as a client-kingship."

"Never!" Calhoun shouted. "Never! Never! Never!"

Several men and women arose and chanted, "Never! Never! Never!"

Calmly, Boadicea pounded the handle of her knife on the table until the chanting stopped. "My friends, my advisors. It is true that the gods gave us the wisdom to make choices, but only the gods can see the future."

Fallon, her age seemingly forgotten, stood and glared at each man and woman until there was a stillness broken only by the sounds of the night. "I have faith in my King and Queen. I have faith in the Priestess, Boadicea. I feel we are doubly honored to have a priestess as queen. My clan will follow the wishes of our leaders. For the sake of the gods, Queen Boadicea performed the five day prayer—not for herself, but for us. Show a little of that same faith yourselves."

Fallon sat. One by one, the clan leaders sat down, nodding their agreement with her wisdom.

For her faith, Boadicea vowed to make certain the woman had extra sheep and grain for the winter. Fallon was strong and powerful in spite of her age, and Boadicea hoped that she would be the same when she had lived that many years.

The best robe that Prasutagus owned was Boadicea's favorite. It was saffron and when he wore it, her husband's brown eyes had depth. She laid his crown with its red, blue, and green gems on the bed. Next to it, she placed his matching gold rings and the torc of his office. Smiling, she smoothed the panel that graced the front of his robe. It had come from a land that was years away. The merchant told Boadicea the people had eyes that turned upwards and hair as black as the inside of a cave. For every important occasion, she had performed this ceremony for her king and husband.

She smoothed the robe once more, then went to the altar room. Standing in front of the altar, Boadicea asked her gods to guide her through the next few hours. She didn't know how long she had been praying when Prasutagus walked quickly into the main hall straight to the altar. She felt his presence behind her, and she turned, her eyebrows raised forming a wordless question.

"They have come. You look stunning, my dear."

Boadicea adjusted her crown of gold studded with as many precious gems as Prasutagus' and smiled. "Thank you." The bracelets on her arm jingled merrily.

"The gods smiled on me the day that we met. I am so fortunate to have you by my side; nay, sometimes in front of me." Prasutagus looked toward the thrones that were in position to the left of the altar, carved generations ago of oak trees from the sacred grove. The backs were sculpted with a swirling design of intricate knots and twisted columns, with arms etched to represent the body of a wolf that ended with the heads facing the visitor. Snarling lips and bared fangs could intimidate anyone with a weak heart. The legs of each throne were the legs of the pair of wolves.

Boadicea took her husband's hand and led him outside. "I want to see how many have come." She looked to the southeast and gasped. The rhythmic sounds of marching mixed with the sound of prancing hooves on the hard ground made her breast-bone tingle from the noise. The sun glittered off the armor of the cavalry as it moved toward them. Behind them, troops marched in double time.

Boadicea shaded her eyes with her hand. "It is true what Keir has told us. They cover their entire bodies with metal. Their heads are decorated. Perhaps they also believe that the head is sacred as we do."

Prasutagus took her arm. "Come, let's prepare to receive them."

"Do not forget that the general was responsible for the death of some of the Dobunni warriors," Boadicea said.

Impatience had haunted Boadicea for many months as to the ways of the Romans she had studied for years, but now that they had finally arrived she was reluctant to see them. She sat tall and stately on her throne to the right of Prasutagus. To her right Sydelle and Neila were seated on smaller, but identical thrones. Noble sat between them, yellow eyes watching the door, her ears forward.

Boadicea knew from her network of spies led by Keir that the Romans did not think women should be in power. Perhaps the trouble caused by an Egyptian queen forced them to think that way. Boadicea frowned. She couldn't remember the Egyptian's name, but she had loved the story when she'd read it in her Greek chronicles.

The doors opened and the governor, Suetonius Paulinus, was presented along with General Cerialis and General Lucian. Suetonius certainly wasn't what Boadicea had expected. He was handsome with his dark hair scarcely touched by the silver of age. She had expected someone who looked like the residue of the underworld. She would have to teach Keir that she needed facts, not emotional stories about the Romans.

To his right stood General Lucian in an easy stance. He had a pleasant face, but it carried the weight of war. He had the same polite manner as the governor and had removed his helmet.

Cerialis, however, did look like residue from the underworld. His hair was gray, his face thin, and his nose bent like a kestrel's was not centered beneath eyes that were too small and too close together. He didn't remove his helmet.

Suetonius removed his helmet. Except for his staring at her, Suetonius Paulinus seemed as any other man to Boadicea. She was surprised at the alarm on his face when he approached too closely to the girls and Noble growled. Indeed, it was unusual for wolves to be pets of young girls. Perhaps she would have acted the same as Suetonius.

This meeting was important. It could either mean peace, or the end of their country, their people. Boadicea could feel her stomach churning at the closeness of the two Romans. She ignored Cerialis, studied Suetonius, then spoke to him in Greek, a common language for tradesmen and travelers.

"Prasutagus and I welcome you to our country. As an honored guest, it is our custom to give you a pair of our finest yearlings. With your permission, they will be sent to your quarters in Glevum Caster."

Suetonius' eyebrows raised. He hesitated as if searching for words, then haltingly, answered Boadicea in Greek, the words stumbling from his mouth. "I thank you for your generosity. I must apologize for using words that have lain dormant in my mind for so long."

"Allow me to apologize for assuming that my Greek was understandable. It has been years since I sat at my tutor's knee and learned his language." She noticed that Cerialis had a stunned look on his countenance. She should not have insulted a guest so, and Boadicea could hear her father's voice admonishing her. It would be a further insult to switch to Latin at this point, so she continued in short sentences with none of the normal flourishes.

Boadicea waved her hand toward three chairs. "Please do us the honor of sitting, Governor Paulinus, General Lucian, and General Cerialis."

"Thank you." Suetonius waited for a pair of servants to place the chairs centrally in front of the rulers before he and Lucian sat. He frowned at Cerialis until the general joined him.

"Allow me to present my daughters, Sydelle, our first born, and Neila."

"My pleasure," Suetonius said. "They are quite beautiful like their mother."

Boadicea blushed at the unexpected compliment. "Have you children?"

The hesitation on Suetonius' part was noticeable. He didn't know how to answer, so he shook his head. "I have been a career soldier." Fleetingly, he thought of Trista and the baby boy that his mother had held and then buried.

"Ah, yes. The rules against family," Boadicea said. "Practical, but unfortunate."

Suetonius looked at Prasutagus. "I have come from my leader, Emperor Nero, to introduce myself."

"Ah, yes. Emperor Nero. The four years that he's been in power have been interesting," Prasutagus said.

"The Parthian War was moderate, but successful," Boadicea said. "However, I fear that his moderation has given way to excesses in both his personal and political arenas."

"A wise observation," Lucian said.

"I think not," General Cerialis said. He folded his arms across his chest and scowled.

"General Cerialis, do you fear losing your head because of treasonous arguments? I agree with the Queen. Emperor Nero is given to excesses." Suetonius leaned back in his chair and smiled at Boadicea. "Please excuse my general. He is loyal to a fault."

"No offense is taken." Boadicea said. "Tell me about Mithras. I understand that soldiers, such as yourself, worship the bull. As a priestess, I find your religion intriguing."

A look of surprise flashed across Suetonius' face. He spoke to Prasutagus. "I did not know your queen was a priestess."

"She comes from generations of Druid priests and priestesses. The power runs strong in her lineage." Prasutagus nodded toward Sydelle. "Our oldest daughter follows my queen's path."

"Druids are everywhere." Suetonius said this more to himself than to his hosts.

"Yes, we are," Neila said in Greek as flawless as her parents. She leaned forward to scratch Noble behind her ears.

Boadicea noted the sly smile on her daughter's face, and she gave Neila a warning glance to rein her in before she insulted the guests. "Perhaps we could compare our religions over dinner, Governor Paulinus. I have found that we share some commonalities."

"Really? How interesting." Suetonius shifted uncomfortably in his chair.

General Cerialis snorted. "We don't do human sacrifices."

Laughter from Boadicea echoed across the altar room. "My dear General, that is a rumor spread by our enemies to the north who practice the same religion that we do. They claim we do human sacrifices so that they have an excuse to make war upon us." She leaned forward. Her voice no longer held laughter. "I have been shown through my meditations that many wars will be fought in the name of the holy. Make no mistake; holy wars are an excuse to take other people's lands."

Suetonius tugged at his earlobe. "An interesting vision, to be sure."

"My queen has many such visions. Our nation as well as neighboring nations often come to her for advice." Prasutagus' voice held unmistakable pride.

"You have priestesses, do you not?" Sydelle asked. "Are they not held in high esteem by your people?"

It took a moment for Suetonius to answer. He seemed to be struggling with Sydelle's Greek intonations. "That is true."

"Is it not common for the Romans to accept other religions as part of their own?" Sydelle asked.

"We take parts of other religions, that is so." Suetonius leaned back in his chair and studied the two girls before him. "How well informed you are for someone so young."

Neila glanced at her mother. "We have excellent teachers. From our mother, we've learned Latin, Greek, and the language of the Germans plus the history of many peoples. From our father, we've learned mathematics, astronomy, to hunt, to raise animals and crops, and we've learned about the foreigner's passion for political intrigue."

"Political intrigue?" Cerialis muttered. "Women have no business being concerned with that."

Sydelle, Neila, and Boadicea looked at Cerialis until he broke eye contact and stared at the floor. The room was so silent that the leaves could be heard rustling in the trees outside the door.

"We've learned that you Romans have a passion for entertainment at the expense of others." Sydelle leaned forward and stared at General Cerialis.

"I know not what you mean," the general said.

"When Rome invades a country and conquers it, the rulers are led down the streets of Rome like animals in a parade for all to see. It happened to the Egyptian Queen so long ago, and it still happens." Sydelle leaned back. "I understand Rome's need to degrade others, but I find it peculiar."

Prasutagus lifted a finger to silence his daughter. "Perhaps we should get to the heart of the reason for your visit, Governor Paulinus."

The look of relief mixed with his distress at General Cerialis was evident on Suetonius' face. "I agree. I hope you women will excuse us while we talk to King Prasutagus about some matters. I'm sure our discussion would bore you." He smiled.

The gasp from Neila was so audible that Noble growled. Suetonius looked to Prasutagus for guidance, obviously confused as to why his statement had brought such a response.

"My queen rules by my side as an equal. She has as much authority as I do as a ruler. As a Druid priestess, she governs everyone, even me, in religious, family, and medical matters. As a warrior, she has been trained since childhood in the ways of war."

"The queen is a formidable warrior," Sydelle said. "I've seen her kill men with the same ferocity as our father. She has taught my sister and I some excellent techniques with the long sword."

"Sydelle killed her first enemy when she was but thirteen summers," Neila said.

General Cerialis' hands gripped the arms of his chair tightly. "When, pray tell, did you kill your first enemy?" His voice was scornful and matched his facial expression.

"It was in the same battle. I took out an old man who looked much like you, General."

"Neila!" Boadicea hissed in her own tongue. "Your manners need mending." She noticed that General Lucian grinned.

"I'm sorry, Mother." Neila smiled at General Cerialis. "Not that someone as inexperienced as I could run you through with the long sword. I harbored no such thoughts. You're scarcely past your youth."

Suetonius cleared his throat to hide a chuckle. "If we Romans trained our women in warfare, I'm afraid they'd run us into the sea. We don't seem to be able to please them."

Prasutagus nodded. "That is true even in our world, Governor."

"There is something else that you may find difficult to understand, Governor Paulinis," Boadicea said. "Our daughters will rule jointly after our demise. It would be a breech of our laws and customs for any of them to be excluded."

"My most humble pardon. I did not fully understand your customs." Suetonius squirmed in his chair. "In Rome, women are not usually in positions of power."

"How barbaric," Neila said.

"I had never thought of it that way," Suetonius said.

"Perhaps we should spend this day in learning to understand each other better," Prasutagus said. "Let's dine, drink, laugh, then meet again tomorrow to discuss more serious matters. We have made preparations for you in our guest hut. I'm certain you'll be very comfortable there. Perhaps you'd like to rest before our main meal. I think you'll enjoy the wine. It is from your country. We have always been fond of your wines, and this is especially good."

"Roman wine? Thank you." Suetonius stumbled over his words.

Boadicea took her husband's hand. It felt warm, and she loved to walk with Prasutagus this time of night. She leaned against his arm as they walked along the edge of the road and looked at the sky. The sun had dropped below the horizon and only its blood-red shadow remained at the edge of the earth. The goddess of the night was reclaiming what belonged to her, and her cloak was being drawn across the sky.

Prasutagus raised Boadicea's hand to his lips and kissed it. "Do you think that the Roman will be true to his word?"

"Which Roman? The Governor, Suetonius Paulinus, or the General, Cerialis?" Boadicea stopped walking and tugged at her husband's arm. "Listen to the birds. They are chirping to each other before they settle in for the night. I always imagine that the parents are trying to get their little ones to be quiet. Like our children, bedtime to them seems to be a time for sharing secrets and dreams."

"Birds? How can you think of birds after today's meeting? And one to come on the morrow?"

"I think of the little things that the gods have given us. It helps me to avoid thinking of the big things that the gods have thrust upon us."

"You spoke of the dreams of children. Do you have dreams, Boadicea? Dreams for our future? Where do the Romans fit into our future?"

"I have dreams and nightmares." Boadicea stopped and turned her husband toward the southern sky. "Our lands run farther than we can see, and I know that we are to protect the people who live on our lands. I hope the gods have helped me to choose wisely our course of action, for I have often dreamed that rivers of blood flowed across these fields. I don't want to think about what the dream means."

"I trust in you. You've talked with the gods. Let's put aside our concerns and live as the gods told us to." Prasutagus put his arm around Boadicea's shoulder. "You did not answer my question."

"Which one?"

"You have always been able to understand people and their motives. Do you think the Roman will be faithful in working with us?"

Boadicea sighed. "I like General Lucian. I don't think General Cerialis can be trusted. Governor Suetonius Paulinus seems to be a fair man, but he will want what Emperor Nero tells him to want. I am afraid of what that may be."

"We can only hope that our alliance succeeds." Prasutagus spread his hands. "If not . . ."

"Let's forget today and remember this evening. See how the sky darkens? Soon the stars will push through the night and decorate the sky. It is a beautiful evening—a good sign from the gods, don't you think?" Boadicea wrapped her arm around Prasutagus' waist. "Let's walk some more."

CHAPTER

XII

SUETONIUS ADJUSTED THE SHEATH that held his ceremonial knife and shifted in the saddle so no one would see his discomfort. He had to ride this morning to think about yesterday's meeting and dinner. Prasutagus appeared to understand his need to ride and think.

"It's time to return," Lucian said.

"Really?" Suetonius looked around and realized that he had led his men farther than he'd realized. The meetings this noon promised to be as exciting as the first one. He felt too old to be riding this far, but it would not do to come in a chariot. A leader of men had to ride in front of the cavalry.

Suetonius looked ahead at the village in which huts were bunched together on the side of a hill. There was the large building at the top of a series of ramparts where they'd had their meeting. Suetonius squinted. That particular building looked like a series of huts put together to form one large dwelling. It was a place fit for a king and queen.

General Cerialis had insisted on coming along on the ride against Suetonius' wishes. He could not easily confer with Lucian when Nero's spy rode with them. Cerialis wasn't a tall man, but on his war horse, Cerialis looked grand. A show of strength was not a bad thing to have, but it should be tempered. Suetonius looked over his shoulder. It was difficult to decide how many men were necessary to show that he commanded respect, but at the same time not be a threat to the Iceni. He had heard from many people that they could be fierce warriors, and yesterday's conversation supported that notion. Caitlin had also told him that the women were warriors as well, but he had thought she was exaggerating—until he had met the queen and her daughters. Women, of course, were unsuited for battle. These women, however, seemed to be an exception.

As they neared the village for the second time in two days, Suetonius leaned over to Lucian. "Do you see anyone tending the fields or the herds? Do you see any women doing chores about their huts?"

Lucian casually glanced around. "I do not even see dogs running about. By now, they should have begun to bark. I admit the silence is disconcerting. Do you sense a trap?"

Suetonius looked at the huts that lined the street ahead of them. He thought he could see faces at the tiny windows and shadows in the doorways. "I pray that they have the sense not to take on the Roman army. If it is a trap, they will suffer dearly from our spears."

"These barbarians cannot be trusted any more than the other primitive people we've had to conquer." General Cerialis wrinkled his forehead and a bead of sweat rolled down his face.

Suetonius snorted. "Do not underestimate the Iceni. These people are not barbaric. You've seen their highly developed civilization. The king and queen are very knowledgeable and highly educated."

"I found the queen's command of our language and the Greek's highly commendable," Lucian said. "I fear that she would be a fierce adversary."

"Hmmph." General Ceralias said. "We Romans have had to save the Brigantes from themselves because of their civil war. Our fine army had to fight alongside blue tattooed savages. They don't wear armor because they believe the gods ride in front of them and protect them. I'm sure the Iceni are the same." General Cerialis' voice was full of disdain.

"Look ahead, Cerialis," Lucian said. "There are your savages. For the second day in a row, they've known where we were and when we'd arrive."

"They have a exceptional communication system. I wish I knew how they did it." Suetonius pointed to the people who lined the streets as the Romans marched through their village. They looked like a living rainbow with their striped and plaid tunics. "Their bodies are not painted, but their clothing certainly is." Suetonius looked down at the solemn faces of the children who stood next to parents. The children did not shy from the army as many children in other countries had done. Either they were brave, or had no idea of the extent of the Roman power.

General Cerialis coughed. "What do they expect of us? Are we to ride to our guest hut or to the meeting hall?"

"You're certainly short-tempered this morning," Lucian said. "And the proper term is the altar room, not the meeting hall."

Suetonius glanced up the road. "There's your answer. A trio rides toward us—no doubt as an escort." Suetonius raised his hand to halt the army, then waited as the men approached on mounts as beautiful as any horses he had ever seen. The coats of the animals were shiny and muscles rippled under their taut skin. Good breeding showed in these horses. He would have to ask Queen Boadicea about their breeding plan.

The men stopped in front of him. Suetonius raised his arm in salute to them, and they returned it. "I have been riding across King Prasutagus' and Queen Boadicea's beautiful land. I am impressed with the bountifulness of the crops and the care they've been given." Suetonius wondered if these men spoke Latin as did their rulers. He was surprised to hear almost flawless Latin as their leader replied.

"You're most kind. I am Keir. I am instructed to take you to Queen Boadicea and King Prasutagus for the second day's meetings. These will be held in the great hall rather than the altar room."

Suetonius, Lucian, and Cerialis followed Keir as he turned his horse and led them up the ramparts to the main section of the sprawling complex. Young boys appeared from nowhere and held the reins of their horses as the three Romans dismounted.

Suetonius followed the Iceni escort up the familiar path, but through a different doorway. He was startled to find himself in a room the size of a small field. His eyes adjusted to the dimly lit room. At the far end, side by side, the royal couple sat on the same heavily carved, wooden thrones. Suetonius was struck by the height of the King of the Iceni, but more so by the beauty of the Queen. Boadicea was even more beautiful today than yesterday. She sat, nearly as tall as her King, back straight, chin up, staring at the visitor.

Suetonius removed his helmet and tucked it in the curve of his left arm. He moved across the room, never taking his eyes off the Queen. A golden crown studded with jewels rested on her head, but her hair far outshone the crown. Auburn, it hung in heavy waves to her waist like a river of silk. Her skin was as creamy as rich milk, and Suetonius imagined it was as smooth to the touch as cream. It was her eyes that made him catch his breath. They were green like emerald stones, and she gazed at him as one might an interesting salamander.

The Queen wore a gold torc about her neck that on an ordinary woman would have been too heavy, but she seemed not to notice its weight. The wide band of gold tubes sparkled in the light. Suetonius saw that it was implanted with gems of turquoise and red. From elbow to wrist were bracelets of gold. Boadicea sat very still, and the bangles did not ring. Her tunic was as colorful as the torc with slashes of red, blue, brown, and yellow in horizontal and vertical stripes. Suetonius had to keep his teeth clamped together to keep his mouth from dropping open. As he neared the thrones, he glanced at the King. His tunic was saffron silk with a broad band of embroidery. He wore an identical crown and torc, and Suetonius noted that both thrones were the same height. The King had hair of deep brown with silver intruding at the edges. His stature was as elegant as his Queen's and brown eyes regarded his visitor with interest.

Suetonius had concentrated on the royal pair so much, that he was startled by a menacing growl. The wolf, of course. He stopped in mid-stride and looked toward the sound. To Queen Boadicea's right were seated Sydelle and Neila. Neither, he thought were as beautiful as their mother.

Between the girls sat the large she-wolf, again, golden eyes glaring, lips pulled back and teeth bared. Suetonius suppressed a shudder. Lucian chuckled and General Cerialis sucked in his breath. Suetonius was as much astonished by the wolf's presence as he was when Sydelle placed her hand on the wolf's head. The growling stopped at her touch.

"We welcome you once more, Governor Paulinius, General Lucian, and General Cerialis," Boadicea said.

Suetonius bowed. He hoped that it would hide his surprise at her flawless Latin, spoken elegantly with the proper intonations. "I am honored to be standing before Queen Boadicea and King

Prasutagus and their lovely daughters. It is an honor to be with you a second day." Suetonius struggled to keep his intonations proper. He had spoken formal Latin so little in the past months, the finer points of the language eluded him. He was shocked to find himself disadvantaged a second time in so many days—this time by his own tongue.

King Prasutagus leaned forward. He, too, spoke Latin, but not as fluently as his Queen. "You have come as an envoy from your Emperor Nero to talk with us about the client-kingship. The Queen and I are willing to listen to one who is ranked as highly as you are in the Emperor's eyes. I understand that you have been awarded many medals for bravery in battle."

Suetonius' surprise was hidden, he hoped. The obvious knowledge in the ways of the world and politics of the King and Queen continued to surprise him. Their network of informers must range farther than he had thought. Suetonius waved his hand to show humility. "The medals have tarnished with age, and there are no new ones to shine upon my breast. I am an old soldier put to pasture in this beautiful land of yours. My days of glory have passed."

King Prasutagus leaned forward. "A soldier is always a soldier, and a valiant leader remains a valiant leader. Please, you and your generals need to be seated."

"Thank you." Suetonius settled in a chair. Again, Suetonius noted that he, Lucian, and General Cerials had to look up at the Queen and King and their daughters. At the first meeting he had dismissed the arrangement as uncouth. Today he knew better. He guessed that Queen Boadicea's seating arrangements had been carefully thought out.

"You have come here to discuss a matter of some importance to our people." Queen Boadicea looked down at Suetonius. "What do you want?"

Her manner was quick and to the point. It was unsettling to discuss policy with a woman. Suetonius looked into her eyes and felt he was drowning in a sea of green glass. If he were to survive this meeting with his pride intact and his goals accepted without a battle, he would have to do more than grasp for a rope. He cleared his throat. "The Emperor Nero has given me the honor of appearing before the Queen and King of the Iceni to ask for their help.

Word of your strength in battle has come to our Emperor. He admires leaders who are able to keep their people safe."

Suetonius waited for permission to continue. Seeing Boadicea nod, he spoke again. "I have been sent to this country to make certain that its people are protected from the armies that come from the countries far to the north. With our soldiers in place, this country will be safe."

Boadicea smiled and moved slightly. A soft jingling sound rippled down her bracelets. "Delicately put, but we know why your Emperor has sent his army to protect us."

Suetonius returned the smile. She enchanted him as no one had done since Trista. "We have a system of government that works very well for all people concerned. Rome wants only what Rome already has and no more. The Emperor Nero has asked only that the great Iceni allow Rome to help you keep out the raiders from across the sea. The Queen and King would remain as is on the throne, for who could better govern and understand the Iceni better than their own leaders?"

"At what cost to the Iceni will this protection be?"

Clearing his throat, Suetonius stumbled over his Latin vocabulary to find a suitable way of answering. "It is expensive to arm as many legions as we have . . ."

"Twenty-five legions throughout the world have expanded to thirty-two. Expensive, indeed," Boadicea said.

Hiding his astonishment at her intimate knowledge of the Roman legions, Suetonius could only nod.

"How much will your Roman protection cost us?"

"One half of your animals, gold, and grain," General Cerialis said.

Suetonius wanted to knock the general from his chair. The old fool had no sense of diplomacy.

"Do we send it to you, or do you collect it? What about wagons? Do you bring them or do we supply them? Forgive me, I do not know your rules of polite plundering."

Suetonius felt his face flush.

Queen Boadicea tapped her finger against the arm of the throne. For the first time, Suetonius noticed the wolves carved into the arms and legs of both thrones. It was an apt symbol, for Queen Boadicea appeared to be both cunning and powerful. She stopped tapping her finger. "There is no point in discussing this further. I have spoken to the gods, and they have answered me."

Suetonius held his breath. He had expected a longer time of negotiations, but the Queen was blunt. Whether it would be war or not between her people and his hinged upon her next sentence. Instinctively Suetonius knew she would be a formidable foe. He could no longer hold his breath and let it out slowly. Why had he not left Cerialis outside?

Suetonius waited for Boadicea's explanation. He did not look at the King, for he realized that she was speaking as a priestess. Suetonius hoped his face did not reveal the incredulity he felt at meeting and dealing with a woman with the same amount of authority as a man. Helpless, he stared at her. Obviously, Suetonius thought, Boadicea was as intelligent as she was beautiful. There would never be another woman in the world like her.

"The gods have told me that we should allow our Roman friends to help us. There could be trouble from our enemies who will now be your enemies. However, we are to rule as in the past—free to govern our people."

Suetonius nodded. "Of course."

Boadicea stared at Suetonius, then she nodded. "Let us have a meal together as a testimony to our new alliance. The details will be dealt with later. We have prepared a banquet for you in celebration." Boadicea snapped her fingers, sending a ripple of noise up her braceleted arm.

Tables and benches were carried into the room and placed in one long line. Women, clad in the same type of colorful tunics as their Queen, carried in platters of meat, seafood, game, and pitchers of drink. The aromas reminded Suetonius that he had not eaten since early morning.

King Prasutagus stood. "You will want to invite your soldiers in for this meal. We have provided for them, too."

Suetonius bowed. "Thank you."

King Prasutagus nodded to a pair of men at the door, and they disappeared. In a few minutes, Roman soldiers entered, puzzled looks on their faces as they stared at the vast room and the large number of tables.

King Prasutagus took his Queen's arm and led her to the table. Their daughters followed them. Suetonius noted with surprise that only a hand signal from the dark-haired daughter was needed to keep the well-trained wolf in place.

King Prasutagus turned to Suetonius. "Please join us."

Suetonius nodded to the men, and they stepped up to the table. At the Queen's command, they were seated. Suetonius was at a loss as to what to say, as were his men, but the Queen softened instantly.

"Please, we would like for you to eat your fill. Our hunters have been very successful." Queen Boadicea smiled at Suetonius, then at Lucian and Cerialis. "Do you find our country to your liking?" She held up a gold cup. "Let us drink to our newfound relationship. May we remain friends until the sky holds no stars and there are no oak trees in our forests. May our gods see you as friends and protect you against our common enemies."

Suetonius held up an identical cup. He saw that General Cerialis stared, and he nudged him. The general raised his cup. A frown flickered across the general's face. He would have to watch that man carefully. Not for the first time Suetonius wished he could have the general transferred, but Cerialis liked it here, and he was a favorite of Nero's.

"May our gods work together to protect us and this beautiful island from invasion," Suetonius said. He noted that Queen Boadicea's face hardened at his choice of words. It was too late to recall the words. She viewed the Romans as invaders, and, he had to admit, she was right. Suetonius followed his hosts and drank. From the corner of his eye, he could see that Petilius Cerialis followed suit, but grudgingly. Suetonius did not doubt that Queen Boadicea could read the general's actions.

"How fares your mother, Governor Paulinus?" Boadicea asked. "I am sorry that she is widowed."

Suetonius set his cup down a little harder than he had intended. Her question startled him. He looked into her eyes and decided the question was genuine.

"I am lucky to have a mother who still lives. I miss seeing her as I miss my sisters and their families. It is one of the problems of serving Rome in a far-away land."

General Cerialis leaned forward. "It is forbidden by decree to be a Roman soldier and to be married."

Boadicea raised her eyebrows. "Really? How barbaric. For what do you fight, then, having no offspring to protect?"

"Why . . . why we fight for the glory of Rome." General Cerialis said.

Lucian choked on a sip of wine. He wiped his mouth with his sleeve. "The glory of Rome? That's an old notion."

"Fight for an abstract concept?" Boadicea said. "How absurd. It is far better to fight for one's family. I pity the person who even contemplates harming any member of my family, my clan, or my tribe. What say you to that, Governor Paulinus?"

"I think that your ideas are much more pleasing to me than the 'old ideas of Rome' as Lucian puts it." Suetonius glanced at Cerialis. He dared him to utter one word of this conversation back in Rome.

"An admirable confession, Governor." Boadicea turned to General Cerialis. "Have you nothing so dramatic to confess?"

Suetonius laughed aloud at Cerialis' horrified expression followed by a scowl. Suetonius could see the merriment in Queen Boadicea's eyes. She obviously liked to win at battles of words. She thoroughly enjoyed bedeviling Cerialis.

Catching Suetonius looking at her, she gave him a sly smile. So! The Queen was a master at manipulation. Suetonius grinned in return.

Perhaps it was the drink, perhaps it was the circumstances, but Suetonius could not help himself. He entered the teasing of Cerialis with zeal. "The good general is very serious about being a soldier. He marches in his sleep."

"I do not!" With that statement, General Cerialis rose. He glared at Suetonius. "I do not have to take this verbal abuse." He stalked out of the great hall. Waves of silence followed him as the Romans and their hosts watched him leave.

"Forgive me, Queen Boadicea. My manners were forgotten. It is not wise to insult one's compatriots."

The Queen leaned forward. "It was my fault, Governor. I made sport with a man who is not the sporting type." Boadicea looked at Cerialis' retreating form. "I hope that I can make it up to him in some way. I should not have let his obvious abhorrence of us distort my judgment. I will send him a gift. Perhaps a fine horse would soothe him."

"I'm certain that it would. If I leave in anger, would you send me a fine horse, too?" Suetonius laughed with the Queen.

"I would rather give you a fine horse because you are a fine man." Boadicea leaned toward Prasutagus and whispered.

The King looked at Suetonius. "My Queen has requested six of our best horses for you and your generals. You shall have them by your leave tomorrow."

Suetonius had to clamp his mouth shut so as to not appear stupid. "It was but a jest. I feel that I have said more than was appropriate, and I feel ashamed to be your guest."

"Don't be so ceremonious, Governor Suetonius," Boadicea said. "If it calms your nerves, then consider it a bribe. I wish to remain in your thoughts as a good friend."

"I thank you." Suetonius looked at Boadicea's fine jewelry. He hoped that he could send for something almost as beautiful from the artists in Rome.

The moonlight was bright when Suetonius was shown to his quarters in a hut at the end of the compound. He looked at the curly-haired youth who escorted him along a path strewn with flower petals. "You are Keir, are you not?" Suetonius asked.

"That is true."

"What do you do for Queen Boadicea?"

"Most of the time I work with her horses to train them. I will do anything that she asks, but she knows that I do my best when I'm with animals." Keir looked down at his feet as they walked along. "I would like to be betrothed to her daughter, Sydelle. She is the oldest and has hair the color of her mother's."

"Love is the same in any country."

"What sir?"

"Nothing. The musing of an old man."

"You are not old, sir. Sydelle and Neila find you quite handsome."

Suetonius coughed to hide laughter. "I appreciate your frank talk, Keir, but I'm not certain this is a proper subject."

"I always speak of that which I'm not supposed to. I have been scolded many times by the women." Keir sighed.

"I, too, have bent the patience of the women in my life with my brash ways. It seems difficult for women to teach us. A sorry lot we are."

"Here we are sir. The generals who have accompanied you are inside as they were last evening. We are sorry that we cannot offer you a private dwelling," Keir said.

"It does not trouble me," Suetonius said, although he did hate the idea of having to contend with Cerialis. "Thank you for attending me." Suetonius watched Keir bow and retreat down the path, and he wondered at the real purpose for his having been escorted.

Lucian was already snoring. That man could sleep anywhere and at any time.

General Cerialis rolled over when Suetonius entered, forcing a greeting from the governor. "Good evening, Petilius. How is your bed?"

"Comfortable."

"Not what one would expect from barbarians?"

"Enough!"

"Sorry." Suetonius was sorry. He should have better manners. "What do you think of the King and Queen?"

"He is a fine warrior. At dinner we talked of battle strategies. She frightens me."

"For what reason?" Suetonius removed his ceremonial armor and sat down on the other bed to unlace his sandals.

General Cerialis clasped his hands behind his head and stared at the ceiling of the hut. "Her people will follow her wherever she wants to lead them. They worship her as a queen and a priestess, but most of all, they worship her as a natural leader."

"You're saying we should try hard to remain friends."

"I have to say that. I wish I didn't. She would be a fearful foe. Let us hope that Prasutagus lives a long and healthy life."

"Why? She can carry on without him." Suetonius dropped his sandals on the hard-packed earthen floor. "Surely you do not believe her strength would overpower that of Rome. Your talk sounds treasonous."

"I speak as an army officer. We are trained to fight one way. She will fight in whatever manner suits the moment. If Queen Boadicea has to fight, she will fight with her heart. Those enemies are the worst to conquer." The general turned over and looked at Suetonius. "We must watch Poenius Postumus. He has cowardly ways. I fear that if any of the Britons rise up against us, he won't help."

"'Tis true he seems to be cowardly. I still cannot believe that he wanted to bring his entire legion to join ours in Glevum Caster instead of staying in Isca Damnoniorum," Suetonius said.

"What would happen if Postumus had to fight our Druid Queen?" Cerialis asked.

"He would not fight her. She is a lioness to his hare." Suetonius liked his analogy.

"If King Prasutagus dies, then Nero will never maintain the client-kingship with a woman," Cerialis said.

"Why not? Queen Cartimandua leads the Brigantes under a client-kingship with Rome."

"It is only because she turned her husband over to us as an enemy to Rome that Nero has allowed her to maintain the client-kingship," Cerialis said.

"Queen Boadicea would have no need to be traitor to her husband," Suetonius said. "She would not be disloyal to him, either. We must strive to make her our ally."

"Before today, I would have laughed at that thought, but now I see the wisdom in maintaining peace with the Iceni. They are fierce warriors. If their women fight as does the queen and her daughters, then we are outnumbered. We must maintain peace or lose our hides."

"A wise idea." Suetonius blew out the torch and lay down. "Sleep, for we have a long ride back."

CHAPTER
XIII

OADICEA HELD THE ROSE-COLORED BOWL above a wreath of fresh oak leaves that lay on the altar. She needed color to lay against the gray rock. Her whole world was made up of color, and she wondered if the other world would be colorful without grays or browns. Her hand went to the torc at her neck, and she ran her fingers across the tubes that were strung together to form rows upon rows of gold studded with turquoise stones and red gems.

Boadicea looked at her daughters. With her death and theirs, everyone that she cared for would be in the other world. Perhaps this was the gods' way of telling her that the world she had known was gone. If the new world contained Romans, then she belonged in the other world. The Romans were barbaric in their actions toward her people in spite of warnings from Governor Suetonius Paulinus. She said his name over and over. It had soft sounds. He was the one honorable Roman she knew, but no longer was that enough.

Boadicea said the prayer of death, then turned to her daughters and repeated the prayer for a safe journey to the other world. It must be a quick journey. Boadicea chanted a prayer to her parents to call them to the edge of the other world so that they would be there to greet her and her daughters. And to Prasutagus. She missed him. She remembered his death with a pain that could not be obliterated. She remembered that her husband's last words were of his love for her. Treasured words from a man whom she loved dearly. The last few months had led her on a path to this moment. She remembered with bitterness, like the wine she was about to drink, the short months between Prasutagus' death and the day that began the war. Both incidents were as clear in her mind as if they had happened yesterday instead of a season ago.

"Mother, why do you look so sad?" Sydelle sat next to Boadicea under the oak tree in the front of their hut.

Boadicea had not expected Sydelle to catch her in this melancholy mood. "Time has made me sad."

"Time?"

"I have watched you and Neila grow from coltish children into young girls. When I see you walking instead of running, I know you've changed. You've seen sixteen summers and Neila fourteen. Time has flown." Boadicea took Sydelle's hand. "Some day you'll meet one of the young men from the village, and you'll forget everything but him."

Sydelle giggled. "Mother, I'm not yet interested in any of the boys. I think they act silly."

"Are you just saying that so I will feel better?"

"No, mother. I mean it. Boys are very silly." Sydelle pursed her lips. "Except for Keir. He's all right."

"You raced out against an army to rescue him." Boadicea laughed when Sydelle blushed. "See, you are getting older."

"He's just fun to be around. He isn't noisy and rough like most of the boys." Sydelle looked down the ramparts to the chattering voices that drifted upwards. "There are my girlfriends. May I join them?"

"Of course. You girls have much to giggle about."

Sydelle jumped up and raced down the ramparts toward her friends. Hair flowed behind her as she ran with the grace of a deer, seemingly forgetting that she was trying to be grown up. It was strange to think of Sydelle as a novice warrior when Boadicea saw the coltishness still in her.

She leaned against the trunk of the oak tree and looked southward toward where she had grown up. She went back to her people regularly, but since her mother's death, the trips had no meaning for her.

She should think about the Roman problem. Governor Suetonius Paulinus still maintained the client-kingship, but General Cerialis had sent her a warning message that, in effect, called her a liar. He claimed that she withheld some of the taxes. He was a fool. She never gave less than what was due, and often she gave more. Why? Without Prasutagus by her side, she was afraid of losing her daughters, so she bribed the Romans.

What a fool she'd been. General Cerialis could not be placated. If he sent that Procurator, Catus Decianus, again to her for an inventory of the Iceni holdings, it would be difficult to contain her anger. After last time she had sent a letter, in Latin, to Governor Paulinus protesting both General Cerialis' accusations and the rude manner of Catus. He had taken his time in replying, apologizing for the delay, but offering no explanation. He wrote that her problem was not great. It was customary to take inventory before assessing taxes. Boadicea had thrown the parchment in the fire. Suetonius Paulinus had missed her point entirely.

Boadicea closed her eyes. The hot sun made her feel sleepy, and she let herself drift to the land between waking and sleeping. A shadow across her eyelids made her stir. Boadicea opened her eyes to see Neila standing before her, two rabbits tied together and slung across her shoulder.

"Mother, I need to talk with you." Neila shifted from one foot to the other. "Father did not go hunting with me, again. He has not been hunting for many days. Is he ill?"

Boadicea looked across the valley toward the hills that rolled on and on toward the channel. She had never lied to her daughters. She looked into Neila's eyes. "I am afraid that he has been ill. He is growing older."

Neila pulled the rabbits off her shoulder and dropped them to the ground. She paced back and forth. "Why does he grow so thin? Why does he not eat as he used to? Why does he sleep, even during the day."

Boadicea shook her head. "I cannot answer your questions. Your father is very ill. He has the sickness that takes people from the inside out."

Neila stopped her pacing and stared at her mother. "No, Mother!"

"I have tried rue and even mistletoe, but your father gets worse each day. He weakens before my eyes." Boadicea brushed a strand of hair away from her face. "All my medicines and my knowledge are to no avail."

Neila dropped to her knees and put her head in her mother's lap. "Why didn't you tell Sydelle and me?"

Boadicea stroked her hair, pulling the wisps away from the beads of sweat that decorated her temple like dew. "I didn't want to admit that your father was fading. I fear he is slipping away from us."

"Why does this happen?" Neila clutched her mother's skirt. "My father is not old enough to die."

"Anyone can be old enough to die if summoned by the gods to go to the world beyond." Boadicea kissed the curls on her daughter's head. "Your father has lived longer than most men, nearly forty-five winters, but I will still feel cheated when . . ."

Neila picked up the rabbits and held them. "I'll go show Father my catch. Do you think he'll be pleased?"

"I do." Boadicea smiled.

"Where is Noble?"

"She lies next to his bed guarding him, I think. Do you believe the wolf will let you in the room without taking your kill?" Boadicea touched the soft rabbit fur.

"Noble is not a scavenger. She has too much pride."

Boadicea watched Neila skip across the yard and into the hut, her rabbits bouncing in rhythm with her movements. Neila's curls floated down her back like endless bracelets of raven colored feathers. Boadicea smiled at the girl who preferred hunting to becoming a priestess. Most of her time had been spent with her father, so had learned the ways of the woods animals, how to break and tame a horse, and how to make a harness.

Boadicea watched Sydelle as she talked with her friends. Though Sydelle was a good hunter, too, she preferred to learn about the priesthood and medicine. She would be a good priestess because she understood people. Boadicea believed that her instincts with medicine would eventually surpass her own, and she thanked the gods for two good daughters.

Her thoughts were interrupted by Neila's quivering call from the doorway. Boadicea sprang up, pulled her skirt above her ankles, and ran across the yard. "What is it?"

"Father is very quiet. He asked for you and Sydelle."

"Run down and get your sister." Boadicea pointed to the group of girls at the bottom of the ramparts.

Boadicea stepped through the doorway and hesitated. It took longer for her eyes to adjust than it used to. Finally, she saw the outline of the altar, and she rushed across the great room to the smaller room beyond. As she stepped through the door to the sleeping room, she smelled the sickness. No longer could she deny it. She stifled a cry and moved quickly to the bed where Prasutagus lay. Noble arose and moved to the end of the bed, her gold eyes following Boadicea. She circled around, then lay down, propping her head on her paws.

Boadicea sat on the edge of the bed and placed her hand on Prasutagus' forehead. It felt as dry and lifeless as parchment. For a moment, she thought he had stopped breathing, but then saw the slight rising and falling of his chest. She blinked rapidly to hold back the tears.

Prasutagus stirred. "My time to go with my ancestors has come."

"It grieves me to hear you say such things."

"The truth is that I am afraid my ancestors are more anxious for my company than I am for theirs."

Boadicea heard a rustling. Sydelle and Neila crept into the room and stood next to the bed. "Your daughters are here to see you."

Prasutagus opened his eyes. "It does my heart good to see my two beautiful daughters. Neila, you must hunt every day to keep meat on the table for your mother and sister. Sydelle, you are to continue learning and studying, for you are to be a priestess like your mother."

Sydelle placed her hand on her father's arm. She choked back a sob and steadied her voice before speaking. "Father, you sound as if you are giving us last instructions."

"Perhaps I am."

"No, Father," Sydelle whispered.

Boadicea caught the sound of the girl's pain. She didn't want to make it any more difficult for her daughters than it had to be. "Are we tiring you? Should we allow you to sleep?"

Prasutagus shook his head. "I have the sleep of centuries coming soon. I want my daughters and wife to spend the last moments of my time on earth with me."

Sydelle placed her hand on her father's forehead. "I have a potion prepared for you."

"No more potions. I have passed the time when your medicine will help me."

Sydelle nodded and a tear slid down her face, dropped on to her tunic, and made a splash of color darker, like blood. She moved around to the far side of the bed and, easing herself down, placed her hand on her father's.

Neila watched her father's face. She glanced at Boadicea, her eyes questioning her mother.

Boadicea put her arm around Neila's shoulders and hugged her. There was nothing she could say to ease the agony for her daughters and herself. Boadicea's breath escaped her in a ragged burst, and she realized she'd been holding it.

Prasutagus smiled at her. "I go first to prepare the way for you. Remember what we've discussed. You must allow the Romans to rule jointly with you in order to preserve our kingdom. They grow too strong for our people."

"I regret that the gods saw fit to allow them to stay in our country." Boadicea stared out the window. "They have slipped into our lives like the snakes that eat the eggs of our fowl."

Prasutagus made an unsuccessful effort to raise himself, then lay still. When he spoke, his voice was barely above a whisper. "I trust our plans will work. To make Nero part heir to these lands and our riches was risky, Boadicea, but you know we had to do so."

"Do not trouble yourself, Husband. I will manage the Romans. We have prepared for the future as best we could. The future is not ours to know, but ours to control. Rest easy, for I can take care of our daughters and our people. We have loyal subjects in the Iceni."

Prasutagus closed his eyes. "I have faith in you, Boadicea. I know that you will win any battle that has to be fought."

Boadicea watched him closely. His breathing was irregular and the drops of perspiration that had lined his upper lip evaporated as his fever rose. Boadicea glanced at her daughters who stared at their father. Prasutagus, King of the Iceni, took one long breath, shuddered, and stopped breathing.

Boadicea sat motionless, stunned at the truth. The expected had become the unexpected. She placed her hand on her husband's chest, but knew that it would not rise. "Let us thank the gods for an easy death." She herself could not cry, but she heard the quiet sobs of Sydelle and the choking cry of Neila.

Boadicea knew that her tears would come later when she retired for the night and found the bed they had shared for seventeen years empty on one side.

Boadicea didn't know how long she sat and watched Prasutagus. It was Sydelle's hand on her arm that brought her out of the dream world.

"Mother?"

"I am fine." She patted Sydelle's hand.

Sydelle had her hand on her father's arm as well as her mother's. She said a silent prayer, her lips moving as the words flowed soundlessly across the body of her father.

Neila interlaced her fingers with her father's. "No more hunting with the two of us. Your hunts will be in the world beneath the sea from this day forth while I will be stuck fast to this world. It will be lonely without you, my father."

Boadicea stood and walked to the door, then turned back to look at her husband. "Sydelle, I go to prepare a funeral for a king. You and Neila should prepare a funeral for a father." She left the room quickly.

The place of burial was on the highest hill. Boadicea felt the wind tug at her skirts as she looked down at the body of her husband in the pit. The cawing of ravens drowned out the rustling of the oak leaves as the wind rose and fell, seemingly in remorse. Even the sky seemed to cry for Prasutagus as gray clouds let loose a gray mist to fall upon the mourners.

Boadicea held each of her daughters' hands as they flanked her at the grave side. The three days that Prasutagus had laid in state were a blur in Boadicea's memory except for dressing him. She had done that herself, laying out his best robe and gold jewelry one last time. She remembered countless ceremonies in which she had laid out these items for him. The last time had come, and she was not ready for it. The king would be buried with his crown, bracelets, and rings. His torc would grace his neck so that the gods would know a king had come their way.

Boadicea listened to the words the people chanted. For the first time, the song wrenched her heart as never before, not even when her father died. She looked up as the singing drowned out the cawing of ravens. There were many people, young and old, far and near, who had come to tell Prasutagus that they wished him gods' speed on the journey to the other world. He was their king and friend. Already she dreaded the empty hours without him.

She heard Neila sniffle, then Sydelle, and she squeezed their hands. The chanting stopped and the people passed by one at a time and threw flower petals in the pit. Petals floated down; colored flakes that covered Prasutagus with a delicate blanket. The last person dropped in more petals and departed. Boadicea watched her go, then turned to her crying daughters.

"It's time."

Sydelle nodded and let go her mother's hand. She bent over and scooped a handful of dirt from the mound next to the pit and threw it into the grave. Neila did the same and both girls stepped back.

Boadicea took the cool earth in her cupped hands and let it sift through her fingers into Prasutagus' grave and made certain it did not cover his face. She wanted to see his face as long as possible. That done, she stepped back and nodded to the grave diggers. Taking the girls' hands, she walked away, hearing the thuds as the dirt closed over him.

"Mother, Keir is riding towards us and throws up clouds of snow. I recognize the horse as one of Thayne's lineage." Sixteen-year-old Sydelle crossed to the fireplace, pulled off her woolen cape, and shook the snow from it. She draped it across a stool and turned to her mother. "He should be here any moment."

Boadicea set a bowl down carefully on the altar. She watched the smoke from incense curl toward the ceiling to carry her message to Prasutagus where he dwelled under the sea awaiting rebirth. She was distressed at the interruption, but knew her daughter would not interrupt unless necessary.

Boadicea spent much of her time in front of the altar now, praying for Prasutagus. She missed him most in the room where they slept and only felt close to him while at the altar. She knew that more and more she let her daughters deal with the day-to-day details while she withdrew from life, but she had no reason to do differently. They were capable.

She frowned because of the interruption. "From which direction does Keir come?"

"From the south." Sydelle cocked her head. "I'll bid him enter." She crossed the room, pushed open the door, and closed her eyes against the swirl of snow that pushed in through the opening. "Come in quickly."

She slammed the door behind him. Keir crossed the room and bowed to Boadicea. "There is an army riding this way. The person who leads this army is the Roman we know as Catus."

Boadicea's hand went to the knife she wore at her waist. "Catus? He's ruthless. He has taken all the grain from other tribes in the southwest. Some tribes have no animals left. Romans! They've taken it all. He whines to General Cerialis. Why does he ride this way?" Boadicea turned toward Sydelle. "Run and find your sister and bring her here."

Sydelle stared at her mother. "What is wrong?"

"Just hurry. I hope nothing is wrong."

Sydelle scurried from the room toward the sleeping area.

Boadicea turned to Keir. "Sound the gong. I want our men and women here immediately."

"Yes, my Queen." Keir backed from the room, pulled the door open, and slipped out.

Boadicea followed him and stepped outside in a flurry of snowflakes. She disregarded the cold and ran to the edge of the yard to peer toward the south. Impatiently she brushed the snow from her eyelashes so she could see better. The wind stilled suddenly, and Boadicea was left with a clear view of the road. There was an important man riding in front of more than two hundred soldiers. At best, she could only get fifty warriors together from their huts, and they would be in great danger.

Boadicea ran after Keir and yelled, "Wait, do not sound the gong! Wait!" She pulled her skirts to her knees and continued running toward the oak where the gong was kept. "Wait!" She was relieved when Keir lowered the hammer and stared at her. "Don't sound the alarm. I will deal with the Romans myself. Be gone so that you are not seen."

"I cannot do that," Keir said.

"You must! We'll be fine. Go! Come back later when you're most needed." Boadicea shivered and ran through the snow back to the warmth of her home. She slammed the door behind her and raced to the altar. Dropping on her knees, she said a quick prayer. When Boadicea arose, she saw Sydelle and Neila watching her.

"We have a problem. I don't like Catus. He is ruthless and he comes with at least two hundred soldiers. This visit is not one of friendship."

"Another inventory?" Neila held up her dagger. "I have my knife. Perhaps we will have to kill a few of them. This is their second inventory in three moons' time. Do they think we can't count?"

Boadicea suppressed a smile. "I don't think they want anything more than a few tokens of our appreciation for their protection. I will do what must be done to save us from slavery."

Sydelle's hand went to her mouth. "Slavery? I don't understand. I didn't think Governor Paulinus would allow that."

"Emperor Nero has a long arm. He orders the Governor what to do. If we do not agree to pay their taxes, then Nero will have us enslaved. The Romans are good at taking what is not theirs to take." Boadicea heard the sound of horses. She held her hands toward her daughters and with a gesture bid them stand next to her. "Stand tall, daughters. Whatever happens, remember that you are daughters of Prasutagus and are of the clan of the Iceni."

The sound of horses' hooves increased, then faded as they passed the royal dwelling. Confused, Boadicea raced to the doorway and looked out. Catus led a detachment of Roman soldiers to the granary that was across from the corral. Some of the soldiers broke away and rode to the corral.

"What are they doing, Mother?" Sydelle ran out into the yard and peered through the snow storm.

Boadicea followed her. "I do not know. We have just sent them half of our yearlings."

"By the gods, Mother!" Sydelle shouted. "They're taking our horses! All of them!"

"Not Thayne and not Father's horse they won't," Neila said. She cut loose with a loud whistle.

"Nor mine, nor yours, Neila," Sydelle said. She whistled as well.

Four horses pricked up their ears, and whirling away from the Romans who had tried to tie them, raced across the corral, tails flying out behind them.

"The Romans rush like ants to close the gate." Boadicea chuckled. "They don't know any better."

The horses thundered across the corral picking up speed. Thayne was first to sail over the gate with Rand and the other two horses close behind.

Neila clapped her hands in glee. "Well done, my trusty friends."

"Look at the faces of the Romans! They think our horses are possessed," Sydelle said.

The four horses trotted over to the women who stood in the swirling snow, laughing at the Romans. Boadicea grabbed Thayne and Rand by the forelock and led them out of sight behind the hut. Neila and Sydelle followed with their steeds.

When Boadicea returned to the front of her dwelling, she was astonished to see the Romans carrying the entire winter supply of grain out of the granary and loading the bags into her wagons. "The demons!" she said.

"Will you write another letter to Governor Paulinus, Mother? If you don't, our people will starve," Sydelle said.

"Another letter!" Neila said. "If the Governor waits as long to answer as he did the last time, we'll all be dead."

"An interesting plan," Boadicea said. "If we starve, then the Romans will have kept their part of the bargain by not attacking us, yet they'll still inherit our lands."

"What shall we do?" Sydelle asked.

"I don't know yet." Boadicea signaled for her daughters to follow her inside. "Come, I don't want to watch any more atrocities by Catus."

Boadicea went to the altar and stood in front of it. She folded her hands and stared at the door.

"For what do we wait?" Neila asked.

"Fate. Fate comes through that door." Boadicea clamped her mouth shut. She had nothing more to say.

The sound of footsteps preceded the banging of the door against the inside wall. The man that stepped through the door was shorter than Boadicea. Catus wore the typical armor of the Roman procurator, complete with a red, woolen cloak. He did not remove his helmet. Six other soldiers came in with him and stood on either side of Catus, but a few paces behind him.

She glanced through the doorway and could see a number of cavalry outside. Horses snorted at new odors that assailed their nostrils. Plumes of white danced from their noses. The horses stamped their hooves against the frozen ground. These horses were not as fine as the ones that belonged to the Iceni, except for the few that were of Thayne's lineage. She made eye contact with one young cavalry office and glared at him for his part in this intrusion into her life. She was glad when he broke eye contact and turned away. He was only a boy playing soldier in a fine uniform.

Boadicea stared at Catus. He appeared soft in the belly in spite of the armor that was laced in place across it. Boadicea raised an eyebrow and stared at him. "Do you not have manners? We usually shut a door after entering."

Catus watched her for a moment, then letting enough time pass so that he wouldn't appear to be obeying her orders, motioned one of his men to shut the door. He continued to stare.

Boadicea stood as straight as she could. She was a head taller than this interloper, and she felt contempt for his manners. He was nothing like Suetonius Paulinus. His fingernails were dirty and ragged. He was no more than a lowly peasant trying to be a leader. He could be dangerous, for these men carried with them both the instincts of the hawk and the vulture—to kill and then to pick clean the bones of the dead.

Boadicea looked down at her adversary. "It is Catus Decianus. Do you have a message from Governor Suetonius Paulinus?"

The man scoffed. "I do not bother with messages from mere governors. I come from General Cerialis, who answers to Emperor Nero himself. I am here to collect what belongs to Rome."

"We have been waiting for your arrival. I see you have found the bags of our best grain in the store houses for our part of the taxes." Boadicea tried not to sound caustic. "We have also raised some fine horses for your cavalry. I see that you have found them. We have already sent our best sheep and cattle to your emperor. We have been generous."

Catus' eyes narrowed. "You are a rich people. You can afford to be generous, but you underestimate your own wealth. Emperor Nero deserves more than grain and sheep. That is fit for a barbarian, but not for the Emperor."

"We have saved the best for your Emperor, but if it is not good enough, then we have nothing to give you. I will write to Governor Paulinius to confirm our agreement. We thought we had more than kept our part of the bargain."

Catus stepped toward Boadicea, his hand on his short sword. "You have much for us to take. I see that you wear a great deal of gold. The Emperor has need for such treasure. You will collect all the gold trinkets together, including what you wear at this moment."

"I will write to Governor . . ."

"Emperor Nero spits on the Governor! He has no power over the Emperor's orders," Catus said. "I act through General Cerialis for the Emperor."

"Then what is the point of having a Governor?" Boadicea took a deep breath to control her anger. "I will write to your Emperor Nero, then. Surely a great man such as he is will keep an agreement that has been written."

"Emperor Nero need not bargain with Druids." Catus spat the words out. "Druids! Your religion needs to be destroyed for all the trouble it's caused Rome." Catus looked beyond Boadicea to the altar. "Is that one of your religious pieces? Do you sacrifice your victims on it?"

"We don't do human sacrifices," Boadicea said. Her hands were cold, and she felt as if the world had disappeared outside the altar room. Was this to be her end? Not this way! Not this way! She reached behind her and held onto the stone altar that had been brought from her home place and put in this room the day after her mother had died. It was the symbol of her ultimate power as the primary priestess now that Durina was in the land of her ancestors.

Catus' eyes narrowed and he grinned. He signaled to his men and said, "Tear the barbarian's altar down. Rome allows no human sacrifice."

Boadicea's voice was cold. "What of the Christians? You sacrifice them to hungry lions. You are the barbarous ones. Stay away from the altar or you will suffer dire consequences."

"Take it down," Catus ordered. He jerked Boadicea away from the altar.

Boadicea gave her daughters a warning glance that meant for them to do nothing. She stood calmly next to Catus as four soldiers, their faces red, lifted the huge altar stone. The men had no time to be surprised when the large paving stones beneath their feet gave way and the four of them tumbled into a deep pit. Stones from the sides collapsed on top of them, driving them down on pointed stakes. The screams lasted a only a few seconds and had stopped by the time the dust settled.

Boadicea could not hide her triumph at the stunned looks of Catus and his soldiers. "I warned you of dire consequences if you touched the altar."

"Your taxes have just gone up. You'll have to pay for the training of four more soldiers. The death of Emperor Nero's men will cost you dearly. It will cost you gold." Catus put his hand on Boadicea's golden torc.

Boadicea looked down at Catus. "Tell your Emperor that the Queen of the Iceni does not give up her treasures to a short, fat ignorant pig. When he sends someone of the same stature as I, then we may discuss gold." Boadicea placed her hand on the Catus' shoulder and pushed him toward the door. "Tell your Emperor that I choose not to give him that which does not belong to him. Forget the grain, the cattle, and the horses." Boadicea leaned over Catus and snarled in his face, spitting out her words. "There is nothing that I would give to your Emperor, not even a lowly rat. You will get nothing from the Iceni. Now, take your smelly self and your pitiful army and leave before I slice you apart."

Catus' mouth dropped open, then he snapped it shut. Through his teeth he hissed out orders. "Seize her!"

His guards, stunned, failed to act quickly enough, and Boadicea stepped out of range, drawing her dagger. The soldiers hesitated, looking to their leader for orders.

"If you come near me, then some of you will die." Without taking her eyes off the soldiers, she called back to her daughters. "Leave by the back and spread the warning that the enemy has invaded this house." She listened for the rustling of their tunics that told her they had moved toward the back of the great room.

Catus yelled, "Grab her, you fools! She is just a woman and cannot hurt you. Get her daughters, too."

Two Roman guards rushed around Boadicea toward Neila and Sydelle. Boadicea realized too late that they were in more danger than she. She stuck out her left arm and grabbed the one guard around his neck and threw him into the pit where the altar had been. She smiled at the sound of metal hitting slabs of stone. She peered into the pit and saw that his head was angled unnaturally, and his eyes stared at nothing. His soul had fled his body. Boadicea observed the death of the enemy at the same time that she slashed at the face of the second guard, and her knife sliced open his cheek. He stopped and stared at her, disbelieving what had happened until he felt his face. Boadicea laughed and lunged at the third guard, but he was larger and was prepared for this woman warrior. His hand shot up, and he grabbed her wrist. He twisted her arm back, but with strength born of hatred, Boadicea managed to jerk free and she slipped the knife into the exposed part of his neck between the bottom of the helmet and the top of his metal jacket. He dropped, gurgling, to the floor and with eyes that held shock, stared at Catus until death claimed him.

"Guards! Guards!" Catus shouted. He bolted for the door and threw it open. "Get that woman and hold her. She will pay for the death of my men."

The guards rushed in and stopped before Boadicea. She held her knife high above her head, the blood of the Romans dripping from its point. Her eyes sparkled like one with a fever, and she laughed. Her hair, usually held in place, was disheveled.

"Come to your deaths, for now I know the Romans are my enemy and all shall die. Come and taste the blade that sends you to the other world." Boadicea leaped toward the closest guard and pushed her arm into his face. Both of them fell to the floor and tumbled over each other. Boadicea rolled on top and pushed his chin up, then brought her knife down against the guard's jugular vein and sliced through just as she did when killing a wild animal.

Boadicea was jerked backwards, and she hit the hard earth of the floor. It knocked the breath from her, but she still fought the four men who came down on her, stripping the knife from her hand. When she knew the odds were against her, she lay still.

"Take her outside so her people can watch. This barbarian witch will be made an example of to her people. No one kills a Roman soldier, especially not a woman."

Boadicea laughed. "You may kill me if you like, but it will do you little good. My people will hunt you down like the animals you are. Romans will die by the thousands for me. Kill me. I do not fear death nor do I fear you, little man." She threw back her head and laughed again.

Catus' nostrils flared and his eyes narrowed as he watched Boadicea. "I see that death is too easy for you. I believe that pride needs to be beaten from those who harbor that vice." Catus grabbed Boadicea's arm and jerked her off the floor.

She stumbled to her feet and pulled her arm away, but was immediately grabbed and held from behind. She smiled, then spit in Catus' face. "Swine."

Catus slapped her hard across the mouth. "Take her to the center of town and tie her to the nearest tree. We will show these barbarians what happens to their obstinate Queen."

The soldiers pulled Boadicea toward the door, but before she could be dragged outside, Sydelle appeared at the back of the room on the right, and Neila stood on the left. Noble planted herself beside Neila. The wolf's eyes, golden in color, stared at Catus. She bared her teeth and emitted a low growl.

Sydelle aimed her bow at the nearest soldier. "Let Queen Boadicea go." Her voice was steady with a thread of deadly calm weaving its way through it.

Catus growled, "Seize the girl!"

The soldier who ran toward Sydelle was dropped before he was halfway across the room. The silence was broken only by the sound of the quivering arrow. Sydelle pulled another arrow from the sheath on her back and placed the string in the notch while Neila held her spear steady.

Catus held his hand up to halt any action. "There are more than twenty of us left. You have only one spear and not enough arrows to kill us all. There are ten times this number waiting outside."

"Sydelle, Neila! Kill as many as you can. Take a legion into the other world with you."

Catus grabbed Boadicea and pulled her in front of him. "Throw your spear at me, girl, and you kill your mother."

"Throw your spear at any one of them, Neila. I do not matter, for I am ready to die." Boadicea stared into Neila's eyes. She saw the wavering, the uncertainty. "I would rather die by your hand than theirs, daughter. Take the chance and kill these swine."

Neila let the spear fly across the room faster than any Roman could move. It struck a Roman soldier in the chest, and he dropped to his knees and fell forward, propped up on the shaft at a forty-five degree angle. Blood dripped to the floor beneath him and soaked into the dirt. Neila stood straight and waited for the rush of soldiers whom she knew would come. When the troops ran toward the girls at Catus' command, Neila stood quietly. Sydelle drew back her bow too quickly and struck a soldier in his arm.

Noble leaped on command from Neila and ripped open the throat of a soldier who came toward the girls. Blood coated her fur as she sprang again at Neila's command. A second soldier died instantly.

Sydelle shot an arrow into a Roman who tried to knife Noble. He dropped to the floor.

"Noble, fetch Keir! Fetch Keir!" Sydelle shouted.

The wolf streaked across the room and leaped out the door before any Roman could stop her. She twisted her way through the crowd of soldiers outside and disappeared.

Soldiers swarmed in from outside and surrounded her daughters. "Fight them with teeth and nails! Fight them with your Iceni strength!" She tried to jerk her arm away from her captor, but Catus twisted it behind her back. She gasped, not from pain, but from the sight of her daughters being dragged into the back part of their home.

Catus yelled after the men. "Rape the bitches! They will pay for the deaths of my men."

Boadicea threw back her head and let forth a howl that sounded like a thousand wolves. She resisted as she was dragged out the door, down the ramparts, and to the center of town. Boadicea cursed the Romans and called on her gods as the soldiers fought her. After much swearing from the Romans, she was tied to an oak tree that grew in the center of the village. She felt the rough bark against her cheek and breasts, and she took strength from the tree of her birth sign. She had to wait until her people were taken from their huts and forced to watch her degradation.

"Do nothing!" she shouted when a group of women started toward her. They were stopped by the dozens of Roman soldiers who pushed them back. "Do nothing to cause harm to yourselves."

The first blow from the whip across her back cut through her tunic. Boadicea cursed the Romans again. The second slash of the whip made her laugh. She arched her head back and let the sounds escape toward the sky.

"You fools! Don't you know that you have given me what I want? You have given me a reason for war!"

The next gash stung, and Boadicea bit her lip to keep from crying out. She felt the hot blood run slowly down her back and follow the path made by her spine. Boadicea laid her head against the oak tree. The bark beneath her cheek cooled her fever and she drew strength from the closeness of the village's sacred tree. She shouted above the noise of the whip. "I will see all Romans dead." With no more energy, Boadicea fell silent and counted the lashes through clenched teeth. When the lashes reached eighteen, she saw her world whirl, then the edges grew black and closed in until the people of her village disappeared in the darkness like a stormy night. She remembered nothing more.

The first sensation Boadicea felt was the inside of her mouth. It was as dry as the oak leaves after winter. She licked her lips. They were dry and cracked. She tried to recall where she was, but couldn't. She opened her eyes and found that she was in her own bed, but she stared at the floor instead of the ceiling that she usually saw upon awakening. Boadicea started to sit up, but fiery pain shot through her from her shoulders to her hips.

In a rush, memory returned to her. She closed her eyes part way and lay still to see if her enemy were near. She looked out beneath eyelashes and searched the room. There was movement to her left, and she quit breathing. The familiar odor of Sydelle's perfume drifted toward her. She moved her head toward the sound.

"Mother, we feared for your life." Sydelle leaned over and laid a cloth on her mother's bare back.

Boadicea winced. "I am filled with pain, but it is soothed by my hatred of the Romans. What of your sister?"

"She is getting cool water from our well."

Boadicea licked her lips. "Good. What of the Romans?"

Sydelle swallowed hard. "They have gone."

"Thank the gods. What damage did they do?"

"They have taken most of our men. Some were able to hide in the woods. The Romans took . . ."

"Who did they take?"

"They took many of the young girls, too. They will serve their manly needs, as they call it." Sydelle's voice caught, and she started breathing hard.

Boadicea opened her eyes and stared at Sydelle's tunic. Between the colors of saffron, yellow, and blue, was the color of dried blood. Blood covered her legs. Boadicea reached for her hand. "What did they do to you?"

Sydelle's eyes filled with tears. The tears washed over her cheeks and dropped onto her torn tunic. "They took what I was saving for my future husband."

"I am sorry, Sydelle. My temper did this to you."

"No, Mother, for it would have happened anyway. The stupid pigs did not know I knew their language and when they finished with me, they bragged about other times."

"Your sister?"

"She comes. Ask her."

Boadicea pushed herself up and swung her legs over the side of the bed in spite of the physical pain. The pain of her daughters was more than she could bear. She watched Neila carefully as she entered the room carrying a bucket of water. Boadicea grimaced as she saw the torn tunic covered with her daughter's blood.

Neila smiled as soon as she saw her mother. "I am glad to see that you've awakened. Sydelle stitched you together, and I have used the Moon Goddesses' myrrh salve for your back. The scars will be light."

"How did you fare at the hands of our enemy?"

Neila raised an eyebrow. "The same as Sydelle, but with a difference. I had a hidden dagger and made a girl out of one Roman.

He would have had me killed, but he bled to death. None of the others would come near me, for I faked madness. I even drooled like an animal diseased. I hope they think they are infected."

"We will avenge what they have done to the villagers and to you," Boadicea said.

"And you, Mother."

"Yes. What else was done?"

"They have taken everything they could, including most of the horses." Sydelle said.

"But not the four we saved. Rhianna chased them away. She's calling them now." Neila shook her head. "She is as stubborn as our father when it comes to horses. I told her she was too old to run the fields and woods, but she told me to worry about you, and she would get the horses. She said we would need them for the war." Neila dipped her fingers into a jar of myrrh and smeared it carefully across her mother's back.

"Rhianna says that you will not rest until the Romans are dead. She says that you will raise an army of all the tribes of the Iceni."

"I will raise the wrath of more than the Iceni. I will get thousands of men and women to fight the Roman plague."

"We will ride with you, Mother," Sydelle said.

"No, you will not." Boadicea winced as Neila touched a deep wound.

Neila pulled her hand away and took a deep breath. She let it out slowly. "We are the daughters of Queen Boadicea and King Prasutagus of the Iceni. After the Romans are routed from this land, Sydelle and I will rule. Do we not belong in the war with our leader and mother? Have we not proven ourselves against the Brigantes?"

Boadicea still held the hand of Sydelle, and she pulled her onto the bed and continued to hold her hand. "Because you are to be the next rulers of the Iceni, you must be protected so that you will not be slain in battle."

Sydelle raised her mother's hand to her lips and kissed it. "Mother, we have lost much. Neila and I want our revenge. We deserve our revenge."

Neila sat on the other side of her mother. "We have been violated in our own home. We have lost our dignity and our land. The Romans have taken from us personally as they have from you."

"It would be dangerous."

Sydelle shrugged. "It is dangerous here."

"Mother, I need to have a part in restoring our lands and our people. Only then will Sydelle and I feel vindicated. Only then will we feel fit to rule our people."

Boadicea shook her head. "I cannot take a chance on losing the heirs to this kingdom."

Neila stared out the window at a sparrow that chirped merrily as if it had no care in the world. "Mother, I believe that the gods will not let our souls rest unless we are allowed our revenge."

Sydelle's lower lip quivered. "I want to kill the Romans for what they did to our people, but mostly for what they did to you, to Neila, and to me."

Boadicea looked at Sydelle's tearful eyes and quivering lip, then she glanced at the flashing eyes of Neila. The room was so silent that she could hear her own breathing. If she did not allow her daughters their retaliation, would they carry open wounds the rest of their lives instead of scars?

"Your arguments are so sound that I find no fault with them. You'll not only ride into battle with me, but you will be by my side as we ride through the country gathering forces. Remember that the scars you bear from this are protection for a wound once opened. We will all wear our scars, hidden or not, as a badge to remind people why we do what we do. Prepare for a journey week after next."

Neila jumped up and whirled around. "Thank you, thank you." She stopped and her hands clasped her stomach. Her face registered pain. She waited a moment, then said softly, "Now I will reap the revenge due me."

Sydelle laid her head on her mother's shoulder. "I will make you proud of me."

"You have always made me proud of you. Sydelle, I want you to prepare a basil and tansy drink to prevent a child from forming. Make it stronger than usual to make certain you and Neila will have no bastard child of a Roman." Boadicea spat out the words. The hatred raged within her, but she knew that hatred would give her strength, so she let it boil and churn.

Boadicea pulled back on the reins to stop a team of horses that had been found wandering through the village. The creaking of the chariot had become a familiar sound the last month. She was as far to the south as she could get and not be in Roman or Brigantes lands. The well-trained horses stopped abruptly, and Boadicea bumped into both Sydelle and Neila who stood in the chariot behind her. She smiled an apology to them, then turned back to look at the crowd of men and women who had gathered. The matched pair of sorrel horses tossed their heads and harnesses jingled. Boadicea had stopped her chariot on the rise of a hill. She faced west with the sun rising behind her. She knew the sun would shine off her hair and make it seem as if she had fire for tresses.

Boadicea faced the crowd who stood a few paces below her. She had instructed Sydelle and Neila to move as she did. She glanced sideways and was pleased to see that her daughters stood tall, their backs straight and their eyes staring straight ahead at the crowd of Cantiaci.

Boadicea raised her arms and felt the sleeves of her white priestess' robe fall back above her elbows. The murmuring that had begun when her chariot came into view stopped. Boadicea waited until she had the attention of the many men who stood below her. Scattered throughout the crowd were women. Boadicea noted their strong arms and sheathed knives at their waists that denoted their warrior status. Boadicea caught the eye of one woman, young enough to be her daughter, with a fierce look on her face. Her blonde hair tumbled down about her shoulders nearly hiding her tunic of bold blue splotches against red. She stood with feet slightly apart, one hand resting on hilt of her dagger. She commanded the space around her. No one crowded close to this grim warrior.

Her arms still raised above her head, Boadicea looked through the crowd at the other women soldiers, but saw none as fierce. She would have to find out this woman's name, for she could be useful in battle when the time came.

"My countrymen and women, I have come to tell you of a great injustice done to the Iceni. I stand here with my daughters who were violated in our home by the soldiers of Rome." Boadicea waited for the gasps to give way to silence, then she continued. "My daughters, born from the loins of King Prasutagus and me, were treated not as the princesses that they are, but as slaves by the invaders. Women and young girls of our tribe suffered similar fates, and our men were taken away to be slaves. Our grain for the winter, our horses, and our cattle were stolen by the Roman invaders." Boadicea paused to let the last bit of information register with her audience. When she saw the angry faces, she knew they had heard.

She raised her voice. "The Romans do not belong here. Before King Prasutagus crossed to the other world, he tried to befriend the Romans. The treatment of our people and my daughters has proven that the Romans cannot be tolerated. They must be driven from this land." Boadicea lowered her arms and untied the girdle that held her robe together. She shouted across the crowd of faces in front of her. "I will show you how much the Romans respect the Iceni." She turned slowly, grasped her long hair with one hand and pulled it around so that it fell down in front. With her back to the tribes-men and women below her, she dropped the robe to her waist. The cold wind would have made her shiver any other time, but her blood raced through her veins in response to her choler. The collective burst of angry voices indicated to her that the audience could see the red welts that crisscrossed her back like the roads that the Romans were building in the lands of the Iceni. Boadicea waited until she heard the words of war shouted out against the Romans. She pulled on her robe and faced her people.

"I am a Queen. Will you let the Romans flog a Queen and live?" The voices were raised as one, and the battle cry was sounded. Boadicea raised her hands to the sky. As if on command, a flock of magpies flew across the clearing and their white feathers sparkled in the sunlight. The birds dipped and swooped toward the people and traveled in a straight line to the oak forest. The birds settled in the tops of the trees. A rustling from their wings and the dried oak leaves sent an eerie message across the field where people stood. The mob quieted.

Boadicea kept her arms raised to the sky. "The gods have given us a sign, for they have sent great numbers of our holy birds to watch over us. I meet with your clan leaders to plan our attack before the sun reaches it zenith. Prepare yourselves for battle in the spring, two months from now. The Iceni shall not be insulted or enslaved."

The roar from the people caused Boadicea's heart to beat faster. The many weeks she had traveled to talk with her people and the leaders of the bordering clans had given her strength and determination. Boadicea had been given hope, for all the tribes with whom she had spoken were more than eager to send the Romans back across the sea. The leaders saw the threat to their countries, and the warriors wanted a chance to spill enemy blood. The young blonde woman raised her dagger to the sky and cursed the Romans.

Boadicea nodded to her daughters, and the girls grasped the wooden railings of the chariot as their mother took the reins. She snapped them across the backs of the horses, and the rig lurched forward. Boadicea drove it down the hill at an angle to keep it upright. She held the horses in check as they made their way through the throng of people toward the meeting hut.

Seeing the blonde woman warrior in front of her, Boadicea pulled up next to her. "Will I see you in the council?"

The woman stared at Boadicea and glanced at Neila and Sydelle. "I would like to be, but I am not one of the leaders yet."

"As a Queen, I request that you be there. I have a job that perhaps you can do for me. Be there. What name do I call you?"

"I am Meara." Her blue eyes never wavered from Boadicea's. "I am a bastard child abandoned at birth, but reared by the Cantiaci. I know only that I came from the north, but not from what tribe."

"It matters not from whence you came, only that you know where you are to go. And under what tree sign were you born?"

"None. I was born on the nameless day. Appropriate, isn't it?"

"Perhaps." Boadicea snapped the reins, and the horses pulled forward. She did not stop them until they were outside a long hut. The council fires had already been lit. Boadicea could smell the food cooked in her honor. She realized she was hungry and laughed quietly.

Sydelle whispered, "Why do you laugh, Mother?"

"I laugh because my mortal body is as hungry as my soul. I think that in order to fight the enemy, I shall have to eat like the fierce boar. Doesn't the food smell wonderful? Why is it that other countries have dishes that seem so much better than our own?"

Neila shrugged. "I don't know, but I am starving as well. When does custom allow us to eat?"

Two young boys, wide-eyed with wonder at the prancing horses, took the pair of reins in their work-worn hands. "I think that we will be served soon. Perhaps we shall eat the hearts of the Romans."

"I hope not," Sydelle said. "I think the Roman heart would be too bitter for my taste."

Boadicea laughed and put her arms around both her daughters. "I think you are right. Look, our hosts are waiting to greet us." Boadicea walked with her daughters to the council hut.

A man stood in the open doorway. He was gray-haired and stooped, but had a bearing that reminded Boadicea of her father and of Prasutagus. She thought that she remembered him, but the name eluded her. He bowed slightly to show homage to a Queen, but not so much that he would lose his own place of honor in his tribe. Boadicea's mind flashed back to a time long ago when she stood next to her father and greeted a tribesman from far away. This was the same man, grown older, but still the deep brown eyes and the long jawline taunted her with clues as to his name. She fought with her memory when just in time, his name pushed its way into her brain and was drawn to her tongue.

"Tremain, it is an honor to see you after these many years." Boadicea was pleased at the startled look in the old man's eyes. "I will value your friendship as did my father."

"I did not think the young child in you would remember me, Queen Boadicea." Tremain smiled, his aged and broken teeth showing between his lips. "Please come to the council table so that we may plan." He stepped aside and indicated to Boadicea that she and her daughters were to enter before him. Boadicea noticed that the packed earth floor was a deeper brown in color than the earth of her great hall. As she walked across the floor, she could feel the tiny pebbles through her shoes. The earth here was much coarser than the earth at home. She stopped at the council table, unsure of where to sit.

The problem was solved when Tremain escorted her to the head chair. It was carved of oak to match the table, but the back of the chair was much higher than any of the other dozen chairs that surrounded the table. The carving on the chair was of oak leaves and acorns in a pattern that continued down the arms of the chair and appeared to wrap the sacred leaves around the person seated.

Boadicea sat in the chair, rested her hands on its arms, and felt the smoothness of the wood. The table had also been rubbed smooth, probably with sand, until the wood grain seemed to take on a life of its own. The illusion of depth was wonderful, and Boadicea resolved to find out which craftsman had built the exceptional table. Sydelle and Neila were seated to her left. The chair to her right was occupied by Tremain. In descending order were the men of the tribe and women who made up the council. Altogether, nine pair of eyes stared at her as she looked at each of them in turn.

Boadicea leaned over to Tremain and whispered, "I would like Meara to be here at the meeting."

Tremain's startled expression gave him away, but he quickly masked his surprise. "Meara is not of an age to be here. She has completed only seventeen summers."

"I have reasons. Is a Queen to be denied?"

"Of course not, but you should know that Meara is of, shall we say, unknown parentage? We do not understand her ways that seem to have been born in her." Tremain's hands fluttered as he tried to wave away the thought of the orphan child in the council chamber.

Boadicea leaned closer to Tremain, so that the others could not hear. "I know of no rule that prevents anyone from being on the council. Does this tribe have such a rule about which I know nothing?"

Tremain struggled with his words. "I do not think so, but there are certain customs."

"Customs are none of my concern. Send for Meara."

"Yes, of course." Tremain snapped his fingers and a young man left his seat at the end of the table and came forward. Tremain leaned over and whispered to him.

The young man's eyes widen in disbelief. When he didn't move fast enough, Tremain prodded him in the thigh with his bony finger.

Boadicea couldn't explain it to herself, but she believed that Meara would be a valuable asset to her. Something about the haunted look in her eyes drew Boadicea's attention to her. Maybe she was like the orphan wolf cub that Prasutagus had brought home; feisty and sure of herself, but lonely. Boadicea smiled at the memory of Noble, gone off to mate with her own kind, but who still returned to them every spring to show off her litter of cubs. It was odd that

Noble had reappeared two days before the Romans had come. She had followed them on this journey for a day before she turned back. The gods must've sent for her to help them. Like Noble, Meara needed her own kind, but she did not know who her people were. She was not as fortunate as Noble.

Meara appeared in the doorway of the council chamber and glared at anyone who dared look at her too long. If she were uncomfortable at being here, she concealed it well. Meara stood, chin up and hair flowing about her shoulders as if she belonged in the room she had probably never seen. Boadicea motioned for her to enter and close the door. Meara bowed her head slightly to acknowledge her Queen and did as she was bid. She stood at the opposite end of the room from Boadicea and waited. Boadicea leaned over to Tremain. "I would like her to sit with my daughters."

Tremain's hand flew to his heart. "I must protest! It is not proper."

"It was not proper for the Romans to flog me and rape my daughters either. I have need of this woman. She will serve me in a way that no one else could. Get her a chair and place her between my daughters."

Boadicea leaned against the carved back of the chair, but winced as the roughness of the leaves dug into her not yet healed welts. She leaned forward, hoping that she hadn't torn the skin on the deepest welt. She waited until Meara was seated between Neila and Sydelle, then nodded to Tremain.

Tremain stood slowly, his arthritic joints obviously giving him trouble. With gnarled hands, he gestured to Boadicea. "Queen Boadicea has been insulted by the Roman invaders and her daughters violated. Because the Romans chose to do this to our neighbor to the north, six days ride from here, they have chosen war. Let us now discuss the plans so that we may wipe these barbarians from our country and send them back across the sea. Queen Boadicea has gone to all the tribes in our nation as well as to tribes in the neighboring nations. At each place, the warriors have declared their allegiance to Queen Boadicea and have pledged war against our common enemy. We are the last country she has visited. It is with honor that we have been chosen by her to help formulate the plan of attack. As with all meetings of this nature, we must make a vow to secrecy. Any who cannot abide by this may leave at this time."

Tremain waited. No one moved. "We will listen to the plans of the Queen and then each will be allowed to speak in turn." Tremain sat down.

Boadicea leaned forward. "I will not reveal all my plan to you, only that which you need to know at this moment. Is there a problem to gathering our forces from our tribal villages across the fields to this village? I have had promise of over two hundred thousand warriors." She waited for the murmuring to quiet. "I do not exaggerate the numbers. These are men and women who believe as I do that the time has come for the Romans to be pushed out of our countries. Do I hear any doubts about the numbers?"

"Do we select our own commanders?"

Boadicea looked at the red-haired man who asked the question. "Yes, but each commander reports to me so that I can plan our attacks."

"Where do we attack first and when?"

Boadicea leaned forward with her elbows on the table and her hands clasped in front of her. "Forty miles north of Londinium is a city that the Romans call Camulodunum in the country of Trinovantes. Here the Romans have built a temple to their former Emperor, Claudius. It is here that the old Roman soldiers retire to continue to be a plague on our land. It is here that the purging of the disease will begin. We attack it first as soon as the earth is dry enough to carry our wagons and chariots." Boadicea looked from face to face. None registered any protest. "Next we will wipe out Londinium and then it is on to Verulamium a half day's march to the northwest. From there, we spread across the land all the way to the Welsh border. We will swoop down like an ocean of blood and drown every Roman in our wake." Boadicea nodded toward Meara. "I ask that I be given leave to take Meara with me. I have a use for her talents. In the time of the second full moon, be ready to ride to Camulodunum. We shall meet on the plains outside my village. Come prepared to bathe the enemy in their own blood. I pray for victory every day. I have said all that I need to." Boadicea sat quietly and waited for discussion. When there was none, Tremain ended the council meeting.

Now that the meeting was over, the odors from the kitchen made her stomach churn and growl. Tremain stood and clapped his hands together. At that signal, trays of food were brought into the room and placed on the table by red-faced servants.

Great platters of roasted lamb surrounded by turnips, carrots, and greens were placed near Boadicea. In the center of the table was a roast boar with baked apples ringing the beast. A bowl of honey was put to Boadicea's left, and she smiled at Tremain. He had remembered her fondness for the bee's nectar.

Boadicea leaned across Neila. "Meara, after we eat, you and I will have a private meeting. Eat well, for I will soon send you on a long journey."

Although the sun was shining, the wind was chilly, and Boadicea had to pull her woolen cloak tighter. She walked with Neila and Sydelle to her left and Meara to her right. The grass was brown from winter, yet it seemed to have life as it wrapped itself about her legs, slowing her walk. Boadicea stopped at the top of a small rise and pointed toward the northwest. "I want you to go to the Island of Anglesey. Tell my sister and brother priests that I need their help. The Druids are to sap the strength of one who is strong and fierce. They are to create a distraction for Governor Suetonius Paulinius."

Meara nodded. "What must I tell them?"

"Tell them that Boadicea, a priestess trained by her mother, Durina, in their ancient ways needs a diversion. Explain our cause and ask that they cross the Straits of Anglesey to attack the Romans. Then they are to race back across the Straits to the safety of their own island. We need them to do this before the next full moon."

"I will do as you ask. When I have finished there, am I to return to the village below us?"

"Is that your wish?"

Meara turned and looked over her shoulder toward the village that was laid out below them. "From here, one cannot see the dirt in the corners. From here, one sees the village as a bird must. From a bird's point of view, there is no unhappiness, no scorn, and no sadness." Meara shook her head. "No, I don't wish to return to the place of my pain. My wish is to remain with you to serve in whatever way I can."

"I ask that you return to me after you've talked with the Druid priests. Tell me what they say. Remember every detail of their manners and speech." Boadicea took Meara's hands in hers. "I see in you a great warrior. I have need of such a person to stand beside my daughters and me. If you need a family, we will be that family."

Meara blinked rapidly and turned her face away. "I will serve you until my death. Your voice will be my command. I will protect your daughters with my life."

Neila took Meara's hand. "We will protect you as well. No longer need you suffer for want of a family. You have ours."

"I, too, have room in my heart for another sister." Sydelle took Meara's other hand. "We three will form a triangle to keep our mother safe."

Boadicea smiled at the three girls. "The day grows late. Meara, you must have packing to do. Have you a good horse?"

"I have an excellent horse. I trained him myself, and he is the fastest in the village. Nay, the fastest in several villages. I shall be ready to leave before dawn breaks tomorrow."

The sound of metal wheels against gravel made Boadicea smile, for that sound always told her she was home. Even though her eyes told her the village was in front of her, she always waited for the sound of her chariot wheels on the main road through the town to celebrate her return. The sun was still high in the sky. The distance had been made short by thoughts of war that had crowded her mind all the way home as well as by fresh horses purchased from Tremain.

Sydelle pointed. "Mother, the villagers are running toward us from the fields. They have seen us."

Neila pointed to the riders behind them followed by a wagon filled with supplies. "I am not surprised, Sydelle, since we traveled with no fewer than a dozen people to ease our trip."

Boadicea held the horses in check as they strained against the harnesses, snorting at familiar sounds. It was good to be home again after so many weeks of traveling. The sound of metal ringing against metal could be heard over the horses hooves and the chariot wheels, and Boadicea turned toward the sound. It was coming from the shed where the smith worked. "Do you hear that sound, daughters?

It is the music of war. Our blacksmith is already busy making swords for our warriors." Boadicea could smell the hot metal as it was removed from the coals, hammered, then doused in cold water.

Boadicea stopped the team of horses before the oak tree in the village square. Anger raged when she recognized a brown stain at the base of the sacred oak. Her blood. Weeks old, but still there, like a sacrifice.

People ran toward her, joy on their faces. These were her people and would help her destroy the Romans. She waited until they crowded around her, then raised her arms to quiet the buzzing crowd.

"I have come with good tidings. Our fellow Iceni, as well as other neighboring tribes, have vowed to fight the Romans. We go to war against the invaders."

The roar of approval from her people was a balm for Boadicea's heart. She smiled at her friends and neighbors. She did not try to quiet them, but let the cheers continue until the crowd was in a frenzy. Only then, did she raise her arms for silence.

"Prepare your shields, your swords, and your bodies. Pray to our gods for vengeance and make ready your chariots and wagons. We go at the second full moon. The Trinovantes, the Coritani, the Cornovii, the Cantiaci, and many others have joined our cause. Remember, the gods promised us a swift and merciless victory.

"When I released the hare nearly a month ago, it went toward the south where the enemy resides. Had the hare gone north, we would have had to wait for another time. We were shown the road to war by the gods. We will fight, and we will kill all Romans. We will have our revenge. Death to the invaders!" Boadicea smiled as the chant was repeated by her people, and she heard over and over "Death to the invaders" until their voices were hoarse.

She signaled for quiet. "My friends and family, you are to go home tonight and rest. Tomorrow at dawn we begin to ready ourselves for war." Boadicea slapped the reins lightly against the team and let them pick their way through the path the crowd created as it parted for them. She smiled as the villagers reached up and lightly touched her. Boadicea held the reins with one hand and returned the touches. She was filled with thankfulness for these souls who were willing to fight, and her heart filled with tenderness. Tonight she would pray until dawn for guidance.

Boadicea stared across the field of faces that stretched in front of her. Each warrior held a spear and a shield of wood with bronze plating. The split cavalry flanked the right and the left of the foot soldiers. Scattered throughout the ranks were women with the blue tattoos of the warrior. They held their shields and spears in front of them. Long hair had been braided. The women looked as determined as the men. Many were as youthful as her daughters, at fifteen and sixteen summers, and many were as old as she was at almost thirty-six summers. Some looked much older, perhaps too old. But what age doesn't have a taste for freedom?

Boadicea wore the robes of priesthood. The white robe glowed like the bark of a birch tree against the gray of the pre-dawn sky. She hoped she looked like an apparition from the other world. The sun peeked across the horizon in front of her. As it did so, her robe became pink. She stood like a statue and waited for the morning sun to rise higher. The beams danced over the sky and draped themselves across the warriors in front of Boadicea. When the rays crept further over the hills and caught her robe, it turned from pink to blood red. The faces of her people were awe-struck. Boadicea stood frozen and listened to the staccato tapping of her team's hooves as they danced in place. The excitement of her warriors, stretched out as far as she could see, filled her heart.

Boadicea's lieutenants waited for her command to move the troops southward. She raised her arm, dropped it down, and slapped the reins hard against the backs of her war horses. They jumped forward, and Neila and Sydelle grabbed her robes in order to hang on in the rocking chariot. She slapped the reins again, the sound of leather against horse flesh making the thrill of the battle a reality. The spray of pebbles that was thrown up from under the wheels mixed with sparks that flew from the iron as it struck the gravel. Wind whistled past her as she slapped the horses again. The war had begun.

Boadicea left the chariot out of sight behind a hill and stepped from it. She walked with Meara and Keir, who had scouted the village for her, to the top. She stood in a small grove of trees and looked down at the sleeping village below. The conquerors had become complacent. No guards patrolled the town limits. Camulodunum was nothing more than a collection of wattle and stake homes filled in with daub and crowded next to each other along narrow alleyways, but inside were enemy soldiers. Romans! The word was as harsh to her ears as its people.

Boadicea's eyes narrowed as hatred filled her heart. The sleeping Romans would pay for their crimes against the Trinovantes. "Did you warn of the plan to our fellow clansmen who have been enslaved by the Romans?"

Keir brushed his hair away from his forehead where sweat had plastered the wheat colored curls tightly against his skull. "I told the Trinovantes to beware the fires of Boadicea that would strike on this date. They have promised to help us from the inside. We are to start the fires from the north as we ride through Camulodunum as a signal to them. They will be with us, for they are also tired of having their lands stolen, their food eaten, and their coffers raided to pay for Claudius' ridiculous temple."

Meara leaned forward, her hair as straight as Keir's was curly. "The town is filled with old Roman soldiers no longer fit for duty. Over there is the temple the Roman invaders forced the Trinovantes to build. This is where the old men will flee for protection by their gods."

Boadicea stared at the city below. "Rejoice, sleeping Romans, in the peace you have now, for it will be your last. After today, Camulodunum will cease to exist." She turned to Keir. "Go and tell the Trinovantes that they shall lead the attack from the north so that their people will recognize them. I will lead the attack from the east and make straight away for the temple. If we do not manage to keep the old soldiers out of the temple, then we will batter in the doors. Tell the warriors there will be no prisoners. All Romans and their sympathizers are to be killed. We attack immediately."

Boadicea marched down the hill toward her chariot. Her daughters waited next to the horses, holding them in place. Boadicea stepped into the chariot, only half-hearing the usual squeak of the wicker lacings that made up the sides as they rubbed against each other. She touched her spear that stood in its holder at the front of the chariot and checked her knife attached to her girdle. It had been specially made for this war, and she rubbed her fingers across the handle. A blue stone was imbedded at the top of the handle to help her go with the grace of the gods. The ten-inch blade was forged of the finest steel and sharpened until it would slice a hair lengthwise. Her daughters and Meara had been given similar knives, forged by the master blacksmith in their village. Boadicea knew the children of Prasutagus would not hesitate to use these weapons.

"Come Neila and Sydelle. It's time. When the day is done, your mouth will be filled with dust and smoke and blood." Boadicea picked up the reins and held the horses in place. The chariot's center of balance shifted as Neila and Sydelle took their customary places behind her. Boadicea signaled to her army as she pulled away from the hill and onto the road that led to her first battle without Prasutagus at her side. She prayed to the gods to allow Prasutagus to be with her.

The unguarded town of Camulodunum grew larger as Boadicea, followed by her army, closed in on it. When they were within a hundred yards of the nearest houses, Boadicea let out a howl that could be heard to the next world. She loosened the reins and her war horses thundered forward. She could smell the firebrands that burned behind her as her army made ready to torch the houses. Boadicea pulled her spear from its holder and held it up, ready for death.

Boadicea laughed as the doors to the nearest houses flew open and the retired Roman soldiers, in varying states of dress, tumbled from them. Sleepy faces registered blank looks, then horror as they realized what the galloping horses, the warriors, and the torches meant. With her chariot swaying, Boadicea braced her legs against the sides and leaned forward. The first old Roman stared into her eyes as she speared him. He fell away from her, taking the spear in his chest. Sydelle jerked it from his body as they flew by. Boadicea took her knife from its sheath. With her thumb, she rubbed the blue stone for the gods, and held it ready. As she passed the second house a man ran toward her with a javelin. Its shaft was old and dusty as was the man who threw it wide of its mark. She leaned out of the chariot and sliced the blade of her knife across his throat. Boadicea laughed as she rode through the narrow, graveled streets, preceding death and destruction. Behind her thundered the cavalry, slashing and burning the houses. Screams of the old soldiers assaulted Boadicea's ears and she laughed, again.

She dropped the reins to allow her team to pick its way past men and women who flocked to the streets. A man screamed in agony as part of a burning thatched roof fell on him. The stench of burning flesh reminded Bodicea of a boar roast. The first of the Romans had died as they had lived.

The white-columned temple loomed in the distance ghost-like through smoke. Boadicea swore as she picked up the reins and guided the chariot toward the hated symbol. She stopped in front of the stone temple. It had been built on the outskirts of town and thus had escaped when houses burned.

Smoke wafted across the sky and turned it as gray as a winter's day. Boadicea jumped from her chariot and, followed by her daughters, ran up the steps between the massive columns to the temple. She pushed against the doors, taller than she by twice, but they were barred, and she knew that some of the Romans had had time to hide inside. It would be fitting that they should die in their own temple. Boadicea motioned for the cavalry to surround the building. It would be a short siege, for the men inside had had no time to prepare.

Boadicea waited for her lieutenant to approach, then she spoke. "Get the battering ram. This door was not made to keep out the enemy."

Three thuds of the sacred oak was all it took to break into the temple. Torches thrown inside caught silk drapes on fire. Pieces of flaming material dropped on the hapless Romans who could not escape without the Iceni slicing them in half. The screams died when the last Roman succumbed to the flames.

Boadicea turned toward the burning town. The houses had been easy to destroy and so, too, the Romans. The memories of what the Romans had done to her daughters made her smile at the sight of the ruined village.

Flames rose so high in the sky that the gray from the smoke had given way to a fiery rose color. The stench of burning wood, clothing, bodies, and animals stung Boadicea's nostrils, and she wrinkled her nose in distaste.

"The smell of victory should be sweeter."

"What did you say, Mother?"

"I said that Camulodunum will be only a memory for the Romans and a monument to us. We have just this temple to pull down, and the destruction will be complete. We're soon on our way to Londinium."

CHAPTER
XIV

SUETONIUS SHIVERED when Caitlin rubbed her hand across his bare back. He sat on the edge of the bed and waited for her question. He knew she was about to ask him to stay with her.

"Do you have to go to this far-away place?" Caitlin dropped her hand to the covers and threaded her fingers through the furs that lay across the bed. "How can you leave such a comfortable nest as this?"

Suetonius still felt warmth where her hand had rested on his back. "It's not what I want, but it's what has to be done." He shivered in the cool spring air. "I'm too old to be riding for four days, then doing battle with a bunch of Druids on an island in the northwest."

Caitlin's laughter sounded like bells to Suetonius, and he turned toward her. He always liked the way her hair, colored like chestnuts, tumbled across her face and shoulders in the morning. He was too old for her, too.

"You are so peculiar, Suetonius, always blaming your age for everything." Caitlin sat up and kissed him on the cheek. "I need to get up and fix a meal. I know that my daughter is already hungry. She is worse than you when it comes to food."

Suetonius slapped her bare bottom as she crawled across the fur and woolen covers. Caitlin yelped, and bounded across the tiled floor toward the temporary firepit. She wrapped a robe around herself and poked the fire with iron tongs. It was a morning ritual he would miss while on his journey. "You will have to oversee the rest of the building of this villa. Do you think you can do that? Thank the gods that we have a decent place to live at last, even if it is Glevum Caster rather than Londinium."

"I'll enjoy telling the workers what to do. Besides, we only have the floors to finish in the atrium and a few statues made. I won't know what to do with my life of leisure. If we had lived in Londinium, then I would have gone to the market everyday. Here, there's only the little bay where the ships come in."

"I know you like the excitement of Londinium, but it's seven days ride east of here and too far for me to command the Legions effectively."

"I know." Caitlin sat back on her heels and poked at the fire once again. "I'm anxious to see the central heat work."

"So am I." Suetonius reached for his toga. "Why don't you have some fun while I'm gone? You could take the ship that comes in tomorrow and sail to Londinium. It would take only four days."

Caitlin clapped her hands together. "An adventure! Oh, I'd love to. I hate to be here when you're not."

"I'll send two of my men with you. What of Darcy?"

"The babe never leaves me. I may buy some blue leather shoes to match the blue silk you bought me the last time we were in Londinium." Caitlin pointed to the floor. "Maybe I could find the tile to finish that."

"Why isn't the floor finished?"

"I had to send the tiles back. They sent the wrong color. It wouldn't do to have two shades of white."

"Of course not. It would be a tragedy." Suetonius laughed at the look he got from Caitlin.

"You ask that I decorate your villa. Don't tease me about how seriously I do my task. You are the Governor of Britannia, and it would be unseemly for you to have a poorly-done floor." Caitlin stood, threw a log on the fire, and walked to the door. "I'm going to see about your breakfast. I shall also send that worthless boy of yours to see about your horse. The journey will be a long one, will it not?"

Suetonius nodded.

"Get dressed. The only time I like you naked is in bed." Caitlin left the room in a whirl of color as her robe flowed around her.

Suetonius smiled at the picture he would carry with him on his journey. He was too old for her, and he wondered how long she would stay with him. She seemed content enough at the moment, but he wouldn't have been surprised to find Caitlin with a younger man at any time, though she did make him feel younger than his years. She had told him that younger men did not have the brains to keep her interested. He chuckled at the memory of her wrinkled nose when she discussed younger men. Caitlin knew her own mind. He could hope that she meant what she said.

He walked to the firepit and held out his hands. He wished the central heating system had worked properly. He should have known better than to depend on local help. What did they know about central heating? By now he had hoped the Roman workmen he'd sent for would be here. Lately, it seemed that nothing was going according to plan. Even the trip to the northwest was unexpected. He had thought that to come to Britannia would be an easy job, away from the sight of Emperor Nero, whom he, among many others, believed to be sliding closer and closer toward insanity each day. Nero had ordered him to destroy the Druids and their religion. Suetonius saw no reason to bother them, for they hadn't interfered with the Roman occupation until now. The uprising on the Island of Anglesey seemed to be an answer to his dilemma of whether to go against his Emperor or follow his own convictions.

Suetonius turned his back to the fire and glanced across the room to a small statue placed in a niche above the bed. He said a prayer to Mithras to guide and preserve him and to protect Lucian while they were forced to do battle. He would be glad when he could return to Glevum Caster.

From the top of the hill Suetonius had a view of the lay of the land below him as it sloped toward the water. He walked away from his horse, held up his arms, and stretched. It was good to be out of the saddle. His horse grazed on patches of grass that grew between the scattered trees, the harness jingling in rhythm with his slowly working jaw.

"I'm getting tired of fighting, Lucian. It's time to think of returning to Rome," Suetonius said.

"You say that, but what would you do to keep busy?" Lucian grinned. "Other than the brothels, I mean."

"Is that all you think about?" Suetonius shook his head. He looked down the hill again toward the water. He could see the Straits of Anglesey through the mists that rose above it. The Straits were wider than he had expected; a full three hundred yards. He glanced back at the soldiers who sprawled on the ground or leaned against trees. They were tired after climbing the thousand-foot hill carrying boats. The boats sat on the ground with the men perched on the flat bottoms. It looked like a fleet sailing across the grass.

It had taken the full seven days to march this far. The twenty-mile-a-day pace was grueling for the men, especially the infantry. Suetonius wished he could let them rest today, but that was not possible. The island that lay across the strait was the Druid's holy place and most of their leaders had come with their followers to use Anglesey Island as a base of operations. The Druids, restless to the point of attacking the Romans in small, mobile bands, had to be subdued. With these island Druids destroyed, Britannia would belong completely to Emperor Nero.

"Lucian, pass the word that we are to make our way down this hill. We'll cross the river in the daylight. I want no surprises." Suetonius returned Lucian's salute, then took the reins of his horse. He walked down the hill, for he was afraid that his old bones wouldn't take any more bumps in the saddle. Suetonius' horse nudged him as he wove his way through the grass. He glanced over his shoulder and noticed that other cavalrymen followed suit. It had been a long ride from Glevum Caster.

Grass at the bottom of the hill was waist-high, strong and tough. Suetonius likened it to the Druids who lived here. The grass cut into his arms and legs, leaving a minute crisscross pattern that would darken when it scabbed over. Suetonius pulled his horse over to a fallen tree swung himself into the saddle. His legs hung down and the grass still engulfed them up to the calves.

He signaled the infantry to place the boats in the water. They would go first to secure the shore and the cavalry would follow.

Suetonius patted his horse on the neck and leaned over to whisper to it. "You have a long swim, but you are of good stock. The Britons do know how to breed a good horse." He loosened the reins and let his mount take its head as horse and man climbed out of the water. The horse took a moment to shake himself before plodding on. Suetonius smiled and rubbed his horse's neck. "I should have named you a long time ago, my friend, but I have been too busy. Only a fine name will do for such a fine horse. What say you to Caius?" Suetonius laughed as the horse shook its head. "Why, for shame. It is a noble name and one that belonged to my own father. Consider the name I always use. How does Victory sound to you?" The horse nodded. "It seems you are happy with my choice, Victory."

He watched the movement of the Legio XIV and XX. He had been determined to win this island and so had brought twenty-five thousand men. They would not lose.

The birds ceased to sing, and Suetonius found the quiet to be eerie. The birds, always quiet when a battle was about to begin, would be back to squawk over bodies like creatures from the underworld. Suetonius always hated the birds after a battle. Their shrieks chilled him and reminded him of tales of the Furies.

Suetonius waited until the last infantry boat was more than half way across the river. He brought his arm down as a signal and kicked his horse. The animal sprinted forward and leaped into the water. Suetonius' breath left him as the icy water assaulted him. He shivered and prepared to suffer as his horse swam the strait, water up to the top of the horse's shoulders and lapping at Suetonius' hips.

The twenty-minute swim must have been invigorating for his horse because the animal climbed the bank with zeal and stamped and pawed the grass. However, Suetonius felt his legs would never come to life. He rubbed his purple-colored legs and swore to the gods that this had better be a victory. He rode to the front of the troops and ordered his officers to have them to spread out, shields and spears ready, and march forward.

The wind chose to attack the already cold men, and Suetonius could almost imagine the sound of teeth chattering in time with the marching feet of the army. It was a good thing they marched, for at least it would help warm them. All thoughts of cold would leave them as soon as they found the enemy.

Screams arose in front of the troops, and Suetonius felt the chill of fear gallop down his spine. He swallowed the lump that arose in his throat, but before he could calm himself, hundreds of garishly-clad men and women appeared in front of him seemingly coming out of the ground. His horse reared and pranced around in a circle. Suetonius was forced to keep turning in the saddle in order to watch the enemy.

The Druids held torches high above their heads and even in the daylight, the shadows that were cast had ominous overtones for the Romans. Suetonius was unprepared for their hair that was long and seemed to have been uncombed their entire lives. It stuck out in all directions with a life of its own and reminded Suetonius of hundreds of Medusas lined up ready to turn all his men into stone. All at once, the attackers shrieked in one high-pitched and loud voice, rattling the heavens above and shaking the underworld below. Again Suetonius shivered. He could not stop. He pulled his horse around and saw that the entire force of fighting men had stopped in place as if they had, indeed, been turned to stone. Horrified, Suetonius watched as the Druids moved toward his army, obviously intent on burning them as the soldiers stood like statues.

Suetonius kicked his horse in the ribs as hard as he could and rode up and down the lines shouting, "Do not let the Druids cast a spell on you! You are the best fighting force in the world. These apparitions before you are only mortal and can be killed like mortals. Here, I'll show you!" He grabbed a spear from one of his men and heaved it with all his might at a Druid who marched directly toward him. The spear found a home in the man's belly. Suetonius started to utter a prayer of thanks to Mithras but stopped when the Druid refused to fall. The stringy-haired, howling priest kept walking. Suetonius doubted his own mind and thought that perhaps he had unwittingly found the gate keepers to the underworld. He pulled back on the reins and forced his mount to step backwards as the Druid put one foot in front of the other. Blood spurted with each step and still he came.

Lucian rode from nowhere and hit the Druid in the back with a mace. When the priest at last fell face down on the ground in front of Suetonius, the man's hand flopped against the horse's leg. The horse's nostrils flared at the smell of blood, and it allowed Suetonius to rein it to the left and leave the Druid in a puddle of his own blood.

"Thanks, Lucian," Suetonius shouted. He smiled at his friend who was always there to protect him.

"It is my duty!" Lucian shouted as he rode behind the line of javelin throwers.

The soldiers shook off their dread of the unknown and saw that the Druids were human. Experts threw javelins, hit their marks, and Druids fell in great numbers.

Suetonius turned just in time to see Lucian lead a band of cavalrymen into the Druids to break the line.

"No! No!" he shouted. "The torches!" He watched in horror as Lucian was surrounded by the priests and priestesses with torches and robes that were already smoldering. Lucian, momentarily stunned, tried to ride through the mob. Three of them pulled him from his horse, and Suetonius cried out when Lucian screamed. The horse whinnied in agony and fell, his mane and tail on fire.

Suetonius kicked Victory in the ribs and raced toward his lifelong friend. A band of soldiers followed him into the fray. He slashed his way through the murderous, screaming Druids who fell in the confusion. Torches fell with them and caught their own robes on fire. Soon screams of revenge became screams of agony as the living were trapped by the torches of the dying. A great wall of flame surged upwards, fed by the wind and the dry grasses of winter. The stench was of burned flesh and winter wheat.

It was too late for Lucian. Suetonius, coughing and gagging, ordered his men to the safety of the strait, and they withdrew leaving the burning priests and priestesses behind them.

Victory jumped into the cold strait and swam for the other side. This time Suetonius did not notice the cold, for the pain of Lucian's death numbed him. He prayed over and over to Mithras.

When he turned back to see the destruction, the sky was black above him and the flames turn the water to red around him. Trees shimmered through the intensity of the curtain of heat that surrounded the last outpost of the Druids. Suetonius shook his head. Ironically, this was no battle at all. Lucian had died needlessly. These people had spent so much time in prayer that they believed they didn't have to protect themselves. They were the elite and learned people of this land, and yet they were not pragmatists. Idealists would never rule a harsh world.

He could not think, so loosened the reins and let his mount take its head as horse and man climbed out of the water. The horse took a moment to shake himself before plodding on.

Suetonius was at a loss. He had always given orders to Lucian who carried them out to perfection sometimes even before being told. He searched for someone to give orders to. He wiped tears from his eyes with his cloak. "Lucian, Lucian. A great hole has been ripped in my life."

He spotted a lieutenant and ordered him to his side. "We're all tired from the long march and this battle. Have the men dig trenches at the top of the hill and set their tents. They can load the boats on the wagons, then camp here until rested." Suetonius waited for the soldier to leave. He frowned. He never had to dismiss Lucian. "Go!"

The lieutenant saluted hastily and rushed away.

A horseman raced toward Suetonius at a breakneck speed. The horse slipped and sent loose gravel down the path in front of him. Suetonius frowned. The rider was in too much of a hurry and it was hard on the horse.

The messenger saw Suetonius, stopped in front of him, and saluted. "I have news for the governor of Britannia, Suetonius Paulinus. I believe you are that man."

"I am. What news have you?"

The messenger reached inside a leather pouch at his waist and pulled out a scroll. "This is for your eyes only."

Suetonius took the scroll. He popped the seal with his thumbnail and unrolled it. His eyes darted quickly across the page, and he cursed. Reading it again for details, he cursed again.

Suetonius nodded to the messenger to dismiss him. "See that you get a good meal. Stay the night. You'll ride to Isca Damnoriorum to see Poenius Postumus, the third in command of Legio II. I'll have the dispatch ready by tomorrow morning."

Suetonius tucked the scroll into his knapsack and cursed his fate once more. His victory over the Druids and control of the last outpost of Britannia was marred by an uprising more than two hundred miles away. He wouldn't even have time to properly dry out his saddle to keep the leather supple.

He slapped the reins against his horse and clambered up the hill. When he got to the top, he found his third in command.

"Quentin, I have a dispatch from Catus. Queen Boadicea of the Iceni has gathered a force made up of the Trinovantes, the Catuvellauni, and the Coritani as well as others. With a force of over two hundred thousand men and women, she has burned Camulodunum to the ground."

"I do not understand, sir. Did you say that the Queen sent her people into battle against us? I find that preposterous that they would go against the Roman army."

"Queen Boadicea led her people herself." Suetonius watched the look of shock on Quentin's face. "She managed to destroy the temple the next day as well as all the soldiers who tried to find shelter inside." Suetonius looked past Quentin toward the eastern sky. It was ironic that on both sides of this land, smoke from burned people rose to blacken the sky. Suetonius found it poignant that the inhabitants of the Roman capitol city, Camulodunum, had lived through battles, had retired, and then had died at the hands of a woman.

Suetonius reached back and pulled the scroll from his pouch. He waved it at Quentin. "See this? It tells me in detail what Catus, in his stupidity, did to the Queen of the Iceni. If we lose Britannia, it is because of this man who took all the Iceni's grain, raped the Queen's daughters, stole their horses, and enslaved their men. The Queen is not just going after Catus, but all of us. We may well lose Britannia."

Quentin snorted. "Lose Britannia? Sir, you astonish me. The Roman army is the greatest the world has ever seen. We cannot lose."

"Quentin, do not underestimate this enemy. I have met the Queen of the Iceni. She will be a worthy opponent." Quentin stared at him. "I know it sounds strange to give a woman manly qualities, but there has never been a woman like this one. I only wish she had not been made an enemy."

"You should send for Catus," Quentin said.

Suetonius tapped his finger against the scroll. "It is too late. Catus took a mere two hundred men to fight the Iceni. When he discovered his mistake, he took to the sea and fled. If ever I see him, I will punish him severely for his stupidity, his cruelty, but most of all, his cowardice."

Quentin's face showed agreement with his leader. "He is despicable for his cowardice most of all. What should be done to prepare for the journey? We will have to undo Catus' damage."

"Gather the cavalry. We ride at dawn with provisions for two weeks. Tell the infantry to follow us as fast as they can. They must also carry provisions for two weeks. We will have to move faster than the supply wagons. Tell them we head east through Cornovii country for two hundred miles. The Cornovii have joined forces with Queen Boadicea and the Iceni. I will send to Lindum for Cerialis and the Legio IX to march toward the rebel army and intercept them before more damage is done. If he finds her, he is to engage in battle." He shook his head, remembering the battle against the Dobunni that Cerialis would have lost had Suetonius not helped him. "May Mithras help us all."

General Petilius Cerialis halted the Hispana IX and looked down the road. It was peaceful—too peaceful. There were no sounds of nature except for the snorting and pawing of the cavalry horses. Cerialis put his hand to his forehead to shade his eyes against the morning sun. He could not see anything, but his soldier's instinct told him that something was amiss.

Cerialis motioned for his lieutenant to come forward. "Tell me, Terence, what do your young eyes see? What do your youthful ears hear?"

Terence held the reins tightly to keep his horse still. He stared down the road. "Nothing, General."

Cerialis nodded. "Hmmmm. Exactly. I hear nothing. Does that not bode ill tidings?"

Terence cleared his throat. "We are within a half-day's march to Camulodunum."

"Then that means we are within a half-day's march of the enemy or less. We should hear the sounds of marching, the squeak of wagon wheels, the voices of the leaders shouting orders. Instead we hear nothing. It is enough to chill a strong man's heart." Cerialis stared down the road again.

"Should we fear a woman, sir?"

Cerialis shook his head. "No, but we should fear her spears as we fear any man's, and we should fear her warriors, for they are mostly men." Cerialis looked out at the plain before him that lay on both sides of the road. "At least here there is no cover for ambush. We ride."

How the enemy came so close to them without being seen was a question that Cerialis didn't have time to answer. They moved at a haphazard pace, nearly tumbling over each other as they raced toward him. Cerialis roared out the command for his cavalry to retreat behind the infantry. He glanced over his shoulder as he raced to place himself behind the double line of javelin throwers. It seemed the earth was a living, breathing beast as the Iceni closed the distance between the two armies. "By the Gods, that woman is mad! Not only has she found us, but she has the audacity to pursue the Roman army!"

Cerialis jerked his horse around and waited behind the lines. Terence pulled up next to him and placed a trumpet to his lips waiting for orders.

Cerialis waited until the unruly horde was forty yards away. He judged the distance with an eagle eye and the patience that had been fine-tuned over the years. He took a deep breath. "Sound the stand to arms." Javelin throwers on the first row stood steady with their throwing arms upraised. A combination of instinct and training took over. "Sound the call for the first wave of attack."

Javelins whistled through the air. Cerialis could hear the thuds as they found their marks in the shields of the Britons. He watched as men fell. Those who didn't had to throw away their shields because it was impossible to withdraw the javelins from them in time to continue the advance. "Sound the trumpet for the twenty-yard throw!" Cerialis watched as more of the enemy found their way to the other world. "Terence, it's almost too easy fighting those who have no sense of warfare."

Terence set the trumpet down on his leg. "They will be sent to their heaven before their time, sir."

"This day is ours, my man." Cerialis looked back toward the front lines of the Iceni. "What is that?" He pointed.

"I don't know," Terence said.

"By Mithras! It must be her—the Queen of the Iceni!" Cerialis had difficulty believing what he saw. A chariot raced from right to left across the battlefield that was driven by a woman taller than most Romans. Red hair flowed out behind her like a signal flag to the troops. Cerialis was shocked to see that the chariot also held two young women, and he recognized the daughters. Stupid Catus! Stupid, stupid Catus! The cause of the insurrection rode in the chariot as a reminder to their troops. Grudgingly he admitted that her tactic was excellent.

Cerialis was jerked from his revery by the realization that the Iceni were being joined by the Cornovii and the Trinovantes. "By the gods, Terence, sound the trumpet for the charge by the cavalry! Where did they all come from?"

Cerialis charged forward with his short sword held waist high. He guided his horse around fallen Romans, his shock grew as he realized that the barbarians, with their bronze long swords, spears, and maces, were slaughtering the finest Roman military machine. Cerialis felt a rage that surprised him. He kicked his horse forward and braced his sword against the leather band that protected his arm. He flew after the woman in the chariot. Her hair was easy to see, and he made that his target.

He closed the gap between them and, as he swooped past the chariot, thrust his sword forward. By the gods, Cerialis was surprised when he felt the metal of a sword instead of human flesh. For one instant his eyes locked onto hers, and he was dumbfounded at the depth of hatred he saw. He didn't have time to do more than spur his horse forward and sweep around for another try at the Queen. Cerialis knew he had to kill her to stop her warriors. With no leader, they would soon disband and return to their villages.

Cerialis kicked his horse and pulled past the chariot. He raced ahead, taking time to run his sword through a barbarian. He had to put his foot against the chest of the falling warrior and push to get his sword out. When Cerialis wheeled his horse around, he saw that the enemy was swelling in number instead of shrinking. A chill rippled down his back, and he forgot his plans to kill the Queen. Cerialis knew he had to race for his life back to his own lines. He let the reins loose and lay against the neck of his horse as much as the high pommel would let him.

Dust whirled around him, and he let the horse lead him through the lines. Cursing and angry with the turn of events, he shouted at Terence. "Sound the retreat! Retreat! We are outnumbered! Go north! Go north to Lindum." Cerialis didn't wait for the infantry to form, but swung his horse ahead of them and ran. He felt like a coward, and he hated the fear that overtook him as it had in the past. He wiped the sweat from his face. "I curse the Iceni. I curse Catus!" He shook his fist at the sky. "But most of all I curse my gods for taking away the chance to kill that damned warrior queen!"

Suetonius threw the scroll to the earth and ground it into the dirt with his foot. "This is an outrage! How can Cerialis be such a coward! He could not even stand before a woman and fight. This Queen has chosen to take on the Roman empire. Well, she shall get the Roman empire." He couldn't direct his anger. He hated the Druids for killing Lucian. He hated Catus for his stupidity and Cerialis for his cowardice. He wanted to hate the red-haired queen who chose to fight his army.

Suetonius whirled around and shouted at Quentin. "We shall continue toward Londinium as planned. The infantry marches double time. The cavalry rides in front. The supply wagons have to travel night and day to catch up with the main body."

"Yes, sir!" Quentin pulled his horse to a mounting stone and leaped up. Quentin pulled his trumpet from its strap on his saddle and sounded the marching orders in clear tones that carried for over a mile.

The city of Londinium lying below Suetonius in miniature, was about to be besieged by Queen Boadicea. A few short minutes ago the report had come in from his scouts. He was glad that he had been able to get here before the red-haired witch. Caitlin and Darcy were in Londinium staying with friends. He wished that he could ride into town and take Caitlin to safety, but it would give away his presence to the red-haired fury. He would rescue Caitlin and Darcy after Boadicea was intercepted. All he needed was the Legio II led by Poenius Postumus. They should arrive any moment.

Suetonius rubbed his cramped thigh. His face itched from an eight-day beard, and he could smell his own acrid sweat, the odor it always had when he was at war, and he wondered if it were from excitement or fear. Suetonius was tired to his bones, and he ached all over. He rubbed his eyes to make certain he was seeing the town right. He pulled on the reins, turning Victory away from the rising sun.

Suetonius stopped next to his second in command. "Quentin, I am concerned about Poenius Postumus and the Legio II. I sent for them before we left the straits. He had a seven-days' march, and he should have been here before now."

Quentin pointed to a cavalry officer who had collapsed under a tree and handed Suetonius a scroll. "He has just arrived from Isca Damnoniorum. This communique is from Poenius Postumus."

"Isca Damnoniorum! That is a three-days march from here!" Suetonius felt the roughness of the vellum as he took the scroll in his hand. He ran his finger under the flap and the seal and separated the edge from the rest of the scroll, and unrolled it. As Suetonius read the meticulous writing, his face turned crimson, then deep purple. He crushed the scroll with one hand and flung it to the ground. Victory tossed his head as his eye caught the unfamiliar item that sailed past his line of sight.

"It is an outrage! I have one general who creates a war, another general who is a coward, and now this!" Suetonius' mouth clamped shut so tightly that the blood was drained from around it leaving a ghostly paleness. "Quentin, this is treason!"

Quentin sat quietly and held the reins of his horse short. "Sir?"

"Poenius Postumus has written his own death warrant. I shall order a slow and tortuous death to this traitor. I will follow Roman law to the letter." Suetonius stared at the city of Londinium. "Postumus has said that he will not ride out with his men through Durotriges' territory. He says that their leader, Dearg, is waiting to ambush them. Roman soldiers do not hole up like terrified hares! Brave Roman soldiers fight their way out, if necessary. It is not Postumus' choice whether or not he join us. It is my choice." Suetonius swept his arm out to take in the city below. "Because of his treachery, I will have to make another choice, terrible and difficult." Suetonius pushed thoughts of Caitlin from his mind lest it taint his judgment. When he spoke, his words were harsh. "With Boadicea's army about to engulf Londinium, I have to decide whether to fight her here or make a stand farther north."

Quentin balanced his helmet on one hip, ran his fingers through his hair, and shook his head. "It is a decision that leaves you with no way to win. What are you going to do about the people in Londinium?"

Suetonius stared at the town below them, then made the decision he had avoided. "The numbers against us are too great without Postumus. We can't win if we make a stand here. Lead part of the cavalry into Londinium to warn people of their doom, then join us. Those who can keep up with our army can go with us for protection. We march due west to Regnum to meet with the rest of our forces. When the infantry joins us, we'll send scouts to find Boadicea and stop this savagery."

Quentin saluted Suetonius and placed his helmet on his head. "I do as you command, sir. When we meet again, may it be with better news."

Suetonius returned the salute. "It can't get much worse. Go quickly, for we pull out immediately." He waited until Quentin was several horse lengths away, then turned Victory toward Londinium. He felt hatred rise in him as he looked at the city that was certain to be destroyed along with its people, and an incredible sadness engulfed him as he thought of Caitlin. Suetonius stared at the center of town with its collection of businesses, the sparkling Thames, and the baths. The times he had been to Londinium had been exciting. He and Caitlin had gone there to furnish his newly built villa. She had loved the international flavor of the port and had exclaimed at every shop about the marvels brought in from the east, Africa, and the far corners of the world. Together they had purchased blue silk from China. Blue silk flowed around his memory of Caitlin. The swirling silk had made her as beautiful as an empress.

Suetonius clenched his fist around his sword. "Poor Londinium. I am forced to assign you the same fate as those who lived and died in Camulodunum. I can't help you, lest I lose all of Britannia. I am in the thankless position of sacrificing a piece to save the whole." Suetonius saluted the town, then abruptly pulled Victory around and galloped away.

Suetonius lay looking at the stars for the fourth night in a row. It was like watching a procession of candles parading across the sky. Sometimes there were so many stars that the sky looked powdery.

The stars looked cold, and Suetonius was reminded that the night was chilly. He pulled his woolen cloak about himself, but the night air flowed in and cooled his back. He squirmed around trying to get comfortable, but the ground was still harder than it used to be when he was young. It was colder, too, and made his bones ache. He wiggled his feet to warm them and cursed the war. He couldn't even have a proper fire or a camp set up without the infantry to dig the seven foot ditches and build the palisades. He never thought he'd miss the smell of his leather tent, but he did. At least with the tent, it would not matter that there was no fire. Perhaps the infantry would catch up with him tomorrow, and he could find Boadicea. He had to find her before all of Britannia was burned.

Someone shook Suetonius' shoulder, and his eyes popped open. Quentin knelt beside him. Suetonius sat up and stretched, carefully, for he was as stiff as old, dried leather. "What news have you?"

"Good news twice over. The infantry is camped less than two miles from here and will be here within the hour at sunrise. The second piece of good news is that Boadicea marches this way from Verulamium toward Londinium, again."

"Londinium? Did she not destroy it the first time?"

"That she did, sir. Boadicea also burnt Verulamium to the ground yesterday. Many were killed." Quentin sighed. "It is a strange war to be fought against a woman."

"This is a strange land, Quentin." Suetonius ran his fingers through his hair and pushed it away from his forehead. "I can't let her force us from this land."

Suetonius stood and looked toward the eastern sky. It was black except for a strip of gray at the horizon. The sun would be up none too soon. "Is there hot water for a shave?" Suetonius waved his hand. "I forgot, there's no fire. Ah, well. Order the cavalry to saddle up. We ride immediately to where Watling Street and the Fosse Way meet in the place they call High Cross. The small garrison there have to be warned. Hurry. We have to intercept Boadicea on her way to Londinium."

Suetonius looked toward the east again. "With every sunrise, I wonder if I am to join Lucian."

CHAPTER

XV

BOADICEA TAPPED HER FINGER against the rose-red dish. Exhaustion wrapped itself around her. Death would be a welcome change from the troubles she'd had the last few months. She could smell the bitter hemlock, or was it her imagination? Her thoughts tumbled across each other in a blend of memories. Prasutagus, Rhys, and her parents mixed with the memories of blood, swords, and screams. Was the price worth it? Would the gods accept her sacrifice? Boadicea stared at Neila and Sydelle who knelt before her. They had bathed in the sacred stream. There was no outward sign of lost virginity, but their constant pain had been visible to Boadicea.

Boadicea looked into the poisoned wine. It was a chance she had had to take. The Romans had no right to be in her country, and they had no right to destroy her daughters. Boadicea had won. The Romans paid dearly for their stupidity.

"Let them go!" Boadicea shouted. "Concentrate on the soldiers, not citizens!" Her chariot clattered down stone streets in front of her army. Flaming torches, thrown at roofs, caught the dry thatching instantly. Soldiers poured from huts in disarray only to be forced back into the burning buildings by hordes of sword-wielding Britons. The stench of burning thatch was joined by the smell of burning hair. Screams pierced the sky and followed Boadicea through the city.

Sydelle and Neila gripped the sides of the chariot with one practiced hand and held their weapons in the other.

Boadicea pulled her chariot up short when she saw a native with a baby in her arms. "Get in!" she shouted. "I'll take you to safety!"

"There's room," Neila shouted.

The woman with chestnut-colored hair stared at her with her mouth agape. She shook her head and clutched a baby to her chest. "Never!"

Caitlin turned and clutched the arm of a fleeing woman. "Take my baby to safety! The gods call to me!" She shoved Darcy into the woman's arms, then pulled forth a dagger hidden in her sleeve.

"There is room for you and the babe," Boadicea said.

Caitlin lunged toward the chariot, knife poised above her head, and climbed up the spokes. She clung to the wicker sides of the chariot, one leg hooked across the top. "You die, you bitch! You killed my family!"

Boadicea was stunned. This woman was confused. She was an ally. Boadicea easily moved out of the way of the slashing knife, but did nothing to stop the woman. "Stop! I am here to rid you of the Romans!"

"I want the Romans to rid me of you!" Caitlin slashed upwards with the knife, but cut nothing more than a fold of Boadicea's gown.

Before Neila and Sydelle could react, their friend and protector appeared from nowhere.

Meara screeched as she rode toward the chariot. "You die! You die!" She had her sword poised for attack and quickly bore down on the assassin. One swipe with the sword and Caitlin fell from the chariot to the street. Blood gushed from a wound to her side and ran between the stones in a macabre mosaic pattern.

"Get out of here!" Meara shouted. "Lead the army to victory! Victory!"

Boadicea slapped the reins and the chariot clattered away. She looked back at the fallen woman whose face in death registered surprise. "Why?" she asked.

"Some woman are deranged by war," Sydelle said.

"I'll say a special prayer to the gods for her soul," Boadicea said. "I am sorry."

Smoke became so thick that Boadicea could hardly see. She loosened the reins and let the team pick their way through the streets and to the far edge of the city. Ahead was a hill; the perfect place to view the destruction of Londinium.

When she looked down on the blazing town, Boadicea was shocked. She'd seen other cities put to the torch, but none burned as furiously as this one. The Romans paid for their treachery.

Boadicea turned from rubbing down her team and stared at Meara. "Do I hear you correctly? Is that liar, Governor Suetonius Paulinus, waiting for us?" She re-folded the rough cloth so the dirt was on the inside and ran it over her horse's hind quarters. Her forehead was furrowed in thought. Boadicea stood. "Oh, this is a happy day, if true." She looked across the fields at the thousands of warriors who were in varying stages of preparation for the next battle. Some sharpened their swords, some stripped branches to make new shafts for spears. Some played knuckle bones, their guffaws and curses attesting as to the winners and losers. Boadicea turned back to Meara. "You are the most valuable scout in my command. Keir admires you. I know not how you do it, Meara!"

"I have the protection of your prayers." Meara's eyes twinkled and she chuckled. "I also have the advantage of being thought of as nothing more than a nuisance, a girl who has no worth and therefore is not dangerous. I find out much by pretending to be a simple female."

"That shows how stupid the Romans are. Can they not see that you have ears and eyes?"

Meara threw back her head and laughed. "Sometimes I think that all the Romans see are breasts and thighs. Their vision is tainted with lust."

Boadicea swept her arms to include the field of warriors before her. "Yes, it is because of their lust that we are here. That and the fact we can no longer pretend we won't be enslaved." Boadicea threw the cloth in the box beside her.

The eastern sky was cloudless and slowly changed from blue to gray of night. The sun set behind her and a cool breeze, freshened by salt from the sea, lifted strands of hair away from her face. Boadicea turned toward the setting sun. "Out there Suetonius Paulinus waits for us. Tell our warriors that we leave tomorrow morning at sunrise for the march toward our final victory. Where are my daughters?"

"They are with Rhianna checking the supply wagons. The last wagon has come in full of grain. I believe the women have already lined up to get their share to make bread." Meara pointed to a crowd of women around a wagon. "The women insist on bringing their children to see their husbands fight our wars. It would be better if we didn't have them following us, for they slow us down."

Boadicea rubbed her temples. "Unfortunately, it is custom, and I do not have time to change it. Later, I will make the change when we build a real military force. That is one thing I've learned from the Romans. Their army is well disciplined."

"They are not as good as we are, and we have them outnumbered." Meara put her hands beneath her hair and lifted it from the nape of her neck. "By the gods, it is hot for this time of year."

"The better for us. The Romans encumber themselves with metal armor while we have the gods to protect us." Boadicea ran her fingers through her horse's mane to untangle it. "Go quickly and tell our warriors to prepare to march and fight."

Meara let her blonde hair drop into place. "It will be like a gift from the gods to have the Romans given to us on the morrow."

"Be careful. Suetonius Paulinus is not like Catus or Cerialis. He is not vengeful, but he is unrelenting. He is not accustomed to losing as is Cerialis, and he wants to win. He is the most powerful foe we have yet encountered. Carry my warning to the men and women who wield the spears and swords."

The sun was not yet to the quarter way mark in the sky as Boadicea braced her legs against the sides of her chariot. She looked at the ivory-colored clouds separated by rivers of blue. The sun was bright and she had to shade her eyes to see the army that faced hers. The sun was behind her, but it seemed to be in front of her as well, for the armor of the Romans reflected it. Boadicea noted that there were not as many men as she had expected, but they stood in neat rows. The javelin throwers were two rows deep. Behind them were the swordsmen, whose swords were shorter than her warriors', and she wondered about the effectiveness of something so small. The cavalry flanked the infantry on either side. Their metal armor gleamed and sparkled like the sea on a summer's day. The bright red of their short tunics was matched in color by red-crested helmets. Even the horses sported red tassels on their harnesses.

"This is a battle that will change our lives forever, my daughters." Boadicea reached out and touched Sydelle on the cheek. "You, my first-born, will remember the day well so that you can tell the story to your children and the children of your children." Boadicea kissed her gently on the forehead. "May all our gods protect you from the spears and swords of our enemy." Boadicea turned to Neila. "You, my child, were the companion to your father and very dear to him. I call upon the gods to give him leave to watch over you." Boadicea placed her arms around Neila and pulled her close. "You are fierce of heart. Let that be your guide today."

Boadicea pointed to the Romans. "I love both of you equally, and if the cause were not so great, I would not have you with me. It is for your own sanity that you are allowed to fight the Romans to undo the harm that was done to you. Make your fight a memorable one."

Neila glared across the expanse that separated her from Suetonius Paulinus' army. "I will have my day."

Boadicea looked at Sydelle. Her daughter also stared at the Roman army, but her face was void of any expression. "Sydelle?"

"Mother, I would rather die fighting the Romans than live with the shame they caused. I am ready."

Boadicea slapped the reins across the rumps of her horses and the chariot lurched forward, its iron-clad wheels cutting a path through the soft earth. She drove the chariot up a hillock that had been built for this occasion and faced the multitude of men and women who stood before her, their spears and swords ready. Boadicea looked over to see a group on horseback and smiled at Meara who sat tall and stately. As she raised her hands, the sleeves of Boadicea's robe slid back revealing gold wrist bands that shone in the sun. The sun warmed the torc that was about her neck and reminded her that that symbol of her office meant she was duty bound to protect her people. Ironically, today she would ask her people to fight to the death once more.

The wind traveled far from the sea and brought relief from the sun as Boadicea shouted to the gathering. "My friends in all things. I come to you today as a warrior first, your priestess second, and your Queen third. Today we fight a most important battle. Today we fight not as men and women, but as warriors who have been unjustly invaded by a foreign army. Today we fight to free not only ourselves and our children, but all the future generations of our great nations. Today we meld our nations together into one strong unit. As different metals when mixed become stronger, so shall we.

"As your priestess, I call upon our goddess, Andraste, who protects us in battle. I call upon our gods to watch over us on this day that is to be the last for some of us. Those chosen this day to go to the other world will go with honor. As your Queen, I ask that you fight for peace and return with me to our own lands."

Boadicea lowered her arms and picked up the reins. She had expected the normal cheering, but she had not expected it to be so loud. It continued, wave after wave ringing in her ears. Finally, after she glanced at her daughters in the chariot with her, she raised her arms. When after a full minute the crowd quieted, Boadicea smiled. "I have only one thing more to say." She snapped the reins and her horses leaped forward. "Follow me into a glorious battle!" Boadicea raced toward Suetonius' lines with her army shouting and screaming as they spurted behind her on horseback and foot, brandishing their weapons in front of their blue-tattooed bodies. Women hastened along with the men, holding swords and spears and cursing the Romans.

Suetonius watched the chariot coming closer with the driver's red hair flaming behind her. He remembered Caitlin and the other innocents and vowed that this day would be Boadicea's last. Momentarily he was taken aback by the horde of unruly warriors who followed her. He sensed the uneasiness of his own men, and he looked at the javelin throwers next to him. Their eyes were wide with terror, and Suetonius realized that they had never encountered such a huge army or one that was as ghastly and unmanageable.

He kicked Victory in the ribs and rode along the front of the line, shouting as he rode. "Listen to me, my men. You are the greatest fighting force in the world. You have been better trained and better armed than any army in history. What you see before you are the multitudes of Britannia, but they are not trained. See, they do not even have proper armor for protection. Look around you. I have chosen this place to do battle because the terrain favors us. We have the forest behind us so that the only direction the enemy can approach us is in front. Be brave, my countrymen! It is only a woman who leads them. There are women in her ranks, but let not that deter you. Send them to meet their gods as they sent our women by fire to meet ours. Stand by for the order to throw the first volley."

Suetonius watched in horror as the swarm surged toward his army. His practiced eye noted that his ten thousand men were outnumbered at least ten to one. His felt his heart rise to his throat and lodge there. He closed his eyes momentarily, but the noise of the raging Britons that penetrated his thoughts terrified him more than the sight of them. "I am a Roman soldier," he reminded himself. "I am not to shirk my duty or let fear be my guide." He rode to the flanking edge of the javelin throwers.

Suetonius held his breath to quiet his beating heart and waited until the enemy was within forty yards. He raised his arm and signaled Quentin who sounded the trumpet. A barrage of spears raised into the air almost as one unit, then fell into the shields of the Britons. The Iceni staggered back from the force of the blows and the unwieldiness of holding a shield with a shaft protruding from it. Warriors were knocked to the ground by the stumbling gait of careless neighbors.

Boadicea raced toward his troops, calling orders to her warriors. When the Britons were within twenty yards, he called for the second trumpet to sound and watched the another volley of spears sail through the air. This time the damage was greater, and Boadicea's men and women fell in large numbers. Suetonius was aware that she had many warriors to spare, and the fight would go on for hours. He looked at the sun. He knew from past experience that when he looked again, it would be setting, and he would be shocked at how fast time had flown and how fast death had come.

Boadicea held her spear high above the horses. She drove straight into the path of the javelin throwers with no fear, for Andraste protected her and her daughters. She looked between the horses, their manes flying and saw a Roman soldier who hadn't had time to draw his sword. She raced toward him and was pleased to see the horror in his face as he knew death rode with her. She swerved the horses and clipped the Roman with their hooves. He rolled to get out of her way, but she leaned over and drove the spear through his armor and into his belly, attaching him to the ground.

Boadicea turned the chariot to come around again and, from the corner of her eye, she watched Sydelle let loose with a sling-shot. A rock felled another Roman and Neila followed her sister's blow with a sword thrust of her own. Neila was quick and pulled a bloody sword from the throat of her victim. Boadicea saw the grim smile on Neila's face, but it was Sydelle's laughter that caught her attention. She hoped that Sydelle would be able to push the demons from her mind after the battle so that she could go on with life.

Boadicea raced back toward her own front lines. "Keep fighting! Keep fighting! We win today. Our lands will be ours once more!"

She pulled up next to Meara. "How goes it?"

Meara smiled. "I killed two from horseback before they knew I was there." She stopped smiling. "Many men fell with the first round of javelins."

"It is to be expected. It has to happen. This is war." Boadicea saw a look of puzzlement in Meara's eyes, and she turned toward the Romans. "What is it?"

"I don't know. Did you hear the sound of their trumpets?" Meara shook her head. "I've never understood why they use music."

Neila chuckled. "It's their dance of death, Meara."

"Haven't you been watching?" Sydelle snorted. "It is how they tell their soldiers what to do. See, they are moving about in some formation."

"I need a better vantage point." Boadicea drove her team to the edge of the battlefield where a knoll rose twenty feet from the rest of the area.

Meara followed her and the quartet of women watched the battle continue to unfold before them.

"See, they form a triangle with their men." Sydelle pointed. "What is it that they do?"

Neila shaded her eyes with her hands. "They have one man in front, two following him, four behind him. They all have their shields in place."

Boadicea stared in bewilderment at the formation. "I don't understand the reason for it." She watched her army on the plains below. Many had fallen, but many others took their places.

"By the gods, it moves as one person." Meara swung her leg over and slid off her horse. "What is its function?"

Boadicea watched, fascinated, as the wedge of shielded legionnaires moved forward in dog trot fashion, neither fast nor slow, spears poking out from between the shields like bristles on a hedgehog. She shook her head. "I must know what new trick this is."

"They go straight for the front lines. Nothing seems to stop them," Sydelle said.

Neila placed both her hands on the smooth oak rail of the chariot and leaned out. "That trumpet sounds the same notes over and over and they seem to march with it."

"Our men will tear them apart." Meara gripped the handle of her sword tighter and peeled the skin off her lower lip with her teeth.

Boadicea watched as the wedge got closer to her men. She smiled when her men spied the Romans in their peculiar formation and rushed toward them, their swords ready for action.

"Now we will see the blood fly." Boadicea heard the first clash of sword against shield as her men surrounded the Romans. She screamed as her men dropped by the tens in front of the wedge. "It is Suetonius' trick! He fights like no man, but like a machine. Quickly, he must not break the front lines or all is lost!"

Boadicea pulled back on the reins. "Meara, get behind the lines and tell our women to move the wagons. They block any retreat we may have to make. I see it now! What a fool I was not to insist on leaving the wives and children further back."

Meara grabbed Boadicea's hands. "Where are you going?"

"I go where I am needed. I go to undo the Roman treachery. Get to horse and ride, Meara!" Boadicea felt the reins in her hands, but she was unaware that she had given any orders to her horses until the chariot lurched onto the stone paved road. As she drove toward the front lines with one hand, she pulled her sword out with the other, and she was once more in the middle of the battle.

Time was moving in a different dimension for Boadicea. It seemed the battle moved at the pace of a snail while she was flailing away more quickly, double time, and although she did not hear her broad sword whack through flesh and bone, she saw the blood fly upwards like a red starling with broad wings. She did not feel the bodies of her countrymen under her chariot wheels as she bumped over them. She drove through the Roman soldiers possessed by anger and despair.

"Boadicea! Boadicea!" Meara rode through the battle lines toward her queen. "You must fly! All is lost. The Romans will kill you."

"I stay. I die with my people."

Meara jerked her horse around, but the mount slipped in the blood-wet earth and went down, throwing Meara to the ground. Meara hit the dirt with a thud just as a Roman cavalry office came riding toward her, his spear poised.

Boadicea screamed and pulled her sword up. She watched in horror as the spear came down toward Meara's breast. Meara rolled just in time, but the spear caught her in the thigh. Boadicea jumped from the chariot and swung her sword at the rider, knocking him off his horse. She ran her sword through his neck, enjoying the spurt of blood that shot his life into the air.

"Meara, are you hurt too badly to ride? You must get out of here." Boadicea looked around for Meara's horse. She sighed with relief as she saw Sydelle quieting the animal. "Is the horse all right?"

"She is fine. Meara, I'll ride the horse, and you get in the chariot," Sydelle said.

Meara grabbed hold of Boadicea and hopped over to her horse. "I'll ride. You belong with your mother."

Neila rushed to Meara and pulled her hand away from the bloody wound. "Let me bind that for you." She quickly cut strip of cloth from her tunic and wrapped it expertly around Meara's leg. "I'm sorry I've no time for myrrh for your wound."

Meara grinned and pointed to Neila's torn tunic. "Let's hope the rest of us don't get hurt or you'll have to finish the war naked."

Meara grabbed her horse's mane, stood on her good leg and pulled herself up with a boost from Neila. "Away!"

"You leave. I have fighting to do." Boadicea climbed back in the chariot and her daughters followed.

Meara grabbed the reins that lay across the front railing of the chariot. "I won't leave without you." She jerked the reins forward and out of their tracings.

"What are you doing!" Boadicea reached for the slithering reins, but she wasn't fast enough.

Meara kicked her horse in the ribs and raced off with the chariot in tow.

Boadicea, stunned at Meara's behavior, began to scream at her when she discovered she was headed away from the battle. "Do not do this, Meara! I must fight with my warriors. I am their leader. Without me, all is lost."

Meara shouted back over her shoulder. "All is lost already. Look to your right. Tell me what you see."

Boadicea's hands gripped the rail in front of her and she stared at her white knuckles, not wanting to see what Meara told her to. She finally forced herself to look. It was then that she realized she had not heard the noise of battle because she had not wanted to know the truth, but now she heard the screams of the women and children as well as her warriors. The Romans cut through her army like a sharp sword through flesh. The wedge was already to the wagons. Soldiers slaughtered everyone who was in their way. They even killed the draft animals. Spears stuck from screaming horses, and Boadicea shivered. The sound of an animal dying was almost as bad as the sound of a person's soul being released to the other world. No one who stayed here would survive this day.

"Meara! Stop! I cannot leave my people."

"It is no shame of yours. You must live to fight another day. We must fly so no Roman will look down upon you in death." Meara shouted over her shoulder, but she did not slow her horse or the chariot.

Boadicea looked back at the bodies on the battlefield, covered with drying blood and impaled with spears. A great rustling of wings caused her to look up. A shadow moved across her face as hundred of ravens gathered, ready to swoop down onto the battlefield to pick clean the bodies. She shuddered.

"There will be no more battles, Meara. Too many were lost. Too much was lost. We are a nation doomed to extinction."

"Meara, we are home. You can stop driving us now." Boadicea allowed Sydelle and Neila to help her from the chariot. She felt like a vessel with nothing inside—like her village. The worst part of coming back was to find the streets empty. There was no one left except for a few old men and women with leathery skin and toothless gums. There were no fields planted, but then there were no people to tend them, and no children to eat the bread from them.

"I am a queen with no subjects." Boadicea said this to no one in particular and no one answered. She was tired all the way through to her bones, and if she had any feeling left, she was certain that her bones hurt, too. Her hair was stringy and full of the smell of death. There was grime on her face. She ran hand down her tunic, the colors obliterated by dirt and sweat. "The stench of war is too powerful for me. We shall go to the sacred grove and wash in the brook. The gods won't tolerate us like this. Neila and Sydelle, go to the house and get fresh tunics for the four of us, then meet us in the grove. Meara and I go ahead of you."

The girls moved slowly up the ramparts, and Boadicea turned to Meara. "As we walk, I have something that I will ask you to do for Neila, Sydelle, and me. I ask as a friend, but I command you as your Queen. It is my last wish and my last command."

Meara unhitched the horses from the chariot in silence, then slapped them on the rump. The horses walked into the corral, shook themselves and looked back at the women before trotting off to look for greener grass. "You sound serious. I am afraid of your request."

"After we purify ourselves, my daughters and I wish to join Prasutagus in the other world." As if the gods were answering Boadicea, a gust of wind whipped her tunic and pushed her hair away from her face.

Meara turned to her Queen, a stunned look betrayed her feelings. "You must not!"

Boadicea looked up to help her form her thoughts. Splotches of lavender and cream colored clouds scuttled across the sky and matched the lifeless lavender gray trunks of trees long dead. One birch tree held its arthritic bleached bone limbs toward the sky. The tree was a reminder from the gods of what was expected of her.

Boadicea slipped the bridle off Meara's horse. "Can you understand the freedom a horse must feel when we remove its bridle after a long, hard day?" She watched as Meara wrapped her arms around her horse's neck and buried her face in its mane. Meara looked up. Tears slid down her face. "Yes." She tugged on his forelock, led the horse through the gate, then pushed her away.

Boadicea watched the horse run across the field to join the others. "I would not have the freedom of the horse. At this moment, Suetonius looks for me and for my daughters. Do you know what they do to captured enemies?"

Meara shook her head. "No."

"They parade them naked through the streets in chains. My daughters and I have suffered enough shame at the hands of the Romans. We cannot tolerate any more ridicule."

Boadicea held her chin up. "I am Boadicea, daughter to Garik and Durina, wife to Prasutagus, and Queen of the Iceni." She smiled. "Do I not deserve a better ending than what the Romans would give me?"

Meara sobbed. Through her tears she answered, "Yes."

"I ask that you help me to a better end. I want you to take the bodies of my daughters and me away from here so that even in death, Suetonius will not see me or know where I am. Our graves shall be secret forever, so that we may not be disturbed. Tell no one." Boadicea removed her wrist protectors. "These are gold. I give these to you now. There will be more gold for you."

"I don't want your gold, my Queen."

"You may need to pay for the journey. Where will you take us?"

Meara pressed her lips together and looked to the north. "I will take you to the lands of my fathers. We will travel by wagon . . ." Meara's voice caught in her throat.

Boadicea kissed her on the cheek. "Tell me where I will spend eternity."

"It is three days from here. We will travel day and night in order to thwart the Romans. I'll find a driver to help me." Meara fell into Boadicea's arms. "I shall want to come with you."

Boadicea brushed Meara's hair away from her face. "If you die with me, then who will tell my story? No, Meara, you must stay behind until your time comes. When you die, then I'll be waiting at the edge of the other world for you."

Meara nodded. "I will do as you wish."

"Come, let's join my daughters and cleanse ourselves."

Boadicea leaned against the altar. She needed the hard stone to give her strength. She looked at Sydelle and Neila who knelt in front of her. "I wish to propose a toast."

Her daughters looked at her, their faces clean and beautiful, the filth of war washed from them. They looked serene, and Boadicea realized that it had been a long time since Sydelle and Neila had had a peaceful moment.

Boadicea held the rose-red bowl to her breast. "I wish a better life for you in the other world. I wish you happiness and peace. Now drink, my daughters. Your father awaits." Sydelle and Neila raised silver chalices to their lips and drank. Boadicea gulped the wine so that she would overtake her daughters and be with them on the journey to the other side.

The poisoned wine burned. Memories of the war tumbled about in her head. Her daughters swirled before her. Poisoned fire burned her throat, but she forgot that sensation as Prasutagus appeared before her. He reached for her. Boadicea stepped out of life and into her husband's arms.

CHAPTER
XVI

SUETONIUS STARED INTO THE FIREPIT. The Roman army had been victorious, but he had lost. He had lost the will to fight, to live, to move. He had lost all will except the will to drink wine. He raised his cup.

"This is to you, Caitlin. You gave me many gifts." He stared at the unfinished floor. Now he would have to find tile that matched. Maybe not. Maybe he would leave the floor unfinished as a symbol for his unfinished life. "You gave me youth and love. You gave me joy." He took a long drink.

"And here's to Lucian who gave me his life. What did I give you? I gave you nothing." Suetonius took another long drink. "I will miss you more than I ever thought possible, my friend."

"Here's to you, infant Darcy. I gave you cold stares, frowns at your tears, and you gave me gurgles, tugs on my fingers, and happiness. May the gods grant you a peaceful haven." Suetonius took another long drink until the cup was empty.

He leaned over and poured the cup full and drank again.

"But most of all, here's to Boadicea, Queen of the Iceni, who taught me the most important lesson of all." Suetonius ignored the tears that flowed down his face and soaked his tunic.

"You taught me not to underestimate the enemy. You taught me to respect a warrior be it a man or a woman. You taught me that the Roman army is vulnerable against an army led by passion and a desire for freedom. Here's to you, Boadicea, a fine warrior queen.

May you rest peacefully." Suetonius raised his cup and drank the wine until it dulled his senses. Maybe tonight he could sleep. Maybe tonight.

EPILOGUE

THE OLD WOMAN HELD UP HER HAND to quiet the audience. "I have not finished. The queen of the Iceni was beautiful and brave. She knew that her time had come. Even in death she was more beautiful than any living woman then or now."

"So where is her final resting place?" A young girl leaned forward and waited for Meara's answer.

Meara smiled. "I am old and can't remember."

"You do remember!" a youngster shouted. "My mother told me you know everything from the old days—even the medicine and the Druid ways."

"I don't remember that which was pulled from my head by the gods." Meara pulled her woolen cloak tighter about her shoulders. The chill in the air was worse each year. Sometimes she could not get warm in spite of sleeping next to a large firepit.

It was her duty to tell Boadicea's story. Over the years she had traveled to more villages than she could remember. The Romans used to chase her away, but she told her stories in the dark of night deep in the forests.

Meara accepted the wine offered her. As was her custom, she raised the cup to the moon and thanked Boadicea for the changes she'd forced the Romans to make. The Romans no longer tried to dispose of the local rulers, but let them to maintain their culture and thus peace. She hoped that Boadicea knew she had conquered the Romans after all.